The Royal Baths Murder

A YORKSHIRE MURDER MYSTERY

J.R. ELLIS

THOMAS & MERCER

Text copyright © 2019 by J. R. Ellis
All rights reserved.

Published by Thomas & Mercer, Seattle

www.apub.com

Amazon, the Amazon logo, and Thomas & Mercer are trademarks of Amazon.com, Inc., or its affiliates.

ISBN-13: 9781542015424
ISBN-10: 1542015421

Cover design by @blacksheep-uk.com

Printed in the United States of America

To my mum and dad

Prologue

The Harrogate Turkish Baths of 1897 survive virtually intact, with many of the original fittings still in place. They have recently been refurbished. The Baths have a Moorish design with Islamic arches and screens. The walls are of vibrant multi-coloured glazed brick. The arabesque-painted ceilings, Italian mosaic floors and polished hardwoods produce a period feel of luxurious colour and elegance.

'And so, ladies and gentlemen, we are delighted to welcome back to this year's festival the distinguished writer Damian Penrose.'

There was enthusiastic applause from the sell-out audience in The White Swan Hotel. It was a pleasant summer evening in Harrogate and the Crime Writing Festival was in full swing. Penrose, seated in an armchair on the stage that had been set up in the hotel's ballroom, accepted the applause with a haughty nod in the direction of the audience. He passed a hand through his hair, ruffling his long and greying locks. He was dressed in a corduroy jacket and wore a cravat.

Penrose had had a long career as a successful, bestselling crime writer and was rumoured to be worth several million pounds. He had also gained notoriety due to his tempestuous private life and his frequent barbed comments about other writers. The latter had led to him being dubbed 'Poison Pen', a title in which he revelled: good writing was always assisted by bad behaviour, which created publicity and boosted sales.

The title of the event was 'The Perfect Crime: Writing a Bestselling Crime Novel', chaired by Ben Poole, a writer, journalist and presenter who was prominent on the circuit of local literary festivals. After Ben had interviewed Penrose, the session would be open to questions from the audience.

'So,' began Ben, 'if I can ask you first of all, where's your starting place when you're writing a crime story?'

Penrose relaxed back into his chair with an air of arrogant nonchalance.

'Inspiration comes in many forms to the mind gifted with imagination. I can see something while I'm driving or walking down the street, or read about some trivial event in a newspaper, and suddenly a plot unfolds before me. It's quite an extraordinary process.'

'And then it's a question of crafting those ideas into novel form?'

'Exactly, and that's where the serious work begins. Of course, after so many successful novels, I've got it down to a fine art, so to speak.'

'Quite. Do you have a set of principles that you follow?'

'Oh, I don't need those. It's only weak and struggling writers who need props like that. Once I sit down to write, it flows without much difficulty.' He turned to the audience. 'My twentieth book is out soon, I'm sure you're all keen to know.'

There was subdued laughter at this brazen act of self-promotion.

'Yes,' said Ben, who was already finding it difficult to get Penrose to talk about anything other than himself. 'What do you think makes a good crime novel?'

'There's no formula for it. I just follow my instinct, and it's never let me down in twenty books. You'll have to ask my readers what makes my books so appealing.'

Ben was tight-lipped and trying to hide his irritation with Penrose's behaviour. 'How far do you base your characters on people you've known?'

'Well, it's a truism that one writes from one's own experience. In my own case, for example, I've taken great pleasure in devising deaths for unpleasant females, based, of course, on my former wives, who tried to extract as much money as they could from me when we divorced.'

There was some nervous laughter.

'And do you tend to incorporate things that have happened to you into your stories?'

'Absolutely. A life as varied and fascinating as mine has yielded some wonderful material.'

And so it went on and, however hard he tried, Ben found it impossible to get Penrose to reveal anything about his methods or make any points that might be useful to a budding writer.

'Well, thank you, Mr Penrose,' said a weary Ben at last. 'Let's open this now to the audience. Any questions? Yes, over there.'

'What advice would you give to a young writer?' asked an earnest-looking young woman.

'Stand on your own two feet and don't expect people like me to help you along. No one did it for me. I get so many unsolicited scripts, most of which are utter rubbish. I don't know what they expect me to do, when they don't show any signs of real ability. It seems to me that there's a terrible dearth of talent around at the moment; we're a long way from the Golden Age that I remember.'

'What do you think about writers who steal ideas from other people?' This question was posed by a woman dressed in jeans and a strappy top, who'd been glaring at Penrose throughout his conversation with Ben. Esther Stevenson was also a crime writer, based locally.

Penrose initially frowned, and then smiled maliciously. 'Obviously I think it's completely reprehensible and it goes without saying that I am always very scrupulous about such matters.'

Stevenson gave an audible snort of contempt.

'It's only writers who lack ideas of their own who steal other people's,' continued Penrose.

'Another question. Yes?' The anxious Ben gestured to the back of the room.

'Do you think it's helpful if writers criticise each other in non-constructive and personal ways?' The questioner was another local crime writer from York, Charles Derryvale.

'It depends what you mean by non-constructive. I tend to speak about things as I see them. If I think a novel is leaden and tedious, I'll say so. If I think the author would do us all a favour by not boring the pants off us with his or her awful writing, I'll say that too. What's more, I think this is better than much of the mealy-mouthed commentary peddled by those halfwits who call themselves critics. "The writer shows potential in his characterisation, but has not yet achieved consistency." In other words, a lot of it was rubbish. That's the kind of thing I mean.'

'You go much further than that, don't you? I'd like the audience to hear this.' Derryvale, who was shaking with anger, started to read from a sheet of paper. '"Derryvale cuts a heavy and unwieldy figure in the world of crime writing and his heavy, turgid prose seems to reflect this . . ."'

A desperate Ben intervened before things got out of hand.

'I'm sorry, I'll have to stop you there. Can we please keep any personal disputes in the private realm? This is not the forum to discuss them.'

Penrose smiled but Derryvale stuffed the paper into his pocket and stormed out of the room. A number of people heard him mumbling something about 'making him pay' and there was a hum of excited conversation.

Ben tried to restore order but only partially succeeded as the session limped on to a rather unsatisfactory close.

'So thank you, once again, to our guest this evening: Damian Penrose.'

The applause this time from the somewhat confused audience was lukewarm, but Penrose didn't seem to mind. He shook hands with his exhausted interviewer and immediately headed for the bar, which was in a large, comfortable room with sofas and armchairs, but Penrose took up a position on a stool at the far end of the counter, from which he ordered a double whisky. He sipped his drink and glanced around, hoping to see some of his admirers, but the seats were sparsely occupied, as many drinkers had moved outside on to a terrace to take advantage of the warm evening. Seconds later, however, he saw a group arriving, which included Stevenson, Derryvale and a man called John Sinclair: a publisher with whom Penrose had had a bitter dispute. They saw him at the bar and clustered at the other end. Penrose smiled as he spotted another opportunity to goad and provoke.

'Ah, look who it is!' he called across. '"When shall we three meet again?" I must say, this hotel is better than the blasted heath. What are you old crones plotting now?'

Derryvale was still red-faced with anger. He stared at Penrose. Stevenson clutched his arm and murmured, 'Don't . . .'

But Derryvale would not remain silent. 'Your downfall, Penrose.' He raised his glass. 'I think we'll all drink to that.'

'You're really quite pathetic, aren't you, Derryvale? You can't contain your jealousy of my success and you resent it when I write the truth about your miserable little efforts.'

'At least they are his own efforts and not stolen from somebody else,' retorted Stevenson.

'Ah, Esther Stevenson, the Queen of Crime, as she likes to think of herself. At least, the queen in these benighted parts of the country, but she daren't come down to London and face the competition where it really counts.'

'Why would I, with people like you around?'

Penrose ignored this. 'And are we still peddling the ridiculous and discredited notion that I stole material from you?'

'Hardly discredited. I can prove it.'

'Go ahead, my dear. I'll see you in court.'

'You might see me there first,' said John Sinclair.

'Oh, Sinclair of Sinclair Books. Are you still around? Is your little business surviving?'

'Yes, no thanks to you.'

Penrose waved his hand in contempt. 'I don't support failing ventures.'

'You don't honour your obligations either.'

Penrose laughed. 'What obligations? I'm not obliged to give you anything.'

'We had an agreement.' Sinclair seemed very upset, almost tearful.

'Oh, please!' Penrose snorted in contempt.

'You're such an arrogant bastard, you're . . .' Derryvale raised his voice, and Stevenson clung to his arm again.

'Calm down, old boy, you'll give yourself a heart attack in your condition.'

For a moment, it looked as if Derryvale was going to throw his glass at Penrose but instead he gulped the rest of the contents down and stomped out of the bar, followed by his companions.

Penrose chuckled to himself and ordered another whisky. A harassed-looking woman came into the bar and frowned when she saw Penrose. It was Patricia Hughes, the festival organiser.

'Damian, can I have a word?'

'Oh dear, it's Patricia. What have I done now?'

'Let's sit over there, shall we?' She indicated a table in the corner of the room that would offer some privacy.

'Very well.'

They sat in armchairs opposite each other.

'Can I get you a drink?' asked Penrose while he sipped his second whisky.

'No, thank you.' Patricia leaned forward. 'Damian, I specifically asked you to focus on writing in that session with Ben, but he tells me that you got into a nasty slanging match with Esther Stevenson and Charles Derryvale.'

'Good Lord. I feel as if I'm in the headmistress's office. Ben Poole's telling lies, Miss.'

'I don't think so, Damian, and it doesn't help if you don't take it seriously. Look, people paid good money to attend that session, hoping to hear you talk about your work and offer some insights into writing crime. Instead they just get you boasting and slagging other people off.'

'They started it by asking provocative questions.'

'Oh, we really are in the playground now, aren't we? "They started it." Why did you have to rise to the bait? We're paying you to deliver a good session for us.'

'They got a good session; they got to see their hero: the internationally successful Damian Penrose.'

Patricia stared at Penrose with something approaching contempt. 'It really is all about you, isn't it, Damian? Just to see you is enough. Do you think people come to a festival like this as pop fans who just want to see their idol? They're interested in literature and its crafting; some of them are aspiring writers hoping for some help and inspiration.'

Penrose simply grunted.

'Well, Damian, I'm very disappointed. You've got another session coming up on Tuesday evening and I hope we get something better from you. If we don't, I can't see us inviting you again.'

'I don't think that will go down well with crime readers. They want to see the top people.'

'Maybe they do, but they also want to hear something interesting. You're not the only person around, Damian, although I know you think you are.' She got up abruptly and left.

'Stupid bitch,' mumbled Penrose as he returned to the bar for his third whisky.

The rest of the evening proved disappointingly uneventful. Penrose stayed around conspicuously, but no one came up to him to say how much they enjoyed his work or to ask for his autograph. But what could you expect from a provincial place like this? The people here had no appreciation of real talent.

Eventually, the bar started to empty except for a group of younger writers who were still drinking enthusiastically and looked as if they were set for a long session, so Penrose, who was staying in the hotel, reluctantly sloped off to bed.

The early morning of the next day found Penrose walking through the quiet town centre. Every year when he was in Harrogate, he enjoyed visits to the Royal Baths. It was one of the few consolations of having to travel to the north of England and stay in a dull little spa town two hundred miles north of civilisation.

As Penrose was not the kind of person who enjoyed mixing with the hoi polloi, even if it was the middle-class hoi polloi of Harrogate, he had taken advantage of the opportunity to book a private session at one of the town's most famous attractions. This was very expensive, and he had to attend early, before the Baths were open to the public. But it was worth it to have the swimming pool and all the steam and hot rooms to himself.

It was 8 a.m. when he arrived at the beautiful late-Victorian entrance. He pressed the bell. Inside, receptionist Carol Ashworth saw him through the glass-panelled door and pressed her switch to release the lock. Carol was a plumpish woman in her forties, with a pleasant smile. She was an avid reader of crime fiction, and looked forward every year to the Crime Writing Festival. She and her friends enjoyed walking round the town trying to spot famous crime writers, and they always treated themselves to tickets for at least one event. She regarded it as a huge stroke of luck that she worked at the Royal Baths, where the famous Damian Penrose came nearly every morning of his stay. During this period, she always volunteered to do the early shifts.

'Good morning, Mr Penrose,' she called breezily and beamed at him.

'Good morning, Carol,' replied Penrose, who enjoyed any kind of flattering attention, especially from a female, and was always quick to return it. 'It's wonderful to have such a lovely greeting so early in the morning.'

Carol blushed. 'Oh, thank you, Mr Penrose. Everything's ready for you, if you want to go down.'

'I will. Thank you very much.'

'We open to the public at nine fifteen, Mr Penrose.'

'Very well.'

Penrose headed down the marble staircase that led to the baths area, his footsteps echoing into the distance. Carol sat smiling at the reception desk. What a charming man he was! She couldn't understand why he had such a bad reputation. A few minutes later Shirley Adams, the cleaner, came out of the office behind her, wheeled her vacuum cleaner into the reception area and began to clean the carpet. Carol answered some emails and texted some friends about meeting up for coffee.

The baths area was below street level. Penrose wandered through a little maze of branching corridors to reach the changing rooms, where he put on his swimming trunks. One of the reasons he favoured the privacy of these sessions was that he knew his ageing body was not so attractive these days. His leg muscles had atrophied, leaving his legs thin and shaky. His belly hung over his trunks in white folds of hairy flab and his backside was shrunken and limp. He was no longer the dashing and debonair writer of his earlier days.

It was satisfyingly quiet down here. The only noises besides the background thrum of the boiler were an occasional gentle hiss of steam and a gurgle or plop of water. Penrose started with a few lengths of the swimming pool. Whilst he swam, he thought with satisfaction about the encounters of the previous evening. He'd seen those three off, and as far as Patricia Hughes was concerned, she could do what she liked. To be perfectly frank, he was tiring of coming to Harrogate, despite the pleasures he was currently enjoying.

He emerged from the swimming pool, dried off and headed past the small cold plunge pool to the interconnecting steam and hot rooms. These were graded in temperature, and the steam smelled of eucalyptus. After a spell in the steam room, he cooled off in the cold plunge pool and returned to the dry hot rooms. The hottest of these reached 65° Celsius. As he sat on a stone bench sweating profusely, the hissing sound increased and a mist drifted in and became dense. He must have left the door to the adjacent steam room open. Surely something was turned up too high? And what was that dark shape moving by the door? Perspiration ran down his face, dripped from his nose on to his chest and formed rivulets over his belly. He sat with his eyes closed and was unaware of the figure now behind him, moving in ghostly silence towards him through the mist.

It was over in seconds; a ligature was passed around his neck and tightened. Penrose struggled and grabbed at the choking cord. He stumbled to his feet, then crashed on to the wet floor. He flapped and floundered like a fat pig caught in a noose, until at last he lay still. The ligature was removed and the assailant flitted away noiselessly.

There followed a strange period of calm and quiet. Penrose remained where he'd fallen, staring across the damp floor of the hot room. Small rivulets of water ran down his face and dripped off the end of his nose. The fragrant steam continued to pour out of the steam room.

In reception, Carol sat behind the desk, glancing at her newspaper and waiting for the rush at nine fifteen. Shirley had almost finished her cleaning and was standing outside having a smoke at eight forty-five when Steve Monroe, one of the attendants and masseurs, arrived for work. He was in his early thirties and very handsome, so Carol gave him another of her wide smiles when he came through the door.

'Hi, Carol, anybody in?'

'Just Mr Penrose.'

'Right, I'll go down and get things ready. Has Shirley finished?'

'Think so – she'll be off in a minute.'

Steve clattered down the steps, but it seemed only seconds later that he called out urgently for Carol to come down. She hurried down the stairs, to find Steve, grim-faced, standing over a body.

'Steve!' she screamed.

'It's Mr Penrose. He's dead.'

'Oh my God! Are you sure? I'll call an ambulance. He might have just fainted in the heat, you know. I've always said they have the heat turned up too high down here and there's steam everywhere.'

'No, he's definitely dead. I tried to find his pulse. But Carol . . .' Steve looked at the receptionist, puzzled and shocked. 'He's been murdered, strangled. Look, there's a horrible red line round his neck.'

'I'll call the police!'

'Did you let anyone else in?'

'No, no one's been in except you and Mr Penrose.'

'Has anyone come back up from here?'

'No.'

'Then I don't know what's going on. I've looked absolutely everywhere and the emergency exit hasn't been touched. There's no one else down here.'

One

Harrogate is the queerest place with the strangest people in it, leading the oddest lives of dancing, newspaper reading and dining.

Charles Dickens, 1858

Detective Sergeant Andrew Carter was enjoying a slow start to his day at West Riding Police Harrogate Division HQ, drinking a cup of coffee and eating a croissant. He still found the pace of things in Harrogate very relaxing after his frenetic days at the London Met, although the latter was now beginning to seem quite a while ago. Unfortunately, his morning peace was disrupted by the call from the Royal Baths. He left immediately, taking a detective constable and a couple of PCs with him.

There was a queue of puzzled people outside the Baths waiting for them to open, and the arrival of the police provoked a buzz of conversation. Inside, Andy found a shocked Carol Ashworth and Shirley Adams being consoled by Steve Monroe at the reception desk. Howard Barnes, the manager of the Baths, a stocky, balding man, had also arrived following a desperate call from Carol. Andy quickly established what they had discovered.

'So the body is still down there?'

'Yes,' replied Steve. 'I turned him over, tried to find his pulse, but there was nothing.'

'Has anyone else touched the body?'

'No. Only Carol and I and Mr Barnes have been down, and they only looked at him.'

'Is that correct?'

Carol and Barnes nodded.

'So three people have been down to where the body is?'

'Yes, but only Steve touched anything,' repeated Barnes, tight-lipped and serious.

'You wouldn't get me down there for anything,' said Shirley, before asking if she could go outside for another fag.

'Have you called for the ambulance?' asked Andy.

'No, we haven't,' said Carol. 'When he was dead, we just thought . . . I'm sorry.' She couldn't continue.

'Not to worry, we'll get forensics.' He nodded to another PC, who called a number.

Steve turned to Andy. 'The first thing I thought was the murderer must still be down there, so I looked all over in the steam rooms, the changing rooms and everywhere, but there's no one, and Carol says I was the only person, apart from Mr Penrose, to go down there.'

'Right, well, we'd better get down and have a look. Is there any way down other than these stairs?'

'Only the emergency exit on to the street, but that's not been touched.'

Andy turned to one of the PCs. 'Seal these stairs off. Stay on guard at the top; no one unauthorised comes down.'

'OK, Sarge.'

Andy and DC Robinson went down. It was hot, misty and eerily quiet everywhere. They passed the swimming pool, empty and still – apart from some disturbance from the pumps circulating

14

the water – and entered the steam room area. Andy examined the body.

'Strangled,' he announced somewhat redundantly as he exposed the deep red line around Penrose's neck.

He looked round carefully for hiding places. There were not many possibilities; the room was open-plan, and there were only bare benches in the steam rooms. Andy went into every changing cubicle but found nothing. There was a door into some kind of boiler room, which was open. It was a warm room with a dirty floor and walls, littered with oily rags and a few tools on a small bench. There was the loud hum of the operating boiler. A search revealed no people and no weapon. Then, in a corner of the changing rooms, Andy saw a large wicker basket. Eagerly he turned it over and emptied the contents out but there was nothing except dirty towels.

'Damn!' he swore to himself and put the basket upright again. Unless the two who'd reported the crime had also committed it, this was looking like a case for DCI Oldroyd, Andy's boss, who seemed to specialise in solving impossible crimes.

Andy looked briefly around the rest of the areas, including the little cold plunge pool and swimming pool chamber, with its high ceiling clearly recently renovated with a modern take on a Turkish pattern. Everywhere was deserted.

'OK, let's go back up,' he said to DC Robinson.

When he got back to reception, he called his boss.

At 9.45 a.m., DCI Jim Oldroyd was standing in his underpants in front of the bathroom mirror and brushing his teeth when the call came from Andy Carter. It wasn't exactly an early start, but he tended to keep his own hours these days. He put in so much

time on cases late at night that he indulged in the occasional lie-in without any feelings of guilt.

'Yes?'

'Andy Carter, sir. I'm at the Royal Baths. There's been a murder.'

'Good Lord, is nowhere sacred? That's supposed to be a place of calm and tranquillity.'

'Not today, sir. There's a big bloke dead on the floor in one of those hot room things, strangled, I think. It's bloody hot down there and stinks of menthol or something. Do people get high when they're down there?'

'No, it's to clear the sinuses, you big ignoramus,' joked Oldroyd, and Andy laughed.

'Anyway, I've got them to turn everything off. He's got a great big red mark round his neck where the ligature was and no rope here or anything, so it couldn't be self-inflicted. The SOCOs are here taking pictures and Mr Groves is on his way.'

Tim Groves was a forensic pathologist who had worked with Oldroyd for many years.

'Good work, Andy,' Oldroyd said. 'I'll be there as soon as I can.'

'OK, sir, but I might as well tell you, it's not going to be straightforward, or I wouldn't have called you.'

'Things are never straightforward when you're working with me. You know that by now.'

'I do, sir.'

'So what's the problem?'

'Well, he's definitely been murdered, but no sign of the murderer. He was down there by himself; he'd booked a private session. Damian Penrose. A crime writer, apparently.'

'There's irony for you.'

'Yes. The receptionist let him in, then later on a bloke who works here went down and found the body. But they both say

16

there was no one else in the building apart from the cleaner, who was upstairs near reception, and we can't find anybody. So unless the people who found the body are the murderers, it's another of those disappearing acts.'

'I see. Well, tell me more when I get there.'

Getting there was no more than a pleasant walk from his flat across the Stray, past Bettys Tea Rooms and down Parliament Street to the Royal Baths. He arrived to find that Andy had everything under control, and accompanied the DC down to see the crime scene. They found Tim Groves and his team at work.

'Good morning, Jim,' said Groves, his tall frame stooping to examine the body. 'I don't think this one's much of a problem. Strangulation: strong, thin ligature, something like nylon rope. We may find a few strands of whatever it was back at the lab. He's not been dead long; not more than a couple of hours, I'd say. How are you going to classify this one?'

Oldroyd smiled. He'd developed a kind of taxonomy of murders over the years, which amused his colleagues: BM for blackmail, LJ for Lust and Jealousy, and so on. 'It's early days for that, Tim, I've only just got here, but I know he was a controversial figure in the world of crime writing. It could be PH for Professional Hatred.'

Groves laughed. 'That's a new one! Well, you'd better get after the culprit while the trail is warm.'

'Thanks, Tim, but according to Andy, there is no trail. No sign of the perpetrator.'

'Oh, not again! You're beginning to specialise in solving the impossible. Are you a detective or a magician?'

'A rationalist, Tim. There's always an answer if you think carefully and never give up.'

'Well, you always seem to get there in the end, so I'll leave you to it. I must say, it seems an odd place to murder someone.

Anyway, I'll send my report in as soon as I can, but I'm not expecting anything unusual.'

'Thanks, Tim.'

'OK, that's fine.' Andy was speaking on his phone to the PC guarding the stairs. 'That attendant wants to come down to get that wicker basket of towels,' he said to Oldroyd.

'I presume you've checked it?'

'Yeah, we emptied it on to the floor and there was nothing but wet towels.'

'Hmm . . . OK.' Oldroyd looked round the steam and hot rooms, the plunge pool, the swimming pool and then into the boiler room. The elaborately decorated Turkish arches and the tiles in a variety of vibrant colours gave the place a weirdly exotic feel. 'So only Penrose, the receptionist, the manager and that attendant came down here?'

'So they say.'

'So, on the surface, those three would be the obvious suspects. We've only got their word for what happened.'

Steve Monroe arrived and went to get the wicker basket. Oldroyd was still in the hot room area looking at the ceiling and the shower fittings. He saw Steve come out of the changing rooms with the basket.

'Just double-check that basket, Andy.'

'It's just towels,' said Steve, and he pulled them all out again. 'I need to get them to the washing machine.'

Andy felt around right to the bottom of the basket and found nothing. 'OK,' he said. Steve lifted the basket on to his shoulder, carried it up the stairs and put it into a room near reception, which acted as both store and laundry.

'So what makes you think they're not the killers?' asked Oldroyd.

'It seems a very poor scheme: murder someone in a way that puts suspicion firmly on you. And then there's the question of motive: I don't think any of them really knew the man, although it seems he was a regular here when he was in Harrogate. We'll find out more when we question them.'

'OK. Good. I remember the time when you'd have wanted to rush in and arrest them because they're the obvious suspects: they had the means and there's no indication of how anybody else could have done it. But you're using your brains and your instincts a bit more.'

'Thanks, sir.' Andy grinned. Ever since he'd come up from London to work for Oldroyd, he'd wanted to impress his boss.

'And I agree with you. There's more to this than meets the eye, so to speak. Nevertheless, we do need to question them carefully. Come on.'

Back upstairs, Howard Barnes ushered the two detectives into his office. 'Of course, I understand we have to close the Baths for the foreseeable future?'

'That's right, I'm afraid, until we've done all the necessary tests and searches. Can you send the receptionist in? Carol, is it? And then the cleaner.'

'Yes. Carol Ashworth and Shirley Adams.'

Carol came in looking very apprehensive. Oldroyd beckoned her to sit down.

'So, is it Mrs Ashworth?'

'Yes.'

'OK, Mrs Ashworth. Just take us through what happened this morning. In your own time.'

'Well, I came in early to work at seven fifty because on Thursday mornings there are the private sessions and I was on duty.'

'Do you have a rota for that amongst the reception staff?'

'Yes.'

'There must be someone else who gets here even earlier than you, to open things up and turn things on.'

'The technician, Sid Newman, gets here first. He comes about five thirty a.m. and starts everything up – you know, the heating, steam generators and all that stuff – and then goes off. Shirley, the cleaner, arrives a bit before me, and she lets me in.'

'OK. Go on.'

'Mr Penrose was booked in and he arrived at eight a.m.; that was the time of his booking. He pressed the bell. I saw him and let him in. We said good morning and then he went straight down.'

'So there's security on the door?'

'Yes, when there's only one of us here. We only let people in who are authorised. I recognised Mr Penrose.'

'Did you notice anything unusual about him? Was he anxious or preoccupied or anything?'

'No. He just seemed his normal, cheerful self.'

'So he went down and what happened then?'

'Nothing. At least nothing strange. I sat here. There were emails to answer from people making enquiries, so I sent off replies. I also sent texts to some friends. Shirley was cleaning this office and then she vacuumed the carpet in the entrance. After that she went out for a smoke and just at that moment Steve arrived.'

'So, for the period between Mr Penrose arriving and Steve Monroe getting here, you and Shirley were here, together, in the reception area?'

'Yes.'

'And neither of you left?'

'No.'

'And what time did Mr Monroe arrive?'

'At quarter to nine. We open to the public at nine fifteen and he has to check round and see if everything is OK.'

'So you let him in?'

'Yes, and he went straight down.'

'And how long was it before he raised the alarm?'

'Just seconds, less than a minute, I'm sure.'

'So he wouldn't have had time to kill the victim?'

Carol looked shocked. 'Steve? No, he wouldn't do anything like that, but he definitely wouldn't have had time anyway.'

'OK. And then you went down and he was there with the body?'

'Yes.' She winced. 'It was horrible seeing Mr Penrose like that. I . . .' Andy noticed a box of tissues on the desk and passed one to her. She dabbed her eyes. 'Thank you.'

'You came back up here and phoned the police?'

'Yes, I did.'

Oldroyd paused to let her recover. 'I take it you knew Mr Penrose because he came here regularly?'

'Yes, and I've read a lot of his books; they're very good, so it was nice to meet him, if you see what I mean.'

'You didn't know him in any other context?'

'No.'

'Thank you, that's all for now. An officer will take a written statement from you. Then I think you should go home. I'm sure your manager will let you.'

'Yes.'

'When you go out, please ask Shirley Adams to come in here.'

Shirley was shaking and looked as if she already needed her next cigarette.

'Please try to be calm,' said Oldroyd with a smile. 'We just want to know what happened this morning, so tell us everything you did.'

She looked anxiously from one detective to the other.

'Well, I got here at seven. I always do. I've got a key to let myself in at the side door, and I did all my jobs.'

'Where's the side door?'

'It's just over there in the room with the washing machine and stuff. It leads to a side street. That door's only for staff and it's kept locked. There's a key at reception but me and Sid Newman have our own so we can get in early.'

'I see. You can't get down to the baths from there?'

'No. You have to pass reception.'

'OK. Go on.'

'I let Carol in at the front door at ten to eight. She was here early because there was a private session.'

'And you clean this office?'

'Yes, and the staff toilets and the carpets by the door and up the stairs to the meeting rooms and in those.'

'You don't go down to the baths?'

'No, that's Steve's area. He does the cleaning down there; has his own stuff. I never go down those stairs.'

'I see. So you and Carol were in reception all the time?'

'Yes.'

'And neither of you left?'

She wiped her brow, as if it was an enormous effort to speak. 'No. I heard someone ring the bell. It must have been about eight; Carol hadn't been here long. That must have been Mr Penrose arriving. I was cleaning the office. I vacuumed the carpets and the next thing was Steve arriving. I'd just about done and I was having a smoke outside. Then about a minute later there was a scream and Carol came running back up the steps saying someone was dead. I couldn't do anything. I can't be doing with dead bodies and stuff. My sister's a nurse; she says I'm squeamish around blood. Anyway,

I just went and sat with Carol in the office until Mr Barnes got here and then the police came.'

'Thank you, that's very clear. Can I just ask if you saw or heard anything unusual between when you arrived and when the body was discovered?'

She thought for a moment. 'No, it was just an ordinary day.' She shook her head. 'I don't know what my Stan will say after this. He'll tell me I ought to leave here if there's going to be murders and stuff. Anyway . . .' Her voice trailed off.

'I'm sure there won't be any more, and thank you very much.' Oldroyd smiled at Andy as Shirley left.

Steve Monroe sat looking very shaken.

'Can you tell us exactly what happened from the time you arrived this morning?'

'Yes. I got here at eight forty-five and Carol let me in. Shirley was outside having a smoke. I went straight downstairs to check everything.'

'What kind of things?'

'That everything's working, that there are fresh towels available, the changing rooms are clean, stuff like that.'

'You work as an attendant and a masseur?'

'Yes. I have a small treatment room near the changing rooms.'

'OK. So what did you see when you got down the stairs?'

'Everything seemed normal. I passed the pool and looked in the steam rooms and saw the body on the floor. I knew it had to be Mr Penrose because he was booked in for a private session. At first I thought he'd fainted or had a heart attack and I was ready to do CPR, but then I saw the red line around his neck, saw his eyes were open. It was very hot in the room, but his body felt cool. I felt for a pulse, but couldn't find one. I was absolutely sure he was dead.'

'Did you move the body?'

'I just turned him a little to get a better view of his neck. That's all.'

'And then you called Mrs Ashworth?'

'Yes, but first it began to sink in that he'd been murdered and his murderer must be down there. I rushed round everywhere, but there was nobody there. There aren't really any hiding places down there and I checked all the changing cubicles. Then I called Carol and she called you.'

'Did you know Mr Penrose?'

'No, except that I've seen him here before. He comes every year at festival time.'

'OK. Thank you.'

It all seemed very plausible, thought Oldroyd, but could this man who found the body have had time to kill Penrose?

'See what I mean, sir?' said Andy when Monroe had left.

'I do. It's a good 'un, isn't it? Murderer disappeared but no way out. First, we must establish that what these three are telling us is true. Have a look at Carol's computer and see if she was sending emails at that crucial time between eight and eight forty-five. Check her texts too. I've been wondering whether Monroe might have had opportunity to quickly strangle Penrose but if she's right about Monroe calling out to her not long after he went down, it hardly gives him time to commit the murder, and it would be a stupid plot anyway. If you were the murderer, why draw attention to yourself like that? The two women's stories seem to corroborate each other nicely, but maybe too nicely.'

'The main problem with them all is the absence of motive, isn't it, sir?'

'Yes, unless we can dig something up, but I agree with you that it all seems unlikely: a crime writer murdered by three people – a receptionist, a cleaner and an attendant, who all happen to work together at the Baths. No, I think we're faced with another cunning, well-planned murder here. My first thought would be that the murderer was already down there waiting for Penrose.'

'Stayed here overnight?'

'Exactly. It wouldn't be too difficult to hide somewhere in the building and lie in wait, then get down to ambush your victim. The difficult thing to explain is how they escaped, given they were down there, and the only way out is past the receptionist's desk. We need to talk to that technician person she mentioned.'

'Sid Newman,' said Andy, looking at his notes.

'Yes, see if he noticed anything unusual. The killer must have been around when he was opening up and doing his jobs.'

'There is another possibility, sir.'

'Yes?'

'Those three may not have been the killers but they may have allowed the murderer to escape. We've only their word that there was no one else down there and no one left the building by the front door.'

'True, but I notice there is CCTV, so we should be able to check that. Also, double-check the emergency exit hasn't been tampered with.'

'Yes, sir.'

There was a knock on the door. Howard Barnes, the manager, came tentatively into the room. 'Can I help at all, Chief Inspector? My staff have had a terrible shock.'

'Yes, they have. What time did you arrive?' asked Oldroyd.

'Not long before the sergeant here.' He nodded towards Andy. 'I got a call from Carol. She sounded distraught, so I came as quick as I could. I was just about to set off for here anyway.'

'Did you know the victim?'

'No. Only that he was a crime writer – famous, apparently.'

'Yes. So you went down when you arrived. What did you see?'

Barnes corroborated what Steve and Carol had said.

Oldroyd mused briefly on the irony of the situation. If things were to continue as opaquely as they were at the moment, they may well miss the victim's skills in solving his own murder.

'Have you noticed anything unusual recently?'

'Nothing, except at festival time you do get an influx of unfamiliar visitors like Mr Penrose. But I've seen nothing alarming or sinister.'

'Fine. Well, please continue to console your staff and of course you'll have to remain closed until I give you the go-ahead to reopen, and I don't know when that will be.'

'OK. I'm going to send Carol and Steve home.'

'Good idea.'

'Oh, and I've called Sid Newman and asked him to come in. I knew you'd want to speak to him.' Outside there was the sound of the door opening and voices. 'I think that's him now. I'll just go and briefly tell him what's happened and then I'll send him in.'

Shortly after, a brawny man with hairy, tattooed arms and dressed in jeans and a T-shirt came into the room.

'Mr Newman?'

'Aye.'

'Please take a seat.'

'What's all this about somebody getting bumped off in th'hot room?'

Oldroyd smiled. 'Well, you've summed it up very nicely. I'm afraid that's exactly what happened.'

Newman whistled. 'Bloody hell! I couldn't believe it when Mr Barnes told me; strangled, was he? Well, I hope yer don't suspect me. It's my job to get everythin' goin' on a mornin'. I don't go round throttlin' folk wi' bits o' rope.'

'I'm sure you don't.' Oldroyd had to smile again. 'The main thing I want to ask you is: did you see anything unusual this morning when you came in? Anything at all? You see, we believe the murderer was probably down there waiting for their victim, so they would have been there when you were going about your business. I understand you have a key to the side door?'

'Yes. I let myself in as normal. Bloody hell! Down there waitin'.' He shook his head and thought for a moment. 'No, I didn't see owt. But it wouldn't be difficult to hide down there when there's nob'dy around. I don't look in all t'changin' cubicles, don't have time. I get t'boiler and t'steam generators goin' and then sweep round a bit in there and that's me done. It's Steve Monroe's job to check t'changin' rooms and t'toilets. I have to get off.'

'Have you got other jobs?'

'Yes, I go on to t'Leisure Centre and do t'same job there, and then to a private gym. When ah've done it all, I go home for a kip. Later on I do any maintenance jobs 'at need doin' and then I come back at night and turn everythin' off again.'

'So you keep everything moving?'

'I do; they couldn't manage wi'out me. Now then, I 'ave remembered summat. T'steam generator wa' turned up to a higher settin' than normal, but that's not my job to decide. I thought someone must have asked for it to be up higher.'

'What would be the effect of having the steam turned up?'

'It'd create more steam, of course, and t'place'd be so full of it, you'd hardly be able to tell where you were and . . . Shit! That's what t'bloody murderer wanted, wasn't it, so that they wouldn't be seen? They must have turned it up! There's no lock on t'door to t'boiler room.'

'I think you've got it. You'll have to come and work for us.'

'Aye.'

'Right, Mr Newman, that's all for now.'

Newman nodded and walked out.

'Sir, I suppose it could have been possible for him to hide in that boiler room and wait for Penrose,' said Andy, after the man had left.

'Yes, but where did he go then? You have to pass reception even to go out through that side door. You didn't find him in that boiler room.'

'We're no further forward, then, sir?'

'No, and I wouldn't expect to be at this point. This is a meticulously planned operation, and whoever's behind it has sat down and tried to think of every possible angle. However, in my experience that's not possible; there's always a chink somewhere, something that gives them away.'

'And it's our job to find it.'

'Of course, and we will. The main task now is to find out more about this Damian Penrose, and that should lead us to someone with a motive. Our starting point is going to be The White Swan Hotel, where I think he was involved in an event last night as part of the Crime Writing Festival. I know the people who organise that. I'm due to take part myself in a few days' time. They'll be very upset.'

As the detectives were about to depart, Carol Ashworth came back in looking excited.

'Chief Inspector, I've remembered something. I don't know whether it's important, but I knew what's happened reminded me of something.'

'Yes?' said Oldroyd.

'You know I told you that I read a lot of crime stories. Well, I read one recently and someone was murdered in a Turkish baths like this, and he was strangled, just like Mr Penrose.' Her expression changed as she remembered the horror of the day.

'I see,' said Oldroyd, 'and who wrote this book?'

'It was Mr Derryvale. He comes to the festival too.'

At The White Swan, preparations were underway for the day's events at the Crime Writing Festival. There was to be a publishers' forum at 11 a.m. and then Abi Derham would be reading extracts from her new book in the bar over lunch. A panel of four writers was to discuss 'Scandi Noir' in the afternoon, chaired by a prominent news broadcaster. In the evening there would be a creative writing workshop.

Patricia Hughes normally worked in the Harrogate Festival office in the town centre, but during the Crime Writing Festival she operated from a temporary office at The White Swan near the hotel lobby. She sat at her desk and sighed. There was a demanding day ahead of her, and she was still furious about the previous night's debacle with Damian Penrose. Penrose was a big draw and she didn't really want to lose him from future festivals. However, the line had to be drawn somewhere when it came to behaviour like that, so did she have to call it a day with him?

Glancing at the programme, she saw that Penrose was actually due to do a book signing at 10.30 a.m. in the outside marquee. It was quite a relief to remember that her deputy, Amanda Rigby, was handling this event, so she could keep away from Penrose for the time being. As if on cue, however, Amanda came into the office looking worried.

'Morning, Amanda. Anything wrong?'

'I hope not. It's just that we've got Damian Penrose scheduled to do his book signing and he seems to have disappeared.'

'What?'

'Well, you know he's staying here?'

'Yes.'

'I've been to the hotel reception and asked if I could speak to him on the phone, to remind him. You know what he's like sometimes.'

'I do.'

'They called his room but no answer, so I thought he must still be having breakfast, so I went to the dining room and they told me he hadn't been down and that's very unusual for him.'

'Doesn't he sometimes go for early-morning sessions at the Baths?'

'Yes, but he always comes back for his breakfast and I've looked everywhere. I'm sure he's not in the hotel.'

Patricia shook her head; what more trouble would that man cause her? He'd probably forgotten about the book signing and gone to York for the day or something. He really was beyond the pale.

'OK, well, maybe he's been delayed at the Baths or something. I—'

She was interrupted by the sudden appearance of the hotel manager, Barry Evans, looking very pale and agitated.

'Sorry to interrupt, Pat, but Damian Penrose . . .' He appeared to be struggling for words.

'What about him? He's got a book signing at ten thirty.'

'The police have just rung. Penrose has been found dead at the Royal Baths.'

'What?'

'They're on their way over here now.'

'But what happened?'

'Apparently he was murdered; they wouldn't give any details.'

'No!' exclaimed Amanda. 'But what about . . . ?' She was about to say 'the book signing' but stopped.

Patricia took a deep breath and went into emergency-planning mode. 'OK, get round all the staff and tell them to come here for a meeting. We need to brief them about what's happened. I'll go over and get a notice put up cancelling his book signing. Luckily for us that's no great loss. No one's paid for that, and, as his last event was scheduled for next Tuesday, we should be able to get a replacement.'

She realised her comments may have sounded insensitive in the circumstances but her responsibility was to the festival and its customers. They were all about to leave the office when a receptionist came to the door.

'Mr Evans, the police are here.'

Oldroyd admired the grandeur of the old hotel as he parked his Saab at the entrance. It was one of several majestic hotels that had survived from the golden era of Harrogate's history as a spa and tourist destination, though some were now apartments. In front of the imposing building were extensive lawns, on one of which a large white marquee had been erected.

In the entrance hall, people were wandering around, presumably waiting for the next event. There were a number of hushed conversations taking place and Oldroyd wondered if rumour was already sweeping through the Crime Writing Festival venue that a real murder had taken place and, irony of ironies, of a crime writer.

Oldroyd and Andy went to reception, where Barry Evans came to take them into his office. The detectives sat facing Evans, who took a seat behind his desk.

'So just to reiterate,' began Oldroyd, 'one of your guests, Damian Penrose, has been found dead at the Royal Baths, and not of natural causes. Consequently this is a murder enquiry. We will need to speak to everyone who had contact with him.'

'I see,' replied a still stunned Evans. 'By all means use this office to talk to people.'

'Thank you very much, sir. And we'll start with you, if that's OK.'

'Well, yes, by all means,' said Evans.

'What can you tell us about Mr Penrose?'

'Well, he . . .' Evans was clearly struggling, having been suddenly plunged into this serious situation. 'He's stayed here for a number of years now when the Crime Writing Festival is on. It's obviously very convenient for him, as we are also the venue for most of the events.'

'Quite. What was your impression of him? Were there ever any problems?'

Evans shuffled uneasily. 'Not particularly. He always paid his bills and stuff like that but I can't say I found him a pleasant person. When he had dinner, he sometimes complained about the food, or the choice of wines. He gave me the impression that he thought everything here was vastly inferior to what he was used to in hotels and restaurants in London.'

Oldroyd frowned at this and Andy smiled, knowing how his boss reacted to any criticism of Yorkshire.

'Did he treat the staff well?'

'As far as I'm aware, no one complained about him, though I did see him flirting with waitresses and female bar staff at times.'

'Have you noticed anything unusual about his stay this year?'

'In what way?'

'Did he seem different in any way? Worried or anything like that?'

'No.'

'Did he have any visitors?'

'I don't think so. He spent time with the festival people, of course, but other than that he seemed to be alone. He went on walks round Harrogate by himself, I think. I was not aware that he had any friends in the town and nobody came with him from London, unless they stayed somewhere else.'

Oldroyd was beginning to form a picture of the victim. Penrose had not been a very pleasant person, but that was not unusual in well-planned murders of this kind. The number of suspects was likely to increase the further the investigation progressed.

Evans continued. 'Apparently there was an incident last night here in the bar.'

'Oh?'

'I only know what a member of the bar staff told me. Penrose got into an argument with some other writers and people who'd been attending an event where he was being interviewed. Pat Hughes, the festival organiser, was here. She'll be able to tell you more about it.'

Patricia Hughes looked under stress – and no wonder, thought Oldroyd. This was all going to be very disruptive for her and the festival.

'How's the festival going this year?' he asked, to try to calm her a little.

'Very well until last night and now this.'

'What happened last night?'

Patricia sighed and looked exasperated.

'That bloody man!'

'Penrose?'

'Yes. He was always causing me problems but this time he was completely out of order.' She laughed bitterly. 'And he's still making life difficult for me now, isn't he?'

'So tell me what happened.'

'He was doing a session with Ben Poole; he was being interviewed about his work, then there were supposed to be questions from the audience. Trouble with Damian was that he wasn't interested in anything or anybody but himself. The idea was for him to talk about how he works and hopefully provide some helpful hints for new writers, but poor Ben Poole couldn't get him to say anything useful. It was basically: "If you've got talent like me, you'll be successful, otherwise forget it."'

'I see.'

'But that wasn't the worst. When we got to the question-and-answer bit, there were a number of his enemies in the audience, who started asking provocative things, and a row developed.'

'Which I'm told continued into the bar.'

'Yes.'

'Did you see any of that?'

'No, but I went over when the others had gone to have a word with Damian.'

'How did he seem?'

'He was smiling; he didn't seem angry at all. He actually liked insulting people and causing controversy. I think he regarded it as good publicity.'

'And what did you say?'

'I told him I'd had enough, that if he behaved like that again I would drop him from our schedules in the future.'

'How did he respond to that?'

'I don't think he believed me. People like him think they're indispensable. But I would have done it, don't you worry.' For a moment her eyes blazed with anger.

'So after that conversation, did you leave him in the bar?'

'Yes.'

'And what did you do?'

'I went straight home. I live in a flat off Cold Bath Road.'

'And this morning?'

She looked at Oldroyd. 'Hold on, Chief Inspector, I hope you're not thinking that I might have had anything to do with Damian's murder. I mean, I didn't like the man, I admit, but—'

'Well, just answer the question, please,' cut in Oldroyd.

'I drove here and arrived at half past eight. We've got a number of events on today. Which reminds me . . .'

'Yes, don't worry, we won't keep you long. Can someone verify that you arrived here at that time?'

'Yes. I spoke to Claudia on reception.'

'Do you know the Royal Baths?'

'Yes, of course.'

'Do you go there? Are you familiar with it?'

'Yes, I do. I go every few weeks and spend an hour or so there. I find it very relaxing. But I don't see what—'

'That's fine. Can you tell me who the people were who were involved in the row with Penrose?'

'Yes. There was Charles Derryvale – he's a crime writer based in York. There's never been any love lost between him and Penrose. Then there was Esther Stevenson, another crime writer. She lives locally in the Duchys. There was a big row between her and Penrose a couple of years ago. She accused him of stealing material from her. I don't know the details, and I don't think it ever came to court. The third person was John Sinclair. He runs a small publishing company here in Harrogate. I don't know what his grudge against Penrose was, but I suspect it must have been something to do with money.'

'Do you know of any other people who might have had a reason for wanting Penrose dead?'

Patricia thought for a moment. 'No, I don't, but he was a man who made enemies easily, so there must have been others. I don't know much about his private life but he's been married twice, and each marriage ended very publicly and acrimoniously.'

'Thank you very much. You've been very helpful. If you have contact numbers and addresses for any of the people you mentioned, that would be useful.'

'Charles is staying here at the hotel. I have an address for Esther, and John Sinclair has an office in James Street. Ben Poole will be here soon. He's chairing another discussion for us today.'

'Thank you. That's all for now,' concluded Oldroyd.

Patricia consulted her phone and wrote down an address. She looked at Oldroyd. 'Chief Inspector?'

'Yes?'

'Will you still be able to attend that session for us, if we're able to go ahead?'

Every year, Oldroyd made a personal appearance at the festival. He usually spoke a little about real police work and how it differed from its fictional depiction, and then answered questions. It was a popular session with the public and with crime writers.

'Well, we'll have to see how things go, but I hope so, yes. You'll probably be under some pressure to cancel things, but my view is that the show must go on. It's important to the town, even if my officers are all over this place.' He smiled. 'But don't worry, they won't be.'

'Thank you.' She left the office looking very relieved.

'Well, she's certainly very angry with him, sir,' observed Andy. 'She has to be on the suspect list.'

'Yes, although spoiling a festival event doesn't seem much of a motive for murder.' Oldroyd got up. 'OK, we'd better get on to this Derryvale character. He should be around, if he's staying here.'

Oldroyd went out briefly to ask Evans, who was waiting nervously in the corridor, if he could track down Derryvale.

'Funny how I called Derryvale a character just now,' said Oldroyd as he returned. 'This is developing into a crime thriller that one of these people at the festival might write. Maybe it'll be one like those by John Dickson Carr and Clayton Rawson.'

'Who were they, sir?'

'Oh, crime writers from the golden age of The Impossible Crime or The Locked-Room Mystery: crimes that seemed to have no explanation. Some of them used to compete with each other back in the mid-twentieth century to see who could devise the most ingenious mystery.'

'We've worked on some cases like that ourselves, sir.'

'We have indeed, and this is shaping up to be another. Don't you think it's a bit creepy that the victim is a crime writer, and he's been murdered during a crime writing festival? It makes me think that whoever's behind it is making a point: look, I can create a real mystery plot, and you won't be able to solve it. And what about the murder being like something from one of Derryvale's books?'

'I don't know, sir, but you've taught me to be rational and keep plugging away until you get rational answers, which are always there, if you look hard enough.'

'Yes.' Oldroyd smiled. 'I need to take my own advice.'

Evans knocked on the door and came in. 'Apparently Mr Derryvale is still in his room, Chief Inspector. He never appears very early in the day. He says you're welcome to go up and talk to him.'

Oldroyd raised his eyebrows and glanced at Andy. 'Very well. If that's the way he wants to do it, we'll pay him a visit.'

The two detectives left the office and climbed up the wide, carpeted staircase to the first floor, where Derryvale had a comfortable suite overlooking the front lawns.

Andy knocked on the door.

'Come in!' proclaimed a confident voice.

Inside, Derryvale was revealed, reclining on a large bed, in a long, striped dressing gown. He was wearing his reading glasses and a book was propped on his ample belly. There was a cup of tea on a bedside table. He waved a hand languidly towards two chairs.

'Please, sit down.' Oldroyd and Andy obliged. Derryvale closed the book. To his surprise, following the conversation he'd just had with Andy, Oldroyd saw it was a classic locked-room mystery by John Dickson Carr. 'Well, a visit from the police to one's hotel room; very intriguing. How can I help you?'

'Have you been informed about what's happened to Mr Penrose?' asked Oldroyd.

'Well, the chappie just said that there's been an incident over at the Baths and Penrose was involved.'

'He was murdered.'

Derryvale whipped off his glasses. 'Good God! You're not serious. Well, well, the old bugger's got his comeuppance in the end.' He couldn't prevent himself from smiling.

'I take it you and he were not close, sir?'

Derryvale broke into raucous laughter and his belly wobbled under the dressing gown. 'I think that's a fair observation. The fact is, we hated each other's guts. It was a race to see who could finish the other off first. It appears I won.'

Andy sat up in his chair but Oldroyd shook his head. He knew the man wasn't serious. 'Well, that confession makes our job easy, sir. If you'd like to come with us.'

Derryvale smiled. 'And so ends the case. That plot would be about as interesting as the storyline in one of Penrose's books, wouldn't it? All style over substance; the lowest common denominator of the populist blockbuster.'

'So I take it you're not really confessing?' said Oldroyd, intent on moving things forward.

'Good Lord, no! I write about murder, Chief Inspector, but committing one is a different matter. Look at the state of me. I'd have a hard time pursuing my victim.'

'You have the kind of mind that could develop a scheme, though, haven't you? And I'm sure you could have persuaded other people to carry it out, given that Mr Penrose wasn't exactly popular.'

'Creating a real murder instead of a fictional one with my arch enemy as the victim! Wonderful!' Derryvale was in raptures over the prospect. 'I could write about all this. It would be some kind of meta-fiction, as I think they call it.'

'Well, maybe you already have written about it. I understand that in one of your books a character is murdered in a Turkish baths.'

'Ah yes, *The Incident at the Turkish Baths* – one of my bestselling crime mysteries.'

'Maybe you used it as a template for the real thing?'

Derryvale exploded into laughter again. 'Chief Inspector, that's wonderful. Maybe you should try your hand at detective fiction – you have a vivid imagination. But I'm sure you've considered the obvious point: why should I draw attention to myself like that if I was the murderer?' He rubbed his hands together. 'Oh, but this is so exciting! I never thought I would be a suspect.'

'So maybe someone was trying to incriminate you? Can you think of anyone who might want to do that?'

Derryvale laughed again. 'No one at all, Chief Inspector, except maybe Penrose, and he's gone before me. I'm a harmless old buffer; most people have a soft spot for me.'

Oldroyd turned to the events of the previous night. 'You were seen in the bar here last night, in the company of a number of other people, engaged in an acrimonious row with Mr Penrose.'

'Correct.'

'Can you tell me what happened, and why there was so much animosity between yourself and Mr Penrose?'

Derryvale went quiet and serious for the first time since Oldroyd and Andy had entered his room, and his lip curled. 'How long have you got, Chief Inspector? Look, before I continue, would you like a drink? I'm going to order coffee.'

The detectives accepted the offer, and Derryvale rang room service.

'Penrose was a nasty piece of work,' he said after hanging up the phone, 'make no mistake about it. He believed himself to be a far superior writer to anyone else and he enjoyed insulting other writers, belittling and humiliating them. There was a definite streak of sadism in him. He could also be very unscrupulous. This never happened to me, but talk to people like Esther Stevenson and they'll tell you he stole material from them.'

'We will. Didn't anyone ever threaten him with legal action?'

'These things can be difficult to prove. His insults were always carefully worded to be susceptible to different interpretations. Also, he's very wealthy and can afford the top lawyers.'

'So you tried to attack him through disrupting events he was involved in?'

'Yes, a group of us: that's me and Esther and John Sinclair, who was let down by Penrose in some kind of business deal. We decided that we'd go along to that session last night and tell the audience some home truths about the man at the front who was taking their accolades. If we can't get at him legally, we can at least damage his reputation.'

'And it got rather heated?'

There was a knock on the door and a waitress brought in a tray containing a coffee pot and three cups, which she placed on a table between Oldroyd and Andy.

'Thank you very much, my dear,' Derryvale said. The room service waitress left the room. 'Would one of you like to be mother?'

Oldroyd glanced at Andy, who got up, poured out the coffee and handed round the cups.

'Thank you,' said Derryvale, who took a sip of coffee and then continued. 'Yes, it did get rather heated. I'm afraid I find it difficult to contain myself when I encounter that man. He has a devilish, insidious way of getting under your skin.'

'Was there anything in particular that annoyed you?'

'He writes reviews that not only condemn the writing, but also contain subtle personal insults. He wrote about me being a "heavy and unwieldy figure" in the world of crime writing, which is clearly a reference to my size, and then he compared this to my "heavy, turgid prose". Of course, he gets away with it because you can't prove it's a personal insult, even if you had the money to take him, or his publishers, to court. They would argue that he was referring to my work as a whole, that my books are heavy and "figure" refers to my presence as a writer, that it's nothing to do with my appearance, and so on.'

'So this disagreement continued into the bar?'

'It did, and I must admit that by the end I was apoplectic. I could have smashed him over the head with a bottle.'

Oldroyd drank his coffee as he listened to these incriminating remarks. 'What did you do when you left the bar?'

'Came straight up here and went to bed. I was so angry, I couldn't sleep for a long time, which is why I've lain in this morning.'

'Can anyone verify that you've remained in this room since last night?'

'I don't suppose so. I've made a few calls, but I could have been up at the Baths finishing that bastard off.' His eyes gleamed with relish at the prospect.

'Do you visit the Baths?'

'Yes, like Penrose, I go there to relax occasionally when I'm in Harrogate, but I steer clear when the festival is on. I'd no desire to bump into him there.'

'So you haven't been there recently?'

'No.'

'And you're based in York?'

'Yes, I have a nice apartment overlooking the river. There's only me, Chief Inspector – always lived a bachelor life. I'm married to my work, as they say. I don't think anyone would have me anyway.'

'You never moved to London when you were younger, then, like most writers do?'

'Absolutely not. I may not sound like a true Yorkshireman – my parents were very middle-class York people and in those days you were encouraged not to sound too broad, so they sent me to an obnoxious little private school in the south – but I am. I've been campaigning for years to get more publishers up here in the north.'

At last Oldroyd found something in the man that he could respond to positively. 'OK. Well, thank you for now, Mr Derryvale. I'm sure you don't need me to tell you that you are a suspect with a clear motive for the crime, so we need you to stick around here for the time being.'

Derryvale smiled. 'Do you know, it's quite exciting being a suspect! I've written about such things so many times, and now I'm going to find out what it's really like. My writing's going to improve as a result; you're actually doing me a favour.'

'By the way,' said Oldroyd as he and Andy got up to leave, 'I notice you're reading John Dickson Carr?'

'Oh yes, Chief Inspector.' Derryvale beamed. 'I just love the ingenuity of those plots, even though they strain credulity at times. And the atmosphere of the 1930s. I've read them all at least once, but I keep coming back. It's so delicious to enter that world again.'

'Have you ever tried your hand at writing one like his?'

'Oh, I don't know, Chief Inspector. I'm not sure they work in a modern setting, but who knows? I might have a go sometime.'

Oldroyd and Andy left the author on the bed in exactly the same position in which they'd found him.

'What do you make of him, then, sir?' laughed Andy as they were on their way back to reception.

'He's what you'd call a colourful character, I suppose, very entertaining but in my experience there's often a great deal of affectation with many people in the artists', actors' and writers' communities. They like to play the role of the eccentric with the outrageous personality – *darling!*' Oldroyd flung out his arms and struck a pose. 'You just have to ignore it and stay focused on the questioning.'

Andy smiled to himself. His boss was quite capable of indulging in dramatic gestures himself, as he'd witnessed on several occasions. 'Do you think he was involved?'

'Quite possibly. He clearly couldn't have done the murder himself, but we've seen several times, haven't we, that carefully planned and executed murders like this involve more than one person?'

'Yes, he would enjoy planning it from the comfort of his bed,' laughed Andy. 'What do you make of this similarity between his book and the murder, sir?'

'Not much at the moment. It's all a bit thin. Much more likely to be a coincidence.'

When they arrived at the desk, there was a man waiting for them. He had longish black hair and was wearing jeans and a leather jacket. He addressed the detectives rather nervously.

'Oh, er, hi, I'm Ben Poole. Pat Hughes said you wanted to speak to me. I suppose it's about Damian Penrose. Sorry to hear that he . . .'

'Yes,' said Oldroyd. Patricia Hughes was working hard for them. 'Can you come this way?'

After the detectives had left his room, Derryvale reached for his phone.

'Ah, Esther, have you heard? . . . Yes, delightful, isn't it? The police have already been to see me. I interviewed them in my room.' He burst into laughter. 'Oh yes, they'll be wanting to talk to you soon, and mind what you say to them, you know what the police are like . . . Well, of course you know what they're like, you write about them all the time.' He guffawed again at his own joke. 'Yes, let's meet up this evening to celebrate . . . What do you mean that's bad taste? I haven't felt so pleased about anything in years, and don't tell me you don't feel the same; that obnoxious bastard . . . Yes. Anyway, I'll see you tonight. Bye. Oh, and by the way, the police have spotted a similarity between one of my books and Penrose's death . . . I know, it's absolutely hilarious, isn't it? . . . Oh, Esther, well, I think it is. Bye again.'

He rested the phone on his belly, lay back on his pillow and smiled. He found it impossible to think about Penrose's death in any way other than with pleasure. He began to sing to himself and eventually to contemplate that it might at last be time to emerge from his bed.

Ben Poole sat stiff and upright on a chair in Barry Evans's office, looking as if he'd been called to the headmaster's study.

'So I hear you had a difficult session with Damian Penrose last night?' began Oldroyd.

'Yes. Pat Hughes warned me about him, but I've chaired events with him before. He's always the same; he makes the whole thing about himself. Whatever I asked in the interview section, he simply brought it back to how good he was. It was supposed to be about him giving some insights into his craft in order to help aspiring writers. He didn't seem interested, just kept talking as if it's all only about natural talent: either you've got it or you haven't, and, of course, he thinks he has.'

'You felt that was a bad attitude?'

'Yes. It angers me when writers are so lacking in generosity to others. You can be sure they've been helped or given a break by someone at some time in their career, whatever they might say. All he wanted was to rubbish the opposition.'

'And then people started to throw contentious questions at him?'

Ben shuddered a little at the memory. 'They did. In a way, I can't blame them. He was so insufferably arrogant, but it got personal and I had to intervene. I tried to get the session back on course but without much success. It just sort of fizzled out. I don't know what the audience thought, but I found it embarrassing.'

'So that wasn't your first encounter with him?'

'No, I've encountered him several times.'

'But you didn't know him that well?'

'No.'

'What did you do after that event?'

'I left the hotel. I would normally go with the guest to the bar for a drink but I didn't want to spend any more time with Penrose.

I walked home. I stopped for a drink on the way back. I live out at Oatlands.'

'OK, and what about this morning?'

'I got up at six, although I didn't sleep well after all that stress last night. I go to the gym early on Thursday mornings. Then I came here. I've got another event this morning, or I had. I don't know if it's going ahead.'

'Can anyone verify your movements?'

'My wife, Geraldine. She's an artist and works from home. Also the people at the gym.'

'Have you had any dealings with Penrose other than festival events?'

Ben hesitated. 'Not directly, but I do some work for John Sinclair. He has a publishing business. Penrose was involved with that but it . . . it turned nasty.'

'What happened?'

'I'm sure you'll be talking to John. He will explain; it was all about money. I think Penrose helped John to start up his business but pulled out when it wasn't making as much money as he'd hoped.'

'I see. Did you ever hear John Sinclair threaten Penrose?'

'John can be short-tempered. He's a passionate man, passionate about books. I have heard him say bad things about Penrose, but never that he would like to kill him or anything like that.'

'He was here last night, wasn't he?'

'Yes, I understand he confronted Penrose in the bar along with a few others who'd been at the event.'

'He did, and it got unpleasant. Do you know the others: Esther Stevenson? Charles Derryvale?'

'Yes, of course. They're local celebrities on the literary scene, colourful characters as well.'

'They also seem to have hated Penrose. Did you ever witness them threatening him?'

'No. But Penrose was a very unpleasant character. I'm sure he had many enemies.'

'Yes, I'm sure you're right,' concluded Oldroyd thoughtfully.

After Ben had left, the two detectives had their first case discussion. Barry Evans had arranged for coffee to be brought to the makeshift incident room, along with some tempting Danish pastries. Andy was tucking in, while Oldroyd struggled hard to resist.

'Well,' began Oldroyd, sipping his coffee and trying not to look at the pastries, 'it looks like we've got another puzzler on our hands. Plenty of people with motives but no idea how the crime was committed. I remember promising you that life would be interesting here in Yorkshire when you first arrived and I've not been wrong.'

Andy smiled and swallowed a mouthful of pastry. He vividly remembered his first day at West Riding Police, when Oldroyd had whipped him off to investigate an unusual case in the potholes of the Yorkshire Dales. Police work was very different here from what he'd known at the Met, but no less demanding.

'Yes, sir. Well, they warned me that it would be challenging working for you and they weren't wrong.'

'No. I always seem to get the difficult ones, but it makes life interesting.'

'Definitely, sir. I wouldn't have it any different.'

'Good man. So what do you make of what we know so far?'

Andy quickly downed the last piece of his pastry. 'As far as the murder goes, someone got in and out of those Baths, so are those people – the receptionist, the bloke who found the body, the cleaner, the maintenance chap, even the manager – lying? It could have been one of them or a group of them, or they could be covering for someone else who came and left before they called us.'

'Yes, that seems the most likely scenario at the moment. The problem is that, although those people had the means and opportunity, they didn't have a motive. All the people with motives were far away from the Baths, as far as we know.'

'We might find they had motives.'

'Absolutely, it's very early days, but at the moment I can't see what a receptionist, a cleaner and a masseur and so on would have had against Penrose that would make them want to kill him. The other problem is that we'd be talking about a conspiracy, and you know how suspicious I always am of those. At least some, if not all, of them would have to be working together, and that always complicates things.' Oldroyd put his coffee cup down, broke off a small piece of pastry and popped it into his mouth. 'What do you think of the people we've seen here so far?'

'That Derryvale bloke's a dark horse. He blatantly makes himself out to be Penrose's worst enemy, as if he doesn't care if that makes him seem suspicious, but I think it's like a double bluff and maybe that similar murder in his book is the same kind of thing. He's trying to put us off, by making it seem too obvious, but in fact he must be the main suspect at this stage. He was here at the hotel with Penrose and could follow his movements. He must have had an accomplice, but I think he could work out a clever scheme – after all, he does it for a living, doesn't he?'

'Yes, I agree. What about Patricia Hughes and Ben Poole?'

Andy shrugged. 'Maybe, sir. I'm not sure either was telling us everything. There's a lot more work to do.'

48

'There is indeed. We've only just started, so I think we should get back to HQ briefly and then get on to John Sinclair and Esther Stevenson. Let's see how they shape up.'

~

Ben Poole arrived back at the festival office to find Patricia Hughes at her laptop.

'How did it go?' she said without looking up from the screen.

'OK.' He sat down, looked round and leaned towards her. 'Do you think we should have told them about Clare?'

Now she did look up. 'No. Why should we do their work for them? They'll find out soon enough.'

'But if they think we knew something, they'll be suspicious of us.'

'Well, we don't know anything, do we? Or do we?' She looked at him more intently.

'No, of course not. It's just that, well, we have to be careful.'

'Look, let's just concentrate on the festival, shall we? I've decided your interview with Jessica Wilson is going ahead. We can't let the people down who've paid for it, so why don't you go and get ready?'

'Right.' Ben sighed and Patricia smiled wanly at him.

'Look, Ben, I'm sorry about . . . you know.'

'It's OK. It's not your fault, but it's not easy to take.'

'No, I understand.'

~

Oldroyd and Andy had just arrived back at HQ when DI Derek Fenton came to Oldroyd's office.

'What can I do for you, Derek?'

'Some help, sir, if that's OK? I know you and the sergeant here are occupied with this Royal Baths case, but I'm dealing with this alleged corruption case at the council. There's going to be a lot of work involved and I wondered if you'd let me have Sergeant Johnson?'

Steph Johnson was Andy's partner and a longstanding member of Oldroyd's team. She'd worked with him ever since she joined the force not long after leaving school. She and Andy had got together soon after he'd joined West Riding Police from the London Met.

Oldroyd considered. He was fond of Steph, with whom he had a kind of father–daughter relationship, and he valued her work for him. However, there was no good reason to refuse Fenton's request; in fact, there were good operational reasons to accept it.

'Fine. I'll just have a word with her and send her up.' Fenton's office was on the floor above.

Fenton left, and Oldroyd went out into the general office to call Steph in from where she was working, writing a report on a recent investigation. The three sat down together.

'How did it go at the Baths?' asked Steph.

'Another puzzler,' replied Andy. 'A writer bloke with loads of enemies was strangled in a steam room but apparently by nobody. You know, the sort of case DCI Oldroyd and his team specialise in.' He grinned at his boss.

'At least it's never boring,' Oldroyd replied. Steph's eyes brightened; she was looking forward to being involved in this. Oldroyd, however, delivered the unwelcome news. 'Steph, Derek Fenton has just been in; he wants you on that council corruption case. I couldn't really refuse him. He needs support and it would be greedy of me to keep both of you.'

Steph was very disappointed, but tried hard to conceal it. 'That's fine, sir. Shall I go up now?'

'If you would.'

Steph left the office grim-faced. She had another reason for not wanting to work with Fenton. His behaviour towards her was unpleasant in a way that amounted to sexual harassment. He stood too close to her at the photocopier and often made comments about her appearance. When she'd tackled him about it, he'd turned hostile, pulled rank and threatened to spread false rumours about her and Oldroyd. Since then she'd tried to avoid him, but she knew he was still watching her and it made her feel uncomfortable.

When she arrived at Fenton's office, her heart sank further. Fenton was behind his desk, and lounging in nearby chairs were two male DCs who regularly worked with him: DC Hancock and DC Turnbull, or 'Cock and Bull', as they were widely known. They were notorious for their unreconstructed behaviour and had both been cautioned in the past for their smutty talk and sexist attitudes, but to no avail. They enjoyed Fenton's protection.

Turnbull greeted Steph with a leering grin. 'Ooh! Aren't we lucky, sir? The chief inspector's let us have his favourite sergeant to work with us.'

'Cut it out,' said Steph firmly, attempting to nip things in the bud.

'Sergeant,' replied Fenton abruptly, 'that's uncalled for. I expect everyone who works with me to be able to take a joke.'

Steph did not reply, and Turnbull smirked like a schoolboy who had got away with a prank. Her mood darkened still further as she contemplated the reality of working with these three.

'Not to worry, sir. I expect Sarge is just a little nervous now she's away from the chief inspector and lover boy,' said Hancock, who sat in a chair with his legs splayed apart, displaying his crotch towards Steph. At the insulting reference to Andy, Steph glared at Fenton.

'OK, that's enough, shut up, you dickhead,' Fenton said to Hancock, but the two DCs just laughed. 'Let's make a move,' said Fenton. 'The sergeant and I are going to do an interview on this corruption case. You two get on with writing the reports on that assault case at The Horse and Groom.'

'OK, sir, enjoy yourself,' said Turnbull, with a revolting leer at Steph.

The DCs left the office and Fenton turned to Steph with a nasty smile on his face. 'At last,' he declaimed dramatically. 'Just the two of us. What I've been waiting for ever since you came here.'

Instinctively, Steph drew back and edged to the door. She didn't think he would try anything on now, but she was going to have to stay on the alert. Clearly she was in for a difficult time.

Two

There is the Sulpher and Stincking spaw, not improperly term'd for the Smell being so very strong and offensive that I could not force my horse near the Well.

Celia Fiennes's Visit to Harrogate recorded in Through England on a Side Saddle in the time of William and Mary 1685–1710

Unaware of Steph's ordeal, Oldroyd and Andy walked through Harrogate to James Street in order to find John Sinclair's office. James Street was a pleasant, arcaded thoroughfare lined with expensive shops. Between two of these shops, Andy found the number Patricia Hughes had given them. It was on a black door, to which a square plate was fastened, announcing 'Sinclair Publications'. Andy rang the bell. Immediately a buzzer sounded and the detectives entered. Steep steps rose in front of them. At the top they knocked on a glass-panelled door.

'Come in!'

Oldroyd opened the door to reveal a cramped office overlooking the street outside. Books covered tables and the floor in high and unsteady-looking piles. A young woman sat at a computer, which was perched on a small table, near a man sitting at a larger wooden desk. He was thin, with longish dark hair streaked with grey, and a swarthy complexion. He looked towards the door over his reading glasses. 'Yes, what can I do for you?'

'Police,' announced Oldroyd as he and Andy showed their IDs. 'We're investigating the murder of Damian Penrose. I assume you're John Sinclair?'

'What?' Sinclair was either genuinely shocked or a very good actor, thought Oldroyd. 'But how? Where?'

'He was strangled this morning at the Royal Baths.'

'Good God! I . . . er, yes, I am, er . . .' He looked across to his assistant. 'Amy, why don't you go for your lunch break now? I need to talk to these gentlemen in private.'

Without a word, the woman got up, slipped on a jacket and left the office. Sinclair seemed too stunned to speak for a moment.

'Er, sit down.' He pointed to two chairs at the side of his desk. The detectives stepped gingerly between the piles of books to reach them.

'Look,' said Sinclair, more directly, as if he'd decided what line he was going to take, 'I'm sure you've got me down as a suspect. It was no secret that Damian and I had a bad relationship, and I expect you've already heard about last night. That arrogant man; he was absolutely intolerable. But I didn't kill him.'

Sounds from people walking in the street below drifted in through the open window. It was quite relaxing, but Oldroyd saw all around him the evidence of a struggling business. Hard graft went on in this room.

'Can you tell us more about this bad relationship?' he began.

Sinclair sighed and ran his fingers through his hair.

'I've known Damian a long time. We were at school together, down in Hertfordshire, a minor public school, bloody awful place, but we had a good time running a school mag when we were in the sixth form. We were always interested in books and writing. I enjoyed the organisation and printing; Damian was the writer, and that's just how things carried on.

'We lost touch for many years; it was all well before Facebook, but I watched the progress of his career as a crime writer with interest. I got into the publishing industry and worked for a number of companies in London. My family came from up here and it was always my ambition to return to Yorkshire and establish my own business. I think it's wrong that the north has so few publishers.'

'I agree, very laudable,' said Oldroyd, pleased to hear this sentiment for the second time. He was keen to see northern writers being able to have their work published locally.

'Anyway, around that time, I bumped into Damian at the London Book Fair and we re-established contact. It was all very pleasant for a while, reminiscing about the past.' He shook his head. 'I should have left it at that, but I told him about my plan to set up a business here. Damian didn't like the north of England, he thought it was the back of beyond, but when I explained that there might be money to be made publishing local writers, he became interested. Despite his image as the urbane, literary type, he's always been very keen to make money. I think that was the main motivation for becoming a crime writer: he thought he could make money out of it and I can't deny he was right about that. However, he said he would help me set up here in Harrogate. I was desperate for some support and nearly bit his hand off. I ought to have trodden more warily, as it turned out.'

'How did he help you?'

'He lent me money; enough for me to start here, rent the office and so on. That was four years ago and we agreed that once things were established he would invest in the business.'

'How did things go wrong?'

'I was too naïve and trusting. It was a gentleman's agreement – you know, old-school loyalty and all that. There was nothing written down. I was a fool. We then had a difficult couple of years and just about broke even. We didn't make any profit.'

'So he turned against you?'

'Exactly. He called one day to ask how things were going and when I told him, he said in that case he'd had enough and wasn't going to invest any more. He wasn't going to support lame ducks and he also wanted his loan paid back within five years. Damian could be like that: very unpredictable.'

'Nevertheless, you were disappointed?'

Sinclair thought for a moment. 'I suppose I was really. I thought that our old friendship meant something but apparently not. It was merely a financial transaction for him. I explained that it was a very competitive market and publishing is undergoing big changes and all that, but he wasn't interested, just said I was making excuses.'

'And has it had a bad effect on you?'

'Absolutely. We're really struggling now. I can only employ Amy part-time, and I work God knows how many hours a week trying to make a go of it. I feel he ditched me just like that, despite all his talk about supporting a new venture.'

Sinclair had been tapping a pen on his desk, and now he threw it down.

'You're obviously very angry with him,' said Oldroyd.

Sinclair frowned. 'Yes, but I know what you're driving at. I didn't kill him.'

'You were there last night in the bar at The White Swan as part of a group who got into an argument with Penrose.'

Sinclair raised his eyebrows. 'I assume you've been talking to the others.'

'We have.'

'OK. Well, I was at that event and what a farce it was! Poor Ben Poole tried to get Penrose to talk about something other than his damned self but without success.'

'Why were you there, given you'd fallen out with him?'

'Good question, Chief Inspector. You could ask the others the same thing. I suppose we have – had – a fascination with the old rogue. We like him to know we're there, that not everyone in the audience is there to fawn on him. Last night Esther and Charles took it all a bit further: they asked awkward questions and tried to unsettle him, and afterwards we all followed him into the bar and continued it.'

'And what happened?'

'It just became a slanging match. You could never get the better of Damian in that kind of scrap: he loved it. Whatever you slung at him, he just replied in kind. The more notorious he became, the more he thrived on it.'

'So were there other ways you could get back at him?' asked Andy.

Sinclair looked at the younger detective and smiled. 'Nice try, but no, we didn't plan to kill him, though I can't see that many people are going to be lamenting his passing . . . except his fans.'

'And what did you do when you left the hotel?'

'I went home. I live over in High Harrogate and I walked it. It helped me to cool off. I got back around midnight. My partner, Ed, was already in bed and I joined him.'

'And this morning?'

'Got up at my usual time about eight and walked back into town and then here. I always walk to work; it's my main exercise. Ed was around – he can vouch for the time.'

'OK. Do you go to the Royal Baths?'

'Yes, occasionally. I think a lot of Harrogate people go now and again. They're such a feature of the town. Ed goes there quite regularly.'

'So you're familiar with the layout and everything?'

'Yes, but I'm afraid I didn't just pop in this morning on my way to work and bump him off. That would be too easy for you.'

'We don't go in for easy cases,' replied Oldroyd as he and Andy got up to leave. 'That's all for now, and I wish you the best of luck with the business. You're right, Yorkshire needs more publishing houses of its own.'

'Thank you.' Sinclair smiled and seemed genuinely grateful for Oldroyd's words of encouragement.

On the way down the stairs, they passed Amy – the assistant – returning from her lunch break, but she looked away and said nothing.

Steph sat rigidly in Derek Fenton's car: an Audi, which was his pride and joy. It was always immaculately clean inside and out and the interior smelled of cheap air freshener.

Fenton always put on dark glasses to drive, and he'd taken off his jacket and placed it on a hanger attached to a rear door. His shirt was pulled tight over his fat stomach and there were the usual sweat stains under his arms. The strong smell of his aftershave combined with the air freshener made Steph feel sick.

'Well, this is nice, isn't it?' He grinned at her in a knowing, lecherous way, which added to her nausea. She moved as far away from him as the seat would allow and looked out of the window. 'I'm sure we'll work well together, don't you?'

'Yes,' she replied tersely, not wanting to be either rude or encouraging.

'You'll find there's nothing like a mature man who knows what he's doing.'

Steph ignored this comment and its crude implications.

'Don't you get tired of working with the chief inspector? It must be like working with your dad all the time.'

Steph felt she had to defend Oldroyd. 'He's taught me a great deal, and I respect him a lot.'

'Aw, that's sweet. I won't ask what you've learned but I bet he's enjoyed teaching you.'

Steph felt angry and bit her lip. Clearly everything she said was going to be turned to smut. They were driving past Ripley, and she caught sight of the castle. She felt as if she was trapped in some kind of dungeon and was relieved when they arrived at their destination: a converted barn out on the road to Nidderdale. Fenton pulled into the drive and switched off the engine. As his hand left the gear stick, it brushed briefly against her leg.

'Anyway, better get to work,' he said. 'This woman's called Clare Bayliss. Her husband, Jack Sandford, is a councillor and he's been accused of corruption – in particular, putting a contract her way. He's suspended from the Procurement Committee at the moment. She's an architect, and the contract was for renovations to the Royal Baths last year. Let's see what she has to say for herself.'

Fenton knocked on the door, which was answered by a woman with short dark hair, dressed in expensive Capri trousers and a halter-neck top. He showed his ID.

'Yes, come in,' she said with a sigh.

The detectives entered a huge sitting room. There was a large window looking out on to a paddock, where two horses were grazing. A wooden spiral staircase led up to a mezzanine floor. Steph could see the skilled work of the architect owner in its design. Fenton sank into a leather sofa and Steph sat well away from him in an armchair. Clare sat on an upright wooden chair and crossed her legs.

'I really think this is unnecessary. I—' she began to say, but Fenton interrupted her abruptly.

'We'll be the judges of that.' Steph winced. Why was he being so rude? 'Your husband's being investigated for corruption. He gave you a contract to do work for the council. What do you have to say to that?'

'Well, I was about to say that it was all a mistake. Jack thought he'd declared all his interests, but apparently he'd forgotten about me.'

'That's a bit hard to believe, isn't it?'

'Not really, if you know Jack. He's very bright and well meaning, but a bit scatterbrained when it comes to detail. And anyway, the point is, he didn't personally give me the contract. It was decided by the Procurement Committee.'

'But he's the chair of that committee, and so he was in a position to steer the other members in your direction.'

'But he didn't.'

'We'll see what they say when we interview them. The fact is, the allegation has been made and he didn't list you as an interest.'

'Made by people in the council who want to get rid of him.'

Fenton ignored this comment. 'It was too good an opportunity to miss, though, wasn't it? A nice juicy contract with the council. Handed to you on a plate and you didn't need to offer any favours in return.' Steph looked up sharply.

'What do you mean by that?' asked Clare, looking flustered.

'We all know what goes on when people are bidding for contracts. People like you use all the assets you have.' He gave her one of his leering grins.

Steph's cheeks went red with embarrassment, but she couldn't say anything.

'Are you implying . . . ?' said Clare.

Fenton laughed, enjoying his dirty innuendo. 'No, not me. I wouldn't imply anything. I'm just saying it was easy pickings, wasn't it?'

'No.' Clare looked angry, and Steph sympathised. 'I put in my bid and the committee decided it was the best. They know who I am and their discussions and decisions are all minuted. The only problem was Jack's oversight, which has been used maliciously by his enemies.'

Fenton continued with his cynical line of questioning, constantly verging on the sleazy and suggestive. He didn't appear to have much of an aim beyond making Clare uneasy. Steph felt angry and ashamed, and wondered what he might have said to Clare had she not been with him.

She sat silently in the car on the way back, considering how she could escape from working with Fenton.

When they were out of the drive, he turned to her. 'Well, you weren't much bloody good in there. You didn't say anything.'

'Did you want me to? I thought you were quite happy making the woman feel uncomfortable.'

He laughed. 'That's the first rule in my book: never mind putting them at their ease, get control over them, show them that you mean business.'

'Did you have to imply that she might sleep with people to get contracts?'

'Ooh! Who's got a dirty mind, then? Who says that's what I meant? Anyway, you're bloody naïve if you think that kind of thing doesn't go on. And women are the worst.'

Steph said nothing. She didn't want to get into an argument with him.

After a while he said, 'Maybe this'll get you talking.' He opened the glove compartment with his left hand, took out an envelope and threw it at her. Startled, she looked at it on her lap. 'Open it.'

She did, took out the contents and gasped.

There was a series of photographs showing a woman topless on a beach. It was her. For a moment she was bewildered, but then realised where they came from. It was several years ago and she'd been in Mallorca with some rather rowdy friends. They'd all got drunk and then photographed each other with their bikini tops off and making lewd gestures. Someone had put them on Facebook, but that was a while ago. She thought they'd all been removed. How had he managed to get them?

'Good, aren't they?' he said, and this time his smile was positively sinister. 'Not pictures you'd want everyone to see, though, are they?'

'Where did you get these?'

'Never you mind.'

Then she remembered. Amelia, one of the friends, had sent her some prints of the images as a joke. She'd sent them to Steph at work with a note saying, 'Dare you to hand these round the office. Quick promotion if you do!' It was just like her. Steph had laughed, stuck them in a drawer in her desk and, like an idiot, forgotten about them. The bastard must have been going through the drawers trying to find something he could use against her. He wouldn't have been able to believe his luck when he struck gold! She could kick herself for being lax about keeping those drawers locked; if only she'd remembered that this stuff was in there.

'You've been going through my personal things.'

'Hey, be careful with your allegations. Anyway, it's a shame to keep such lovely pictures secret, don't you think? Or would you rather they weren't shown to your colleagues at work?'

'Are you blackmailing me?'

'Oh, that's such a nasty word.'

'Can you think of a better one?'

He turned to her. 'Whatever. Anyway, you should have thought about that when you were posing like a whore for those photographs. I don't think DCI Oldroyd would be impressed if these became public. Do you think you'd be taken seriously again by the powers above? And what about that Cockney boyfriend of yours? I don't think he'd want pictures of his girlfriend's tits being shown around HQ. It'll make you look like a real slapper.'

It took all Steph's self-control to stop herself from slapping him across the face.

'But don't worry, there are ways we can stop that happening,' Fenton continued.

Steph said nothing. She didn't want to hear the revolting details. Nothing else was said until they arrived back at HQ. As he stopped the car, he put his hand on her leg.

'Take your hand off me.'

'Ah, ah, no need to be so touchy. Think about what I've said. It would be a great pity if all those male officers suddenly saw you in a different light. Could you face them again once you knew they'd had a good look at your nipples in a photograph?'

Again she said nothing. She went straight inside, locked herself in a cubicle in the toilets and sobbed.

Esther Stevenson lived in a house in the Duchy Estate, an area of handsome stone-built houses in various styles, many of which had elaborate and well-maintained gardens. Her house had pointed, tall gables and rooms on three storeys, but was rather shabby in appearance and the garden was somewhat overgrown at the front with leggy rhododendrons and rampant pink geraniums. Grass grew between the paving stones on the path.

'Well, she's not a gardener,' remarked Oldroyd as he knocked on the door. A dog barked in the hallway.

'Too busy writing, I expect, sir.'

'Well, writing didn't stop Vita Sackville-West creating one of the great gardens at Sissinghurst.'

'Absolutely, sir,' said Andy facetiously. He'd worked with his boss long enough now to know that Oldroyd was fond of throwing in snippets of obscure information from his rather arcane interests in order to tease him.

There was the sound of a muffled voice from within. 'Just a minute, I'm on my way.'

The door was opened by Esther Stevenson, who was wearing purple dungarees. Sharp eyes behind round-rimmed glasses assessed the visitors. 'Oh, you're the police; I can tell straight away. You'd better come in. Shut the door behind you. Be quiet, Toby!'

She turned and led them down a passageway, where an Airedale Terrier sniffed at them but decided they were OK. They went through a small conservatory and out into a similarly overgrown back garden, where she'd been sitting and writing. There was a wooden table and a number of chairs. A cat lay curled up on one of them and on the table lay a notebook and pen.

'Take a seat. I like to sit outside and write when the weather's good, and I get sick of tapping away at the keyboard, so I revert to the old pen and paper now and again.'

'I'm sure I'd do the same,' replied Oldroyd. 'It's only people of his generation' – he nodded at Andy – 'who can sit at screens all day.'

'Quite,' said Stevenson, looking at Andy, who grinned at her politely. 'Sit down.' She indicated two vacant chairs as she took a cigarette from a packet and lit up. 'You're here to find out if I killed that bastard, Penrose, but I'm sorry to disappoint you; it wasn't me.'

Oldroyd enjoyed the blunt attitude and the Yorkshire tones in her voice. 'How did you find out about the murder?' he asked.

'Charles phoned me earlier to give me the good news.'

'You clearly didn't have a high opinion of Mr Penrose.'

She took a drag and blew out the smoke. Andy, who strongly disliked cigarette smoke, winced a little.

'Damian Penrose, the doyen of the crime novel,' Esther said, with undisguised contempt. 'What you have to realise is that Penrose was not only a highly unpleasant individual with his general arrogance and nastiness, but he was also a charlatan who brought the whole writing profession into disrepute.'

'What do you mean?' asked Andy.

'I mean that a lot of material he used was stolen. He owed a lot of his success to what he took from other people, and that is a terrible crime in the literary world: passing other people's work off as your own.'

'He plagiarised?' said Oldroyd.

'Oh no, he was too careful for that. He never copied from stuff that was already in print. What he did was steal ideas.'

'How?'

'When you attain a certain level of fame and popularity, as he did, you get a lot of aspiring writers sending in their writing, hoping that you will look at it.'

'I thought writers were too busy to do that? Isn't that what the agents are for?'

'Yes, but Penrose was a devious bastard. He let it be known that his agent would pass on certain things for him to look at, and so lots of people sent things in, in the hope that they might get his help or his endorsement. He got his agent to do a kind of filter and then he read some of the more promising efforts, not with any intention of helping anybody, but purely to see if there were any good ideas he might use himself. If there were, he would send a note back saying that the book wasn't very good, have another try, et cetera. The poor writer would probably abandon that project only to find that ideas from it popped up in Penrose's next novel.'

'You say "probably" – what evidence do you have for any of this? Didn't anyone try to sue him?'

She laughed contemptuously. 'I don't know anything for certain. He was a clever sod. The ideas he stole were always subtly changed so that he, or his solicitors if it ever came to court, could argue that there were significant differences and it was therefore just a question of coincidence.'

'You seem to have a thorough knowledge of this.'

'It happened to me years ago and I've been conducting a long campaign against him ever since. I try to contact anyone who's been treated in a similar way. We know what he does, but so far we haven't been able to pin anything on him.'

'How many times do you allege that this has happened?'

'Quite a number. I've got a dossier of people who've been his victims, and those are only the ones who've come forward.' She stubbed out the remains of her cigarette. 'Look, I'm going to get a drink; talking about Penrose always sets my nerves on edge. Do you want anything?'

'Just water, thank you,' replied Oldroyd.

She went briefly into the house and returned with a gin and tonic, and two glasses of water.

Oldroyd accepted his water before continuing. 'Surely if what you say about Penrose is true, it would have caused a scandal by now?'

She smiled, implying that he was being naïve. 'Of course, there are lots of rumours in literary circles, but no one dares make anything public. Penrose would have been on them like a ton of bricks.'

'What about his publishers? Don't they mind him using other people's ideas?'

She shook her head. 'I don't think publishers give a damn, as long as it's not too risky and the books sell. And, of course, his did. It gave Penrose a lot of power.'

Oldroyd paused. 'I'm getting the strong impression that you are very angry and frustrated with this whole situation with Penrose, and I'm wondering if the lack of success in your campaign led you to attack him in a different way.'

She took a sip of her gin and lit another cigarette. 'Nice try, Chief Inspector, but no.'

'You were there last night with Charles Derryvale and John Sinclair, having a go at Penrose.'

She smiled. 'Oh yes. I never missed an opportunity to remind him that I was still here, and would continue to be a thorn in his side. Charles and John were more than ready to give me a hand.'

'And afterwards?'

'Came straight back here. My partner, Leo, was still up, and we went to bed shortly afterwards.'

'And this morning?'

'Never moved from here. Leo left for work at eight thirty – he's a solicitor – and I decided to have a working day. I've got a deadline to meet for my next novel. It's called *Witches' Fever*. It's an historical crime novel set over in Pendle at the time of the persecution there. I hope you'll both read it.'

'It sounds interesting,' replied Oldroyd. 'Do you go to the Royal Baths?'

'Where he was murdered? No, I don't go at the moment but I might after this. It will be very interesting to see where he got what was coming to him.'

Oldroyd got up, thinking just how intensely Penrose had been disliked. It almost made him believe, against his better judgement, that many people could have been involved in his murder. 'OK, we'll leave it there for the moment. Don't get up, we'll see ourselves out.'

'Do you know,' she continued, ignoring what Oldroyd had said as she blew out cigarette smoke, 'I'm almost sorry the old bugger's dead. I'm going to miss trying to bring him down, and he'll never pay for his crimes.'

She picked up her notebook and was writing before the detectives had reached the door to the conservatory.

'What did you make of her, then, sir?' asked Andy as Oldroyd drove them in his old Saab back to HQ. 'A forceful character, and seems to have hated the victim. She made no attempt to hide it.'

'Yes, which may suggest she's nothing to hide, but then again it could be the old double bluff. She talks up her hostility to put us off the track.'

'There seem to be a lot of people she could have planned it with too, if she's telling the truth about this cheating business,' said Andy, echoing Oldroyd's thoughts.

'Again, who knows? We're going to have to investigate that and it may reveal other people with a motive to get rid of Penrose, whether or not they were working with Esther Stevenson. I'm afraid it looks like another case with plenty of suspects that we'll have to slowly weed out.'

'She seems to be big pals with that bloke Derryvale too. They could have formed an alliance.'

'Indeed. I'm afraid at this stage the possibilities are many.'

'Sinclair obviously hated the bloke too, so maybe the three of them planned it together.'

'Possibly, but it all seems a bit too obvious, somehow. There they were at that event causing disruption, having a big public argument with him in the bar, and then next morning he's murdered. It almost seems as if they were deliberately drawing attention to themselves.'

'Why, sir?'

'I've no idea at this point,' replied Oldroyd as he swung the car into the car park at HQ.

'I can't see any real connection between any of them and the Baths,' continued Andy. 'Admitting to going there now and again means nothing, but they must have had at least one accomplice, because somehow I can't imagine any of them actually committing the crime. Can you, sir?'

'I can imagine them planning it, but no, not carrying it out. If we're not careful, though, we'll end up with four or five people involved, and you know what I think about big conspiracies.'

'They don't work.'

'Exactly. They usually fall out with each other and someone talks.'

'Maybe someone will.'

'Yes, we'll have to see.' They arrived back at the office. 'I wonder how Steph's doing with Fenton.'

Andy hesitated. He didn't want to make any comment that could be seen as unprofessional and protective of Steph, but he didn't like her working with Fenton and his team.

'I hope he hasn't got those goons, Cock and Bull, working with him. Those two are a pain in the arse, sir.'

Oldroyd grimaced. He knew all about the two boorish detectives' histories. 'Indeed they are, but we're watching them; another false move and they've had it.' He sat down at his desk and yawned. It was now very late afternoon and they'd been working solidly. 'Well, it's been a long day but we've done well to interview all those people. Tomorrow we need to—'

Steph came into the office.

'Ah, Steph, so how've you been getting on?' asked Oldroyd.

'Oh, fine. It's an interesting case. I'm not sure I like his style of interviewing but each to their own. How's the murder case?'

'Complicated as usual; killer disappeared, lots of suspects with motives but it doesn't seem likely that any of them could have actually carried out the murder.'

'Sounds like normal, then.'

'Yep.' Oldroyd stretched in his chair. 'Anyway, you two might as well get off. I'm going myself soon. Lots of things I need to go home and think about.'

'Take a break, sir,' said Andy. 'You can't work all the time.'

'You're right, but great detectives like Sherlock Holmes and myself need to ponder things, often deep into the night. The only difference is that he played the violin, whereas I just listen to my CDs.'

Steph and Andy laughed.

'One of these days I expect you to turn up in a deerstalker and smoking a pipe, sir,' said Steph as she and Andy got ready to leave.

Andy had sensed that something about Steph was not quite right.

'Are you OK?' he asked as they got in the car and he began the drive back to Leeds. 'You look as if you've been crying.'

'Oh, well. It's that time of the month; you know how I tend to get a bit emotional. It wasn't easy with Fenton. He had those two idiots with him.'

'Cock and Bull?'

'Yeah. Luckily they didn't come out with us, but they're a real pain.'

'I know, but you don't have to put up with it. I'm sure if you asked the boss, he'd—'

'Yes, but I can't go running to him if things get difficult, and I shouldn't have to. They're the problem, not me. If the boss moves me, they've won, haven't they? Their behaviour isn't challenged.'

'You're right, but it can't be easy to deal with it by yourself. Do you want me to do anything?'

'What? Threaten to go round and beat them up? "Leave my girlfriend alone." Then I'm like a child who has to have their parents stand up for them.'

'OK. I'm only trying to help.' Andy admired her desire to fight her own battles, although he remained very concerned. He didn't like the idea that three men, one of them her superior, were treating her like this. But it was difficult to see how he could help.

Steph sat in the passenger seat, quietly reflecting on what had happened, and what she was going to do next. The problem with Andy and many other sympathetic men was that they thought mostly in terms of protecting women from sexist behaviour and harassment, and not enough about stopping the behaviour itself.

She didn't want those pictures made public. Humiliating and embarrassing things like that tended to stick, and people formed opinions based on them. She could put up with some knowing glances and raucous laughter from male officers she had no respect for, but she valued her reputation with Oldroyd and DCS Walker, Oldroyd's superior, and did not want this to be damaged. Even though it wasn't her fault, it didn't look good that she'd had the pictures taken and then allowed them to fall into the hands of other people. But what that disgusting Fenton might have in mind as payment for not showing the photos around made her cringe. She didn't feel she could tell Andy. His response might be angry and violent, and she couldn't go to her boss because she didn't want Oldroyd to know about the photos.

She was trapped in a bad situation, but she had to sort it out herself.

Oldroyd was back in his flat overlooking the Stray. He'd lived alone since separating from his wife, Julia, several years ago. Julia taught in a sixth-form college in Leeds and lived in Chapel Allerton. Some time ago she had told him that she would be considering a divorce if a new relationship she'd started with a colleague from the college worked out. That had been a year ago, but he'd heard no more about it since. He saw his wife occasionally to talk about their family, but she never discussed her private life.

Oldroyd's daughter, Louise, had just graduated from Oxford with a first in History. She had no real idea what she wanted to do next but she had funding to do a Master's if she decided to go back to academia. She intended to take a year out first and was currently in London working in a women's refuge. When she was in Yorkshire, she tended to divide her time between her parents, and Oldroyd was missing having her around. At least he still had his sister, Alison, nearby. She was a vicar in the village of Kirkby Underside, between Harrogate and Leeds.

He sat at his computer, a glass of red wine next to the mouse mat. Due to his continued loneliness, and following a suggestion from his daughter, he had finally submitted to getting involved in something he never thought he would entertain: online dating.

He remembered how he'd started. Louise had coached him along, insisting that lots of people did this nowadays and there was nothing sad or sleazy about it.

'I just don't like the idea. How do you know what they're really like?'

'You don't for sure, but what's wrong with trying? The thing about you, Dad, is that you never go anywhere to meet anybody, so I can't see what alternative you've got if you really are interested in a new relationship.'

He was forced to acknowledge the truth of this. Work dominated his life, it always had, and his marriage had suffered. He felt uneasy about the whole dating thing but he was weary of the loneliness of being single and living by himself.

'You don't understand how difficult and awkward it is for someone my age. It's years since I did anything like this. I'm not used to forming new relationships and it feels like I'm trying to be a teenager again.'

'That's rubbish, Dad. You don't have to be young to be romantic and meet someone new.'

Louise, like her mother, was always very reticent about her own personal life. Oldroyd was hoping that this might be the moment when he learned a bit more, but she didn't say anything. She was sitting at the computer with Oldroyd and rattling through web pages at the kind of speed that left people of Oldroyd's generation feeling dizzy.

'This seems like a good site: Forty-Plus Dating, Leeds and Harrogate. Yes, let's look at some profiles.'

Oldroyd found it too excruciating to look.

'There's one here. Look.' Reluctantly, Oldroyd peered at the screen. 'She sounds really nice; interested in classical music and walking. I think you should contact her. You'll have to send a photograph.'

'Whoa! Hold on. I don't know if I'm ready for this yet!'

'And when will you be, Dad? You'll just put it off and off and you'll still be moaning that you're by yourself. Just do it, OK?'

Oldroyd shook his head at the memory. He'd followed Louise's advice and exchanged details with the woman, but he hadn't really found her attractive in the photograph and didn't take it any further. On the positive side, just getting that far had seemed to break the ice for him and he now felt much more relaxed about contacting people online. However, he'd still not got to the point of actually arranging to meet anybody.

He clicked through various profiles. What was he looking for? The perfect woman? The problem was that he'd always felt that he'd got that in Julia. He'd never wanted anyone else, and even now he still found it hard to accept that he'd lost her. And it was all his own fault. He shook his head. No good going down into self-criticism and self-pity again.

The details kept coming up: 'Fifty-year-old professional woman, Leeds, enjoys country walking and eating in country pubs. Loves dogs and cats.' He sighed; it wasn't much to go on. The walking and dining sounded OK but he wasn't much of a pet person. The whole business was much more difficult when you were older. It wasn't like being a teenager and playing the field; you were much choosier, and you didn't want to waste time seeing unsuitable people.

He was quite relieved when the phone rang.

'Hi, Jim. How are you?' It was his sister, Alison. They'd always been close and she'd kept an eye on him since his separation from Julia. She knew the loneliness of the unwanted single life, having lost her husband, David, to cancer several years before.

'OK. Just got going on an interesting case today: a murder at the Royal Baths. You like to go there, don't you?'

'Well, I did,' Alison laughed. 'But it might feel contaminated now if there's been a dead body there! Anyway, typical of you. I ask you how you are and you immediately start talking about work. I want to know how *you* are, not what West Riding Police are up to.'

'Yes, all right, good point. Well, if you must know, I'm sitting at the computer looking at internet dating sites.'

There was a pause.

'Oh dear. Has it come to that?'

'Ah, you're like I was. You think it's sad, but Louise showed me how to do it and she said lots of people meet partners this way.' It sounded like he was justifying himself.

'Yes, I'm sure she's right. If it helps you find someone, it can't be bad. I don't suppose it's any different from those Lonely Hearts columns you used to get in newspapers and magazines. How does it work?'

Oldroyd explained to her what Louise had explained earlier to him.

'So you put your details and a picture in?' Alison said. 'Sounds good. I think Louise is right: you should just get on with it. I can't see it'll do any harm. The worst that could happen is that you spend a whole evening with someone you don't fancy and who bores you to tears . . . or vice versa!'

Oldroyd had always felt that his daughter and sister had a lot in common in their good-hearted feistiness. He enjoyed having them around to tell him what to do!

'Anyway,' continued Alison, 'I was wondering if you fancied a walk on Saturday. The forecast's good. We could go up Simon's Seat. And don't tell me you're too busy.'

'Fine, great idea. I'll pick you up. What time?'

The walk was duly arranged, and Oldroyd returned to his desultory examination of the dating sites. Was it any wonder that, faced with the difficulty of personal relationships, he sought refuge and consolation in his work? After scanning through profiles for another half-hour, he sighed and shut down the site. He yawned and rubbed his eyes, and then his attention was caught by the screen. A big picture of a chameleon had come on as a screen saver. He looked at the strange creature with deep interest, marvelling how it could modify its colour to blend in with its surroundings. It gave him the beginning of an idea.

On the next day, a Friday, Oldroyd and Andy returned to the Royal Baths. Carol Ashworth was back at work on reception, though under-occupied, as the Baths were still closed to the public. She was spending most of her time answering telephone enquiries about when the Baths would reopen.

'Good morning, Chief Inspector. Sergeant,' she said, and smiled at the two men as they made their way down to the baths area past the officer still on guard. Then the phone went again.

Oldroyd paused at the bottom of the stairs.

'Right, we need to have a really careful look around here. There must be something we've missed. The murderer got out of here somehow.'

'I've heard that before, sir,' replied Andy, remembering previous cases in which murderers had disappeared from a concert hall, and a locked room. 'Anyway, at least it's not so hot down here today, now that everything's turned off, and you can see clearly.' He was looking at the ornate mosaic floor. 'This place must have cost a fortune to build, sir. Look at these floors. The Romans used to have these in their villas, didn't they? I remember learning about that at school, and then we made our own mosaic by cutting up bits of coloured paper and sticking them on to a piece of card.'

'Wonderful! Yes, they're very impressive. I think Italian craftsmen came to lay them.'

They began their second search in the hot room, where Penrose had met his death. Apart from the stone benches at the side of the tiled floor, the room was bare. The steam room, devoid of steam today, and the adjoining cold plunge pool, with its greenish water, yielded nothing. They spent some time in the short corridors looking for any ways of getting out. The windows down here below ground level were high, and on the outside were at street level. Through the frosted glass, Oldroyd could see the occasional pedestrian passing by. It wouldn't have been easy for anyone to get up to those windows, let alone escape on to a busy street without being seen. That is, if any of them actually opened.

They reached the changing rooms and examined all the lockers and cubicles. It was from just outside this room that Steve Monroe had removed the wicker basket of towels. Suddenly a strange feeling passed over Oldroyd. He'd seen something the day before that wasn't right. He hadn't registered it properly because his mind was on other things. What was it? Frustratingly, the vague memory would not solidify into anything clear. He moved to the swimming pool and gazed at the still water and the blue tiles on the bottom. The pool was an original late-Victorian feature. The thick, curved, white-tiled edges overhung the water. These were good for diving but they made it difficult to get out of the pool. Exits from the water had to be made via one of the sets of metal steps that were attached to two sides of the pool. These were clearly a later addition, being made of shiny stainless steel with the usual curved tubular handles at each side. Oldroyd imagined that they would have originally been made of wood. It was all very unusual and interesting but the search appeared to have revealed nothing about exits or hiding places. Andy joined him.

'Any ideas?' Oldroyd asked.

'No, sir. It's baffling. It's the second time I've looked round here and it drives you mad. I've had another look at the emergency exit but it's not been tampered with. There's just no way out of here except back up those stairs.'

'Right, well, get a team down here to give it another thorough going-over to see if they come up with anything. They might see something we've missed.'

It was beginning to sound desperate.

Back at HQ, Oldroyd glanced through some of the newspaper coverage. The press were having a great time with the delicious ironies of a crime writer being murdered in the very town where a crime writing festival was being held and where Agatha Christie herself was discovered after she had disappeared from her home in the 1920s.

> Poison Pen Meets Grisly End in Agatha Christie Spa Town

> You Couldn't Make it Up – Real Life Trumps Fiction at Crime Writing Festival

> Author Dies in Plot Worthy of His Books

> Did Author Plan Own Death as His Last Bow?

The last headline in one of the more lurid tabloids announced the ludicrous notion that Penrose – who was apparently either terminally ill or bankrupt, according to different accounts – had somehow arranged his suicide to look like murder and so have the last laugh over everyone.

'And so he finally lived out one of his own mysteries,' said Oldroyd aloud to himself, shaking his head. He knew when a case hit the headlines, he would soon be called in to see his boss, DCS Tom Walker. Matthew Watkins, the generally despised Chief Constable of West Riding Police, always started to get jumpy when the media highlighted a case, and he would immediately get on to Walker, asking what progress was being made, etc. As Oldroyd predicted, the call soon came and he made his way upstairs to Walker's office.

He actually got on well with Tom Walker, who had risen through the ranks and served many years as a detective in the tougher parts of Yorkshire. He and Oldroyd occasionally met socially. They shared the same beliefs about police work and were both Yorkshire to the core.

'Have a seat, Jim.' Walker, a portly man, was sitting at his desk in the bare office, cutting a rather forlorn figure. Oldroyd knew that the old boy really preferred active police work to administration. Walker was stroking his moustache, a sure sign that he was not happy. 'Well, I probably don't need to tell you what's happened. I've had the bastard on the phone.'

The 'bastard' was Watkins. Much to Oldroyd's embarrassment, Walker never made any attempt to disguise his contempt for his superior, whom he regarded as a phoney careerist.

'I never hear anything from him unless there's something bothering him, and that's usually to do with publicity that he thinks will reflect badly on him. It's all about him, the slimy little—'

'What's the problem, Tom?' Oldroyd cut in to pre-empt Walker's rant.

'He's picked up on this murder of the crime writer. He wants to know what leads we have and do we expect a quick arrest and so on. Bloody hell, it's only the day after the bloody murder, what does he bloody expect?! It's all because he wants to be seen as the head of a wonderfully efficient force but without doing any of the work, of course. It's a bloody disgrace.' He stopped, looked at Oldroyd and then continued almost apologetically. 'Anyway, how's it going?'

Oldroyd outlined what they'd done and what they knew so far.

'Well, that's a damned good day's work, in my view,' said Walker, 'and I'm going to bloody well tell him so. But you say it's a puzzle how the bloke was murdered, and you've also got a lot of suspects?'

'I'm afraid so.'

Walker frowned. 'Sounds like you've got a lot to do, then. Just keep me posted. I must admit, it's a bit of a funny do, isn't it? Bloody Crime Writing Festival on and one of the writers gets killed. Bloody hacks love it, don't they? Do you think there's any connection?'

'Not directly, but the fact that Penrose was here in Harrogate gave the murderer their opportunity. The killer must be someone with local knowledge, but others would have been involved, and the festival brings in people from all over the country.'

'Yes, I can see it's complicated. Well, don't worry, I'll keep the bugger at bay. It might be a good idea to talk to the press. You're good at it, and they like to get the chance to question us. It gives them a sense of power, pathetic as they are.' Walker paused and looked at Oldroyd again. 'By the way, we haven't been out for a drink for a while.'

'No.' Oldroyd didn't mind the occasional social meeting with Walker. He knew how to handle him and keep him off his pet hates. He was interesting to listen to when he talked about his early years in policing. 'How about next week sometime?'

'Can't do that, I'm afraid. The mother-in-law's coming to stay. Ninety-six and deaf as a post, but I need to be around all the time to help Gillian if her mother needs to be lifted or anything. Maybe the week after.'

An evening was arranged and Oldroyd returned to the office feeling an increased sense of pressure.

Oldroyd decided to hold the press conference at The White Swan. It satisfied his sense of drama and appropriateness, and no doubt that of the reporters too. A table had been set up in the ballroom and he sat behind it, flanked by Andy Carter and facing the ranks of reporters eager for succulent bits of information.

Oldroyd quite enjoyed these press conferences. He played a game with the reporters, which he always won by adroitly staying a few steps ahead. They tried to extract things they could use in their sensationalised reports, and he cleverly frustrated them.

He began, as usual, with an outline of what had happened and an appeal for any member of the public who had information to come forward. He then proceeded to questions.

'This Poison Pen bloke, he must have had plenty of enemies to get a name like that. Could they all have got together to do him in? You know, like in *Murder on the Orient Express*?'

'Well, I agree with your first point,' replied Oldroyd, smiling contentedly as he enjoyed his control over the assembled reporters, and various recording devices were thrust in his direction. No more scribbling shorthand in notebooks these days. 'Mr Penrose was not a popular individual and there are already a number of suspects in this investigation. However, I have to say that the idea of a large number of people taking part in a conspiracy to murder him is extremely unlikely. *Murder on the Orient Express* is a great story, an ingenious twist on the question of who among the suspects is the killer, but that is not how these things actually happen in my experience, although we do believe more than one person was involved.'

'Maybe no one was involved, Chief Inspector. If Penrose was dying, as we've heard, then he could have arranged his own death to be like one of his stories – you know, his final mystery. He could be having his last laugh at your expense and a final bit of posthumous limelight.'

Oldroyd raised his eyebrows. He was used to elaborate ideas like this from tabloid reporters, who yearned for things to be as sensational as possible. 'Well,' he replied, 'I have to congratulate you on your imagination. Maybe you should try your hand at writing crime fiction. I'm sure they'd welcome you at the festival. But unfortunately the answer is no. It's not possible that this was a suicide. It's very difficult to strangle yourself with a rope just using your hands, but even more difficult to dispose of the rope when you're dead.'

This brought some laughter, but the reporter was undeterred. 'But could he have arranged for someone to kill him and then disappear, thus creating the mystery?' The reporter looked very pleased with himself.

'I see,' said Oldroyd. 'Well, not impossible, I suppose, but maybe I could go philosophical for a moment. I'm sure you've heard of Occam's razor, yes?'

The reporter was silent.

'In essence,' Oldroyd said, 'it's the idea that when solving problems, simple solutions are generally to be preferred to complex ones. In this case there doesn't seem to be any sound reason to prefer your fantastical notion of an outlandish death involving a disappearing accomplice who has now made themselves a murderer, to the disappointingly mundane idea that somebody just did him in.'

Laughter again, and the reporter was silenced.

'You mentioned the Crime Writing Festival, Chief Inspector. That will be getting a big publicity boost out of this, won't it?' asked another reporter.

'Maybe,' said Oldroyd cautiously. He wasn't sure what was coming next. These people could still surprise or shock him on occasions.

'So could someone have . . . you know?'

Oldroyd realised what the man was driving at: that someone involved in the Crime Writing Festival had killed Penrose to gain publicity. It was outrageous, and he moved to quash it.

'I can see why you haven't spelled out what you mean. The implications of what you're implying are quite scandalous, so I don't think we'll go down that road. In any case, it's even more incredible than the previous suggestion.'

This caused a hubbub of conversation, and then a female reporter asked a more sensible question. 'Chief Inspector, you referred to the killer disappearing. Is it true, and do you have any leads on that?'

'OK. Mr Penrose was murdered in the Royal Baths by an as yet unknown person. We're not sure at this stage how that person managed to leave the scene of the crime without being seen by the staff at the Baths or by police officers who arrived quite soon after the body was discovered. This trick, or whatever it was, implies that the killer was a local person who had detailed knowledge of the building and knew of a way out that we have so far failed to discover. I would again like to ask at this point for anyone with any information about this or any other aspect of the case to come forward.'

Afterwards Oldroyd felt satisfied, as he usually did, that the press conference had gone well. But as he and Andy returned to HQ, he began to think about some of the ideas the reporters had presented and to wonder whether they were in fact as far-fetched as he'd initially thought.

Could the whole thing have been somehow staged? The three people who had confronted Penrose in the bar that night were all writers or publishers with plenty of style and imagination. How spontaneous *was* that row in the bar? Had everybody been acting? Maybe there were reasons why Penrose wanted to end his life and to do it in the style of a murder mystery in Harrogate, echoing the strange behaviour of Agatha Christie herself in 1926. The disappearance of the killer could be part of an elaborate trick to fool his audience for one last time.

Penrose's physical and mental state of mind and his financial affairs would have to be thoroughly investigated, and they would need to delve much deeper into his relationship with those three suspects. As usual, Oldroyd was finding that at the beginning of an unusual case like this, matters became more complex once you began to scratch the surface of the characters and events involved.

Oldroyd and his sister, Alison, were making slow progress up the steep path that zig-zagged through the bracken on the slopes of the western fells of Mid-Wharfedale. Above them loomed the strange and massive sandstone formations collectively known as Simon's Seat. The day was warm but the sky was a complex mass of heavy cloud and patches of blue, suggesting that the familiar combination of sunshine and showers would be the pattern of the day.

Alison paused and looked back. 'That's Parcevall Hall on that hillside,' she said, pointing across the valley to an ancient manor house surrounded by ornamental shrubs and parkland. 'I love that place; it's so beautiful and peaceful. I went on an amazing retreat there once about eastern meditation. It was run by a Buddhist monk from India.'

'Do they know in the parish that you dabble in the spirituality of other faiths?' asked Oldroyd mischievously.

'Some do, some don't. If anyone voiced any disapproval, I'd tell them to live in the twenty-first-century world with its inter-faith dialogue.'

'Even old Major Frobisher, or whatever his name is?'

'Hawkins. Ralph's OK when you get beneath his crusty, conservative exterior. He's got a very kind nature, just too rule-bound. Like many religious people.'

The track left the bracken and took a direct line upwards through gullies lined with fruiting bilberry plants.

'Look at these,' said Oldroyd, picking the small, dark-purple berries. He popped one in his mouth and enjoyed the strong, tart flavour.

'Yes, I wish I'd brought a bag,' said Alison. 'Bilberry pie is one of my favourites.'

At the summit they sat near the trig point and ate their lunch. They were surrounded by a huge series of millstone grit, flat-topped buttresses, which, from a distance, formed the shape of a giant seat.

'How are things in Kirkby Underside anyway? How long do you intend to stay?'

Alison replied between mouthfuls of hummus and red pepper sandwich. 'I'm still on sabbatical.' Most of Alison's time as a Church of England vicar had been spent in the inner city and in campaigning on social justice issues. She had moved to the more tranquil rural parish of Kirkby Underside after the death of her husband. 'I'm taking my time, but it does get a bit tedious occasionally. People get very uptight about things. We have these two readers who are licensed to preach, you know.'

Oldroyd nodded as he munched a slice of pork pie. He was familiar with the structure of the Church of England from his childhood, when he and Alison had been taken to church regularly by their mother.

'Well, one of them accused the other of stealing material from him to put in his sermons. Can you believe it? It got very unpleasant.'

Oldroyd poured out two cups of tea from a flask, took a drink from one and handed the other to Alison. 'Actually, that kind of thing has cropped up in this case I'm working on. One suspect claims that Penrose, the victim, stole ideas from her and used them in his own stories. She made no bones about the fact that she hated the man. This stealing of ideas goes deep, doesn't it? People get more worked up about it than when objects are stolen.'

Alison drank her tea and offered Oldroyd a chocolate biscuit. 'Yes. Although I was making fun of those church readers, there is a serious aspect to it. People feel violated when ideas and written material are stolen and passed off by someone else as theirs. Something deeply personal has been taken from them.'

'And it's unfair, isn't it?' continued Oldroyd. 'Like plagiarism in academic life. It's cheating and it's benefitting from somebody else's work and imagination.'

'Indeed. Which makes the victim extremely angry.'

'And capable of violence?'

'Yes, though I'm pleased to say that my readers have not come to blows as yet.' Alison laughed as she got up. 'Shall we move on? Look at that incredible view.'

Before they began their descent, they gazed out towards Upper Wharfedale and the distant fells of Great Whernside and Buckden Pike. The path passed across heather moorland, which would be purple in another month or so, and then came down through woodland to the River Wharfe. The last stretch of the route was a beautiful meander among woods beside the river back to Appletreewick, where the car was parked.

Oldroyd had done this walk many times, and just before the path entered the woodland, he liked to pause and look at a poignant memorial to a young woman who had died of cancer back in 1960. She had been an underwater diver and had managed to spend time exploring deep pools in the river in the last months before she died.

There it was, the little stone tablet by the side of the path, rather worn now but still clearly legible. On this occasion reading the words made him think. He was quiet and distracted for the remainder of the walk. Could that really have been what happened? He shook his head and dismissed the idea as impossible. Surely?

'Do you fancy a drink at the Barden Arms, Jim?'

Oldroyd came out of his reverie at the prospect of some beer.

'I'll drive back,' she continued. 'Don't worry, I know how much you like your pints of bitter. An orange juice and soda water will suit me fine.'

Oldroyd gave her a hug. 'Thanks, sis, you're an angel!'

'Not yet,' replied Alison, laughing.

Three

From the sixteenth century onwards, nearly a hundred mineral springs have been found in Harrogate. They contain chalybeate (iron), sulphur and salt. They became a popular health treatment in the seventeenth and eighteenth centuries, and Harrogate developed as a spa town. The town's motto is Arx celebris fontibus: *'a citadel famous for its springs'.*

On Monday morning Steph came into Oldroyd's office, tired with the effort of acting normally while she was struggling with the horrible feeling of being trapped by Fenton. She was trying to think of a way to deal with the situation and was still determined to do this by herself and not involve Oldroyd or Andy. But it was proving particularly hard to keep things from the latter, who still believed that something was wrong, especially when she seemed reluctant to do much over the weekend. She'd spent the morning researching the case she was investigating with Fenton and had discovered a link with the murder of Penrose, which had proved a welcome distraction.

'Hi,' said Andy. 'How's it going with Fenton today?'

'OK. I've been researching the backgrounds of the suspects and I've found something useful for you. I've discovered that Clare

Bayliss – she's the architect at the centre of this corruption investigation – was married to Damian Penrose for six years.'

'Whoa!' exclaimed Andy. 'That's weird! Are these cases connected?'

'More likely a coincidence,' said Oldroyd.

'Maybe, sir, but the project that her husband allegedly put her way was a partial redesign and refurbishment of the Royal Baths.'

Oldroyd perked up at that. 'Good Lord! Well, that's different. I get suspicious when coincidences mount up. We'll have to get out to see her, and soon.'

'Do you think her connection with the Baths might have some bearing on the murder scene, then, sir?' asked Andy.

'Well, as the architect, she will have been all over that building in great detail and may have discovered something.'

'You mean a secret way out or a hiding place? Is it likely that she found something that nobody else knew about?'

'It doesn't sound likely, but neither is the total disappearance of the murderer from the Baths. We've got to follow up every lead. Moreover, what if she had something built into the fabric that could help her in her revenge against her ex-husband?'

'That sounds a bit far-fetched, sir,' said a sceptical Andy.

'Well, I'm not talking about anything as complicated as a custom-built hidey-hole, but here is a woman with a motive, who's had access to the Baths and knows the construction of the building. It's a lead we have to follow. Well done, Steph, and you're not even on the case.'

'Glad to be of use, sir,' replied Steph, smiling.

Andy thought her smile was forced. Her face looked drawn and tense. He'd noticed that when he'd asked about Fenton, she'd only commented on what she was doing and not said anything about how she was getting on with the detective inspector. Something was wrong.

'No time like the present. Let's go. She lives out on the road up to Pateley Bridge, doesn't she?'

Steph gave Oldroyd the address and the two men left. Steph stayed and sat down in the chair she usually occupied in her boss's office. A huge debilitating wave of anxiety washed over her. What the hell was she going to do? How could she prevent Andy from getting more and more suspicious that there was something wrong? She'd been sleeping badly, and was starting to doze off in the chair when a knock at the door startled her.

'Come in!' she called.

A young DC called Sharon Warner came in. 'Hi, Sarge, I've brought these files in for DCI Oldroyd.'

'OK, Sharon, put them on his desk.'

Steph watched her leave and suddenly realised what the answer was: she was surely not the only one. Fenton would have approached and harassed other female officers. How many others had suffered in silence, afraid to say anything because of his rank and power as a detective inspector? It wouldn't be easy but she needed to find out and then persuade them all to stand together and challenge him.

She got up from the chair. Sharon was young and inexperienced and might be afraid of speaking out but there were other officers who might be more forthcoming. But Steph knew exactly who she needed to speak to first.

Clare Bayliss was shocked when she opened the door to find the police there again. 'What's going on? I had an inspector and a sergeant here the other day. Don't you people talk to each other?'

'We're not here about the council matter,' said Oldroyd. 'We're investigating the murder of Damian Penrose; your former husband, I understand.'

She sighed. 'You'd better come in.'

She led Oldroyd and Andy into the same room in which Steph had recently sat very uncomfortably with Fenton. Clare sat in an armchair facing the two detectives on the sofa.

'I suppose I knew this would come out at some point,' she began. 'I was just hoping against hope that you might overlook it. How did you find out? Was it Pat and Amanda at the Crime Writing Festival?'

'No, my colleague working on the corruption allegations made the connection. Why did you mention those people?'

'Just because they know all about Damian and me. I met him when he was up here for the Crime Writing Festival years ago. I was a volunteer in those days. I've always been an avid reader of crime fiction and it was so exciting to meet writers. Damian was a particular favourite of mine.'

'It was like meeting your hero?' suggested Oldroyd.

'Yes, I was dazzled by him and when he showed an interest in me, it was so thrilling that . . .' She tailed off, looked away and seemed lost in thought and memories.

'So it was what you'd call a whirlwind romance?'

'Yes. He swept me off my feet. Think of all the clichés you can – they all apply. I was quite young and not very experienced with men. I was studious; architecture is a long and demanding course, and I'd worked hard to get my degree and then to establish myself.'

'He must have been quite a bit older than you.'

'Yes, that was part of the fascination: this successful celebrity writer, who was confident and knew about the world. I was infatuated. So he divorced his wife, and I married him and went off to London.'

'I see.'

'Yes, it was easy to get work there, although he didn't encourage me. He seemed to want me to stay at home and attend to all his needs. That was the first warning I had that things were not going to be as I'd expected.'

'What had you expected?'

'I don't really know. I was very naïve. I thought being married to a writer like him would be glamorous.'

'But it wasn't?'

'No. It was actually very dull. He went out a lot without me to events and meetings with his publisher and so on. I felt quite lonely and I realised that I didn't really know him. He turned out to be moody and bad-tempered and he soon lost interest in me after he'd paraded me round to all his friends, boasting about his young wife. It wasn't long before I found out that he was seeing other women.'

'I presume that made you angry.'

'Yes, but it also made me face up to the truth: that I'd been a fool and I wasn't going to continue being one by putting up with his behaviour. I left him, came back to Harrogate and filed for divorce. The whole business put me off men for quite some time but eventually I met Jack.'

Oldroyd looked at her closely. 'It all sounds like a very painful episode in your life.'

She shrugged. 'It was. It's the kind of mistake people make when they're young and there are people around who want to take advantage of them.'

'So how do you feel about him now?'

Clare smiled. 'I didn't hate him enough to want to kill him, Chief Inspector, if that's what you're implying. In fact, I think he was a very sad person, completely locked into his own ego and relishing his image as the nasty writer – all that Poison Pen stuff.'

'How did you feel about him coming up to Harrogate every year?'

'I ignored him. Sadly, I don't go anywhere near the Crime Writing Festival anymore and funnily enough I've gone off crime fiction.'

'Not surprising in the circumstances. Can I ask you where you were on the day your ex-husband was murdered?'

'I mostly work from home these days, so I would have been here.'

'Anyone who can corroborate that?'

'Jack leaves for work at about eight fifteen, so he saw me before he went. Other than him, I'm afraid not.'

'You mentioned your work. Although we're not concerned with the issue of how you got the contract from the council, we are interested in your design for the Royal Baths.'

'It was just a partial refurbishment and improvement. I put in a new roof light in the main staircase area; made it less gloomy and more like an atrium. I also redesigned the ceiling in the swimming pool area.'

'What about the baths themselves?'

'I reconfigured some of the changing rooms, but that's all. You can't touch that area; it's all original Victorian tile and brick and it's listed.'

'I see, so you didn't redesign the baths or steam rooms in any other way?'

'No.'

Oldroyd had finished his questioning and stood up ready to go. 'Thank you for being cooperative, and I hope the other matter is resolved as soon as possible.'

'I hope so too,' she replied as she saw them out, but her expression gave nothing away.

❧

'What did you make of her, then, sir?' asked Andy as they drove back to Harrogate via the delightfully named village of Bedlam. 'As we said, she's got a powerful motive, she's based here and she knows the Baths.'

'All true, and I'm not sure I believe her when she says she's put the disaster of her marriage to Penrose behind her. She was treated very badly by that man and the scars must be deep. No, I think the motive is very strong, but I'm less convinced about this Baths refurbishment business. I think we may be clutching at straws on that one. I can't really see how anything she did would have helped her plan the murder, and she would have needed an accomplice if her husband can supply the alibi for that morning. We need to look carefully at all the architectural plans and have the place carefully examined for secret hiding places, but somehow I'm not optimistic.'

'What are your current ideas about how it was done, then, sir?'

Oldroyd sighed. 'At present, Andy, I haven't a single notion that really makes sense. I've got one or two wild theories, but they're not worth sharing with you.'

Andy smiled. He was used to his boss's habit of not sharing everything with his team until he was fairly sure about things. He also knew that, with Oldroyd, a 'wild theory' often turned out to provide an accurate account of events.

Steph went down to the canteen at Harrogate HQ and immediately saw the person she was looking for sitting alone drinking coffee. It was the perfect opportunity.

DC Nicola Jackson was an attractive, curvaceous brunette, who'd had lots of mostly brief affairs with male officers of various ages and ranks. This included a fling with Andy soon after he'd arrived in Yorkshire, but before he and Steph had got together. This history made the two women wary of each other, but Nicola was the kind of confident and uninhibited person who might well be prepared to speak out if she had suffered any unwanted attention.

Steph paused. This would need careful handling. She got a coffee and went over to Nicola's table.

'Hi, mind if I join you?'

Nicola looked up from her phone, eyed Steph suspiciously, then shrugged her shoulders. 'No, be my guest.'

Steph sat down and sipped her coffee. Nicola returned to her phone and was tapping a message.

'There's something I'd like to talk to you about,' said Steph.

Nicola looked up in surprise and then frowned. 'Me? What about? It's not that car parking business, is it? I told that Metcalf to park his bloody great big Audi properly and not take up two spaces and—'

'No, it's not about that. It's about Derek Fenton.'

'Fenton! What about him?'

Her expression and tone of voice conveyed something to Steph that gave her hope. She searched carefully for the words.

'Has he ever, you know, tried anything on with you?'

Nicola drew back, looking very suspicious. 'Well, Sarge, I'm not sure I'm prepared to say anything about that sort of thing to you. Why do you want to know, anyway?'

Steph looked at her very directly. 'Do you think I'm spying for him or something? Quite the opposite: he's been harassing me for ages and now he's got me into a bad place.'

'How?'

Steph had decided to take the calculated risk of telling Nicola about the photographs and Fenton's blackmailing. She hoped that this frankness would gain her trust.

'Bloody hell!' exclaimed Nicola after Steph had explained. 'What a bastard!'

'Yes, so now you know I'm not on his side. What I'm trying to find out is who else he's been bothering. If we act together, we can do something about it.'

Nicola laughed sardonically. 'Who hasn't he tried it on with, more like? Everyone makes an effort to keep out of his way. He kept coming up behind me at the photocopier and putting his hand on my arse and fondling me.'

'What did you do?'

'One day he did it when there was no one else around, so I turned round quickly and grabbed his bollocks hard. He never touched me again after that.'

Steph laughed. 'I'll bet he didn't. Good for you!'

'You have to look after yourself, stand up to the bullies. That's what men like that are really.'

'You're right, but not everyone's as strong and capable as you.'

'You mean they don't know as much about men as I do.'

'No, I didn't mean it like that. Think of people like Sharon Warner. She's very young. If Fenton or anybody else did anything to her, I can't see her getting hold of their balls.'

Nicola shrugged again and went back to her phone.

'Don't you think we should do something about it?' continued Steph, determined to persist.

'Yeah, maybe. But it's the old problem, isn't it? No one wants to speak out against people in authority.'

'But that makes it easier for them to carry on,' said Steph. 'Think of the Me Too movement; we can't just leave these things to other people. Surely we have to do something?'

Nicola sighed and shut her phone case.

'Yes. OK, look, I agree. It's a good idea to stick together but you'll have a hard job getting people to say anything. Think about it: who's in charge? Mostly men. They cover for each other. I've heard rumours that Fenton has friends in high places, men who will protect him on this.' She looked at Steph with a hint of admiration. 'But if you can manage it, I'll support you. It would be great if we could bring that slimeball down.'

'And give out a warning to any others who might want to try the same thing.'

Nicola nodded. 'Yes. Good luck.'

'Ben! Could you make some coffee, please?'

Ben Poole's wife, Geraldine, called down from the attic room of their neat little terraced house in Oatlands, which she'd furnished as her studio. In the back room downstairs, Ben called out, 'OK,' and went to put the kettle on.

He was preparing for another session as chair of an event at the Crime Writing Festival by reading about the authors involved. The income from this was very welcome. Neither of them had regular employment. Ben had been an English teacher in high schools but the stress of the job and the desire to be more creative had made him decide to leave teaching. Geraldine made a reasonable amount selling her work. She had displays in a number of local art shops. Ben wrote children's stories, with limited success, and was also establishing himself on the literary circuit as a competent chair of literary discussions. He also did a little freelance journalism of the investigative type and he had a few contacts in the newspaper world. None of these sources of income brought in very much and money was always tight. Sometimes he had to undertake some supply teaching so that they could make ends meet.

From the kitchen, a narrow one-storey extension, Ben looked out on to a back lane that was currently full of bins, as it was collection day. He could hear the beeping of the refuse lorry as it began to reverse down the lane. He made the coffee in a small cafetière and took two mugfuls upstairs, passing their small son's bedroom on the first floor. Ben ascended the second narrow staircase and entered Geraldine's artist's cave, as he called it. There was an organised chaos of paints, easels and partially completed canvases. The walls were covered in paintings and line drawings.

Ben put the coffee down, sighed and rubbed his eyes. Geraldine looked at him. She was wearing a paint-smeared smock and had her hair tied back. Her narrow face looked strained.

'Are you OK?' she asked anxiously. Her hands were trembling a little.

'Yeah, just tired; didn't sleep well again last night. Don't worry.'

'This Penrose thing's really getting to you, isn't it?'

'I suppose so. It's a shock to be talking to someone in the evening and then they're found murdered the next morning. It's made the atmosphere at The White Swan very tense and everyone's talking about that and not what's happening at the festival.'

'That's inevitable, isn't it? Especially with all the press coverage.'

'It doesn't make my job any easier; audiences don't seem to be concentrating. It seems that the real events are more interesting than anything the writers have to say.'

'Terribly ironic, isn't it?'

'Oh yes, the layers of irony are many: a crime writer murdered mysteriously at a Crime Writing Festival associated with Agatha Christie, leaving the police baffled. Is it real? Or is it a gigantic publicity stunt? Maybe Penrose will reappear in a few days and he'll earn himself more wonderful press coverage. His next book will fly off the shelves and the postmodernist cultural observers will be salivating at the complex meanings to be disentangled.'

Geraldine laughed a little uneasily. 'You don't mean that, do you?'

'No, of course not. The police who interviewed me were real enough, but basically it's ruining the festival and I wanted things to go really well this year. It might be the last . . .' He stopped abruptly. Geraldine looked at him sharply.

'What?'

'Oh, nothing. You know I'm always worrying about whether things will carry on. I hate having to earn money doing supply teaching. Anyway, I'll let you get on.'

He went over, kissed her on the forehead and went downstairs, leaving Geraldine very thoughtful. Sometimes Ben kept things to himself, especially when there was something bothering him.

Half an hour later, he left to go into Harrogate. Geraldine went downstairs and rummaged through a pile of mail. She knew that she'd seen a letter arrive from the Crime Writing Festival office. Here it was, stuffed back into a torn envelope addressed to Ben. She looked towards the door. He wouldn't be back for a while yet, so she pulled out the letter and read it quickly. It was from Patricia Hughes and it didn't make pleasant reading. She wrote confirming the recent conversation she'd had with Ben concerning his future as a chairperson at festival events in Harrogate. It was unlikely that this role would continue after the present festival because of 'the recent trend towards literary events being introduced and chaired by established writers'. She claimed that audiences now expected that not only guest speakers and panel members would be celebrity writers, but also the person who chaired the event. The clear implication was that Ben was neither sufficiently well known, nor a crime writer. Reluctantly she was going to recommend to the festival committee that a new policy, etc., etc.

Geraldine put the letter back into the envelope and sat down. She knew that this would have been a huge blow to Ben, not only in loss of earnings, but also in the rebuff contained in this rejection. It would have confirmed all his fears about not being successful as a writer, and he valued the prestige that his chairperson role gave him. No wonder he was in such a negative mood. Then a stab of anxiety went through her. It must have been doubly hard for Ben to cope with the antics of Penrose a few nights ago, knowing he was about to lose his job. Did he blame Penrose in some way? Surely that didn't mean . . . ? It was ridiculous but she found herself thinking carefully through what had happened the morning Penrose's body had been discovered. It was not reassuring. On Thursday, Ben had left the house early to go to the gym in town, so he would have had ample time to . . . No, that was stupid. Ben would never get involved in anything like that. But . . . She looked up at the wall and saw a picture of Ben with their son, Adam, on his shoulders. Sometimes an idea was so terrible it gained power over you, however unlikely it was to be true.

'No, that figure's too high — surely you can do it cheaper than that? . . . Yes, the margins are tight; tell me about it. It's the story of my life . . . OK, I'll speak to you later in the week.'

John Sinclair came off the phone and sighed. It was enormously difficult as a publisher being a small fish in a big sea. He'd been speaking to the printers; it was hard to negotiate a good deal when you lacked the clout of the big players. He looked over at Amy's desk, where she was tapping away at her keyboard. If things didn't improve, he would have to let her go completely, and then it would just be him.

It was all Damian's fault, damn him! John sat back in his chair and put his hands over his face. There was another dimension to his relationship with Penrose that he hadn't mentioned to the police. He and Damian had once been lovers. It was a long time ago now, during that phase of his life when he'd been mesmerised by Damian, part of whose flamboyance had been his bisexuality.

After school, John had gone to university in London and Damian was hanging around in the capital on the fringe of literary groups, leading a hedonistic kind of life and sleeping on sofas at the flats of various friends. He and John became lovers when it was John's turn to put his friend up for a while. They revelled in the freedom they had in anonymous London after the restrictions of life at boarding school. It was Damian who had enabled him to acknowledge his own homosexuality at a time when that was not an easy thing to do.

The relationship hadn't lasted long before Damian had moved on to new lodgings and to a new lover. John had not wanted things to end, and the break-up had been bitter. He felt betrayed and their friendship had not survived. They'd lost contact until they'd re-met years later, as John had described to the police. He rarely spoke about his love for Damian. It had been years before he told his partner, Ed, about his previous lover. His love for his old friend was still there, deeply buried and bound up with the thrill of being with the most exciting person he'd ever known.

And then to be betrayed again over the business by the man he loved! It was too much. How could anyone not feel a terrible animosity towards a man like that who'd treated him so badly? Enough to want to . . . He shook his head and refused to think about it anymore.

'Mr Sinclair? Are you OK?'

He came out of his reverie to see Amy looking at him. He still had his hands over his face. He sat up in his chair.

'Yes, fine. I was just on the phone to Mallinson's. They drive a hard bargain. It's bloody stressful.'

'Right.'

'I'm going out for a while.'

'OK.'

John went out to nearby Café Nico, which was also regularly visited by Oldroyd, who wasn't there today. He ordered a double espresso and grabbed a newspaper. Stories about the murder were no longer front-page news but were still prominent. The theme of the article in this paper gave him a jolt. On the third page, there was a picture of Damian with the headline: 'Does the Answer to Poison Pen's Murder Lie in his Secret Past?'

At four o'clock in the afternoon, Oldroyd was in Riverstone's Bookshop on James Street, a place in which he frequently enjoyed a good browse. There was a nice café on the second floor. One of the perks of rising to a high rank in the force was that you could occasionally take off during the day for an hour or two and no one would question you.

Today he was perusing volumes rather nervously as he was waiting for someone to arrive – a woman, in fact, and they were going to have coffee together. He'd eventually taken the plunge and contacted this person through the online dating site: Deborah Fingleton was her name, and she'd stated that she was interested in theatre, classical music, walking and eating out. In her photograph, she looked warm and intelligent, and he'd thought, why not? His daughter was right: no point in either self-pity or living in the past. Deborah sounded interesting, but to take things a step at a time, he thought it sensible to arrange a brief meeting first, rather than a whole evening out together.

He'd arrived early and had decided to go to the crime section out of curiosity. Here there were novels written by Penrose, Stevenson and Derryvale. In fact, there was a separate display of their books as it was the Crime Writing Festival, and some of them were local writers. It was rather spooky to see Penrose's books on a special cardboard display shelf in the centre of the room. It contained a large photograph of the recently murdered author behind the books. Oldroyd shook his head. The old rascal was dominating his rivals even in death.

'Hello, you must be Jim.'

Oldroyd turned to see a smiling face he recognised from the website. She looked striking in a sleeveless red dress and espadrille sandals. 'How did you know it was me?' he asked, in a jocular manner. 'You only saw me from behind.'

'Process of deduction. You are a police officer and here you are, looking at crime fiction. And now I can see that it is definitely you.'

'Well, with respect, that's not very convincing. Everyone knows that police officers wince when they read crime stories. They're never realistic when it comes to police work,' said Oldroyd.

'It's the same with all the professions. If you see a teacher in a drama on television, there are only about ten people in the class instead of thirty. And you don't even see people like me. We're far too threatening.'

Deborah was a psychotherapist in Harrogate with her own practice. Oldroyd already liked her sense of humour and her wit, and they went upstairs to the café. A few minutes later Oldroyd was sipping his usual cappuccino and watching as Deborah downed a double espresso. They sat near a window and there was a brief silence as they both looked down into James Street.

'So who's supposed to talk first?' began Deborah, who seemed very relaxed about the situation.

Oldroyd smiled. He liked her directness. 'Why don't you tell me all about yourself first, and then you can hear about me?' he said.

'OK, I'm divorced and have a son in America – he's an academic, a scientist – and my daughter's in London, following in her mother's footsteps studying Psychology. It's all a bit gender stereotypical, I'm afraid, but there we are. I live in Knaresborough and my practice is here in Harrogate. You don't want me to recite my interests again, do you? Jim?'

Oldroyd was looking out of the window and turned quickly. 'No, I mean, yes, I was listening. It's just that I noticed something down there, which . . .'

Deborah put her head on one side and looked at him quizzically.

'You're working, aren't you?' she said.

'What do you mean?'

'I saw you on the telly. I thought, how exciting to be meeting a celebrity. I know you're in charge of this case of the crime writer being murdered. I bet you saw something out there that gave you a clue, right?'

Oldroyd was flabbergasted. 'Well, yes, you're right and I'm sorry. It just happens that way with me. You become hyper-observant and something quite trivial suddenly strikes a chord. It was those men down there in the street. There's a van parked and they're loading it with containers and it reminded me of . . . Anyway, never mind.' He looked sheepishly at her.

She laughed. 'Well, I ought to walk out at this point, as you seem to prefer watching lorry men to listening to me, but I won't, because I want to hear all about you and why you're a workaholic.'

Oldroyd's expression must have shown discomfort. This shrewd remark was too near the painful truth behind the problems in his life.

She drew back. 'Oh, I'm sorry, that was far too personal. That's my professional issue; I'm always analysing people's motives and personalities, and sometimes I blurt things out. I'm sure you didn't come here to be analysed.'

'Not to worry, and you're right. Work was the reason I'm separated from my wife and why she wants a divorce. But don't worry, if things go well I'm sure I'll be able to fit you into my schedule.' This made her laugh again, and they spent the rest of the next hour speaking frankly and laughing about various things. They really enjoyed themselves and they made arrangements to have a meal together.

When the date was finished, Oldroyd walked back to HQ with a spring in his step. It had been a successful afternoon in many ways.

At The White Swan, Patricia Hughes was working hard to keep the Crime Writing Festival together after Penrose's murder. She spent all day flitting between the various tented venues in the grounds of the hotel, talking to people and trying to keep up morale. It was a difficult situation. There had been some questions in the local press as to the propriety of continuing with the festival in these circumstances, and there was to be a committee meeting soon. In the meantime they just had to soldier on.

In the booksellers' tent, representatives from Riverstone's Books looked sombre and seemed to be whispering to each other. It didn't seem very inviting for customers.

'How are we all today?' she said breezily, and got a subdued response. It was a little better in the huge wigwam, which housed the bar and café. The staff were more upbeat, but there seemed to be fewer people eating and drinking there than she would have expected. You could never judge how the public would react, she reflected, as she made her way to the box office tent, past a scattering of people sitting on the lawns in deckchairs. You might expect they would flock in to stare ghoulishly at the place where Damian Penrose was last seen alive. But no, maybe there was fear that the killer might strike again, and that it was dangerous to be at The White Swan. The box office was also quiet. Luckily, tickets for events had sold well before the murder, so even if people didn't turn up, the festival still had the revenue. But the remaining tickets were going slowly.

She returned to the festival office to find Amanda hard at work, and Jade Darton, who did some PR for the festival, waiting for her.

'Hi, Pat,' Jade said, smiling at her. 'I've just popped in to see if I can be of any help. I know things must be difficult for you after what's happened. And don't think I'm looking for another contract or anything. I just thought you might need a hand.'

Patricia sighed. It was so reassuring when people gathered round to support you.

'That's very kind of you, Jade. It's all a bit up in the air at the moment. I think—' There was a knock on the door. 'Excuse me.' She opened the door and let in Barry Evans. He looked rather sombre.

'How's it going?' he asked.

'Slowly, as you might expect. Everybody's stunned, the staff and the public. No one quite knows how to react.'

'No. It was about this that I wanted to have a word.'

'Oh?'

'We've had some complaints from members of the public saying that the rest of the festival should be cancelled. It's bad taste and disrespectful to continue when a famous participant has been murdered.'

She looked at the manager's inscrutable face. 'I see. The local press have been saying similar things. And how do you feel about it?'

'Obviously I don't want to be part of anything that is going to damage the reputation of the hotel, but I don't see how we can disappoint all those people who've paid money to attend our events.'

106

'Quite.'

'Also, as far as the long-term interests of the hotel go,' continued Evans, 'this festival is a great boost to us every year, and I don't want to damage our relationship. So don't worry, I'm fully behind us continuing. I just thought you ought to know what's being said by some people.'

'Thanks,' said Patricia, sitting tensely in her chair. 'I'm glad that's your view because, to be frank, the thought of sacrificing the rest of the festival, for which we've worked hard all year, for the sake of that man, is something I couldn't countenance, even if he was murdered.' She was angry despite Evans's reassurance.

Evans held up his hands. 'I understand; don't worry. He was a thorn in your flesh every year and yet you couldn't afford not to have him here.'

'Yes, something like that, but I was getting near the end of my patience with him, I can tell you, after the other night. This might well have been his last year, even if he was a big draw.'

Jade had been listening to all this. 'Sorry to interrupt,' she said, 'but maybe I can help. This is a PR issue, isn't it? You want to continue with the festival, but you're worried about how that might appear to the public.'

'Yes, you're right, Jade,' said Evans.

'So it's a question of handling things sensitively and hitting the right tone. I've got some ideas about how that can be done.'

Patricia looked relieved. 'Well, thank you, Jade. That would be really helpful.'

'OK, well, I'll go off now and draft a few ideas for you, and, as I say, no obligation.'

Jade left, and Evans got up. 'OK, full steam ahead, then. If you get any complaints or awkward people, refer them to me. It's your festival, but we are the hosts, so I take responsibility. See you later.'

'Thanks.'

Evans left the office. Amanda looked up from her computer.

'It would be terrible if we had to stop. I'm glad he' – she nodded after Evans – 'doesn't want to give in either. And Jade is such a help.'

Patricia rubbed her eyes. She was tired. 'Yes,' she said with a yawn. 'I'm sure we'll get through, if I can persuade the committee that it's for the best. It still irks me that Penrose's murder is going to be the main talking point for the rest of the festival. The bastard's sabotaging us even when he's dead.'

Geraldine had been nervously waiting for Ben to return for several hours. It was late in the afternoon and she'd been unable to concentrate on her work. She tried to control herself by thinking reassuring thoughts about Ben's character and affirming to herself that he would never do anything so terrible. Nevertheless, the timeframe on the morning of the murder continued to torment her. Whichever way she looked at it, it was possible for him to have killed Penrose, his enemy. Someone must have helped him, but . . .

She heard the door. He was back at last.

'Ben!' she called from the kitchen, where she was sitting with a glass of wine. He came into the room.

'Hi,' he said, looking uncertain. 'A bit early for drinking, isn't it? Are you feeling anxious again?'

She didn't reply but pointed to the letter, which was on the table. He picked it up, saw what it was and sighed.

'I should have put this away. I was going to tell you about it soon. I didn't want to worry you. I'll make up the money in other ways; we'll be fine.'

'It's not that I'm worried about,' said Geraldine, taking a gulp of her wine. 'Did you blame Penrose for this? He was difficult, wasn't he? And now he's dead and you went into Harrogate early that morning and . . .' She blurted everything out and seemed to be losing control.

'Whoa! Calm down. What on earth's going on?' He went over and put his arm around her shoulders. 'You surely don't think I had anything to do with Penrose's murder?'

She was weeping now. 'Well, I don't know what to think sometimes. It's just that he's dead, and you hated him and . . . I just don't want anything horrible to happen to us.'

'If you're feeling this bad, maybe you should go back on the tablets. It's better than drinking.'

'I'm not taking those again. The side effects were awful.'

'Then you've got to be firm with yourself. These things are all in your mind.'

She put her hand on his arm. 'I know, but you know what I'm like when I get an idea in my head.'

'I do, but everything's fine.' He smiled, stroked her hair and felt her become more relaxed. Then he saw the letter on the table and his expression changed.

Patricia Hughes sat in a corner of the lounge at The White Swan, nervously sipping at a gin and tonic. There was a raucous group of people at the bar getting steadily drunk as they discussed books and writers and tried to outdo each other in making deliberately outrageous and provocative comments.

As she'd dealt with the repercussions of Penrose's murder, the one thing she'd not really given any thought to was who might be responsible; after all, that was the police's job. Until now. This evening, while she was still at the hotel on late duty stewarding one of the festival events, a jolting realisation had suddenly hit her.

Of course there was something she knew that might be relevant to Penrose's murder. Why had she not remembered before? She'd been too preoccupied with other things. It could be important. She went into the bar to sit down and consider what to do. The group at the bar were annoyingly loud, and she found it difficult to think. Should she contact the police? Maybe that was premature when she wasn't sure. There was someone she should ring first. She consulted her Contacts folder, touched the screen and waited. The noise from the bar would be quite useful in concealing her voice as she spoke on the phone.

'Hello?' Her pulse raced but she held her nerve in the conversation that followed. She explained her concerns and received reassurances. Then she made another mistake in addition to not contacting the police. The person she was calling remarked on the noisy background and asked her where she was. Patricia joked that she was in the bar at The White Swan, surrounded by drunks.

She felt relieved at the end of the call. The outbursts of laughter from the group at the bar were becoming louder and more frequent, so when she'd finished her drink she left the hotel to begin the walk home.

It was a warm night but the clouds that had covered the sun all day were now obscuring the moon and stars, so it was dark on the tree-lined avenue that led from the hotel towards the centre of Harrogate. Patricia passed the large model of a white swan on a wooden pole that formed part of the hotel sign. The swan creaked slightly in the gentle breeze and she noticed for the first time that the heavy model was chained to the metal sides of the sign so that it couldn't be blown off. There was something creepy about this, and she shuddered as she left the grounds and the lights that illuminated the hotel. On the quiet avenue, swifts swerved and screeched around the solid stone buildings which were set back from the road. Unluckily for her, the street was also deserted. She could just hear the sound of music coming from the hotel behind her as the light faded away. There was a jazz evening in progress. Ahead she could hear the soft sound of traffic in the town centre.

But she never made it to the more open, better-lit streets near The Crown Hotel, because when she was halfway down the avenue, a figure emerged silently from behind a large plane tree and struck her a deadly blow on the back of the head. She fell on to the grass verge. The killer paused to check there was no one around, then stooped over the body, grabbed the victim's handbag and ran off.

Incident tape surrounded a section of the grass verge and the crackles of police radio could be heard as Oldroyd and Andy arrived at the scene of Patricia Hughes's murder. Tim Groves was removing his rubber gloves as the body was stretchered into the ambulance.

'Morning, Jim,' he said in his usual urbane, unflappable manner. 'Our old friend the blunt instrument to the back of the head. Been dead a good ten hours, I'd say; must have been attacked last night in the dark. Actually, I wasn't expecting to see you here. Does this mean she had something to do with that murder at the Royal Baths?'

Oldroyd was looking at the ambulance as the doors were shut. It was a very ironic end for a person whose working life had been devoted to organising events for the creators of fictional crime. He needed a new acronym for this demise. Maybe it could be TSTF: Truth Stranger Than Fiction. He turned to Tim Groves.

'She was the organiser of the Crime Writing Festival, and on our list of suspects in the Penrose murder.'

'I see. Well, the plot thickens, as it were.' Groves chuckled to himself at his little joke. 'I'll be off, then, and I'll send you my report.' He got into his car.

Oldroyd turned to the DC who'd been called to the scene. 'So the body was found by Amanda Rigby?'

'Yes, sir. Her assistant, I understand.'

What a terrible shock for her, thought Oldroyd. 'Any sign of a struggle?'

'No, sir. It was a vicious blow from behind. She must have been unconscious before she hit the ground.' He glanced down to where blood stained the grass. 'Her handbag's missing. It could have been an overzealous mugging.'

'Maybe. OK, carry on.' Oldroyd turned to Andy as the DC returned to supervising the crime scene. 'Do you think that scenario's likely on a summer's night in genteel Harrogate?'

'Not impossible, sir,' said Andy.

'No, but it's a bit of a coincidence, isn't it? I think it's much more likely either that she was involved and the plotters have fallen out, or that she was innocent but knew something and so she's been silenced. Come on, we'd better talk to her unfortunate assistant.'

The two detectives walked the short distance to The White Swan, where they found a distraught Amanda Rigby sitting in Barry Evans's office. As she drank from a cup of coffee, her hands were shaking. Her white face was tear-stained. Oldroyd gently asked her to tell them what had happened.

'I was walking down Swan Avenue towards the hotel. We base ourselves here during the festival and we always get here very early to start preparing for the day's events. I live out at Rossett. I get the bus into town, get off at the bottom of Cold Bath Road and then walk up to here. I was halfway down when . . .' She stopped and looked as if she was about to cry.

'Take your time,' said Oldroyd.

'It looked like a pile of clothes, then I saw a leg, and I thought a homeless person was lying there under the tree. When I got close, I saw it was a . . . a woman. And there was blood. I managed to get a look at the face, and it was Pat.' She burst into tears. Oldroyd and Andy waited. 'I knew she was dead,' Amanda continued through her sobs. 'I touched her skin and it was cold. Her eyes were staring. It was horrible!' She covered her face with her hands.

'So did you come straight into here?' asked Oldroyd.

'Yes, I ran into Barry's office; I was nearly hysterical. He called the police and calmed me down. I don't know what happened after that. I've been in here all the time.' She took a sip of her coffee. 'I still can't believe it.'

'Was she OK yesterday? Did she seem her usual self?'

'Yes. It was a busy day as usual during the festival. We don't get a lot of time to chat, but I didn't notice anything wrong. We take it in turns to stay for the evening sessions. There always needs to be someone on duty in case there are any problems. It was her turn, so I said goodbye to her at about five thirty and that was the last . . .' She shook her head and couldn't carry on.

'What time did the evening event end?'

'It was scheduled to finish at nine thirty, but you can't leave straight away. I know Pat often went to the bar for a drink to wind down before she went home.'

'What was that event about?'

'It was a discussion about originality and the issue of plagiarism. A panel of two writers and a publisher.'

Oldroyd raised his eyebrows: the panel topic was certainly interesting in view of the controversy surrounding Penrose. 'Did Pat have any enemies that you know of? Anyone who would want to do her harm?'

'No. The only person I ever saw her really angry with was Damian Penrose, and it couldn't have been him, could it?'

'No.'

'But that man always made her life difficult. I can't help thinking this is his fault somehow.'

'What do you mean?'

She looked angry and desperate. 'I don't know. He was a curse on the festival and now it's ruined. This is what he wanted. What on earth are we going to do without Pat?'

Charles Derryvale and Esther Stevenson were indulging in Afternoon Tea at Bettys Tea Rooms, a local institution. They sat at a table overlooking Montpellier Hill and were served by waitresses in the traditional black-and-white uniform. A three-tier tea stand in the centre of the table was laden with small sandwiches, scones and cakes. Tea was served in a silver teapot, as it had been since 1919 when the café was founded by Frederick Belmont, a Swiss confectioner and baker. Derryvale poured the tea with difficulty, his large, clumsy frame contrasting with the daintiness of everything else.

'There we are. Oh dear, I'm very sorry.' He apologised for spilling some tea from the cup he passed to his companion, but the minor mishap did not affect his jolly mood. He loaded his plate with the sandwiches and kept popping them whole into his mouth throughout the ensuing conversation.

'Well, I must say, Esther, I've never enjoyed a Crime Writing Festival as much as this one, and you know why.' He couldn't restrain himself from beaming at her.

'Yes, I think I do,' she replied. 'I must admit it feels good not to have his baleful presence hovering over it all. Nasty man.' She shuddered, took a sip of her tea and a nibble of her cucumber sandwich. Derryvale used the sugar tongs to plop three sugar cubes into his tea.

'Things have turned out extremely well. If they hadn't, I was half-inclined to go back to York, but now there's such a frisson around here, such a fascinating atmosphere. I feel I could use it in a creative way. Imagine, here we are at the festival and an actual murder has taken place, and not any murder, but that of a famous and infamous writer.' He rubbed his hands together. They were slightly greasy with butter. 'If you wrote a plot like that, they'd accuse you of being totally unrealistic. Anyway, I'm definitely going to stay at the hotel for the duration.' He was already moving on to the scones. He scooped strawberry jam and clotted cream on to his plate.

Stevenson continued to sip her black tea but showed little interest in the food. 'I must admit I do have this feeling of anti-climax,' she said.

'What do you mean?'

'Well, I've spent so much time scheming and planning to bring the bastard down, and now that's all finished. There's nothing more I can do.'

'Oh, the "Duncan is in his grave . . . Treason has done his worst . . . nothing can touch him further" sort of thing?'

'Maybe. I'm not sorry he's gone, but somehow I feel a bit cheated.'

'You'd like to have seen him publicly humiliated in the courts and forced to pay out large sums of money to the writers from whom he stole. That was never going to happen, was it?'

'I don't suppose so.'

'I must say, these scones are excellent. Can I tempt you?'

'No, Charles, go ahead. I might just manage another small sandwich.'

Derryvale's greedy little eyes glistened as he helped himself to another scone. 'Well, try to see the positive side,' he said between mouthfuls. 'Take my approach. You've got plenty of material to use. Your pursuit of Penrose and his subsequent demise could form the basis of a wonderful piece of crime fiction.'

She smiled for the first time. 'That would be audacious, to say the least, in the present circumstances, don't you think?'

Derryvale had finished his second scone and was turning his attention to the delicious-looking cakes on the bottom tier of the tea stand. He placed a small pink iced French Fancy on to his plate and took up a little silver cake fork.

'I think it would be marvellous poetic justice if you could make money out of him after he cheated so many people, including you.'

'Maybe,' said Stevenson as she looked out on to Montpellier Hill. 'Oh, look, it's John!'

Derryvale, who was sitting with his back to the window, turned to see John Sinclair looking through the tea room window. He was waving and saying something to them that wasn't audible. Stevenson shook her head, and Sinclair pointed to the tea room door and walked off.

'Looks like he's going to join us,' said Derryvale.

In a moment Sinclair arrived at their table. 'Well, that was fortuitous,' he said. 'I was about to ring you both.' He paused, as if unsure how to continue. 'It's just that . . . someone's told me that Patricia Hughes has been found dead. On Swan Avenue.'

Derryvale was arrested in the act of manoeuvring a slice of Victoria sponge on to his plate. 'Good Lord,' he said, 'intrigue upon intrigue.'

'Charles! Really!' said Stevenson.

At the Royal Baths, the atmosphere remained very strange and tense. The whole of the downstairs area, including the pool, steam rooms, changing rooms and massage facilities, was closed. There was a line of incident tape blocking off the stairs, with a PC on guard at the top. The police were allowing rooms on the first floor to continue to be used for meetings, and a temporary space for massages had been established in one of these rooms.

Carol Ashworth was spending most of her time on the phone explaining to people that the Baths were still closed and that, no, she didn't know anything about who had killed Damian Penrose. She rightly concluded that most of these calls were nothing to do with the Baths and when they might reopen; they were from people trying to satisfy their curiosity about the murder by asking silly questions.

Steve Monroe and Sid Newman had little to do at the moment. Steve was bored anyway. He felt his life had got into a terrible rut and lacked any kind of risks, challenge and excitement. He was capable of far more than was involved in this job.

Carol saw him lackadaisically sweeping the steps down to the baths area. 'Hi, Steve,' she said, 'do you fancy a coffee?'

'Thanks.'

Carol went behind the office into a little kitchen area and made two mugs of instant coffee. Steve sat behind reception on a chair next to Carol's. She handed him his mug.

'How are you today? It's all weird, isn't it?' she said.

'Too right. I haven't got enough to occupy me and keep my mind off finding that body.' He shuddered and took a drink of his coffee.

'That was such a shock, finding the body like that. I think you were very brave.'

He shook his head. 'Thanks. I still can't believe there wasn't anybody else there.'

'No, and neither could the police. Look, you need a break. Have you got any leave coming up? How's Jade? You two need to go off on holiday together.' Jade Darton, the PR freelancer, was Steve's girlfriend.

'It's a good idea, but Jade's busy at the moment. She's doing a bit of work for the festival and she's also got this contract with a hotel chain. She's spending quite a bit of time in London. Maybe later in the summer, if she can spare the time.'

'Yes, there might be some last-minute deals. You can fly off to somewhere hot and relax.'

Steve grinned. 'Thanks, Carol, you're very thoughtful. I'd like to get away from here, to be honest. It feels like a haunted mansion, and we've no idea when we can open again and get things back to normal, have we?'

'No, I think the police are just as puzzled as we are, and they won't let the public in while down there's a crime scene, and one they can't explain.' The phone rang again. Carol sighed and answered it. 'Hello? Oh, hi, Shirley. I wasn't expecting . . . What? You're joking! No . . . That's terrible . . . Yes, I will . . . OK. I'll see you tomorrow.' She put the phone down and looked at Steve with a shocked expression. 'That was Shirley. She knows someone who works at The White Swan. There's been another murder.'

'What?'

'Yes. A body was found this morning on Swan Avenue, near the hotel. Apparently people were saying it's the woman who organises the Crime Writing Festival. Isn't that Patricia Hughes? It can't be her, surely. I've known her for years. If it is, that's two people to do with the festival who've been killed.' She shook her head.

'God,' said Steve, gripping his mug tightly. 'Do you think there's a connection? If her body was found in the street, it sounds like a mugging to me.'

'Maybe it was. What's the world coming to when you can't walk the streets of Harrogate without someone attacking you?'

Carol closed her eyes to try to shut out the horror of that prospect.

Back at Harrogate HQ, Oldroyd was unpacking a bag of materials sent up by the London Met. He intended to spend much of the afternoon going through them. The bag contained documents discovered in Penrose's London flat that could be relevant to the case. There were lots of bank statements and letters from publishers and his agent, but nothing to suggest that he'd been in any financial difficulties. There was a folder haphazardly stuffed with correspondence from his solicitor about his divorce from Clare Bayliss, but the emotionless legal language conveyed nothing to Oldroyd.

What he was much more interested in was a number of volumes of what was clearly Penrose's diary, written in Moleskine notebooks, those jotters beloved by writers since the time of Ernest Hemingway. He was grateful to the thoughtful London detective who had selected them for inclusion. They were very likely to contain personal information that might furnish Oldroyd with important clues. Penrose had not had the opportunity to alter or even destroy them before he was murdered, so here were the famous writer's unedited views and opinions.

Oldroyd made a pot of tea and sat down in his office to read them. Andy was over at The White Swan finishing off the routine work connected with Patricia Hughes's murder. Penrose's entries were not meticulous or regular. He appeared to have used the diary to sound off about people and events that annoyed him, mostly the former. The entries were short and hastily written in flamboyant handwriting, with liberal use of exclamation marks. Together they formed a pompous and arrogant man's diatribe against the many people who had offended him in different ways. Here was a comment about a critic who must have given one of his books a bad review:

> *That miserable scribbler at the* Daily Crap, *what a bloody idiot!! He knows bugger all about crime writing anyway, praised that pile of utter rubbish by Andrea*

what's her face!! No standards anymore – people don't recognise real quality . . .

This was the angry verdict on an agent:

Why am I paying these useless people barrow loads of money when they can't be bothered to get off their bloody arses and get me a better deal than this shit they're offering me?!! To say I could do better myself is a bloody under-statement of the highest order!!!

He never seemed to have a good word for any of his fellow writers:

I see Dark Noon *has won the Gallery Prize – utterly preposterous: no plot, no characterisation, no atmosphere, no talent!! How can anyone take these judging panels seriously when they make such unbelievably stupid decisions?!!!*

Oldroyd suspected that one of Penrose's books might have been on the shortlist. He sat back and enjoyed himself. He was finding the whole thing an outrageous and entertaining read whilst remaining on the lookout for anything that might offer some insights into the case. Many of the entries were undated, which didn't help, but Oldroyd worked out which volume was the most recent and began to find some interesting material. There were entries from the time of Penrose's divorce from Clare Bayliss:

Like all men, I'm getting taken to the cleaners by the system; it was just the same with Susan: they always side with the poor woman and the man has to pay up!!! Why can't they go out, get a job and keep themselves?!! The sooner she packs herself off to the wild north again, the better, as far as I'm concerned. I'll be taking a wide berth when I'm up there for the festival – bitch!!!

That reference to Penrose's first wife alerted Oldroyd to the fact that she was someone who would need to be followed up. Also, it didn't seem that his divorce from Clare had been at all amicable. He seemed very bitter. Was she angrier about it than she'd suggested when they interviewed her?

The next discovery concerned John Sinclair:

John's just been on the phone again. He really disappoints me: no head for business – does he really think I can carry on pouring money into his failing little enterprise just for old times' sake?! It's sad, though, when I think of the past and how much in love we once were.

Oldroyd raised his eyebrows. That would seem to add another dimension to Penrose's character and to that relationship. John Sinclair would soon be receiving another visit. Sexual jealousy combined with money issues produced a potent cocktail of motives.

A third series of entries was more mysterious, as Penrose never used a name. There was some dispute going on with a woman. This entry was typical:

I'm not giving way to that bloody woman; these people don't realise that writers often use ideas that have been around before. It's the skill with which they rework them that counts. Anyway, it's a 'whore's vengeance', as they say, and I'm not giving in to the little bitch.

Clearly this was related to the disputes about Penrose stealing ideas from other writers, so was he writing about Esther Stevenson? If so, Penrose seemed to be implying that they'd had an affair and her accusations were fuelled by bitterness. Oldroyd thought this odd, and he found the reference to 'the little bitch' offensive but also puzzling because Esther Stevenson was quite tall. They would have to follow this up with her. Oldroyd sensed that someone else was involved, a person who might prove to be significant, and that the mystery was deepening.

The next day Steph continued her difficult and delicate mission: to discover how many female officers had suffered from Derek Fenton's unwanted attentions, and to find this out without scaring or offending them. She tried to make a judgement about which women might have been his particular targets, though Nicola Jackson had implied that most women had been his victims at some point. She also needed to select women who were prepared to speak out.

Cynthia Carey was a detective sergeant who had once worked with Fenton, but had been transferred to another detective inspector. Steph wondered whether that indicated there had been some problems. Cynthia was a single parent with two school-age children. She was an attractive woman with auburn hair, which she often wore in a ponytail. She ran a lot, and kept herself very toned and physically fit. It seemed a fair assumption that Fenton would have paid her some unwelcome attention. Steph asked her to come into Oldroyd's office while he and Andy were out.

'Well, this is very nice, Steph,' said Cynthia, looking round the office. 'You're lucky working with Oldroyd. He's very informal, isn't he? Doesn't pull rank all the time like some of them.'

'No, he's great, Cyn. He makes you feel part of his team. Sit down, will you? I wanted to talk to you about something personal.'

'Oh! OK.'

Cynthia sat down next to Steph.

'It's about Derek Fenton,' Steph said. 'I'm having problems with him and I was hoping you could help.' She described Fenton's behaviour and explained what had happened with the photographs.

'Bloody hell! What a bastard!' said Cynthia, exactly echoing Nicola Jackson's response.

'I know,' replied Steph. 'The thing is, though, I'm determined to do something about him, and I've already got Nicola Jackson on my side; he's harassed her too. I wondered if you'd had any – what shall I say? – experiences with him?'

Cynthia laughed. 'Oh yes,' she said. 'I thought everybody knew why I'd asked for a transfer, although it was never talked about. He's a sex pest, he wouldn't leave me alone. I don't know whether he thought I was easier game because I'm separated from Francis and I don't have a partner, but he was constantly making remarks, touching me, leering at my tits. It was impossible to work with him, and I was getting quite depressed about it. One evening when it was dark and there was no one around, he followed me out to the car and got hold of me, trying to make me kiss him; said he knew I wanted to really. I pushed him off and got into the car. The next day I asked to be transferred, but I didn't mention what he'd done.'

'Why didn't you ask for help?'

'Why don't you?' replied Cynthia directly. 'It's not easy, is it? Men in power – you always feel they'll cover for each other. Maybe not Oldroyd, but there aren't many like him. When I asked DCI Morton for the transfer, he agreed without asking me why. I got the feeling that he knew what Fenton was like, but he turned a blind eye. He just moved me so things didn't get out of hand.'

'Nicola said the same about this male conspiracy of watching each other's backs, but my argument is, if we don't do something, it'll get worse, and I talked her round. How about you?'

Cynthia frowned. 'What do you have in mind?'

'If there are enough of us, we can confront him and threaten to go to the authorities, right up to Chief Superintendent Walker if necessary.'

'He's a bit of an old buffer, isn't he? I can't see him doing much about it.'

'He wouldn't have any choice in this day and age if there are a number of us and we stick together.'

'Fenton might call our bluff and just dare us to report him.'

'If we went to the top, none of the bosses could ignore sexual harassment like that, after we'd called it out. It's staying quiet that's the problem.'

Cynthia went thoughtful for a few moments. Then she nodded and said, 'Yes, you're right. We need to call time on the Fentons of this world. I'm with you all the way.'

Four

Agatha Christie went missing on 3 December 1926 from her home in Berkshire. Her disappearance caused an out-cry amongst the public, and thousands of police officers and volunteers searched for her. On 14 December she was found at The Swan Hydropathic Hotel in Harrogate, now called The Old Swan, registered as Mrs Teresa Neele. Neele was the surname of her husband's lover.

At The White Swan, Oldroyd and Andy were holding their second press conference. It was now almost a week since Penrose's murder, and one day since Patricia Hughes's body had been found. Progress was slow, and Tom Walker was getting twitchy. He wanted Oldroyd to 'keep the buggers at bay so that that idiot Watkins doesn't get on our backs'.

Policing at that level, mused Oldroyd, seemed to be almost entirely about PR. Here we go again, he thought, as he stared at the ranks of reporters and their expensive-looking cameras. He suddenly remembered Agatha Christie and her strange sojourn in the town. He didn't remember her sleuths having to deal with the media like this, and as for Sherlock Holmes: the great man would have considered it far beneath his dignity! Of course they were private detectives, who didn't have to deal with the day-to-day stresses of the job.

'Two victims now, Chief Inspector. Are you sure they're related?'

Quite a sensible start for once, thought Oldroyd.

'That's a good question. We can't be sure that they are, and the second victim, Patricia Hughes, could have been attacked by a mugger, who stole her handbag. However, given the fact that muggers don't usually deliver such vicious blows to their victims from behind, it seems to me that the motive was murder rather than robbery. Patricia was also the organiser of the Crime Writing Festival and knew the first victim, so we are working on the assumption that it is likely there is a link, although at present we don't know what that is. If any member of the public saw anything in this hotel or on Swan Avenue at around ten thirty on Monday night, I urge them to come forward.'

'It's bit weird, isn't it, Chief Inspector: these murders at a Crime Writing Festival?'

'I think we've all registered the irony of that,' remarked Oldroyd.

'But what do you think is going on?' the reporter from a prominent tabloid continued. He had designer stubble, an earring and a tight T-shirt over his beer belly. The faded logo on the shirt seemed to include a profile of Freddie Mercury. 'Is someone acting out a crime story instead of writing one? Some crazed lunatic who couldn't get his works published, so he's taking it out on a successful writer and someone involved in the book world?'

'Well, it sounds as if you'd match him for lurid imagination,' replied Oldroyd. 'We had a number of these – how shall I describe them? – imaginative schemes presented at the last press conference, and I said then that it's much more profitable to begin with the simpler explanations. At the moment we are concentrating on establishing motives for both murders, and we are still working on how the first murder was carried out.'

'Do you think more people are at risk?' This from a bespectacled female reporter, who looked very serious.

Oldroyd paused. This was always a very tricky issue: say no, and if there's another killing they roast you; say yes, and the headlines create panic in the neighbourhood.

'I cannot say for certain that there isn't any further risk, and clearly everyone should remain alert, but neither do I think we have a random killer at large. What I suspect is, given the clever way in which the first murder was planned, that this is really about Damian Penrose, and that maybe Patricia Hughes knew something that could have led us to the murderer.'

'So she was silenced?'

'Probably, but we don't know for sure. I ask again for anyone with any information, however trivial they think it is, to come forward.'

'Do you think the answer lies in Penrose's past? We've found out some interesting things about him. He wasn't exactly popular, was he? Been through two marriages; rumours that he pinched all his ideas from other people; must have had lots of enemies.'

Oldroyd winced. This was exactly the kind of press attitude he detested: the arrogance in presenting themselves as detectives, implying the police weren't doing a very good job, followed by the lazy, imprecise and exaggerated way that allegations against Penrose were made.

'He had a murky past, didn't he, Chief Inspector?' concluded the reporter.

'Don't we all?' replied Oldroyd, not willing to speculate about Penrose's private life. 'Yes, we are pursuing leads concerning relationships and events in Damian Penrose's past, but I would have thought it was obvious that all cases of this kind have their origins in the past lives of people, so I'm not sure about the relevance of your point.'

This put-down caused some smiles and murmurings, and the reporter remained silent.

After the conference was finished, Oldroyd and Andy returned to HQ on foot. Oldroyd had started to insist that they did more walking around Harrogate for the health benefits, and also because it was greener. Andy was sceptical; he liked his cars.

'That should keep everyone happy, at least for a short while,' said Oldroyd, puffing a bit as they arrived back at his office. Andy, who was showing fewer signs of exertion, put on the coffee. 'It's time we sat down and reviewed the evidence. Let's go through the suspects.'

Andy took out his notebook. It was a quaint habit of his to keep notes on everything in the old-fashioned way. He said that writing things down helped him to think.

'OK, sir, so his fellow writers,' he began. 'Derryvale and Stevenson. Alibis confirmed for the night before the first murder, but they both hated him: Derryvale was insulted and Stevenson had a big grudge about this pinching ideas business. Like all the suspects, they would've had to have help.'

'Yes, they clearly had motives and the imagination for a murder plot, which they would've enjoyed devising. It would have appealed to their sense of irony: a crime writer murdered by other crime writers in an impossible crime scenario.' He poured out the coffee, opened the tin that contained their favourite chocolate digestives and offered it to Andy, who took a couple for now but worked nearly all the way through the tin as they were talking.

'The ex-wife, Clare Bayliss,' continued Andy between mouthfuls of the crumbly biscuit. 'An ex-partner is always good suspect material. Her alibi is not confirmed, as she was working from home. She knows the Baths really well, having designed a refurbishment, and she may have more bitterness against her ex-husband than she lets on. Now, at the festival we've got Ben Poole and Patricia

Hughes, both of whom also hated Penrose. Ben Poole was definitely at the gym, as he said. The fact that Hughes is now dead means that she knew something. Always assuming that the two murders are connected. This means that either she was involved herself and was disposed of by her partners or that she'd worked out who the murderer was and that person found out.'

'Remember her phone was stolen,' Oldroyd said. 'There was a reason for that. I think she'd been in contact with her killer not long before she was murdered. It would be very interesting to know who she called before it happened.'

'I've got people working on it, but it's going to take some tracking down when we haven't got the phone and we don't even know the network she was on. She was divorced and lived alone, so there's no one to give us information.'

'Keep on that one. It could prove crucial. Also, go over and have a look around at her flat. See if you can find anything interesting. We'll have to trawl through alibis again for Monday night, but it was relatively easy to lie in wait for her in the street.'

'You would have had to know she was at The White Swan that evening, sir.'

'True, but a lot of people must have known that, given her job. Also, during the festival, the ground floor of the hotel, including the bar, is open to people to wander round. She could easily have been spotted by someone.'

'OK, sir,' Andy continued, consulting his notes again. 'Then there's John Sinclair, who fell out with Penrose over money for his publishing business, and Penrose's diary refers to them as having been lovers. His partner supported his alibi, but you never know – he may have been complicit.'

'Two motives there,' interjected Oldroyd. 'Now, what about other people who don't appear to have a motive but who definitely had the opportunity?'

'That's people at the Baths: Carol Ashworth, receptionist; Steve Monroe, attendant; Shirley Adams, cleaner; Sid Newman, technician; and Howard Barnes, manager. Monroe and Ashworth were first on the scene of the murder, Newman could have been hanging around down in the baths area. As you say, though, the problem with all these people is the apparent lack of motive.'

'So far,' added Oldroyd as he drank his coffee. 'Well, that's quite a lot of people, and none of them have been positively ruled out yet. Who do you think is the most likely suspect at this stage?'

Andy thought for a moment. 'I think the most suspicious people are the ones who were most hostile towards the bloke: that's Sinclair, Derryvale and Stevenson. But somehow I'm not convinced. It seems too obvious, and they've made no attempt to disguise their feelings, apart from Sinclair, even though that draws suspicion on to them. I think we need to dig deeper and find out who else might have had a motive. I don't really have a frontrunner at the moment. We've still got a lot of work to do checking alibis for Penrose's murder, never mind Patricia Hughes. I've got a team on it.'

'Good, I agree, and that's the right approach: trust your instincts, look for evidence but keep an open mind. Anyway, any more ideas about how the murderer got in and out of the Baths?'

'I've never had a single idea, sir, never mind any more than that,' confessed Andy ruefully. 'We've also got people going through that building with a fine-tooth comb, looking for exits and hiding places.'

Oldroyd smiled. 'It's a teaser all right. I'm working on a few theories but they're pretty wild. I'm convinced the answer lies in going through the events of that morning really carefully and thinking deeply about them. And I think—'

There was a knock on the door. A detective constable came in. 'Someone's at the desk, sir, asking to see you; says she has information on the Penrose case.'

Oldroyd and Andy hurried straight down to the entrance to see a tall, stylishly dressed woman standing by the reception desk and wearing a haughty expression.

'Are you Chief Inspector Oldroyd?' she said.

'Yes.'

'I'm Susan Lawrence, Damian Penrose's first wife. I can't get any sense from the police in London, so I've come all the way up here. Can you tell me what on earth's going on?'

Clare Bayliss was driving her black BMW along the narrow, picturesque lanes east of Ripley and the A61. She was meeting her husband for lunch in their favourite country pub in a secluded village south of Ripon. It was something they often did mid-week when they wanted to escape from work pressures for a while.

She arrived at the pretty village, and drove past the duck pond, the stocks on the green, and the medieval church with its squat tower. She drew up in front of The Black Sheep and got out. It was very quiet and peaceful. She saw that her husband, Jack, was already there as his red Mercedes was in the car park.

Inside she found him sitting at their usual table in the dining section of the bar, with its low oak beams. He was drinking a pint of beer. She sat down. 'Hi! How long have you been here?'

'Not long. Only just started this pint but it tastes good – pity I can only have the one.' He flashed a smile at her.

Jack was a tall and handsome man, with thick black hair, now greying at the sides. Clare found him charismatic and attractive but also very straight and trustworthy after her ordeals with Damian.

He had a son and daughter from his first marriage, who they saw regularly. Clare felt that they regarded her as a second mother.

'What do you fancy, then?' Jack passed a menu across.

'Just my favourite, I think: the fish pie,' she replied without even looking at the menu. 'What kind of a morning have you had?'

Jack ran a consultancy specialising in transport and urban planning. He was spending more time in his Harrogate office after his suspension from the council committee. He had serious allegations to face about favouring his wife and others with council contracts.

'Fine. I'm getting back into it all really easily. Andrew's done a great job running things while I've been on the council. They don't really need me. I could make myself redundant.' He smiled again. 'I'm going to have the Cumberland sausage and cheesy mash. It'll go well with this beer. Shall I get you a drink?'

'Just a tonic water.'

'OK.' He went to the bar to make the order. Clare watched him go. He always maintained a cheery demeanour, but she knew he was feeling the stress of recent events. She'd woken a number of times in the middle of the night recently to hear him downstairs watching television.

He returned from the bar.

'Have you heard anything?' asked Clare.

'No. Things move slowly on the council. Goodness knows when they'll get round to making a decision.'

'It's all your own fault,' said Clare, sipping her tonic water. 'You're good at ideas but you've always been slack on detail. In my job, if you don't get the detail right, it can have serious consequences.'

'It was just an oversight.'

'Yes, so you keep saying, but an oversight that gave your enemies on the council material to use against you.'

Jack took another drink of beer. 'I don't know why they had to involve the police at this stage. The enemies you referred to are clearly still at work.'

'They are, and I've an idea who might be receiving information and causing mischief,' said Clare.

'Who?'

'Never mind. Leave it to me. There's something I think I can put a stop to. Anyway' – she changed the subject – 'that Inspector Fenton behaved in a nasty way. He had a sergeant with him. I think she was embarrassed by some of the things he said.'

'Probably, but she won't be able to say anything if she's on a lower rank, and the police always protect one another. Anyway, you don't need to worry about him. You must have really had enough of the police with that chief inspector coming round later about Damian.'

'Yes, but he was very nice.'

Jack smiled again but not quite as pleasantly as before. 'They're wasting their time on that one. I'm glad that bastard's gone.'

Clare glanced quickly round the room. 'Keep your voice down.'

'Who cares? It's going to be much better for everyone with him out of the way, especially for you. I hate thinking about the pain and humiliation he caused you.'

'No need to be so brutal about it and broadcast it to the world. You never know who might be listening and getting ideas. We're in enough trouble as it is – at least you are.'

'Relax, darling. They can't pin anything on me. And I've got people on my side, remember.' He held up his glass as the waitress brought their food. 'Cheers,' he said with a twinkle in his eye, but Clare shook her head. She wasn't sure where all this was going to end up.

∼

'Please take a seat.' Oldroyd and Andy had taken Susan Lawrence into the office. 'This is Detective Sergeant Carter.'

Susan nodded and sat down. 'Well, what on earth's happening in this dreadful business? Are you going to arrest who did it? Why is it taking you so long?'

Oldroyd looked at her, trying to control his animosity. He was familiar with people like this: arrogant, over-assertive, asking ridiculous questions and making unrealistic demands. He could handle them, but they didn't make things easier. He made a big effort to remember that her first husband had been murdered, so maybe she was distressed.

'It's a complex case and it's going to take time to solve. In the end I'm sure we will arrest someone. In the meantime, I'm quite interested in why you've come all the way from London to check on the investigation?'

She seemed a little nonplussed by this question. 'I told you, I can't get any information from the London police.'

Oldroyd had to smile at the audacity of rocking up at a police station belonging to a force that wasn't even conducting the murder enquiry and expecting to be told details of an investigation taking place elsewhere, even if you were an ex-wife of the deceased.

'Is that all? I'm sure you realise that details of investigations are confidential.'

'Yes, but I also thought that maybe I could help you.'

Oldroyd suspected that she must have other reasons for turning up like this and he wasn't surprised by her response. 'Very well,' he said. 'In what way?'

Her demeanour became more serious and she looked from Oldroyd to Andy as she spoke in a lowered voice. 'As I'm sure you've found out, Damian was not a popular man. He had many enemies in the literary world, but I don't believe anyone would kill him over a characterisation or a plot. You have to look at his relationships and the people involved in his personal life.'

'Anyone in particular?' asked Andy.

'Of course, it's obvious: that scheming minx Clare Bayliss, his second wife. She lured Damian away from me, but then she wasn't happy when he wasn't fussing round her all the time. Damian started to stray again, that's his nature, and she left him. The point is, though, I'm sure she never forgave him, and here she is in Harrogate, ideally placed to plan his death. Look no further; open-and-shut case. I can't understand why you haven't already arrested her.'

Oldroyd was unimpressed by this, although he had to admire the sheer effrontery. 'Well, I have to say, there's a breezy simplicity about your theory, but I'm afraid in the police we have to look for annoying things like evidence and opportunity. Even if your "guilty" person had a motive, it seems to me that it was no stronger than yours as another wronged and deserted wife. She has an alibi for the morning of the murder. What about you? How do we know you've only just arrived from London? Can anyone confirm you've spent the last few days in the capital?'

Andy smiled to himself as his boss yet again upstaged someone who was being difficult.

Susan was shocked. 'Well, really! Of course I've only just got here from London. You can check with my housekeeper. How dare you place me on the same level as that woman! Damian always thought far more of me than her. I was the love of his life. She's a cunning so-and-so and she—'

'I really think we've heard enough of this, madam,' said Oldroyd. 'Unless you've got some proper information that might be genuinely useful to the investigation, I think we need to end this interview. Groundless allegations against someone you don't like are not of interest to us.'

Susan's mouth dropped open. 'Well, really!' she repeated. 'I've never been spoken to like that in all my born days. Who on earth do you think you are?'

'The chief inspector in charge of this investigation, and I don't have any more time to waste on this.' Oldroyd's patience was wearing thin.

Susan got up. 'I have to say, I expected better. If you won't investigate this properly, then I shall have to do it myself. I'll be staying at The White Swan until I bring that woman to justice,' she declared melodramatically.

'I strongly advise you not to interfere with the police investigation.'

'What investigation?' she said contemptuously, and started to walk out of the room.

'Before you leave, madam, Sergeant Carter will accompany you back to reception and someone will take some details and a statement from you.'

Susan's mouth opened, but she was speechless.

Andy left with her but soon returned laughing. 'Bloody hell, sir! I've left her with DC Jones. What did you make of that?'

Oldroyd shook his head and also laughed. 'Very entertaining, wasn't it? I don't know whether she's a drama queen who likes the limelight or there's something deeper going on. I don't buy the "I'm the first wife who still loves my husband even though he deserted me years ago" line.'

'"Hell hath no fury" and all that, sir. She obviously wants to get her rival into as much trouble as she can.'

'Yes, but why? It may be to throw us off the trail, a trail that might lead to her. Of course, if she was involved in Penrose's murder and manages to blame the hated second wife, how delicious is that for her? Destroying both of them. We're almost back yet again in the world of crime fiction. We don't seem to be able to escape it in this case, and I still wonder if someone is trying to create a real-life crime story, or something even weirder. Who knows, with all these writers involved?'

'If she was really intent on incriminating Clare Bayliss, though, sir,' said Andy, 'surely she'd have some actual evidence for us, even if it was fabricated.'

'True, but let's see what happens. Contact the Met and get them to find out as much as they can about her and check whatever alibi she gives. That will show we're serious and that we're not going to take any more nonsense and insults. However, I don't think we've heard the last of her. It's going to be very intriguing while she's staying at The White Swan. Meanwhile, we'd better get back to John Sinclair and see what he has to say about his romance with Penrose.'

They were about to leave when the detective constable came back.

'Yes, Jones?' Oldroyd said.

'Some important information, sir. We've been out checking all the alibis for the morning of Mr Penrose's murder. There's this chap' – he looked at his notes – 'Sid Newman; he's a technician at the Baths. He claims he was there early to switch everything on and then went on to the Leisure Centre, where he has a similar job. We've checked at the Leisure Centre and he never came that morning. His son, Terry, came instead; apparently he covers for his father if he has any problems. So that means his whereabouts for the time of the murder are unaccounted for.'

'I see,' said Oldroyd. 'Thank you.' He turned to Andy. 'Well, it's been a very interesting morning. We'd better go and see Mr Newman and leave Mr Sinclair until later.'

In her house in the Duchys, Esther Stevenson was suffering from writer's block. She sat with her laptop in her upstairs study, then moved downstairs to the kitchen table. She drank several cups of coffee, but was still unable to write anything. Finally, in a bad temper, she slammed the laptop lid down and took her notebook, pen and phone outside into the garden, where she had been when the detectives called. Maybe another change of venue and technology would do the trick.

The garden was peaceful, but contained many things to distract her. There were always jobs to be done and she found gardening a chore. She could see roses that needed deadheading and flower beds that should be hoed for weeds. Blue tits and goldfinches were pecking at the somewhat depleted bird feeders. Her black-and-white cat, Rosemary, was looking up at them longingly. Overhead a heron flapped slowly past and two red kites hovered low, just above the trees. The breeding programme established at Harewood some years before had been such a success that the big birds of prey were now a familiar sight all over the area. It was all very beautiful and intriguing to watch.

The life of a writer was not so glamorous and free as it was generally considered to be, Stevenson reflected ruefully, as she sat doodling aimlessly in her notebook. Not only were the earnings of most writers so low that it was impossible to live on the money, but it could be a very isolated existence, in which all your demons could torment you, gnaw at your concentration and prevent you from writing. She had been lucky as far as the income side of things went. Her partner earned a good salary, but she struggled with the process of creative composition and it often caused her to be depressed and moody. This in turn affected her relationship.

At the moment, the turbulence in her mood and her problems with maintaining focus were being affected by all that had happened at the Crime Writing Festival. That bloody Penrose! Still haunting her! It was a great shame about Patricia Hughes, but . . .

Her train of thought was interrupted by her phone ringing. She knew who it was likely to be: at least one of a certain group of people.

She picked up the phone. 'Hi, Liz . . . Yes, I'm fine, though it's been a bit of a rollercoaster . . . I know; he's gone. It's amazing, isn't it? He won't be stealing from any more writers now . . . No, I can't tell you anything about it . . . I know; it's a great pity. She did a great job running the festival . . . Leo's fine, thanks . . . Well, that would be great. Give me a call when you're coming up . . . OK. Bye.'

Liz Simpson was part of the group of writers she had brought together over the years. They'd all been badly treated by Penrose. She lived in London, and had suffered a great deal of sexual harassment from him before he stole the main idea from what would have been her first crime novel. Esther was getting a series of calls from them all and the content was always the same: relief that Penrose was out of the way. No one seemed interested in what had actually happened. They were just glad to see the back of him. It felt different to her being 'on the ground', as it were, in Harrogate, having to live through the trauma of constant questioning by the police. However, when she heard the relief and positive pleasure in people's voices as they celebrated the fact that the old scoundrel was gone, she felt it had all been worth it.

She yawned. She was not sleeping well at the moment. She reached for her pen in order to have another try at writing, but hesitated. She remembered the festival and the fact that Patricia Hughes was no longer there to run things. How on earth would Amanda Rigby cope? It was in all their interests that the festival was a success. Maybe she should call Amanda and offer to help. She put down her pen and took up her phone again.

Sid Newman lived in an outer suburb of Harrogate, on a large estate of social housing. Oldroyd and Andy drove through the dull, rundown streets of standard council houses built between the 1930s and '50s. Andy was surprised.

'Well, sir, I didn't think there were any poor areas in Harrogate. I thought it was all pretty well off and genteel,' he said, noticing a down-at-heel group of people waiting at the bus stop.

'There are poor areas everywhere in this country, Andy; they're just hidden away from view. Anyway, this is it.'

He stopped outside a house with overgrown privet hedges. The scraggy bottoms of the shrubs were stuffed with litter. The detectives walked down the crumbling concrete path and knocked on the door. Immediately there was the sound of a dog barking and a woman shouting, 'Lexi! Shut up! Quiet!' Then there were footsteps and the voice shouted again, 'Just a minute!'

Andy frowned at Oldroyd. 'Sounds like we might get savaged here, sir. I'm not a great dog lover; been attacked too many times by Rottweilers and Alsatians at some of the places we had to bust when I was in the Met.'

'That's the problem,' replied Oldroyd. 'Dogs know if you don't like them; they can sense it.'

'Maybe, sir, but I've met a few that were clearly trained to go for coppers.'

Oldroyd laughed. They heard footsteps, and the door was opened by a woman holding back a growling Staffie. Her short-sleeved T-shirt revealed muscular, tattooed arms. 'Yes, what do you want?'

'We're police officers and . . .' began Oldroyd. Then, looking down the entrance hall, he caught sight of Sid Newman's head peering round the kitchen door.

'Oh, shit!' exclaimed Newman. Then he slammed the door.

Oldroyd turned to Andy. 'Better get after him, he's making a run for it!'

Without a word, Andy rushed past the woman and shot through the house, following Newman through the back door into a scrubby garden.

'Hey, what the bloody hell do you think you're doing? You can't just barge in like this!' the woman said.

'I think we can, madam,' said Oldroyd, brandishing his ID. 'We're detectives investigating two murders, and we need to ask Mr Newman some questions.'

'Why? He hasn't done nothing.' She stood defiantly in the doorway.

'Then can you explain why he made a run for it when he saw us? I think you need to let me in.'

Sullenly she stood aside, shut the dog in the living room and followed Oldroyd back into the kitchen, from where muffled barks and occasional scratchings on the door to the living room could be heard.

Andy was ushering Newman back into the house. 'Got him as he was trying to climb over the fence at the back, sir.'

'Yeah, and you've torn me bloody shirt,' said Newman as he sat down at the orange pine table and examined the torn sleeve.

Oldroyd and Andy also sat at the table, while the woman remained standing by the door.

'Running away from the police is never a good idea,' said Oldroyd. 'It suggests to us that you have something to hide.'

Newman seemed deflated. He shook his head. 'I haven't. It's just that I panicked when I saw yer. I've had a few run-ins wi' t'police over t'years and I get a bit, yer know, edgy.'

'Maybe that was because you didn't tell them the truth. And here you are still at it, because you told us that you went straight to the Leisure Centre from the Royal Baths on the morning of Damian Penrose's murder and that wasn't true, was it? Your son went to the Leisure Centre, not you.'

'Don't get our Terry into this – he just helps his dad out,' said the woman.

Oldroyd turned to her. 'Into what exactly?'

'Just keep quiet, Irene,' said Newman. 'You're makin' it worse.' He turned to Oldroyd. 'OK. Terry covers for me occasionally because I get some work doin' other stuff.'

'Moonlighting?'

'I suppose so.'

'What kind of stuff?'

'Just labourin' work. A bloke I know has a business layin' paths and patios and I do a bit of work fer him now and again.'

'Cash in hand, no tax, no paperwork. That's a bit naughty when you should be at your regular job, isn't it?'

Newman shrugged.

'So that's where you were that morning and not murdering Damian Penrose?'

''Course I wasn't; I was down at t'builders' merchants helpin' him load up his van for t'day.'

'And what about Monday night? I'm sure you know there was another murder near The White Swan late in the evening.'

Newman thought for a moment. 'I was at t'pub, T'Bilton Arms, 'til late; lots of people saw me.'

Oldroyd glanced at Andy and then got up. 'OK. We'll be checking those alibis, otherwise we'll leave it there for the moment. I say again: don't lie to the police. All you do is get yourself into more trouble. If you'd come clean with us at the beginning, we wouldn't have had to waste all this time.'

Newman said nothing. Oldroyd and Andy went back to the front door. The barking and scratching reached a crescendo as they passed the living room.

'Waste of time, then, sir, as you said,' said Andy, as Oldroyd drove back to HQ.

'I think so. You'd better get his alibi checked out and then I'm inclined to leave it at that.'

'What he's up to is a bit dodgy, isn't it, though?'

'Yes, but that's how poor people survive in our society: on their wits. I'm not about to shop him to his employer or the tax people, not when the rich bankers and multinationals are avoiding taxes on an industrial scale and getting away with it.'

Andy thought about his friend, Jason Harris, who worked in the City and openly admitted that the system was like a gigantic casino, except you played with other people's cash. Jason made a packet of money, and how many of his practices were strictly legal? It wasn't easy when you were a policeman charged with upholding the rule of law, but he tended to agree with his boss.

'Ooh! Good afternoon, Sarge. It's very nice to see you, as always.' DC Hancock welcomed Steph into Fenton's office in the usual leering manner. DC Turnbull smirked in the background. Unfortunately for them, they'd forgotten to ensure that their protector was there for them to hide behind. Fenton was out of the office.

Steph had been summoning up the calm courage to enter that office again and try to ignore what was said to her, but now she took her opportunity.

'Don't take that tone with me, Hancock. You're like a pathetic teenage boy. If looking at me turns you on so much, why don't you just go off into the toilets and have a good wank?' The grin disappeared from the faces of both of Fenton's DCs.

'Steady on, Sarge, that's a bit much. It's only a bit of fun,' muttered Hancock.

Steph laughed derisively. 'Is it now? Well, I don't find it funny. You like handing out all this stuff, don't you? But you can't take it when it comes back. How many women officers here do you harass with your smutty talk and dirty looks? Well, I'd make the best of it, if I were you, because things are going to change here before too long.'

Turnbull looked towards the door of Fenton's office.

'I'm afraid he's not here to protect you, Turnbull,' continued Steph. 'What a shame! You're also a couple of cowards, aren't you? Hiding behind the boss.' At that moment there was the sound of someone coming up the stairs. 'That's probably him now. Well, I dare you to tell him what I've said. "Please, sir, she's been nasty to me."' Steph glared at them both, and they looked away, sheepishly.

Fenton came into the office. As usual his sweat-stained shirt was drawn tight over his fat belly. Grubby hair stuck to his balding head and he needed a shave. He saw the three of them. 'OK, cut it out, cut it out. Fancy that, Sergeant – I'd never have thought you were into threesomes.'

Hancock and Turnbull returned to their sniggering. They always laughed obsequiously at their boss's jokes, like the pathetic hangers-on they were.

'Anyway, anybody doing any work round here? Walker wants a report on our investigation into this corruption thing, so maybe you can get your pretty head working on that, Sergeant?'

Despite Fenton's sexist remark, Steph welcomed the suggestion, as it meant she could return to her work, and not have to endure the company of these three. 'Fine,' she said.

'You two,' continued Fenton. 'We're going to that warehouse off the Leeds Road. There's been a big robbery and there'll be plenty of statements to take.'

Turnbull and Hancock left the room without looking at Steph.

Before he followed them, Fenton turned to her. 'I hope you're giving my suggestion plenty of thought. I think you'd enjoy the way out of your difficulties more than you think.' He gave her a disgusting wink and he drew his tongue slowly over his top lip. Steph thought she might be sick.

As soon as they'd gone, she returned to the general office. She had the opportunity to continue her recruitment to the cause. Sharon Warner was the next person. She was a very attractive young woman and another obvious target for a man like Fenton. Again, she would have to take things very carefully, as Sharon was an inexperienced police officer. Steph knew she may well be afraid to divulge anything that had happened.

Steph found the young DC at her desk and called her into Oldroyd's office.

'Sit down, Sharon. I'm going to use your first name because I want to talk to you about something personal.'

'OK, Sarge,' replied Sharon, looking a little alarmed. Steph went to the door to double-check that neither Fenton nor either of his sidekicks were around, then she sat down next to Sharon.

'Look, this isn't easy, so if you don't want to say anything, just tell me. OK?'

Sharon nodded.

'Have you had anything to do with Inspector Fenton?'

The look of alarm in Sharon's eyes told her that something had definitely happened.

'What . . . What do you mean? In what way? I don't . . . work with him,' Sharon said with obvious difficulty.

'Has he said or done anything in a sexual way that has made you feel uncomfortable?'

Sharon looked down, mumbled something and suddenly burst into tears. Steph put her arm gently on her shoulder and gave her a tissue. She was very angry. The girl was barely more than a kid just out of school. How dare that bastard treat her like this! He was old enough to be her father, the nasty, dirty . . . ! She had to take a deep breath to stop herself from bursting out in a rage.

'I'm sorry,' Sharon said between sobs.

'Don't be; it's not your fault but it's important that you tell me about it, whatever he's said to you about keeping quiet. You're not the only one he's treated like this, and together we can stop him.'

Sharon looked at Steph, her blue eyes wet with tears. 'I don't know,' she said. 'My dad said not to say anything; it would be held against me.' She put her hands up to her face. 'Oh God, I sound pathetic . . . telling my parents about things.'

'Why? It's natural to go to them for help when you're not very experienced and not sure of yourself. I used to talk to my mum all the time about what was going on here when I first started: who I liked, who I didn't, what I found hard. But I have to say, I don't agree with your father on this. As I said, keeping quiet makes it easier for people like Fenton, and worse for you and the rest of us. It's bullying and the rule of fear.'

Sharon's hands were nervously working the tissue. 'I'm just frightened, I suppose. He's an inspector, and who would listen to me?'

'That's exactly what he wants you to feel. These things are worse in an organisation like the police, because there are all these ranks, and we have to obey our superiors. It's a perfect place for these predators to flourish. The power over us is part of the kick he gets out of it. He wouldn't try it on with a woman who was the same rank.'

'What will you do if I tell you? You won't say anything to him?'

'No. I won't do anything straight away. I'm talking to a number of women who've had the same kind of experience with him. If we stay together, I think we can do something about it.'

Sharon took a deep breath. 'OK. Well, it began almost as soon as I started here.'

'How long is that now?'

'Six months. He complimented me on my first day here, and at first I just thought, Oh, that's nice and friendly. But then he carried on. Every day he was saying something about my appearance, and asking if I had a boyfriend. I tried to laugh it off, but it made me feel uncomfortable. I didn't think I could say anything to him because he's an inspector.'

'Understandable,' said Steph.

'He started stalking me. He always seemed to pop up when there was nobody else around and he would come up too close to me and sort of leer at me and say things like had I thought how much better older men were as lovers.'

Steph nodded. Somehow the fact that he obviously used the same clichéd line with all his victims seemed to make Fenton doubly pathetic.

'I wondered if I'd said or done something to encourage him. Was it my fault?'

'No, you mustn't think that. You are the victim here, you're not responsible for the way he's treated you.'

'I'm glad you've said that because I just didn't know what to make of it all. Then there are those two men who work with him,' continued Sharon.

'Hancock and Turnbull, yes, I know them – a couple of immature idiots who just feed off Fenton.'

'Well, they started to say stuff as well and . . .' Sharon started to cry again as the memories returned. 'It really upset me. I got to the point where I dreaded coming into work.'

'That's awful.'

'It was then I told Mum and Dad. They were sympathetic, but Dad said there was nothing I could do. I would just have to put up with it and not let it get to me. No one would listen to a junior person like me over a senior man like him.'

'Right,' said Steph. 'You've told me enough, and thank you, I know it's been hard. I promise I won't say anything until I've asked for your permission and that won't be until we're ready to act together.'

Sharon dabbed her eyes. 'Thanks. I feel better now I've told someone.'

'I'm sure you do. In the meantime, if he carries on saying things, do your best to ignore it and avoid being by yourself anywhere he could come in and trap you. As for those goons, Hancock and Turnbull, again just steer clear. I've given them a piece of my mind today, so they might be a bit more subdued.'

'Well done, Sarge.' Sharon smiled for the first time.

'If Fenton tries to get you working for him in his office, tell me. I'll have a discreet word with DCI Oldroyd and we can stop it without giving too much away to anyone. OK?'

Sharon nodded.

'I'll let you know what's happening,' Steph said, 'and you can always come and talk to me if there's anything else you want to go through or you're upset about anything. And remember: this is not your fault. You are the victim and you are not weak.' She smiled at the young DC, who got up to leave.

'Thank you, Sarge,' Sharon said as she left. Steph could hear the relief in the other woman's voice.

Alone in the office, Steph sighed. What she'd heard from Sharon had made her all the more determined to do something about Fenton.

∾

John Sinclair found being interviewed for the second time by Oldroyd and Andy much more challenging than the first.

He descended the stairs from his office on his way out and opened the door on to the street to find the detectives barring his way.

'I'm glad we caught you, sir,' said Oldroyd, formally but genially. His grey eyes were cold. 'If we can just go back up to your office? We need to ask you some more questions.'

Sinclair looked at Andy, but the DS's serious expression offered no support.

'Very well,' Sinclair said, turning round reluctantly and ascending the stairs down which he'd just come. 'What can I do for you?' he asked rather lamely when the three of them were sitting in the office.

'I think it would have been wise,' began Oldroyd, 'if you'd told us about your romantic involvement with Damian Penrose.'

Sinclair frowned. 'It's my private life, and I didn't think it was relevant.'

Oldroyd laughed. 'Even though it gives you a second motive for his murder?'

'I didn't murder Damian!' cried Sinclair. 'I loved him.' He covered his face with his hands and appeared to be weeping.

Oldroyd paused before continuing. 'Unfortunately, you don't need me to tell you that the two things are by no means incompatible, otherwise we wouldn't have the whole business of the *crime passionnel*, as the French put it, would we?'

Sinclair said nothing.

'I can see this is traumatic for you,' Oldroyd said. 'Please take your time.'

Sinclair picked up a tissue and wiped his eyes. 'How did you find out about it?'

Oldroyd told him about the diary.

'I see,' Sinclair said. 'I didn't even know Damian kept a diary. You must understand,' he said in a voice that kept breaking, 'another reason I don't talk about my time with Damian is that I haven't said much to my partner about it. Maybe that was a mistake, but it was a long time ago and I don't want it to affect my relationship with Ed. He knows I had a relationship with Damian, but not how intense it was and how I still had some . . . feelings for him. If anything came out now, things could be . . . difficult.'

'Yes,' replied Oldroyd. 'We understand. Nothing will be revealed unless that proves necessary.'

'You mean if you decide I'm involved in Damian's death?'

'Indeed.'

'In that case, I'm not worried. My conscience is clear.'

Oldroyd pressed on, despite Sinclair's protestations of innocence. 'When did you develop the relationship with Penrose and how long did it last?'

'Oh, it was something that went right back to our time at school together. We were close friends in the sixth form and we met up again in London.' He sighed. 'I always found Damian an exciting character. I was quieter and less confident; I suppose it started out as hero worship. The romance developed later in the freedom of London.' Sinclair was speaking more calmly now. He seemed to be welcoming the chance to talk about his troubled feelings. 'The thing is, I knew I was gay from an early age, but it was Damian who enabled me to acknowledge it. That was a difficult thing to do in those days.' He paused and seemed momentarily lost in memories.

'But I was never really sure about Damian and his bisexuality – whether it was genuine or just part of his image as the bohemian writer with an unconventional lifestyle.'

'But the relationship clearly meant a lot to you,' said Andy.

'Yes, it did. I was in love with him. It was very painful for me when we broke up. He moved on to another partner – a woman – and they eventually married.'

'Was that Susan Lawrence?' asked Oldroyd.

'Yes. I was angry and bitter. It made me feel as if his relationship with me had just been a form of dalliance, an amusement; his real self required a female partner.'

'So there was history between you before all those problems with money?'

Sinclair sighed. 'Yes. It didn't make it any easier, and after our rows about money, our relationship deteriorated to the point where he seemed to despise me. That night before he was killed, he said such cutting things in the bar about my business being a failing venture – he was so contemptuous and cruel, I couldn't believe it was the same person I'd been close to for all those years.' He shook his head.

'You obviously felt very sad and angry,' said Oldroyd.

Sinclair looked at him. 'Yes, but I think you can see that deep down I still cared for him, despite everything. I could never have killed him,' he repeated. 'I was just hoping to keep all this personal history out of the picture.'

'Not wise; we usually get there in the end,' observed Oldroyd.

'Yes, I appreciate that now, but on Monday I was afraid the press were getting on to something. There was a headline about Damian's past holding the key to his death or something. The last thing I want is anything in the press about all this, especially if it's implying my guilt.'

'I wouldn't worry too much about that,' said Oldroyd. 'The press are always claiming sensational breakthroughs and discoveries in high-profile cases that they've managed to achieve without the police. It almost always ends in nothing. If they had anything substantial, they would have published it by now.'

Sinclair nodded. 'To tell you the truth, although I didn't kill him, I'm glad everything's over with Damian. It was all too painful and over too many years of my life.'

Oldroyd nodded back, while still considering whether Sinclair could have taken steps to rid himself of the man about whom he had such powerful and ambivalent feelings.

Susan Lawrence was making herself comfortable in her room at The White Swan. It was a pleasant evening, overcast but warm. She prepared herself a gin and tonic from the minibar and sat by the high windows looking out over the hotel gardens and down the avenue where Patricia Hughes had met her end. Festival-goers were still moving in and out of the marquees, and from one of these in the distance she could hear the intermittent sound of an amplified voice and periodic applause. Clearly there was some kind of awards ceremony in progress.

She sipped her drink, smiled and thought about the clever lies she'd told the police. She wasn't here to find out who'd killed her husband. She was here to protect her interests by doing everything she could to pin the blame on that slut Clare Bayliss: the woman who'd taken Damian from her. It was reassuring to know that the police had her on their list of suspects, and who knew? Maybe she actually did it. That would make things a lot easier. Unfortunately, the police didn't appear to think Clare was a prime suspect, and now two people were dead, which complicated Susan's plans.

She didn't know what was in Damian's will. He may well have died intestate, but she calculated that there was a good chance he would have left some of his estate to his ex-wives, maybe as compensation for the awful way he'd treated them. Damian was capable of the occasional gentlemanly gesture like that. It was his public schoolboy code: 'Treat women as you like, but don't be a complete cad; see they're all right in the end.' If that was the case, then Clare would likely forfeit any inheritance from Damian if she was convicted of killing him. Susan would get her solicitors to argue that she should then receive more.

It was all a huge and rather desperate gamble, but the stakes were high. Now that Damian was dead, the generous maintenance allowance that her solicitors had screwed out of him would dry up, and her very comfortable standard of living would take a serious hit. She might even have to look for a job. Her lip curled: perish the thought!

She finished her drink and went to change her clothes for dinner. Detective work was new to her, but she fancied herself as an amateur sleuth, especially one who was trying to build a case against a particular suspect. That should be a lot easier than conducting an objective investigation, and it was not a bad idea to start here at the hotel. Who could she speak to who might be able to give her information? She applied the finishing touches to her make-up and looked at herself in the full-length mirror. She was every inch the rich and elegant woman: a resourceful and deadly one at that, for she had a backup plan if her main scheme didn't work. She had another idea as to who might be involved in Damian's murder, a suspicion that might prove useful for a little bit of blackmail. She smiled before she left the room. She was very pleased with herself.

❧

Down in the busy hotel bar, Charles Derryvale was perched on a stool, drinking from a tumbler of whisky and chatting to the people behind the bar. He was taking great pleasure in sitting in the place that Damian Penrose used to occupy. Although he was genuinely sad about Patricia Hughes, he still felt a lightness of spirit following the death of his obnoxious rival, and continued to enjoy himself in the hotel and around the town. He'd always regarded the Harrogate Festival as an opportunity to meet his fellow writers while enjoying a bit of a holiday from the writing itself. Penrose had always threatened to blight his enjoyment, but with him out of the way he felt positively blissful.

'Can you tell the writers from the other people when they come to the bar?' he was asking a young barman with a hipster beard.

'Oh yes, usually.'

'Oh? How's that, then?'

'Because they don't buy drinks; they have them bought for them by their admirers.'

Derryvale exploded into laughter and his fat chin wobbled. 'Wonderful! Yes, you're right, we're a set of stingy bastards! We never get a round in if there are members of the public around to buy them for us! I think we'd rather—'

'Ah, Charles Derryvale. I thought I recognised you.'

Derryvale turned to see Susan Lawrence regarding him with an icy stare. He peered at her with his rheumy eyes.

'Good Lord! Is it Susan? I haven't seen you for years, not since—'

'Yes, well, the less said about all that, the better. I can't say I've missed coming all the way up here to this festival. It's so provincial. Damian used to complain about it every year. I don't know why he kept coming – well, I do actually: he couldn't resist being the centre of attention at a small event like this.' She looked around the bar with a supercilious smile on her face and then at Derryvale. 'I see you still make the pilgrimage,' she remarked sarcastically. 'Well, come on, Charles, don't look so flabbergasted, and buy the lady a drink.'

Derryvale had indeed looked as if he was about to fall off his bar stool in surprise at this breezy reappearance of someone he had never expected to see again, and certainly not in Harrogate. 'Yes, of course,' he replied weakly.

'Excellent. Gin and tonic, please, double gin. Let's go and sit over there, shall we.' She pointed to a couple of vacant easy chairs in the corner of the room. 'There's something I'd like to talk to you about.'

Derryvale soon found himself sitting opposite his enemy's former wife without feeling as if he'd had any choice in the matter. He settled himself into the softly upholstered chair and regarded her suspiciously. She sat quite upright and moved her Chanel handbag from the floor to the coffee table, where it was most likely to be noticed.

'What on earth brings you to Harrogate, Susan, especially at this juncture? I would have thought Damian's murder here would have confirmed it as a place you'd want to shun in perpetuity, so to speak.'

'Quite the reverse, Charles. As I told the police, they're making a complete mess of the investigation. The answer's obvious.'

'Oh?'

'Of course. It was Clare. She never forgave Damian for cheating on her, though she seemed to forget she'd seduced him into cheating on me. The police need to get on with it and arrest her.'

Derryvale sat back and looked at her archly. 'And I suppose you're doing this just to ensure that justice is done. There's no self-interest involved.'

'What do you mean?'

'That it's an opportunity to settle an old score and clear the way to be Penrose's sole heir, as he had no children . . . At least that we know of.'

Susan picked up her gin and tonic. 'You're not a crime writer for nothing, are you?' she said. 'Anyway, why not? I deserve something from that bastard after what he did to me.'

'Well, I think you've already had plenty, if what I heard at the time about the divorce settlement is true. But, of course, that allowance comes to an end now, doesn't it?'

'Yes, which is why I'm trying to secure my future. I would have thought you'd have been on my side. There was never much love lost between you and Damian.'

'Indeed, but I draw the line at interfering with the police and trying to get someone convicted.'

'It must have been her. No one else had such a strong motive, and I've heard about her new husband and the shenanigans going on with the council. It just shows she's got a criminal mind, and it was all about the refurbishment of the Royal Baths, so she's got a detailed knowledge of where Damian was killed. It all adds up; plain as the nose on your face. It was her.'

Derryvale laughed. 'I've never heard a finer example of fitting the facts to the outcome you want. What did the police make of your ideas?'

'Oh, they just go on about evidence, evidence. There *is* plenty of evidence. I don't know why they can't see it,' she replied.

'It all fits together well in your mind because you want it to. The police, however, have to be more objective.'

'Oh!' she said in frustration. 'Anyway, Charles, I was thinking that, as I'm not getting anywhere with the police, you could help me solve the mystery of how she did it. What do you think of that? We'd make a splendid pair of private detectives.'

'Steady on!' spluttered Derryvale. 'Count me out on that one. I'm too old and slow to chase murderers. I'll stick to writing about them, thank you very much. In fact, this conversation has given me some good ideas for my next book: the woman who tries to pin guilt on her rival in love. But you wouldn't like the ending: it turns out she was the murderer all along and was trying to distract attention from herself.' Derryvale exploded in laughter again.

'Really, Charles, you're absolutely preposterous,' said Susan, downing the last of her gin and tonic and getting up. 'Well, I'm off for dinner. I'd be obliged if you'd inform me if anything comes to your attention that might help me to prove her undoubted guilt. Good evening.'

'Good evening,' replied Derryvale, shaking his head as she left.

'And he was so drunk that by the time we'd followed him to his house to arrest him, he'd passed out and collapsed outside his front door. He'd not managed to make it inside so he could drink some alcohol in the house and foil our attempt to breathalyse him.'

Deborah laughed at Oldroyd's story of the drunk driver who'd abandoned his crashed car and tried to reach home in a failed attempt to evade the law.

She was wearing a green lace dress this evening, and Oldroyd was very impressed. She wasn't afraid to stand out. Although things were going very well, the pessimistic part of him was thinking that it seemed too good to be true. How come a woman like this had no partner? Did she have a lot of – what was the modern word? – baggage? Was there a shock in store?

They were in the bar drinking cocktails at Edward's, a rather expensive restaurant on Cold Bath Road. Oldroyd had suggested it because it was fairly quiet and had generously sized tables: a good venue for conversation, which is what they wanted. A waiter came to take their order. Oldroyd chose mushroom soup for starter, followed by rack of lamb; Deborah chose goat's cheese tart followed by shellfish risotto. They were going to share at least one bottle of red wine.

'You're not vegetarian, then?' asked Oldroyd.

'No. What made you think I might be?'

'Well, nothing really . . . Just . . .'

'Ah, making assumptions. You see me as probably a leftie and a bit alternative, so you thought, she won't eat meat.' She took a sip of her cocktail and her eyes sparkled mischievously at him. 'Actually, you're right about the leftie bit, and I suppose I'm what you'd call flexitarian. I'm trying to reduce my meat consumption all the time.'

Oldroyd was relieved about the politics. He knew he would find it very difficult to relate to someone with right-wing views. He was intrigued by her views on meat eating. 'Is that for health reasons or animal rights?'

'Both, added to which meat eating is helping to destroy the planet.'

As the waiter came to take them to their table, they were conducting a lengthy discussion about issues to do with vegetarianism and veganism.

'I can't disagree with you,' conceded Oldroyd. 'But my problem is that, having been brought up to eat meat and eaten it for over fifty years, it's very difficult to change. Maybe we should be bringing up all children as vegan.'

'It wouldn't be a bad idea, but it's never too late to change, Jim. You can't use that as an excuse.'

'No, I suppose not,' replied Oldroyd with a smile. 'Look at you. What a model of good practice you are for me.' She laughed again. They were both enjoying this banter. 'Anyway, I'll try my best to eat my lamb without feeling too guilty.'

'I'm sure you'll manage it.'

The conversation continued in this easy manner throughout the meal. Oldroyd felt that he'd known her for years. She was interested in why he'd become a detective.

'You don't strike me as the type of person who would enter the police force.'

'Ah, who's making assumptions now? Policemen are macho and tough; they don't go in for literature and classical music? Apart from Morse, of course. But he's fictional.'

'OK, I stand corrected, but I'm still interested in why. You seem a very independent sort of character, not someone who would conform easily to the authority structure of an organisation like the police.'

'Well, talk to the unfortunate people who've been my superiors over the years and they'll tell you I'm a bit of a maverick and don't always follow the rules.'

'Ooh! I thought that sort of carry-on only happened in television dramas.' She sipped her wine and looked at him teasingly.

'No, sometimes you have to bend the rules to get results. My present chief superintendent, Tom Walker, is fine. We've known each other a long time and he's very pragmatic. He lets me alone to get on with things and doesn't ask too many questions.'

'You're lucky there. When I worked in the NHS, it was the managers who always got in the way and ground you down. But you haven't answered my question.'

The waiter had removed the starter plates and brought the main courses. Oldroyd looked at his substantial portion of lamb with dauphinoise potatoes.

'Wow, this looks good!' He picked up his knife and fork, attacked the lamb and proceeded to speak between mouthfuls as Deborah picked more delicately at her risotto.

'For me, the attraction of the job is that you're clearly performing a public service by catching dangerous people and bringing them to justice, but at the same time you're solving a puzzle. I've always loved a good mystery and wanted to know the answer. I used to watch magic shows as a kid and wonder how the tricks were done, and I was fascinated by the Loch Ness Monster and whether it existed or not. I got books out of the library and looked at all the old photographs. It was the same, when I was a bit older, with the assassination of President Kennedy and other conspiracy theories. I loved reading about them.'

'Do you believe in any of it now?'

'No, I became more and more sceptical over the years. The more elaborate a mystery is and the longer it persists without any conclusive evidence, the more likely it is that there's no basis to it. In my case, it's just a desire to crack the puzzles but I came to realise that other people seem to have a lot invested in a theory and spend their whole lives trying to prove something in which they really seem to believe. This is where you come in.' He pointed his fork at Deborah. 'What do you make of it in psychological terms?'

'Yes. I don't think there's one explanation. Some people have a need to believe in otherworldly things, whether it's monsters, fairies or UFOs. Maybe they're uncomfortable with the limits that rational thinking places on the world. Other people morbidly distrust governments and politicians, so they will always believe that they are not being told the truth, whether it's Kennedy or the Twin Towers or the moon landings.' She took another sip of wine and looked at him again with her head on one side. 'In your case, my diagnosis is that you find it difficult to deal with uncertainty and so you need an explanation for everything.'

Oldroyd drank his wine and nodded his head. 'Actually, I think you're right, but it's a quality that's stood me in good stead in the job. I can't give up on a case until I've solved it, and sometimes the obvious answer doesn't seem right and I have to dig deeper. I'm like a terrier once I get involved.'

'And that's where your obsessive work ethic comes from. It gets personal, doesn't it? You have to prove to yourself that you can find the answer.'

'Bloody hell! This is getting deep!' laughed Oldroyd. 'I didn't know I was going to get psychoanalysed so soon in our relationship.'

'You see, I'm a bit like you,' replied Deborah. 'I'm always thinking about what people say and do, and wondering about their reasons why. Maybe all professionals are the same. We can't just leave our work at the workplace; it's part of our identity.'

Oldroyd put down his knife and fork for a moment and reflected. 'You're right, but in my case it went to extremes and ruined my marriage.'

'You were always working?'

'Yes. It was all my fault.' He sighed. He hadn't expected to be talking about such personal things so quickly with her, but she seemed so easy to talk to and so perceptive. It seemed right. He felt he could ask her things too. 'What happened to your marriage?'

'Much simpler. He was a cheating bastard and did it once too often. I'd already forgiven him for straying, stupid, gullible woman that I was, and he promised he would never do it again. Turned out he was also a lying so-and-so.'

For the first time, Oldroyd saw a serious expression as her eyes flashed with anger. 'That's awful. At least that was never an issue between me and Julia. Our separation was amicable.'

'And you've been hoping to get back together with her?'

Another perceptive remark, thought Oldroyd. 'Yes. Until recently. She's met somebody else. My daughter helped me to realise that I needed to move on.'

'She sounds as if she's got her head screwed on the right way.'

'She certainly has – wise beyond her years.'

The conversation moved on to children and what they were all doing. It was interesting to compare notes on how you related to your offspring when they were living at a distance. It wasn't until they got to the coffee that things went a little quieter. Oldroyd sat back in his chair.

'Well, thank you for a lovely evening. I've really enjoyed myself,' he said.

'Me too.'

'It just so happens that there are some things coming up in the next few days that you might be interested in. I'm appearing at an event at the Crime Writing Festival tomorrow night and we could meet in the bar afterwards for a drink. Then on Friday there's an outdoor performance of *A Midsummer Night's Dream* at Ripley Castle, followed by the Murder Mystery Evening at The White Swan on Saturday.'

'OK. Well, I'm busy early on tomorrow evening but I'll pop down later to meet you. As for the other two, I wouldn't want to miss either. I love drama and theatre and I've always wanted to go to one of those crime mystery things. Lucky for you, I'd nothing planned for this weekend.'

'That's settled, then. We'll know whether we want to continue to see each other after all that, but' – he looked at her – 'I think I already know.'

'I see,' replied Deborah, returning his gaze. 'We'll have to see, won't we?'

As they were leaving, Oldroyd turned to her. 'There was one thing I wanted to ask you,' he said.

'Ah, this is the work bit, isn't it? At least you've left it until the end of the evening so as to not let it intrude on things. Fire away.'

Oldroyd gave her a wry smile. By God, she was sharp! 'Penrose, the first victim, was a plagiarist. He stole ideas from other writers, mostly women. I just wonder what you think of that as a motive for doing him harm.'

'I think it would cause great anger because he's stolen something that was someone else's creation, and in some ways that's worse than stealing a possession – part of themselves went into that. Even worse if they were women. I expect they would feel violated by this powerful man who's cheated them, but they might find it difficult to get back at him. I expect the world of publishing is as male-dominated as every other walk of life.'

Oldroyd told her about Esther Stevenson and her long and persistent campaign against Penrose.

'I can understand it. But did they get anywhere? I can imagine pent-up anger and frustration boiling over into violence. So yes, I do consider it a powerful enough motive for murder.'

'Thanks,' replied Oldroyd. 'Very interesting.' He'd ended this lovely evening with plenty to think about on both a professional and a personal level.

Five

Brimham Rocks is a collection of bizarre rock formations on a hillside in Nidderdale. They were caused by millstone grit being weathered by water, wind and glaciation. The shapes have suggested names for the rocks such as The Dancing Bear, The Sphinx, The Watchdog, The Camel and The Turtle.

It was early on Thursday morning before Andy got a chance to go to Patricia Hughes's flat. He took DC Robinson with him. The flat was up the hill out of the centre of the town, off Cold Bath Road. It was a section of a Victorian villa that had been split up into separate dwellings.

As he was opening the door, there was the noise of loud meowing.

'I think we've got a hungry cat in here who hasn't been fed for a while.'

'Sounds like it, Sarge.'

Inside, a black-and-white cat, not expecting strangers, backed away and looked at them cautiously, but then continued to plead in the most urgent manner. Andy picked up a few pieces of mail and they went through to the kitchen. DC Robinson found a bag of dried cat food and fed the poor animal while Andy looked around.

There were all the usual sad signs that the person who lived there had expected to return soon, though now they never would. He'd seen it many times before: fridge full of food; little reminder notes and a shopping list left on the table; washing drying on a rack; a pair of glasses on the arm of a chair and a book with a bookmark in it; quite a few dirty cups and plates by the sink ready to be washed up; and the cooker hob rather dirty. She'd been very busy right up to her death with the festival, and domestic chores had suffered.

'Funny how death can happen so suddenly, isn't it? And when you don't expect it.'

Robinson looked over at him. 'Steady on, Sarge, that's a bit deep. You sound like the gaffer. It's just like him to come out with stuff like that.'

'True – perhaps I've worked with him long enough to start getting like him. Actually, I think I'd rather go like that myself. You know, quickly, over and done with before you know anything about it. Better than lying in hospital for ages in pain, don't you think?'

'I don't really think about it, Sarge, can't see the point. We're all going to go, and we can't do anything about it. If you start thinking too much, you just make yourself miserable.'

This was very philosophical for DC Robinson. Andy was impressed by his sensible practicality. 'I think you're right. Let's get on with the job.'

'Are we looking for anything in particular, Sarge?'

'Any clues as to what she might have known that led someone to kill her.'

They wandered through the flat with its eerie stillness. The cat had gorged itself and disappeared through a cat flap. Arrangements would have to be made to find it a new home. Andy paid particular interest to a small room that had obviously been Hughes's study and library. There were shelves lined with books, a PC and a handwritten phone book containing lists of numbers. He'd once had one like it and found himself pondering on life again: this time on how rapidly technological change overtakes you. He shook his head. This was becoming serious; was he getting middle-aged or something?

He took the phone book and the PC for analysis by the techies. One shelf contained some neatly stacked ring binders, all labelled. These were clearly records of the Crime Writing Festival from the time before everything was stored digitally. They went back to the early 1990s. He leafed through a few and saw that they were all similarly organised: planning notes, details of events, venues, writers who were appearing, etc., and lists of staff involved, including volunteers. This last item could be useful. They might be able to identify someone significant from these lists. He'd brought some bags, and began filling them with the files.

DC Robinson joined him. 'Can't see anything unusual, sir; seems like a pretty ordinary flat to me.'

'No, I don't think there's much here, apart from all these records and the PC. The answer to these crimes often lies in the past, and there's a good chance that somewhere amongst all this she's written something that could help us.'

'Be my guest. Never let it be said that I have no manners towards ladies.'

Fenton had opened the front door of his Audi and, in an elaborate show of gallantry, was beckoning Steph to take a seat. She would rather have boarded a council lorry going to Harrogate sewage works but she knew she had to get in. She moved sharply and kept facing him as long as she could to avoid giving him an opportunity to pinch or smack her bottom.

'Ooh, aren't we prim and proper today?' mocked Fenton as he went round to get in at the driver's side. 'Wouldn't it be awful if I caught sight of a bit of leg?'

'Where are we going?' said Steph, abruptly getting him off the subject and sitting well away from the brake and gearstick.

'Council offices. To see what Bayliss's other half has to say.'

He drove off at high speed and remained silent for the duration of the short journey. Steph tried to distract herself by thinking about what she and Andy might do at the weekend. There were some good jazz bars in Leeds and she needed to do something relaxing.

Jack Sandford, as debonair and confident as ever, met them at the entrance to the council building dressed in a dark suit and tie. He showed them into an upstairs office. After introductions, he offered coffee, which was refused, but Steph accepted a glass of water.

'So, Inspector. I think we can clear all this up pretty quickly. It's all a silly oversight on my part. No malpractice intended.'

Fenton sat with his legs crossed. 'I don't think it's quite as simple as that,' he said.

'Oh?' Sandford looked supremely unflustered.

'No. It looks extremely suspicious, doesn't it? Your wife is awarded a contract and you didn't declare your connection with her as an interest.'

'No, but as I explained, it was just a mistake. It shouldn't have happened, I know, but things go wrong when we're under pressure, don't they? I'm sure we've all done it.'

'Has your wife been awarded other contracts from the council while you were an elected member?' asked Steph.

Fenton frowned at her, as if to indicate she should stay quiet.

'No, certainly not, Sergeant. This was the only occasion.' Sandford leaned forward conspiratorially. 'You see, what you've got to understand is that this is all really about politics. I have enemies on the Procurement Committee who are intent on undermining me. What better way to do it than make allegations about corruption? The press always love stories like that. Once the mud is slung, some of it sticks, as they say.'

'That sounds a bit paranoid, sir,' continued Steph, undaunted by Fenton's attempts to quieten her.

Sandford bridled a little at this. 'Well, I don't agree, Sergeant. I don't think you realise what a murky world politics can be. I can see that you're still quite young and inexperienced, but believe me, some people will stop at nothing.'

Fenton smirked at Steph after this put-down. Steph sat silently, trying to stop her face going red with anger. Fenton said nothing to support her, but she didn't expect him to. He seemed to enjoy humiliating people over whom he had some power.

'So your story is that you simply omitted to declare your interest before the committee. It was an oversight,' repeated Fenton.

'Exactly.'

'We'll need a statement from you to that effect.'

'Of course.'

Fenton didn't seem to want to pursue matters any further, so the two detectives left.

'I don't think this is going anywhere. I'm not much inclined to take it any further,' he said as he drove back.

Steph was surprised. 'Aren't there other people we need to interview? What about the others on the committee? We need to know how Sandford behaved in the meetings. Did he argue for his wife's business?'

'Naw, it's a no-no. I don't even think that any crime's been committed. At worst it's a breach of their ethical code. I think whoever reported it to us was overreacting or had it in for Sandford.'

'But we can't just accept what Sandford said about that. Of course he's going to say anyone who makes a complaint against him is just against him personally.'

'I think he's probably right, though.'

'Don't we need to interview the person who made the complaint?'

'Already done.'

'And what did you conclude from it?'

Fenton turned to her, looking exasperated. 'Just leave it alone, will you? I'm not giving you chapter and verse now. I'll make a decision when I've reviewed all the evidence. There are more urgent matters that you should be thinking about. I'm looking forward to a nice answer from you. You won't regret it.'

Steph ignored this change of subject and sat thinking. Something didn't seem right. Abusing public office as Sandford was alleged to have done surely was a criminal offence. Why was Fenton giving up on the case so easily when it clearly merited a much more thorough investigation? It was time to conduct her own enquiries.

'Is that Chief Inspector Oldroyd?' The voice was female, with a Scottish accent.

'Yes.' Oldroyd answered into the phone. Andy was back in the office but Steph was out with Fenton.

'My name's Fiona MacPherson, National Trust. I'm calling from Brimham Rocks. I've been reading about this murder case and I've got some information for you.'

'I see. What can I do for you?'

'I work here at the information centre. I read quite a lot of crime fiction and I've seen Damian Penrose at the Crime Writing Festival a few times. You see, I saw him here at Brimham Rocks, just a couple of days before the murder. He was with someone, a woman. They were arguing, and, well, I overheard some of the things they were saying. It was in the Visitors' Centre at the top of the hill. I'm sure you know it.'

'I do. What were they saying?'

There was a pause. 'I'd much prefer it if you'd come out here so I could explain it to you. It's so difficult on the phone.'

'I'll send someone out to take a statement from you.'

'Oh, Chief Inspector. I'd much rather you came yourself. I want to explain it to you personally because, well, I'm frightened, to be honest. I've seen people watching me . . . and, well, maybe I'm paranoid but . . .'

'No, not to worry. I'll come out straight away,' said Oldroyd. 'I'll be there in half an hour.' He put the phone down. 'Well, that's curious.'

He explained to Andy what the caller had said.

'That's odd, sir. Penrose at a National Trust property. What is it? A stately home or something?'

Oldroyd beamed. 'Oh no, it's quite a special place and very good for a private meeting. It's off the beaten track and I can imagine Penrose finding it quite atmospheric. We'd better get off; I've had too many cases of potential informants being got rid of before I could speak to them. Let's not take any chances. Come on, I'll tell you about it on the way.'

The rain was heavy as they were driving up Nidderdale. Andy was subjected to one of Oldroyd's periodic lectures on aspects of Yorkshire's landscape and history. Although the detail was sometimes overwhelming for a city boy from Croydon, he always indulged his boss, even if he had to feign interest at times. He knew that Oldroyd derived a great deal of sustenance from his love of the Yorkshire countryside and actually most of what he said was interesting to a man who had adopted Yorkshire as his home.

As they drove up the main road through Nidderdale, the tops of the fells were covered in mist, and flashes of white showed where swollen streams were crashing down the hillsides. The car splashed through huge pools of water, which were threatening to inundate the road. At Summerbridge, Oldroyd suddenly turned off right, on to a steep and narrow road between some old cottages. There was a brown direction sign with the characteristic oak leaf of the National Trust saying 'Brimham Rocks'.

'You're not going to see much today until we get near them,' said Oldroyd as they drove up into the mist, wipers still flashing across the windscreen. 'It's a proper summer downpour; should ease off soon.'

Before long, some large and strange rock formations started to appear on the top of the hill they were climbing, like a series of unusual sculptures.

'It's a while since I've been up here,' said Oldroyd, looking round wistfully. 'My dad used to bring us when we were kids and I brought mine when they were young. It's a great place to climb and explore. It wasn't National Trust when I was little. There were cars parked all over the place and a funny old bloke in plus fours used to go round trying to get people to pay an admission fee. We used to call him "Baggy Pants".' Oldroyd laughed and shook his head at the memory. 'Now there's a car park here and cars can't go in among the rocks.'

He parked the car and they got out and put on waterproof jackets. Andy looked around at the impressive rock formations, some as much as thirty feet high, dark, gritty structures thrusting up from the hillside like giant fungal growths. Some were jagged, others rounded. There were some crazy structures of enormous boulders supported on slender pedestals and huge blocks with holes worn through, standing on platforms. Erosion had created shapes and contours suggesting birds and animals. There was something weirdly prehistoric about the overall effect. Andy would not have been surprised if a brontosaurus had lumbered into view, striding between the massive structures. The rain had eased, but the mist remained, clinging to the top of some of the biggest rocks and creating a sinister atmosphere.

'Right,' said Oldroyd. 'Up this main path to the Visitors' Centre.'

Andy followed his boss up the path, which wound its way between the towering rocks. The rain had driven most of the visitors back to their cars and they met no one. Rounding a corner, the path was blocked by yellow tape and a diversion sign pointed left.

'They must be doing path repairs,' said Oldroyd. 'This way.'

Andy was about to follow, but he felt that something was not right. There was no real path in the direction of the arrow. Oldroyd's enthusiasm was dulling his instinct for danger. Andy looked around urgently, not sure what to expect, as Oldroyd headed towards a narrow gap between two of the rocks. Andy glanced up to the top and fleetingly caught sight of some movement. Suddenly he realised what was about to happen and lunged forward.

'Sir, look out!' he yelled, and collided with Oldroyd, sending both of them hurtling forward as the boulder dropped down towards them. It crashed behind and split open with a terrible grinding sound. Andy lay on the wet rocks, his trousers wet and torn.

'Sir? Sir, are you OK?'

Oldroyd was laid out just ahead of him with blood streaming from a head wound. He'd hit his head on a sharp rock as he fell and seemed unconscious.

'Shit!' exclaimed Andy, looking back and up to the top of the rock. Was there going to be another attack?

He quickly checked Oldroyd over. The chief inspector's pulse was normal and he was still breathing. Andy needed to get help, but where from? He couldn't leave his boss here when the murderer might strike again. He got out his phone but, as expected, there was no reception here amongst the rocks. He couldn't call for medical help or reinforcements. He would have to try to revive his boss and help him to safety.

'Sir, sir!' He tried gently slapping Oldroyd's face, and there was a moan. Much to Andy's relief, his boss opened his eyes.

'What the hell's going on?' he groaned. 'My bloody head!'

'It could have been a lot worse, sir – someone tried to kill you. They tipped a boulder off the top. You fell on the rocks where I pushed you. It just missed us.' He pointed to the split boulder lying behind them. It was actually not that big, and could have been moved by two people, but it was big enough to kill someone if it hit them from that height.

'What?' Oldroyd was still too dazed to take it in.

'We've got to get to that Visitors' Centre, but we've got to go carefully. Which way is it?'

'Over there, keep going up to the top of hill. It's right at the top.' His voice was weak. He put his hand up to his head and saw the blood. 'Bloody hell.'

'Can you make it if I help you?'

'Yes. Let's get moving; they might have another go.'

'That's what I'm afraid of.'

Andy got to his feet carefully and found that he'd twisted his knee. He helped his boss to stand up, rather uncertainly to begin with, then he put his arm around Oldroyd's shoulder and the two men limped and staggered out of the gully. Looking back, Andy thought he had a brief glimpse of a figure watching them from high up on one of the tallest rocks, but it quickly disappeared from view.

Andy had no idea where they were but he knew they must stay in the open and not walk between the rocks, to avoid further things being thrown at them from above. He thought it unlikely that anyone would attack on the open ground, but he still had to find his way to the elusive Visitors' Centre. Luckily the mist had come down further and was thick enough to confuse their pursuer. He picked up a chunky piece of stone to use on anyone who pounced on them.

They stumbled along, trying to head for the high ground. There was nobody about. Where were the public when you needed them? Andy was sure they'd passed the same place at least twice. Were they going round in circles? They were floundering in the eerie quiet of the mist, in which huge rocks kept looming up in front of them.

'I think this is wrong,' mumbled Oldroyd as they continued through the mist, desperate to find the main path. 'Too far to the left. Watch out for . . . Stop!' He pulled Andy back. They were on a stone platform near the edge of a precipice with a drop of a hundred feet.

'God! Well, thanks for returning the favour, sir. That would have been the end of us if we'd fallen down there. We haven't been in so much danger since we went down those pothole things.'

'At least you don't get this mist down there. But I think this place is what they call The Huntsman's Leap, and at last I think I know where we are. Let's follow this track.' He pointed to a path that ascended and curved to the right and they continued along, passing outlandish rock formations until suddenly some light broke through and the mist began to melt away.

'Good. We must be near the top. Yes, I can see it! Over there.'

Andy could see a solid, low building made of the same mill-stone grit as the rock formations. It too seemed to grow out of the landscape. They made it to the door and stumbled through. Safety and help were rapidly provided and it didn't take long to establish, as the two detectives now fully expected, that there was no such person as Fiona MacPherson working for the National Trust at Brimham Rocks.

Ben Poole sat in a corner of an old pub in the centre of Harrogate. The dark, wood-panelled bar had retained its original gas lights, including one on the counter by the beer pumps. It was an atmospheric, half-lit place and perfect for a clandestine meeting. There was another reason he wasn't sleeping well at the moment that he hadn't shared with Geraldine, in order to protect her from anxiety. In his role as a freelance journalist, he was involved in a secret investigation into Harrogate Council, which was on the brink of revealing the existence of corrupt practices. He'd arranged to meet his contact in the council at this venue, where it was possible to hide from public view. He had a drink of his beer, looked at his watch and checked that there was no one he knew in the pub. He shook his head. Fancy arranging such clandestine meetings in Harrogate, of all places! He almost laughed out loud as he thought of himself as an agent in Berlin during the Cold War. Nevertheless, there was a real sense of danger in confronting powerful people; you never knew to what lengths they might go to defend themselves.

'Hi,' whispered the figure who had entered from a door at the rear of the pub and had shuffled quietly into a seat opposite Ben. He was wearing dark glasses and a coat with the collar up. This was more than ever like a spy story.

Ben spoke in a low voice. 'How's it going? Do you want a drink?'

'Thanks, I'll have a whisky. It's nerve-racking. I'm having to be really careful. I don't think anyone suspects anything yet.'

Ben went to the bar and returned with the drink. He had another look around the pub, which was almost empty. 'Have you managed to get anything solid? Any evidence of what's going on that we can use?' he asked.

'It's difficult. He covers his tracks. I blew the whistle when he forgot to declare his interest in that Royal Baths contract. That was very careless of him.'

'You mean his wife's business?'

'Exactly. The problem is, I've heard the police have dropped the case: lack of evidence. I find that very dubious.'

'What do you mean?'

He downed the whisky in one gulp, looked around then leaned forward to Ben. 'I think he's being protected by the police.'

Ben whistled. 'Wow! You mean someone in the police is in on it?'

'Yes. That's how these things work, isn't it?'

'Bloody hell! Bent coppers. This thing's getting bigger.'

'Yes, which is why I'm getting nervous. We could bring a lot of people down here, if they don't get to us first.'

'Steady on, we're not talking about the Mafia. I don't think you'll be found in the stream in the Valley Gardens with your throat cut.'

'Maybe not, but there's a murderer on the loose in Harrogate, isn't there?'

'Yes, but that business has nothing to do with Sandford, has it?'

'Don't be too sure. You know that Clare Bayliss was Penrose's second wife?'

Ben was surprised for the second time. 'God. No, I didn't know that.'

'I think it was a bit before your time. He met her here at the Crime Writing Festival, several years ago. She went off to London with him but the marriage didn't last and apparently it all ended bitterly.'

'Do you mean she could have bumped him off?'

The man shook his head. 'I don't know. It's doubtful, but we may well be dealing with some ruthless people capable of violence and they may be getting more desperate. Sandford is effectively involved in two police investigations. This is serious stuff. It might not be just my job and your reputation at stake if we get this wrong.'

'So what's the next move?' Ben could scarcely disguise his excitement. This was what brave investigative reporting was all about. Geraldine would have to be kept entirely in the dark.

'We need to find out more about who's protecting him. We've got a lead. The detective inspector who came to interview him was called Fenton. He had a female sergeant with him. If he decided not to continue with the case, he could be the one.'

'I see. I'll talk to my contacts in the police, see if I can find out anything.'

'It might also be worth doing some tracking – you know, see if we can catch him meeting a police officer.'

'OK, well, he doesn't know me, so I'll see if I can follow him. It'll take some time.'

'And it won't be easy. Jack Sandford's a devious bugger, I can tell you, so take care. If he knows someone's on to him, he'll be even more wary and it'll be even more difficult to pin anything on him.'

A silence followed as they both contemplated the difficult and dangerous venture in which they were getting ever more deeply involved. They finished their drinks, arranged another time and venue to meet up again and left the pub by different doors.

⁓

'Blast it! What a damned idiot I've been! Walked straight into the trap! I must be losing my grip.'

Oldroyd was lying on a bed in the first aid room at the Visitors' Centre at Brimham Rocks. First aid had been administered by the friendly staff, and an ambulance called, despite Oldroyd's protestations. He was politely but firmly informed that no risk could be taken with head wounds. Andy sat in a chair next to him, resting his leg, which was bruised but not broken. Despite his painful head, Oldroyd was managing to drink a cup of tea and eat a generous slice of National Trust cake.

'Never mind, sir. I was on hand to save you.' Andy grinned.

'You were. And I can't thank you enough.' Oldroyd looked thoughtful. 'It's getting bloody serious now. There are some determined people behind this. But it's also a good sign. They feel threatened by us, so we must be on to something. The problem is, I don't really know what it is yet.' He chuckled and then grimaced as the pain shot through his head.

'I thought it was a funny set-up, sir, to be honest – couldn't imagine Penrose coming to a place like this.'

'No, you're right. And I should have been on the alert when the caller insisted I come out personally. The trouble with me is I leap at any chance to drive out here into the Dales and I was off my guard.'

'Good place to try to kill someone, isn't it, sir? Lots of hiding places, dark corners. I wonder if they knew there was a good chance of this mist coming down?'

'Probably. You plan it out and then take your chance, don't you? If some member of the public had somehow got in the way, they'd have just abandoned it and no doubt had another try later. Did you see more than one person?'

'No, sir, but I reckon there must have been at least two to manoeuvre a boulder like that into position.'

'Yes, but you'll probably find that that big rock they were standing on above us is embedded in the hillside. There will be an easy access to the top from some point, otherwise they couldn't have got that boulder up there. They would have rolled it to the edge of the gap through which we were passing, and pushed it over. They must have been watching us arrive and then quickly rigged up that diversion sign so that the big stupid copper would walk straight into the ambush. Maybe it's time I retired myself before someone does it for me. Or worse.'

There was the sound of a vehicle drawing up.

'That's probably the ambulance. Here, take the car keys and I'll see you back at work tomorrow.' He threw a bunch of keys over to Andy, who caught them one-handed.

'OK, sir. Take it easy.'

Andy helped a still-groggy Oldroyd off the bed and out into the ambulance. The vehicle drove off down a winding back lane that serviced the Visitors' Centre. The sun had come out and the mist had entirely disappeared. Andy looked back down the hill and over the weird rocks, which were massed together like a gathering of ancient giants turned to stone in a Tolkien story. He tried to pick out the one from which they'd been attacked and the gully they were walking through when it happened. Which route had they taken to the top of the hill? Where was The Huntsman's Leap? He couldn't make out anything. Down there amongst the complex of paths and gullies, it must be quite easy to get lost even when the weather was clear, but covered in mist it became a sinister maze of entrapment, where it was near impossible to get your bearings. The perfect place for a murder.

'Brimham Rocks! What on earth were you doing there? You look wrecked!' Steph was in the office when Andy limped in covered in mud, with his trousers torn.

'We were lured out there.' He told her what had happened. 'I thought it was strange, but the boss was keen to get out there. He was off his guard and someone outwitted him. The boss outwitted: that's a collector's item!'

'I know, but bloody hell, you were lucky to escape,' said Steph as she made Andy a mug of tea. 'Are you OK?' She gave him a hug, even though physical contact was frowned upon while they were at work.

'Yeah, I've just strained the ligaments a bit,' he replied as he massaged his knee. 'The boss fell heavily and cracked his head on a rock. He's gone for a check-up but I don't think there's any damage done. He—'

There was a knock on the door and Fenton walked straight in. 'Oh, sorry, I'm not interrupting anything, am I?' He looked from one to the other and smiled lecherously.

'No,' replied Steph. 'Sergeant Carter's been attacked and hurt.'

'Oh dear,' said Fenton, showing no interest in what had happened. 'He'll need some care and attention, then. Lucky man. Anyway, just come up to my office; I need to brief you about something.'

Steph followed him out, glancing at Andy and casting her eyes upwards.

Upstairs she sat down in Fenton's office, relieved that Hancock and Turnbull were not around. Fenton sat behind his desk looking at some papers but he didn't appear to be reading them.

'I've decided that we don't need to take any further action in this council case. There's insufficient evidence to continue.'

Steph had been half expecting this since his comments on the way back from interviewing Sandford, so she didn't argue with him.

'Does that mean you don't need me anymore?'

'Well, of course, I need you really badly, but not in the way you suggest. No, you can toddle off back to the DCI, but remember: I'm getting impatient.'

Steph ignored his salacious comments and promptly left the office. Something was definitely wrong. Why was he abandoning the case so abruptly? She didn't believe that he'd really investigated it thoroughly. Unless – the thought suddenly struck her – was he involved himself? He was just the kind of sleazy police officer who could be involved in dodgy stuff. It would be worth keeping a discreet watch on his movements. There might yet be material of a different kind that could be used against him.

Oldroyd sat resting in his flat after his ordeal at Brimham Rocks. It was a pleasant early evening, and he had the window open. The mowers had been out on the Stray that afternoon and the smell of the newly mown grass wafted into the room.

He drank a mug of tea and tried to rest. His head was still sore, and there was a large plaster over the cut he had received earlier. He knew he ought to stay in and have an early night but he was due to appear at the Crime Writing Festival later on and then he and

Deborah were meeting in the bar at The White Swan. He didn't want to cancel these engagements, so he decided to lie down for a while when he'd finished his tea and try to regain his strength.

In the meantime, he knew he ought to contact Chief Superintendent Tom Walker and report on what had happened. Although it was late, the old boy would still be at work. Oldroyd suspected that Walker's home life was not particularly good. He seemed to spend his time divided between his office and the golf course.

Sure enough, the gruff Yorkshire voice answered the phone. 'Jim. Well, I'm glad you've rung. How are you? I've had a brief report from Sergeant Carter. He said you were at Brimham Rocks and things turned nasty. What the bloody hell were you doing up there? It's a funny place that; I've never liked it – gives me the creeps.'

In private, Oldroyd and Walker were on first-name terms. They'd known each for many years and respected each other's abilities. 'I'll live, Tom, as they say – got a bump on the head when I fell. Not as bad a bump as I would have had if Carter hadn't had his wits about him.' He explained how Andy had realised the danger and pushed him out of the way.

'Good lad,' said Walker, 'but it doesn't sound like you to be caught out like that. What was going on?'

'Oh, I fell into the trap all right – made a big fool of myself. You know me, I can lose concentration when I'm away in those landscapes.' He told Walker how they'd been lured to Brimham Rocks. 'But don't worry, I'm on the alert now. These people are clearly very dangerous and determined if they're prepared to go for the police like that.'

'Yes, but they must also be scared of you, so you must be on to something.'

'That's what I told Sergeant Carter. The problem is, to be honest, Tom, I haven't got a clear idea of what it is I'm on to but they must think I'm a threat nevertheless.'

'Yes, so you'd better be careful. Don't go around by yourself, and make sure all your venues for interviewing people are safe. Bring them into the station if you can, rather than going out to them. I'm sure the whole thing'd be a lot easier if there wasn't this bloody Crime Writing Festival going on. So many people swanning around, gabbing about the crimes and muddying the waters.'

'It'll soon be over,' replied Oldroyd, who thought it judicious not to tell Walker that he was actually taking part in the festival.

'Good. Well, I don't need to tell you that Watkins is still bleating on to me, especially after that poor woman was murdered. You're sure the two are connected?'

'Pretty sure, Tom. She was bumped off because she knew something.'

'Yes, you're probably right. We don't get many violent muggings in Harrogate. It would be too much of a coincidence. Anyway, just get on with it, but take the day off tomorrow if you're feeling groggy.'

'Righto, but I think I'll be OK.'

Walker rang off, and Oldroyd went to lie down. He was looking forward to the evening but was also quite nervous, not about the Crime Writing Festival event, but about meeting Deborah later. Having been married and faithful to his wife for so long and having had no relationships since they separated, the whole business of getting to know a woman and establishing a relationship was now very strange to him. He'd not done anything like this since his student days, when he met Julia at Oxford. He felt awkward and clumsy. It was like being in your early teens again and trying to link up with the opposite sex for the first time.

He put on a recording of Beethoven's early piano sonatas and lay on the sofa. He also found it hard not to think of it as wrong; meeting Deborah felt like adultery. He knew there was no reason to feel like this. Julia had made it clear that she had a new relationship and she was considering a divorce. He had no religious principles about such things; it was just that he found it hard to accept his new freedom. It was not something he'd ever expected or wanted.

Nevertheless, his canny and wise daughter, Louise, was right: unless he shed all these inhibitions and made an effort, he would continue to be alone, maybe for good, and that was not a destiny he wanted to contemplate.

He was entering a relaxed state and about to doze off when his phone went. He was surprised to hear the voice of Carol Ashworth from the Baths.

'Oh, Chief Inspector, I'm glad I've caught you; it's just that there's something I want to tell you.'

'Yes, Mrs Ashworth?' Oldroyd tried not to yawn.

'You see, I think it's happened again.'

'What has?'

'Remember I told you that Mr Penrose's murder was like a murder in one of Mr Derryvale's books?'

'Yes.'

'Well, I've heard about poor Pat Hughes being murdered near The White Swan and I realised that there's a book called *To the End of My Days*, and in it a woman is killed in a dark street near a hotel, just like Pat.'

'And who wrote this one?'

'It's by Liz Simpson. She comes to Harrogate now and again. I once went to a book signing at Riverstone's. I think she's a friend of Esther Stevenson's.'

'OK, well, thank you for the information . . . Yes, bye.'

Oldroyd rang off and lay down again. There was no quelling the enthusiasm of the amateur detective once it was aroused. A woman killed on a dark road near a hotel – that was even more likely to be a coincidence than the murder at the Baths. Surely there couldn't be anything in it.

Or could there?

Steph and Andy were driving home to Leeds. Steph was very quiet, and Andy, who was driving, looked sideways at her. He'd had a sense for a while that there was something going on with his partner but he couldn't get anything out of her.

'Are you OK?' he asked.

'Fine. I'm just thinking about this case I was working on with Fenton.'

Andy slowed down as they reached the narrow crossing of the Wharfe at Harewood Bridge and gave way to a 36 bus on its way to Ripon. 'I thought it was over.'

'That's what he said. It's a relief not to be working with him and those two clowns.'

'Too right.'

'The thing is, though, there are still things that puzzle me.'

'Oh?'

'Yes. He's dropped the case very quickly and prematurely, in my view.'

'Why do you think that?'

'Well, this bloke at the council, Jack Sandford – his explanation of what happened was a bit weak. He just claims it was an oversight that he didn't declare his interest, but you'd think Fenton would want us to interview other people at the council who knew him or were involved, to check his story and the background and so on.'

'Well, didn't you?'

'No. We only spoke to Sandford and his wife. When I asked Fenton about it, he said he'd spoken himself to all the other relevant people at the council and there wasn't enough evidence to proceed. The thing is, I don't believe him. I don't think he's interviewed anybody else.'

'Why would he lie to you about it?'

'That's what I'm wondering. He got very edgy when I pursued him on it. Don't you think it's odd?'

'Maybe, but he's an experienced detective inspector, even if he's a bit of an arse on the personal level. You know the saying "Ours is not to reason why"? If that's what he's decided, then you'll have to accept it. At least you've got away from him.'

They were crossing the last section of open countryside before the urban area of Leeds began. The blue water of Eccup Reservoir lay to their right amongst the patchwork of fields and hedges. It was looking very beautiful as the sun set in the west behind it.

Steph was tempted to tell Andy more about her suspicions concerning Fenton's involvement with Sandford, but decided not to. She badly wanted to confide in someone, but she needed firmer evidence before she could involve anyone else. Also, sorting out Fenton was still something she wanted to undertake herself; she felt it was her mission. Andy was wrong: she hadn't got away from Fenton. In fact, she was increasingly locked in a struggle with him that was becoming deadlier as time went on. The man was not only a sex pest but most likely a bent copper too, and that had serious consequences for the force. It was now her duty to bring him to justice.

At the Royal Baths, life was slowly returning to normal. After numerous searches of every corner of the building, the police had finally allowed the Baths to reopen to the public.

The final customers of the day had departed as Steve Monroe cleaned the floors of the sauna room with his squeegee. The Baths were booked up solid for several days ahead. People were being turned away at the doors. There was clearly a grim element of wanting to see where the murder had taken place. Steve found it obnoxious. He felt like putting up a notice: 'This is the murder room. Take care!' Maybe that would satisfy their gruesome curiosity. The whole business had put him off his job at the Baths even more. He would never feel the same again about the place after everything that had happened. He felt it was time for a change. He wanted to be his own boss and in control of things. He'd always been too timid about life and now was the time to break out and fulfil his potential.

The temperature was still high in the hot rooms and steam room. As he cleaned the floors, a voice called out.

'Steve, is that you?'

'Hi, Sid. What are you doing here at this time of day?' He walked out of the hot room and saw the technician grinning at him.

'Oh, it is you. Ever since that murder, I've been a bit edgy comin' down here. Daft really. Anyway, they asked me to come and do some extra servicin', you know, because everythin's been turned off for a while. Just to make sure it's all workin' properly. It's nice to get back and get paid again.'

'Don't you get a regular wage here?'

'Oh no, casual contract, mate. I only get paid for th'hours I do, no sick pay, holiday pay or owt like that.'

'That's terrible. How do you manage?'

'Bits and pieces, here and there; there's lots more people in the same position where I live. I've got some other jobs and I do a bit o' moonlightin' – got into trouble wi' t'police over that. It wa' my own fault. I wa' off doin' summat on t'day of t'murder, so me alibi didn't stand up. I think I got away wi' it, though.'

'You want to be careful.'

'Naw. Coppers aren't really bothered about stuff like that. They've got more important things to think about, like who's murdered those poor sods.'

'Yeah, I suppose so.'

'It gave me a shock, though, when they came to th'house. I lost me nerve and ran for it.' He described what had happened.

Steve laughed. 'You daft bugger. When you do that it only makes them more suspicious.'

'Ah know. Anyway, I think they went away satisfied.' He looked around and into the steam room. 'It's a bit weird down here, isn't it, since you found that body? It feels a bit spooky.'

'Yeah, I've had enough of it, actually. I'm thinking about giving in my notice.'

'Are yer?'

'Been thinking about it for a bit. When Jade's finished working part of the time in London, we're going to move away from here and start our own massage and therapy business. It's too expensive to rent anything here in Harrogate.'

'Good idea. It's nowt in my line but it's popular, isn't it, all that massagin' and that romeotherapy? People pay a lot o' money for it.'

'I think you mean "aromatherapy",' said Steve, grinning. 'Yes. Jade's done some courses in that and reflexology.'

'What's that?'

'It's where you massage parts of the feet and get a healing response in other parts of the body.'

'Bloody hell! Well, I pity anyone who ever had to massage my feet; they're a right bloody mess.'

Steve laughed. 'Well, who knows? It might do you some good – make you feel relaxed.'

'A few pints are all I need to feel relaxed. Anyway, I'd better get on with t'job. See you later.'

Newman went off and Steve continued cleaning the floors until he was satisfied that everything was ready for the next people to visit the 'Murder Baths'.

Amanda Rigby was exhausted; she would be relieved when the festival was over, and she was counting down the days. As Patricia's deputy, a big responsibility had been thrust upon her in terrible circumstances. Not only was there the awful murder of Damian Penrose, but she'd also had to endure the shock of finding Patricia's body near The White Swan.

Following this, she had been invited to a hastily convened meeting of the festival committee. The committee had been intending to meet after the murder of Penrose and now things were even more urgent. They decided that, if possible, the festival should continue; otherwise very many people would be disappointed. But they had made it clear to Amanda that, in the circumstances, they fully understood if she wanted to step down from her position. This option was tempting, but she knew that there wasn't really anyone who could take over at this point and the festival would have to be cancelled if she didn't continue. She felt strongly that this was not what Patricia would have wanted, so she insisted that she was capable of carrying on. She saw the relief on the faces of the committee members when she said this.

She returned to the festival's temporary HQ at the hotel and occupied Patricia's desk. To be honest, she wasn't just doing this for Patricia's sake; it was a big opportunity to take responsibility for a major festival and she wasn't going to miss it. If she could demonstrate her capabilities, she would be a strong candidate to do the job permanently.

There was a knock on the door, and Jade Darton came in. She looked shocked. 'Hello, Amanda. I can't tell you how sorry I am about Pat. I worked with her for a few years and she was great.' Amanda saw that there were tears in her eyes.

'Sit down, Jade.'

'Thanks. I won't take up much of your time. It's just that I promised Pat I would put together a few ideas about how to proceed with the festival without offending people – you know, after Damian Penrose's murder. I suppose it's even more difficult now.'

'Yes, but the committee has decided that we should continue, so I'm sure your ideas would be welcome.'

'OK.' Jade looked at some papers she'd brought. 'I'll email this to you, but one suggestion I have is that you present Damian Penrose with some kind of posthumous award, maybe the "Lifetime Achievement" sort of thing, so you would be honouring his memory and his contribution to the festival. His fans would be really pleased with that and it would show that the festival is being sensitive, while at the same time continuing with the events.'

'That's a really good idea, Jade.'

'Thanks. And as far as carrying on goes, place the emphasis on not wanting to disappoint people who've paid money to attend events, so it doesn't look as if you're continuing because you want to avoid a loss.'

'Excellent – you're right. I can't thank you enough, Jade. Surely we must owe you for this.'

'No. I said to Pat: I don't want any money. It's just a few ideas.' She smiled. 'If you like, it's in my interest, isn't it, because I'll hope to get the contract for your PR next year.'

'Well, you certainly will, and thanks again.'

Jade left and Amanda turned her mind to the upcoming evening. There was to be an event in the same room in which Penrose had made his final appearance. Ironically, Detective Chief Inspector Oldroyd, who was leading the enquiry into the murders, was to appear for his annual slot at the festival as a real police officer. It was usually a popular session but this year it would obviously be a sell-out. She had wondered whether he would cancel in the circumstances, but he'd rung to say he couldn't see any reason why he shouldn't go ahead. Like her, he felt that it was what Patricia would have wanted.

She looked at the clock. It was six o'clock and the event was at seven. There was no time to go home before the evening events. She was working twelve-hour days at the moment, but at least she had the opportunity to catch up on some of the paperwork. She was existing on a bad diet of pizzas delivered to the office, burgers, Pot Noodles and endless cups of coffee to stay alert. But at least she was here. She kept thinking about Patricia, and wanted to cry.

She finished her task, closed down her PC, left the office and walked over to the ballroom. It was six twenty. Ben Poole was going to chair the session with DCI Oldroyd: yet another irony. It felt like some malign deity was playing jokes on the festival. Maybe the gods didn't like crime fiction! One or two members of the public were hanging around outside and discussing other things they'd seen that day. These were obviously the really keen ones.

Amanda went past them and into the large room, checking the seating and lighting. Ben always arrived early and was already ensconced in his chair on the stage, looking through his notes. She joined him on the stage and checked the microphone, then was satisfied that everything was ready. 'Hi, Ben,' she said. 'Are you OK? This can't be easy after what happened the last time you were here.'

Ben put down his notes, yawned and shook his head. He was weary with the demands placed on him by his different roles and by the effort of keeping his anxious wife reassured. 'Sorry. I'm fine, just a bit tired. I'll be OK when we get going.'

'Good. Well, why don't you go and have a quick drink before we start? You've just got time.'

'No, I'm OK, thanks. Alcohol just makes me sleepy. I want to be sharp for this one. It's going to be a full house, I think.'

'Yes, DCI Oldroyd is quite a draw, especially with what's going on. I just hope nothing else happens.'

'What do you mean?'

She shook her head. 'Oh, I don't know! I'm just being silly really. This festival seems jinxed. I wonder what else could happen?'

'Has it affected attendances?'

'Well, the good thing is, not really. There was a blip for a couple of days, but I think the people who have been put off are being balanced by those who have a ghoulish fascination with what's happened.'

'I thought it might work that way for you in the end. There's nothing the public likes more than a good murder, real or imaginary.'

'Yes, I know. Oh, there's the chief inspector. What on earth's the matter with him?'

Oldroyd appeared at the doorway with the dressing and plaster still on his head.

'Hello,' he called as he walked to the stage. 'Are we nearly ready?'

'Just about,' replied Ben. 'What happened to you, Chief Inspector?'

Oldroyd's hand went up to the plaster. 'Oh, nothing, I'm fine. Let's just say it was an injury sustained during the call of duty.' He would say no more about it and reassured Amanda that he was well enough to continue. He sat on the chair opposite Ben Poole, just as Penrose had on that fateful night just over a week ago. Ben had a terrible feeling of déjà vu, but Oldroyd seemed relaxed, sipping water as people began to file in.

'This evening we welcome Detective Chief Inspector Jim Oldroyd to talk about the work of the police. Chief Inspector Oldroyd generously gives of his time for nothing every year at this festival, and it's always very interesting to hear a voice from the real world of crime fighting. It sets the fictional world into a kind of context, I think. So, Chief Inspector Oldroyd.'

Oldroyd nodded as he received applause. During Ben Poole's introduction, he'd scanned the audience and noted with a wry interest that a number of suspects in the case were in attendance. Charles Derryvale and Esther Stevenson were sitting together near the back. At the front, looking very excited, was Carol Ashworth from the Royal Baths. Midway down on the left was Susan Lawrence, already looking a little bored and distracted. It was very interesting but frustrating: what did it all mean? Where was the pattern? Was there a sinister reason why they were here? Was one of them going to take a shot at him? Surely not: two attempts on his life in one day would be excessive! He dragged his attention back to Ben Poole.

'I think you enjoy reading crime fiction, Chief Inspector. Is that correct?'

'Oh yes. I tend to be a little old-fashioned in my tastes. I like the novels from the Golden Age: Agatha Christie, Dorothy L. Sayers, Margery Allingham. I think it's because the world they depict is glittering and exciting but quite remote. Those writers tended to use private detectives rather than police officers to solve the crimes. The police take a back seat and they often come across as plodders compared to the likes of Miss Marple and Lord Peter Wimsey.' Gentle laughter rippled through the packed audience. 'However, I have to say there is a part of me that loves a bit of theatre, and I have been known to imitate some of the great fictional detectives if I get the opportunity.' Oldroyd was remembering a recent case at nearby Redmire Hall, and thinking how wonderful it would be if he could engineer another Hercule Poirot-like session, slowly revealing the murderer in this present case. How extra-satisfying that would be here, in the context of the Crime Writing Festival!

'Is that why you prefer them? Because they don't deal with police procedures?'

'I suppose so. I accept that police work can never be accurately depicted in a crime novel. There's far too much routine stuff. It would make the story too boring to read.' More laughter. 'But it does grate at times, when crimes are solved so quickly and the story is full of amazing and dramatic twists and turns that would never happen in reality. It makes me wonder what kind of image the public are forming of the police from these stories. Of course, it's much worse on television: all these super-detectives with their tortured private lives triumphing over diabolical serial killers, after having evaded death themselves. It makes the ordinary, hard-grafting, unattractive guys like me look extremely dull.'

More laughter as the audience warmed to Oldroyd's witty style.

'Do you find your work dull?'

'Not really, I was only joking. In fact, I find it endlessly satisfying. It keeps the old brain ticking over, and we're bringing some dangerous people to justice, so it's all worthwhile, just not as glamorous as it's depicted in fiction.'

'I see. So Hercule Poirot's comment about his "little grey cells" is accurate?'

'Yes. It's an intellectual challenge to solve the puzzle, especially in the kind of cases I seem to get. The stress lies in the fact that you're not trying to solve it in a leisurely way, reading a book in your armchair. You're working against time, particularly when there's a threat that the murderer may strike again.'

'As in the current case here at the Crime Writing Festival?' asked Ben. There was an expectant silence in the room.

'Nice try. I know it's on everyone's mind, but of course I can't comment on any actual case, and especially not this one, which is still very much live.'

'You appear to have encountered some difficulties recently, judging by your appearance.' Ben nodded towards the plaster on Oldroyd's head. 'I assume your injury was sustained during your investigations, or did you knock your head on a cupboard door?'

A ripple of nervous laughter.

'Well, you're not going to give up, are you?' replied Oldroyd, still jovial. 'But I have nothing to say on that subject.'

'It's true, though, that your work can be dangerous, isn't it?'

'Indeed. If desperate people know they're being hunted down, they'll sometimes take desperate measures. There have been a number of attempts on my life over the years. Thankfully, none of them has been successful.'

An outburst of laughter this time. After a few more questions of his own, Ben invited the audience to contribute. Charles Derryvale caught his eye. 'Chief Inspector,' the author said, in a tone that suggested he found the whole situation rather amusing. 'I'm sure you're familiar with the phrase "Truth is stranger than fiction". Here you are addressing an audience, in which there are a good few crime writers, while you are in the midst of an investigation into the mysterious murder of one such writer here in this very same town. I wonder what you're making of it all, just as an experience, you know.'

Oldroyd looked at the knowing expression on Derryvale's face. Was the man taunting him somehow? 'Well, Mr Derryvale, I agree that in some ways the whole business seems like a plot that one of you could have devised, doesn't it? Or maybe it would be regarded as too far-fetched.' His grey eyes fixed Derryvale very directly. 'My response to the situation is to assure you that, however quirky and ironic the situation is, I will continue to focus on the task in hand. I suppose you could say that I share certain things in common with the writer of the fictional crime: we both move the story to an end by finally bringing the perpetrators to justice.' Derryvale nodded to Oldroyd, but the smile never left his face. There was a spatter of applause from the audience.

A few questions later, Esther Stevenson raised her hand. 'Chief Inspector, I understand that when undertaking an investigation like the one you are involved in at the moment, you act as a team with your subordinate officers.'

'Correct.'

'Does that mean you always acknowledge the contributions of the members of the team?'

'Of course.'

'You would never pass off their ideas as your own and take credit for them?'

'No, certainly not. That would be unfair and would destroy the important relationships I have established with the two detective sergeants who regularly work with me. Good teamwork is absolutely essential.'

Oldroyd had a continuing sense of the oddness of the situation. It was bizarre to be questioned by people he'd already questioned himself as part of the investigation, and again he couldn't fathom what the questioner was really driving at. Was she still on her hobby horse of deploring plagiarism with this reference to stealing other people's ideas or was she making some other point? It was all very disconcerting. Esther Stevenson nodded and looked around the audience with a satisfied expression on her face.

Susan Lawrence raised a languid hand. 'Don't you think you'd be better off working on the case than wasting your time here? I mean, never mind "Truth is stranger than fiction", truth is more important than fiction, I say.' A buzz of conversation began at this point, and she had to raise her voice to be heard. 'You know what you need to do, so why don't you just get on with it? It's outrageous that—'

Ben Poole intervened. 'I'm sorry, I'll have to stop you. That's not a relevant question. The chief inspector has made it clear that he cannot answer questions on an actual case.'

Susan Lawrence got up, made a gesture of contempt and strode out of the hall. The audience continued discussing this unexpected interruption in loud voices.

Ben leaned over to Oldroyd. 'Do you know who she is?' he asked quietly.

'Her name's Susan Lawrence; she was Damian Penrose's first wife. She thinks she knows who killed him and that I should just get on and arrest them. I think she's had a few drinks.'

Ben frowned. 'More than a few. Strange woman; well, we'd better carry on.' He raised his voice. 'Ladies and gentlemen, if we could continue, please!'

Carol Ashworth was eager to ask a question. She beamed up at Oldroyd. 'Thank you for coming tonight, Chief Inspector, especially as you must've had a nasty accident. I just wondered: has there ever been a case you couldn't solve?'

Oldroyd was feeling hot and the voices seemed far away. His head had started to ache again. Maybe it had been a mistake to come here this evening. He should have stayed at home and rested. He drank from a glass of water.

'Well, none of us are infallible, are we? Again, I can't comment on actual examples, but I have been involved in cases that have remained unsolved. The main reason for this is lack of evidence.

If there is a single crime, the trail can go cold and then we have to wait, sometimes for years, before fresh evidence becomes available. I'm sure you've all seen cases reported in the press that have been solved years after the initial crime. This can happen where a murderer has committed a number of crimes and then stops, but very often, where a killer is on the loose and carries out a series of attacks, they eventually make mistakes, which lead us to catch them.' He felt he was rambling. 'I hope that answers your question.'

'Yes, thank you.' Carol seemed very pleased. Surely her question had not had any kind of hidden intent?

Oldroyd had had enough and was glad when Ben wound up the proceedings. He received an enthusiastic round of applause and was then able to escape to the bar.

Deborah was waiting for him, sitting at a table and drinking a glass of wine. 'Oh, look at you!' she exclaimed, immediately noticing the plaster on his head. 'You have been in the wars. How very exciting! I'm seeing a man who risks his life in the cause of bringing people to justice.' Oldroyd had called her to explain what had happened at Brimham Rocks but he hadn't told her how close he'd been to being killed. If she'd known the truth, she might not have been so jocular about it. Being less than frank about the dangers he sometimes faced was habitual with him. He'd never told Julia when he'd been under threat. Why worry people unnecessarily?

'I'm glad you appreciate the sacrifice. I have to say, my head's still thumping.'

'You need a drink. What do you want?'

'A pint of bitter would be great.'

Deborah got up and went to the bar. Oldroyd sat quietly until she returned with his glass and another wine for herself. He was too tired to think about anything.

Oldroyd took a long drink of the beer, sat back in his chair and sighed. 'I have to say, that session didn't help.'

'Why was that? I was just going to ask you about it.'

'I don't know; maybe it's because I'm under the weather, but it all seemed a bit weird. There were people in the audience asking me questions whom I've questioned about the case, and they're suspects. How odd is that? Talk about role reversal!'

Charles Derryvale and Esther Stevenson entered the bar.

'That's two of them over there.' Oldroyd pointed them out to Deborah. 'They're both crime writers and they hated Penrose for different reasons.'

'There does seem to be something vague and arty about them,' said Deborah, straining to get a good view. 'I'd have picked them out as writers even if you hadn't said. They don't look like people capable of violence, though. They might write about it, but would they do it?'

'Oh, people like that get others to do their dirty work for them. I've seen it many times, but they're just as guilty as the henchman who fires the gun or twists the knife. Blast, they've seen us! I'm not in the mood for small talk with them. I shouldn't really be speaking to them at all, as they're suspects.'

Derryvale ambled over, clutching his gin and tonic, followed by Stevenson. 'Well done, Chief Inspector, very interesting,' he said. 'It's always useful to hear things from the other side, so to speak.'

'I'm glad you enjoyed it,' said Oldroyd. 'But if you'll excuse me, I can't really socialise with you in the middle of the investigation. It could be very compromising.'

'Yes, we understand,' said Stevenson. 'I'd just like to say that I valued your comments about integrity. It's good to know that not everyone is motivated by self-interest.'

'Yes.'

'We'll leave you in peace, Chief Inspector. But I'm sorry about that Lawrence woman; fancy making a scene like that! What on earth was she playing at? Very odd.'

'Indeed.'

The two writers went off to another part of the bar, talking as they went. Oldroyd rubbed his head.

'Who was he talking about?' asked Deborah.

'Oh, Penrose's first wife, who turned up yesterday telling us whom to arrest for the murder. Surprise, surprise, she believes it was Penrose's second wife!'

Deborah laughed. 'No ulterior motive there, then; just a simple desire to see justice done.'

'Yes,' laughed Oldroyd. He liked her wry sense of irony and humour. She reminded him of his daughter. They would get on well together. 'Then she turned up tonight and started haranguing me for wasting time and not getting on with the case.' His hand went to his head again. 'Look, I hope you don't mind but I don't think I can stay long tonight. It's been a long and difficult day and I'm exhausted.'

'Oh, don't worry. I think it would be good for you to stay here a little while to wind down, though. If you go back too early, your mind will be full of stuff and you'll not sleep. I'm having a fascinating time people watching. It's a very colourful range of characters compared to your average psychology conference, where everybody looks extremely well informed and worthy.'

'Good, I'm glad you're enjoying yourself.'

'It's very exciting to think that there may be a murderer here, sort of hiding in plain sight. They're there but somehow you don't notice them. Jim? Oh, not again.'

Oldroyd was distracted. Even when he was tired out and his head hurt, that part of his brain which was working on a case somehow continued to be on the alert and ready to receive a flash of insight. 'Sorry. Something you just said made me think.'

'You don't say,' replied Deborah archly as she finished her glass of wine.

Susan Lawrence had indeed had plenty to drink. After she flounced out of the ballroom, she staggered up the stairs to her room, got another drink from the minibar and lay sulking on the bed.

Things were not going according to plan. She'd spent the whole day trying to find out as much as she could about Damian's murder, and whether there was anything she could use to incriminate Clare. At the Royal Baths, where the old rogue had met his end, she had felt no emotion except a grim satisfaction that he'd got what was coming to him, and her visit had yielded no clues. She had spoken to people at the hotel and the Crime Writing Festival, but nobody had had any useful information. The only interesting aspect was that she learned a little more about the scandal involving Clare and her husband, who was a councillor. Unfortunately, she couldn't see any way this could be linked with Damian's murder, unless he'd somehow found out about it and was using it against her. But that was not credible: blackmail was not Damian's style – far too ungentlemanly, although, curiously, plagiarism didn't seem to bother him. It was all his fault really; he'd been such a charismatic but deeply untrustworthy character. He'd treated her badly and she wasn't going to be denied her compensation. But how?

She knocked back her glass of gin in one go, and frowned. No wonder she'd lost it at the event with the chief inspector. He was far too much his own man and not malleable enough, in her view. Her plan was starting to look silly. Why had she thought she could just come up here and somehow get Clare convicted?

She looked at her empty glass. She was drinking far too much. Was she losing it? Declining into frustration and delusion? It was time to activate plan B, in case plan A completely collapsed. This promised less financially but at least had some foundation in fact. The more she learned about the circumstances of Damian's murder, the more she was beginning to see that this line of pursuit may prove more fruitful. She poured herself another drink, took up her phone and dialled a number. Someone answered.

'Yes, that's right, it's me,' said Susan. 'No, I'm sure you weren't expecting me to call . . . What do I want? Well, I'm in Harrogate, you see, and I've been thinking a lot about Damian's murder and putting two and two together. I was hoping to pin it on that bitch, Clare, but failing that I have another theory about who might be responsible. Maybe we could meet up and I could explain it to you? . . . No need to react like that; you're making me think I must be on to something. I—'

The person rang off, leaving Susan with a satisfied smile.

Six

Betty Lupton, the 'Queen of the Well', served water from the Old Sulphur Spring to guests for fifty-six years in the late eighteenth and early nineteenth centuries before the Pump Room was built. On retiring in 1843, she was given a pension of seven shillings by the Harrogate Improvement Commissioners but unfortunately she died two weeks later at the age of eighty-three.

When Oldroyd woke next morning, his head felt tender but he'd slept well and felt quite refreshed. It was Friday and the next few days were going to be very busy. As he was eating breakfast, his phone rang. It was Louise.

'Hi, Dad. Well?'

'Well what?'

'Doh! How did it go? Stop pretending to be dim!'

Oldroyd had texted her to say he'd met Deborah, that the initial meeting had gone well and that they were going out for a meal.

'Fine. It was . . . fine,' he repeated.

'Did you go out for a meal?'

'Yes, we went to Edward's.'

'Ooh, that's posh. I'll bet she was impressed. And? God, it's like getting blood out of a stone! Did you get on with her? What did you talk about, et cetera, et cetera?'

Oldroyd smiled. He was deliberately winding her up. He was actually very pleased that she was interested in his life and welfare. He knew many young people of her age had little contact with their fathers.

'She's nice. I like her. Very sharp and a good sense of humour. She sends me up when I get distracted about work, you know. She met me for a drink last night at The White Swan.'

'Good! Well, she sounds as if she'll be right for you. When are you seeing her again?'

'Hey, hold on. You'll be asking me when we're getting married next.'

'You don't need to do that – probably a bad idea. Anyway, you're still married to Mum.'

'For the time being.'

'Yes, but we've been through all that, and you haven't answered my question.'

'Which is?'

'When are you seeing her again?' Louise could be insistent, even hectoring, when she'd decided on a course of action. She'd been a feisty character since childhood.

'Tonight. We're going to a promenade production of *A Midsummer Night's Dream* at Ripley Castle. I'm hoping the weather will hold. And then we're going to the Murder Mystery Evening at The White Swan on Saturday. They always end the festival with that. I've never been. It always sounded too much like work, but Deborah fancies it, so why not?'

'Wow! That's great – that's nearly every day this week you're seeing her!'

'I know, but it just so happens that these things are on now and we don't want to miss them.'

'Great! Well, she's really getting you out and doing things – much better than mouldering away by yourself in the flat. I can't wait to meet her when I come up.'

'Hey, slow down! I've only just met her myself!'

'Aw, shut up, Dad! I can tell it's going well. Your voice is completely different. You sound much more upbeat and you've not even mentioned work.'

Oldroyd laughed. 'Good. Well, we'll see how it goes. I think you'll get on well together. She's partly vegetarian – flexitarian, I think it's called – and she likes making fun of me, so you've got a lot in common.'

'Good for her.'

'By the way, have you heard from Mum?' He could never resist pumping Louise for information about his wife.

'Not recently. Her and Peter are still together, I think, but you know what Mum's like: she never says much about stuff like that. She's been on holiday to France. That's all I know, but anyway, you need to stop tracking her; you've got another relationship to focus on now.'

'I know, but it seems strange. I'm not used to it. You know, after all this time.'

'No, I can understand that. You were with Mum for a long time and you've obsessed about work so much that you're out of practice with people.'

'I suppose so.'

'You'll be fine. Just relax and enjoy it. Anyway, have to dash. I'm working with some difficult clients today: women who've been badly abused and knocked about by their partners and they're in here with their little children who've witnessed it. Bastard men, eh? So if you think you've got problems – bye!'

'Bye.' Oldroyd put the phone down, smiled and shook his head as he felt the familiar sense of role reversal that he often experienced with his daughter.

Derek Fenton walked purposefully through the backways of Harrogate town centre, keeping away from the main streets and looking around constantly to see if there was anyone he knew. He paused behind the Royal Baths and consulted his phone. As he read a text, a figure leaned gingerly around the corner of the building behind him and checked that he was still there. Fenton stuffed the phone in his pocket and headed off through a ginnel behind the Winter Gardens. Steph followed at a careful distance, feeling sure that Fenton was on his way to the council offices in Crescent Gardens. This could be interesting. She'd seen Fenton leave the station, and on a hunch followed him. Unexpectedly, he hadn't got into his car but had headed for the town centre on foot. She saw that he was a bit edgy and was looking ahead and to the side for people who might recognise him. He didn't look behind, however. He didn't expect anyone to be following him.

Fenton crossed the Winter Gardens, with their ornate bedding, and, with a last look round, increased his speed and disappeared round the council building and into Swan Lane. Steph was some distance behind due to the lack of hiding places, but she crossed the road quickly and headed up a steep bank. At the top was a clump of trees, from which it was possible to see down Swan Lane while hiding behind the foliage. She crouched behind the gnarled old trunk of a sycamore tree and peered towards the building. Fenton was waiting outside one of the rear entrances, but concealed behind a wall. After a couple of minutes, a man emerged from inside and greeted him. Steph felt a tingle of excitement.

'That's Jack Sandford coming out of the offices, and I think that's Inspector Fenton,' said a voice behind her quietly.

Steph jumped in surprise and turned. There was a man crouched just behind her. He was holding a camera with a large zoom lens and he took some pictures of the two men together. Then he held out his hand. 'Ben Poole, writer and journalist. I know you're an officer with West Riding Police and you were working on the Sandford case with Fenton, and I've seen you with Chief Inspector Oldroyd. But somehow I don't think you're on official police business at the moment.'

'How do you know all that?'

'Any good investigative journalist has his contacts. I know people in the West Riding Police.'

'Do you? It sounds very dodgy to me. Any officer giving information to the public like that would be in serious trouble.'

'Yes, but it's all in a good cause and no money exchanges hands, I assure you. Sometimes we journalists can get to places the police can't, but it can be necessary to – how shall I put it? – shortcut the system.'

They were still watching Fenton and Sandford in the distance, and the conversation went on in whispered voices.

'Why do you think I'm not on official police business?'

'It's odd that you're skulking here by yourself.'

Steph felt outmanoeuvred. 'OK, you're right. I have my personal reasons for following that officer. I could ask you the same question: what are you doing here?'

'I think you'll approve of my motives. I'm trying to expose some corruption in the council. I've got a contact in there who's telling me all kinds of stuff about Sandford – backhanders, nepotism – but we can't explain how he keeps getting away with it. I've suspected for a while that he has a contact in the police.'

Steph's heart leaped: she could be about to strike gold! 'Good. Well, I have my reasons to suspect that officer of corrupt involvement in the same business; he *is* Detective Inspector Fenton, by the way. But we'll have to move carefully. Those pictures of them meeting will be very useful but we'll need more evidence.'

Ben looked at her quizzically. 'Why can't you report your suspicions to your superior officers?'

'I have my own reasons for that, which I'm not going to divulge. It's nothing criminal. Just let's say we've both got a motive for bringing this pair down.' She gestured towards the two men, who were still talking. Then, as abruptly as he'd appeared, Sandford disappeared back into the building and Fenton headed off down an alleyway towards Ripon Road. He was presumably taking another route back. Luckily, this took him away from their spying position.

Steph and Ben moved from the tree to hide behind a building so they couldn't be seen from Swan Lane.

'OK,' said Ben. 'I'll go with that, no questions asked, if you can pin this on Fenton.'

'I'm Detective Sergeant Stephanie Johnson. I was put on the case of Jack Sandford and the contract his wife was given. I was working with Fenton. I went with him to conduct interviews and so on but Fenton suddenly shut the case down – said there was insufficient evidence. I thought it was very strange. He couldn't possibly have investigated it properly. And it makes it all the more irregular that here he is talking to the main suspect in a case he's just been investigating.'

'I see. Well, my contact at the council is on the same Procurement Committee. He's been suspicious of Sandford for some time, and has been monitoring him. Now we've identified his police contact, we need to try to track their meetings and get as many photographs of them together as we can.'

'I can find out more about Fenton back at the station.' She looked at Ben. 'So do we have a deal? We're going to work together on this without involving anyone else. You can't tell anyone about me, even your contact at the council.'

'Fine,' replied Ben, smiling but still a little puzzled. 'Aren't you taking a big risk? If it ever got out that you've been investigating on your own like this, you'd be in real trouble, wouldn't you?'

'That's my problem. You just keep to your side of the bargain. Anyway' – she looked round – 'we should move on; don't want to be seen together by the wrong people. Let's exchange numbers, and I'll be in touch.'

Esther Stevenson enjoyed walking her dog, Toby. He was an Airedale Terrier, and very lively. Her favourite venue for dog walks was the Valley Gardens and up into the Pinewoods. Today she parked at the edge of the gardens near the top entrance by the children's playground. It was a pleasant morning, with the sun and fast-moving clouds forming changing patterns of light and shade on the wide areas of grass. She got Toby out of the back of her old Volvo estate car and put his lead on.

'Come on, boy!' She pulled on the lead and the dog barked in excited anticipation as he trotted beside her. They walked through the old stone gates past the playground, the crazy golf course and the tennis courts, and then turned right down the hill towards the bandstand and the Sun Pavilion. Esther liked to do a circuit down to the bottom entrance, taking in the flowerbeds and stream, before walking back up to the open areas towards the Pinewoods, where she could take Toby's lead off.

She walked briskly down the hill and turned at the bottom. She was walking back up the hill by the stream when a voice called out to her from one of the benches that lined the path.

'Ah, Esther! I thought I might find you here. You were always fond of your dogs, weren't you?'

Esther stopped and looked towards the speaker. For a moment she was puzzled, before she recognised Damian Penrose's first wife. 'It's Susan, isn't it? Well, I haven't seen you for years. What on earth brings you to Harrogate?'

'That's exactly what your old crony, Charles Derryvale, said the other night when I caught up with him in the bar at The White Swan. I assume you and he still consider yourselves the masters of Yorkshire crime fiction? Why don't you sit down? I'm hoping that you'll be able to help me.' She indicated a space next to her on the bench. Esther regarded her with distaste and remained standing. Toby was sitting obediently beside her.

'It's been a while but I see you haven't changed, Susan. I don't know how you think I can help you and with what. I take it you must be here in connection with Damian's death in some way, but I've no desire to start raking over the past.'

'Oh, it's not the past that concerns me, Esther; it's the present and more importantly the future. My future, to be exact. We all know who's responsible for Damian's murder, don't we?'

'Do we?'

'Of course. It has to be Clare. She had the most to gain, and we know she planned the Royal Baths refurbishment. It's obvious. She had the motive and the means. She must have created some secret entrance to those Baths and then she or her accomplice went in and killed Damian. I've told the police and Derryvale but they won't listen. You and I could investigate the matter. I thought it might appeal to you as a crime writer.'

Esther was forced to laugh at the absurdity of what she'd heard. 'I'm not surprised they didn't listen. Don't you think that's all very far-fetched? What actual evidence have you got? If I wrote a novel with a flimsy plot like that, no publisher would go anywhere near it. It sounds like wishful thinking to me.'

'What do you mean?'

'I presume if Clare were to be convicted of murder, that might leave you to gain more from Damian's estate.'

'Well, what if it did? I deserve it anyway. She stole him away from me, remember?'

'Yes,' replied Esther, looking closely at Susan. 'Maybe there's more to it than that. This could be an attempt to divert suspicion away from you, the real killer.'

'What? Preposterous!' exclaimed Susan, and Esther laughed.

'Well, I wasn't serious but who knows? Your reaction seems to indicate a guilty conscience. Maybe I should investigate you.'

'I'm not staying here to be insulted. But I'll say this. I have other fish to fry in this matter. One way or another, I'm going to benefit from that man's murder. What he did to me in life, he will pay for in death, or at least someone will.'

With this melodramatic announcement, she got up from the bench and strode off haughtily back up the path towards the Pavilion.

Esther looked down at the dog, still sitting obediently on the path. 'What did you think of all that, then, Toby?'

Toby growled in the direction of Susan Lawrence, and then barked excitedly at Esther. He knew it was nearly time for his run over the fields.

Susan Lawrence walked briskly up to the Magnesia Well Tea Room, a circular structure with Edwardian-style ornamental ironwork, ordered a coffee and sat at a table outside.

This was the end of her pursuit of Clare Bayliss. She was clearly not going to acquire any support from anyone, so now it was full steam ahead with plan B. Again she had no real evidence for this theory about who killed Damian, but that didn't deter her.

She used her mobile to call the same number as she had from her hotel room. 'It's me again . . . Don't ring off this time; I don't think that would be wise. Remember what I know about you and how that would interest the police . . . Yes, so I think it's time we met up and discussed things. We can come to some arrangement so that I keep quiet, can't we? . . . No, I can't prove anything, but that's not the point, is it? You don't want the police on your back, do you? Anyway, you have a good think about it and call me back soon. Don't leave it too long. I'm getting impatient and I want to get back to London.' The call ended.

Susan sat back and sipped her coffee. At last she felt she was making progress.

Geraldine Poole was at work in her attic studio when the doorbell rang. She went swiftly down the two flights of stairs and reached the hall as the bell sounded for a second time.

'Coming!' she shouted. She opened the door. It was Clare Bayliss, smartly dressed as usual, but looking very severe. 'Clare! Well, what a surprise! Come in.'

Some years previously, Geraldine had started a degree in Architecture at the University of Leeds and had done a work placement with Clare. She'd dropped out of the course after two years due to her poor mental health and done a diploma in Art at a nearby art school instead. She hadn't seen Clare since that time.

Clare walked in, looking very serious. She followed Geraldine through to the kitchen and sat at the table.

'Can I get you some coffee?' asked Geraldine rather nervously. There was something about Clare's demeanour that she didn't like.

'No, thank you. I can't stay long. How are you? Have things worked out for you?'

'Fine, thanks. I've never regretted my decision, though I know you wanted me to stay on. We do OK, Ben and I; Ben with his journalism and stuff and me with my paintings. We've got a little boy now. Adam. He's asleep at the moment.'

'Yes. I heard you'd had a baby. Congratulations.' Clare's tone changed to signal she was putting an end to the small talk. 'Look, it's your husband I've really come to see. Is he here?'

'Ben?'

'Yes.'

'No, he's out at work doing his research.'

'Yes, poking his nose into other people's business.'

'What!' The abruptness shocked Geraldine. Clare gave her a hard stare.

'I'm sorry to say this to you, Geraldine, but I know he fancies himself as Harrogate's heroic investigative reporter. I'm afraid I'm here to warn him to stay away from my husband and his affairs.'

'What do you mean?'

'Don't tell me you haven't heard about the accusations that my husband persuaded a council committee to award me the contract to redesign and refurbish the Royal Baths? It's rubbish, of course, but we don't want any tittle-tattle to get into the local rags, and that's where your husband comes in.'

'But he hasn't done anything.'

'Good – well, let's keep it that way. Tell him to steer clear. We don't want things to get nasty.'

'Nasty? What do you mean?'

'I'll leave that to your imagination, Geraldine. Now, I'm afraid I have to leave. I have work to be getting on with. Sorry I can't spare any time to reminisce about when we worked together.' She smiled icily at Geraldine. 'I hope things continue to go well for you.'

Geraldine shut the door behind Clare with a trembling hand. Saying she would 'leave that to your imagination' had had exactly the effect on Geraldine's anxious personality that Clare had presumably intended.

She sat down at the table and fumbled in her pocket for her phone. It was a shock. She'd never seen Clare behave like that; she'd always been so kind and helpful. Anxious thoughts raced through her mind: could Ben get into trouble? Might he lose his income from his journalism? How would they manage then? By the time she'd rung his number, she'd worked herself up into a panic, but unfortunately he did not reply, and all she got was the request to leave a message.

'How are you, then, sir? Have you recovered?' asked Andy.

Oldroyd and Andy were walking down to The White Swan to interview Susan Lawrence, the strange loose cannon in this case. The Met enquiry had not come up with anything significant about her, but Oldroyd wanted to press her for more information about Penrose's past.

'I'm fine, thanks.' Oldroyd was feeling much better and was in one of his mischievous moods. As they entered Crown Place, Oldroyd stopped by the Royal Pump Room.

'Have you ever been in there, Andy?' he said, pointing to the elegant nineteenth-century stone rotunda.

'No, sir, what is it?'

'Oh, it's an important part of Harrogate's history. You know this town grew up as a spa, where people came to drink the mineral waters? Well, this was built over one of the most important springs, so the water could be served to people. Let's go in and have a quick look.'

They went in through the Edwardian glazed extension with its copper roof and had a brief glance at the museum exhibits. They stood by a wooden bar with pumps like those in a pub.

'So all the rich people with their gout and ulcers came here to drink this stuff, thinking it would cure them?'

'That's right. And they pumped it up like beer.'

'I prefer beer and the National Health Service.'

'No doubt.' There was a glint in Oldroyd's eye. 'But why don't you try some? Here, drink this.' There were some glasses of the mineral water to sample; he picked up a glassful and handed it to Andy. 'It can't do you any harm.'

Andy shrugged and downed the contents of the glass. His face contorted. 'Oh my God, sir, that's disgusting! It tastes like rotten eggs!'

'That's because it's sulphur water and there's lots of sulphur in eggs.'

'Bloody hell!' continued Andy, clutching his stomach. 'And they drank that to improve their health! It seems more like the murder weapon in one of our cases!'

Oldroyd was in fits of laughter. 'Thousands of glasses of it were drunk every day. There was a woman called Betty Lupton, who spent sixty years dispensing the stuff in the early nineteenth century. There was a hospital too, where people went for what they called hydropathic treatments: bathing in the water, massages and stuff.'

'It reminds me of those treatments we learned about at school in History,' said Andy, who was still grimacing. 'You know, blood-letting and putting leeches on you and stuff like that. The cures probably killed more people than the diseases.'

'I'm sure you're right,' said Oldroyd. 'Anyway, we'd better be off. I want to catch this woman and ask her some questions before she causes any more trouble.'

As they left the Pump Room, Oldroyd chuckled to himself. He hadn't told Andy that in the now defunct Royal Baths Hospital, the toilets had had extractor fans fitted, such were the foul smells produced by the people who had imbibed the waters.

They found Susan Lawrence drinking coffee in the guest lounge at The White Swan after having lunch in the dining room. She was elegantly dressed as usual in linen trousers and a silk shirt, and wore her customary haughty expression. The detectives sat on a sofa opposite her armchair.

'Oh, Chief Inspector and Sergeant Sidekick,' she said. 'What a pleasure! I take it you haven't made any progress in bringing that woman to justice.'

Oldroyd shook his head. 'So you're still on with that? Take my advice and leave it. You can't make a person guilty just because you want them to be.'

'But she's—'

'No, I don't want to listen to any more,' said Oldroyd firmly. 'And if you go around causing any more trouble, you might end up getting arrested yourself. I didn't appreciate your petulant performance last night.' His steely grey eyes fixed her.

'Well, I'm sorry about that. I'd had a few drinks and lost control a bit.'

'Maybe you should be careful what you drink, then. Anyway, I want to ask you about your ex-husband.'

'What about him?'

'You knew him for quite some time. Did he have any enemies? Anybody who would want to harm him?' He raised a finger. 'And don't even think about mentioning his second wife.'

She paused before answering. 'No one except the people you know: Charles Derryvale, Esther Stevenson. Writers seem to hate each other.'

'What about John Sinclair?'

'Yes, well, I knew Damian was bisexual. He'd known John since their schooldays. Their affair was all very complicated and ended badly. Also, I think there was trouble later about money but that was after Damian and I had divorced.'

'Your husband had a reputation for plagiarism, didn't he?'

'So I understand. I didn't take much interest in his work. Damian wanted me for, how shall I put it, intimate relations, and to look glamorous. He liked to show me off.' She frowned. 'When I got a bit older, he traded me in for the newer model, as they say – that woman, who . . .' She stopped herself. 'It's Esther Stevenson you want to question about that stealing ideas business. She's collected a group of writers around her who claim Damian abused them.'

Oldroyd continued to look at her very directly. 'And what about you? You've just told us how bitter you are about your husband dumping you. Did you decide to get your revenge?'

Susan laughed. 'By killing him? When I was in London? I thought you said I was the fanciful one.'

'You may not have been the person who actually carried out the murder, but you may have been involved. It was obviously a clever plan and must have involved more than one person.'

'No, Chief Inspector, you're wasting your time. I got my revenge on Damian all right. When I knew he was having an affair with Clare, I conducted several of my own amours. I was well even with him by the time we parted.'

'I see.' Oldroyd fixed her again with his penetrating eyes. 'Anyway, why are you still here when it's obvious your scheme to pin the blame on your rival is not going to work? I don't think Harrogate is a place, let's say, where you would normally tarry. If you know anything else, you need to tell us. It's an offence to withhold information from the police.'

Susan sniffed. 'Well, you surprise me, Chief Inspector. You've shown no inclination to take any notice of what I've said up to now, so why do you think I would know anything important?'

'OK, well, I've warned you. Also, I would be careful about playing games with dangerous people.'

'Don't worry about me, Chief Inspector. I can look after myself.'

'I hope you're right,' concluded Oldroyd. The two detectives left the hotel, with Andy desperate for a drink to get rid of the lingering taste of sulphur in his mouth.

John Sinclair and his partner, Ed Smith, had a decent patch of garden behind their Victorian house in High Harrogate, and they were both keen gardeners. As Ed, who ran a small hairdressing salon, was constantly complaining that John worked too hard and that they didn't spend enough time together, John had consented to leave work reasonably early on Friday afternoon and make a trip to their favourite garden centre. Ed had left his business partner, Lesley, in charge of the salon.

The garden centre was out on the Ripon Road near Ripley.

'How have you been feeling today?' asked Ed as John drove the car out of Harrogate, past the Exhibition Centre. Ed was quite a bit younger than John, about whom he worried a lot.

'OK. You know things are difficult at the moment.'

'I do, and I know who I blame.'

John sighed in exasperation. 'I know you do but there's no point going through all that again.'

Ed turned to him and his eyes sparkled with anger. 'I can't forget it so easily. That bastard was so nasty to you.'

Ed knew about John's long-ago relationship with Damian Penrose and about Penrose withdrawing his financial help. John was not sure which of these caused Ed more anguish, but he suspected there was a strong element of sexual jealousy in his hostility towards Penrose.

'If it wasn't for him, you'd be flourishing now. He withdrew his support just at the most critical time.'

'Maybe, but the publishing world is tough. I knew that when I went into it. It's not surprising that people are reluctant to put money in.'

'Huh, sounds like you're making excuses for him.'

'No, he went back on his word and let me down, but I can see why. He just thought it was too risky.'

'Why are you so keen to defend him when he treated you badly before that too?'

'I'm not. It's just that we should be fair and not blame him for everything.'

Ed went silent and sullen until they arrived at the garden centre. John knew that Ed suspected him of still harbouring feelings for Damian. Was he right? Damian would always be someone who reminded him of the excitement of his youth; when they were both rebellious, carefree and later in love with each other. But it was all so long ago. How could he convince Ed, who had a jealous temperament, that it had all been over between him and Damian many years ago?

John drove along the garden centre entrance road, which was lined at either side with ornamental shrubs and areas of immaculate summer bedding. It still styled itself in the traditional manner as 'Ripley Nurseries'. They parked, got out and wandered up and down the neat rows of herbaceous plants, roses, fruit trees and shrubs arranged in alphabetical order. There was always so much that was tempting to buy. The problem was that their garden was already so full of plants that it was difficult to fit anything else in!

'I think we need a little more colour for the autumn,' said Ed. 'I've always fancied a hibiscus. Look at this one: it's coming into bud – beautiful mauve flowers, according to the picture on the label.' He examined the palmate and coarsely toothed leaves with his sensitive hands.

'It looks beautiful. There's a space for it in the pinks-and-whites section near the hydrangea,' replied John. 'What about one of these Bishop of Llandaff dahlias? Look at that chocolate foliage and those single red flowers.'

'Absolutely gorgeous! It'll go next to that *Cotinus coggygria* "Royal Purple".'

By the time they'd finished, they'd loaded a trolley with various pots, large and small, including rockery perennials. They laughed at the absurdity of it, but they'd had a really enjoyable time.

'Where are we going to put all this stuff?' asked John.

'Oh, never mind, we'll put some more stuff in pots if necessary. There's always room for another pot on the patio.'

The total price came to a ridiculous amount but they just shrugged it off and loaded it all into their capacious estate car.

On the way back, the atmosphere in the car was much pleasanter, both men having been calmed by their contact with flowers.

'Sorry I went on about Damian on the way here,' said Ed.

'That's fine.'

'He's dead now, so we can forget all about him.'

'Yes.'

John thought how he would always remember Damian with some measure of affection but he decided not to share this with Ed. He drove on, looking forward to a restful weekend together planting their acquisitions.

∼

Back at police HQ, Oldroyd and Andy were conducting another case meeting. There was the usual cafetière of coffee, and chocolate biscuits on the desk. Andy, trying to show restraint after Steph had told him he was getting chubbier round the waist, picked up just one of the biscuits and nibbled at it slowly throughout the meeting.

Oldroyd sat behind his desk, leaning back in his comfortable but battered old chair. Midway through an investigation, he liked to get Andy or Steph to recap what they knew about a case while he thought about it, sometimes with his eyes closed and his hands behind his head.

'So what further progress have we made, Andy? By the way, where's Steph? I haven't seen her for a while.'

'She said she's got some paperwork to do for Derek Fenton, so I assume she's up there with him. You know, sir, I'm a bit worried about her, to be honest.'

Oldroyd looked up. 'Why?'

'Ever since she started working with Fenton, she's not been right; she looks worried. Sometimes in the night I know she's got up, which is unusual for her; she usually sleeps like a log.'

'She hasn't said anything.'

'No.'

'Well, she's probably fed up working with him and his DCs. I can't imagine they're a bundle of laughs. But that's the way it is, I'm afraid; you can't work with who you want all the time in this job. I used to work for a DCI who was the most miserable bugger imaginable. He used to shout at you if you made the slightest error. I wouldn't worry about her. She's pretty tough.'

Andy didn't reply, but he was still unhappy. He looked at his notes and sighed. 'We're flatlining, to be honest, sir. According to the reports, Penrose was in reasonable health at the time of his murder and also his finances were excellent, so that finally eliminates any ideas about him staging his death. I thought that was a bit wild anyway, though this is a strange case.'

'You're right there.'

'We haven't discovered anything yet to incriminate any of the suspects. I think we've always known none of them could have actually committed the murder anyway, but we haven't discovered any accomplices. This woman Susan Lawrence, though. She's a dark horse. Her alibi for the day of the murder was confirmed. She was still in London but now she's here, trying to pin the blame on her rival. I wonder if that's some kind of smokescreen to cover up her own involvement.'

'You may well be right. She certainly knows more than she's told us. She hesitated when I asked her if she knew about any enemies her husband had had. If she wasn't involved in the murder herself, she might well have a good idea who was behind it.'

'Why not tell us?'

'It could be good old blackmail. She's determined to gain some benefit out of her husband's death and her silly idea of getting Clare Bayliss arrested has clearly not worked. But I told her she needs to be careful; there are some ruthless and dangerous people behind this, as we know.'

'Too right, sir. Anyway, I take it you haven't yet worked out how the first murder was done?'

'Not entirely, but I'm getting closer. The secret lies in camouflage, Andy.'

'Camouflage, sir? You mean like concealing something and hiding?'

'Yes – think about it.' It was an eccentricity of Oldroyd's that he believed in training the minds of his young detective sergeants by not immediately revealing his theories, and getting them to think.

'How could you camouflage yourself in those baths? It's all tiles and empty space, and there's nothing to hide behind.'

'Well, you carry on thinking about it. I'm not there myself yet. There are still things that puzzle me.'

'So what's next, sir?'

'Any information about Patricia Hughes's phone calls?'

'Apparently they're on to it, but they're having a few problems with their software.'

'Blast it! That information is vital. If we can find out who she called that night, it could open everything up.'

At that moment Steph came into the office.

'Well, hello, stranger,' said Oldroyd. 'Hasn't Fenton finished with you yet?'

'Just about, sir; just popped in to say hello. How's the case going?'

Oldroyd gave her a quick summary, while she thought to herself that Fenton might think he'd finished with her and was in control, but she was about to prove him wrong.

It was late in the afternoon. Steph, Nicola Jackson, Cynthia Carey and Sharon Warner were meeting in Oldroyd's office. Steph had checked that Fenton, Hancock and Turnbull were all out of the building. Oldroyd had told her that she could use his office anytime she needed it if he was out.

'We'll have to make this quick, Steph,' said Cynthia. 'I've got to pick the kids up soon.'

'Me too,' said Nicola.

'Don't worry, I haven't a lot to say. The main thing is that I wanted us all to meet up, and to say thank you for coming forward.'

'I can't tell you how much better I feel, now that I know it's happened to all of you as well and I wasn't the only one,' said Sharon, sounding very relieved.

'We all feel better when we know that we're not alone,' continued Steph. 'There's strength in numbers, even against a man in a powerful position. If we can make an example of him, it will act as a warning to other men that they can't get away with it.'

'Yeah, fine words,' said Nicola. 'But I'm still not sure what we can actually do about him.'

Steph had decided not to say anything about Fenton's involvement in the corruption with Sandford. She wanted to keep the two issues separate, but she had a plan concerning what to do about Fenton's behaviour towards women and his blackmailing.

'OK, well, I've been giving this some thought, and what do you think about this as a plan?'

Charles Derryvale was not in a good mood. He felt that the atmosphere at The White Swan was not the same since that wretched woman, Susan Lawrence, had arrived. She had spoilt the – what was it? – the *feng shui* of the place. She was always around with her supercilious expression. He saw her at breakfast. She hung around the lounges during the day and the bar in the evenings, making it an inhospitable place for him. He felt driven away from his customary position on the bar stool. The fact was, he had no desire to get into any further conversations with her. She was a madwoman, with her ridiculous theories, always trying to recruit people to her cause. He'd even felt sorry for Damian Penrose in the years he'd been married to her, though heaven knew why he'd ever hitched himself to such a dragon.

During those years, she had usually accompanied Damian to Harrogate. She spent her time complaining and harassing staff running the Crime Writing Festival and the hotel, making it clear that she considered Harrogate to be a tiresome provincial backwater. Derryvale stayed in a different hotel during the festival in that period in order to get away from them both. No wonder Penrose had started his affair with Clare during one of the festivals. And it wasn't the only time he'd dallied with women while he was in Harrogate. Usually young and vulnerable ones. Disgusting man!

Derryvale was at a bit of a loose end. After lunch at the hotel, he had an empty afternoon ahead of him. He'd done all his appearances at the festival and his book signings, but he always stayed until the very end of the festival in order to attend the Murder Mystery Evening: an event that he enjoyed. It appealed to his sense of humour: he regarded it as a wonderful bit of knockabout entertainment. Also, The White Swan put on an excellent dinner. The food there was always very good, which was why he'd returned to stay there in recent years, even though Penrose still commanded the same suite every year. Penrose himself had been just about tolerable: Penrose and his obnoxious first wife were not.

There was one more day to go before the Murder Mystery Evening. He thought about doing some writing, but he never found the festival atmosphere conducive to that. He was a writer who had to be in his regular writing place in order to be creative. In Derryvale's case this was in the room he called his study in his flat in York, overlooking the River Ouse.

As it was a fine day, he decided to wander into the town and take a walk in the Valley Gardens, keeping a lookout for Susan

Lawrence. He didn't want to be surprised by her again, as he had been a couple of nights ago in the bar. He ambled around the stream gardens and past the ornamental dahlia display, where the plants were just starting to bloom. He admired the variety of colours and shapes for a while, and then sat on a bench and reflected. People were active on the tennis courts behind him, and he could hear the thwack of balls being hit by rackets. Penrose was gone at last! Everything seemed calm, and it was such a relief not to have to worry about that malevolent force creating discord wherever it went. Obviously things were not calm for the police or for the family of Patricia Hughes. He was sorry about her. Poor Amanda was having a hard time too. However, he could not disguise his satisfaction that he had won the unofficial bet he'd had with Penrose and survived him, although – and he smiled sardonically to himself – in a curious way, he was going to miss the old villain. Already things seemed rather flat – calm, but flat. It had been exciting to plan ways to undermine Penrose with Esther, John and other enemies of the old boy. He'd enjoyed the intrigue.

Suddenly he had an idea. He took a small notebook out of his jacket pocket. No end of people, including himself, had been making witty comments about the merging of fiction and fact – the murder of a crime writer and so on – but maybe there really was a way to use what had happened in his writing. He'd had an idea for a most unusual and quirky crime story.

After a while, he got up and walked back through the gardens and along to the Mercer Gallery, where he spent some time wandering through its varied collection of artworks. There was an exhibition about the relationship between painting and photography, which he found especially interesting.

After this he found his way back to The White Swan. Near the hotel entrance, he saw that some of Penrose's fans had erected a kind of makeshift memorial, and people were leaving messages. He couldn't bear to read any, so he went to have a final wander through the publishers' and booksellers' stands, which were housed in various tents. He sniffed in disgust to see how Penrose's publisher was still making a big feature out of the dead man's books. He would probably sell even more now that he'd died in such dramatic and intriguing circumstances. Dying had been a good career move for Penrose, thought Derryvale, and chuckled to himself at the black humour.

He chatted for a while to various reps on the stands, including his own publisher, and then saw Amanda Rigby talking to a woman at the entrance to the tent. For a moment he thought it was Esther, but when she turned round he saw that it was Catherine Burnett, who wrote historical crime mysteries set in nineteenth-century England. He'd never understood why anyone would want to do that. It was difficult enough to think of the plots and characters without also having to recreate some historical era in an authentic manner. Amanda spotted him, excused herself and came over.

'Charles, how are you today?'

'Oh, fine. I'm just lazing around as usual. I can never get any work done when I'm here at the festival. There's always too much going on, especially this year. It's different for you, of course. You must be exhausted with what's happened and having to take over from Patricia and all that.'

'Oh, well!' she said jauntily and smiled, but there was no disguising the strain on her face. 'Not long to go now. I thought I'd just remind you that we're starting the awards in a few minutes. It's going to be in that tent at the side of the hotel.' She pointed. 'The bigger the audience, the better, and,' she added slyly, 'there'll be some nibbles and glasses of Prosecco.'

'Ah! Well, thank you for reminding me. I'll toddle over in a few minutes. I take it I haven't been nominated for anything this year or I would have been informed.'

'Not this year, Charles, unfortunately. We're concentrating on awards for young writers, women writers and writers from ethnic minorities.'

'Oh, I see. Well, I certainly don't fit into any of those categories, but I'm sure it's all very worthy, and I shall come along to clap them. I believe in encouraging other writers, not undermining them . . . unlike someone else I could mention.'

'Good.' Amanda looked at her watch. 'Well, I'd better be getting over there.' As she left the tent, she called over her shoulder, 'By the way, Simon Jones from BBC Radio 4 is presenting the awards, so it should be fun.'

'Oh, really, well, that is interesting.' Simon Jones presented an arts programme on Radio 4, and Derryvale was an avid listener. He followed Amanda over to the tent to find that it was already very crowded and he had to stand at the back. He saw that Esther Stevenson was sitting down to one side and he waved to her. A stage with microphones had been erected, and it wasn't long before Amanda went up, welcomed everybody and introduced Simon Jones. He thanked the organisers for inviting him and made a few humorous comments, which established a jocular and informal atmosphere.

There followed a series of awards of the type Amanda had described, and Derryvale had to admit that it was heartening to see young writers and people from different backgrounds rewarded and encouraged. He clapped with enthusiasm for each one and then Amanda announced some special awards.

'This year, as you are aware, ladies and gentlemen, we have lost two people in tragic circumstances who were very important to us here at the Crime Writing Festival. First of all, Patricia Hughes.' Amanda's voice appeared to crack, and she took a moment before she continued. 'We have so much to thank Pat for. She was the force behind this festival and its success for so many years, and I feel privileged to have worked with her. The committee has decided that from next year there will be a new award at the festival: the Patricia Hughes Prize, which will be awarded to a female writer for a debut crime novel.' She brushed away a tear as there was thunderous applause and shouts of 'Hear, hear!'

'The other person we have lost is Damian Penrose.' The room went silent and Derryvale knitted his brow. 'Damian came up from London most years to appear at this festival. Often a controversial figure, he sparked lively debate and was a great draw. His presence was a boost to us. The committee has decided, therefore, that there will also be an award to honour his memory.'

Derryvale spluttered in an attempt to stifle his response to this, and there were some murmurs around the room. Penrose had not been quite so universally welcome at the festival as Amanda had implied.

'The Damian Penrose Lifetime Achievement Award will go to a well-established writer with a long career behind them, in recognition of their contribution to crime fiction over a substantial period of time. I might say that if Damian had lived, he would undoubtedly have been the first recipient of his own award.'

There was some polite laughter at this. Some people clapped, others looked stony-faced. It was a contentious act of appreciation for a divisive figure. Derryvale's mouth had dropped open and he was speechless. He caught Esther Stevenson's eye and she shook her head. Amanda wound the proceedings up, thanking Simon Jones again and everyone else for attending.

Derryvale shuffled out of the tent in shock. A memorial award for that bounder! That cheat! That thoroughly nasty piece of work! He stumbled towards the bar. He needed a drink after that.

Esther joined him, and they sat disconsolate in a corner. 'Well, I don't suppose we should be too surprised,' she said. 'He did get plenty of people to come here, if not always for the right reasons.

The festival people liked it: they want this to be a success; they're not concerned about plagiarism and insults and what kind of character you are, as long as you're not a criminal. In fact, his notoriety was a great attraction. We knew that.'

'I expect you're right but it's still a shock to see the old bugger honoured like that. What are they thinking of?'

Esther leaned forward and lowered her voice. 'I don't think this would have happened if Pat had still been in charge.'

'Oh?'

'No, she had no time for Penrose and his behaviour. I'm sure she was on the verge of dropping him from the programme in future. Amanda, though . . . Well.'

'What are you implying?' asked Derryvale, leaning forward conspiratorially.

'It makes you wonder what kind of relationship there was between her and Penrose, doesn't it? All those kind words, and I'm sure she's been the impetus behind this award. I'm sure it didn't come from anyone on the committee. I'll bet she suggested it. And how did she feel about Pat's hostility to her – what shall we say? – lover?'

'I see! How intriguing!' replied Derryvale, who was already considering this further ramification in the real crime story of this year's festival and wondering how he might use it.

When Ben Poole arrived home in the evening, he found Geraldine in a very anxious state. She'd been crying. Adam was crawling around on the floor and playing with Duplo, but his mother seemed to be taking little notice of him. She was lying on the sofa. It took Ben a while to get her to tell him what had happened.

'I've never seen her like that before; she was horrible. Ben, what if they get you into trouble and then you lose your journalism job? We won't have enough money to live on and . . .'

'Hey, calm down,' urged Ben. Her catastrophic thinking had got her worked up into a panic again. 'They can't do anything. They're the ones who are going to be in trouble. At least, the husband is.'

Geraldine looked at him sharply. 'Then you are investigating him? You never told me. Please don't, Ben. Can't you stick to stuff like reporting on local events?'

'House fires, road accidents, burglaries, births, deaths and marriages? Do you want me to die of boredom? No one pays much for that kind of stuff these days, but a nice juicy scandal at the local council? Well, that's different.' His tone was light-hearted, but she was not reassured.

'It's too risky. I don't want you to do it. Promise me you won't,' she pleaded.

'Look, I won't do anything that could get me into trouble, OK?'

She looked at him sceptically. 'What does that mean?'

'What I say. Yes, Clare Bayliss's husband is under investigation, but not just by me. You mustn't say anything to anybody, but the police are involved.' He saw that Geraldine was reassured by this. 'And if I get the story first, that's going to be a big bonus. I'll do well out of it; *we'll* do well out of it. You've been getting yourself all worked up again over nothing.'

Geraldine sat up and seemed much more relaxed. 'OK. If you promise it won't be dangerous.'

Ben went over, drew her head into his chest and kissed her hair. 'I promise,' he said, but he didn't look her in the face. And he couldn't tell her that the police, in the form of Steph, were only involved unofficially in an unauthorised investigation, which could spell trouble for them both if it went wrong.

All day, Oldroyd had been hoping that the fine weather, which had characterised the day, would hold. He'd been constantly clicking on the Met Office app on his smartphone and updating the page. The forecast was promising: fine and warm weather was set to continue into the evening and after dark. There was no threat of rain.

This was quite a relief because he'd invited Deborah to an open-air promenade performance of *A Midsummer Night's Dream* in the grounds of Ripley Castle. The play-goers were encouraged to bring a picnic, to be enjoyed on one of the large lawns before the play began.

Oldroyd, who had uncharacteristically spent some considerable time deciding what to wear, had decided on chinos and an Oxford shirt that Louise had bought him for Christmas. Deborah looked cool and immaculate in her white linen trousers and black sleeveless top, so he was glad he'd made the effort with his own attire, especially when she complimented him. As Oldroyd drove the old Saab on the short journey from Harrogate to Ripley, Deborah was as relaxed and talkative as ever, which he welcomed. He was still finding the business of establishing a new relationship quite challenging.

'Well, I'm really looking forward to this. I enjoyed Shakespeare at school; we had a good teacher. I did English Lit for A Level. We studied *Hamlet* and *Measure for Measure*. I think we did *Romeo and Juliet* for O Level.'

'Probably; they often do that or *Macbeth*. The plots are simple and they think kids like the romance or the violence,' replied Oldroyd.

'Yes, well, *Romeo and Juliet*'s got both, hasn't it?' She laughed. 'Romance turns to tragedy. Well, not always, I hope.' She gave him an arch little smile. 'I don't know the comedies, though. Enlighten me.'

She already knew that Oldroyd had studied English Literature at Oxford.

'I love them; they're subtle and elegant and humorous at different levels. There's plenty of knockabout humour, and the Bard's witty language and sharp observations of people. Lots to make you think too, or it wouldn't be Shakespeare. *Twelfth Night*'s my favourite, but *Dream* is great. It's got all the business of the fairies with the confused lovers and the workmen with their play, which is hilarious.'

'You're very enthusiastic; did you ever think about going into teaching? You could have really motivated the kids.'

'Not me – haven't got the patience for it.'

'Surely you have to have plenty of patience in your job.'

'True, but it's patience with yourself as you think hard to solve the puzzle. It's not patience with teenage bad behaviour. I don't think I could put up with that.'

'I think I'd be the same. I much prefer relating to people one to one.'

The car moved at a leisurely speed through the lush summer countryside. They passed a local cricket ground. The players, in white, stood out against a background of fields and trees. Their shadows were starting to stretch a little across the grass in the early-evening sun.

The car turned off the main road to Ripon and entered Ripley, one of Oldroyd's favourite pieces of Yorkshire eccentricity. It, and the castle, had been owned for generations by the Ingilby family and, in the nineteenth century, the Ingilby of that time had demolished the village and had it rebuilt in the French style, complete with a *hôtel de ville.*

Oldroyd parked near the church, got out and opened the boot, from which he lifted an old-fashioned wicker picnic basket. 'I'll carry this, if you can manage the rug and those folding canvas chairs. They're very light.'

'No problem,' replied Deborah, and off they went towards the entrance to the castle and grounds, joining a steady stream of people carrying hampers, chairs and bottles of wine. The lake in front of the castle reflected the evening sky, and deer in the parkland beyond stood still and watched the arriving visitors with curiosity.

The picnickers were settling down on a large area of lawn bordered by beds of perennials and flanked by two ancient orangeries. Oldroyd looked at his watch.

'We've got a good hour yet,' he said. 'Let's have a drink.' He opened a bottle of Prosecco, which immediately spumed over the side and down on to his trousers and shoes. 'Blast it!' he cursed as Deborah laughed.

'You should have known it would have been lively after carrying it all this way!'

'Never mind!' Oldroyd smiled as he poured two glasses and wiped his trousers with a tea towel. 'Cheers!' He unloaded the French bread, pâté, cheese, grapes, quiche and mini pork pies, which he had bought in different specialist shops in Harrogate, and they tucked in. They finished with some little pots of crème brûlée.

'Wonderful!' said Deborah, leaning back rather precariously on her canvas chair. 'All I need now is a cup of coffee, but never mind.'

'What do you mean? We've got everything here. In fact, we're "short o' nowt we've got", as my granddad used to say.' He produced a small thermos flask and two cups. 'And proper filter coffee, no instant rubbish.'

'Wow, Jim! You've gone to lots of trouble. Thanks a lot.'

'Well, you know . . .' He was going to say she was worth it, but shyness prevented him.

It was soon time for the play to begin. As the sun slowly went down, Shakespeare's magical play of comic spells, dreams and confusion was played out in various locations within the garden and woodlands that adjoined it, the audience following the actors around in promenade fashion. Never had Oldroyd experienced the night woodland scenes of the central part of the play in such a realistic setting. They were in the woods near Athens! He was, as Bottom is described in the play, 'translated', removed from his normal self. Theseus eventually declared that the 'Iron tongue of midnight hath told twelve' in an exquisite setting, against a backdrop of the lake as the sun finally set behind the actors and ducks settled on the water. To the left, the castle became a dark mass against the night sky. Enthusiastic applause greeted the end.

And yet, being Oldroyd, there was still that part of him, however small, that was always on the alert for clues to help him solve a case he was investigating. As he walked back to the car in a kind of daze and holding Deborah's hand, he couldn't help ruminating on a certain line spoken by Helena in Act 3.

'And though she be but little she is fierce.'

Seven

Hydropathic treatments offered at the spas of Harrogate included: Saline Sulphur Baths for gout and rheumatism; Alkaline Sulphur Electric Baths for muscle weakness and atrophy; Carbonic Acid Baths for heart disease; Harrogate Massage Douche for lumbago and arthritis; Intestinal Lavage Treatment for constipation and mucous colitis; Peat and Paraffin Wax Baths for sciatica, lumbago, stiff joints and rheumatism. Treatments were available until 1969.

At The White Swan Hotel the Crime Writing Festival, much to Amanda Rigby's relief, had finally come to an end. The marquees had been dismantled, leaving areas of flattened, brownish grass. The booksellers had packed up their displays; all the talks, discussions and award ceremonies were over. There was only one event left.

The traditional finale of the Harrogate Crime Writing Festival was a Murder Mystery Evening at The White Swan. This was quite a swanky event, with a champagne reception followed by a grand dinner and dancing in the ballroom. It was always a good fund-raiser for the hotel and the festival. A professional company was employed each year to play out scenes throughout the evening. The guests had to look at their programme notes and observe the action for clues as to the identity of the murderer. There were prizes for people who correctly identified the culprit.

The sombre atmosphere that had descended on the festival after the murders of Damian Penrose and Patricia Hughes had dissipated a little as there had been no further unpleasant incidents and attendances at events had continued to pick up. The good weather that had lasted for most of the festival, except for the day of Oldroyd and Andy's adventures at Brimham Rocks, had now broken and it was a rainy evening.

A steady stream of guests arrived at the hotel after walking through the wet Harrogate streets huddled under umbrellas to protect their smart clothes from the rain. Formally dressed, Amanda Rigby and Barry Evans greeted them at the entrance, and directed them to the bar for the champagne. This was another tradition: the festival organiser and the hotel manager did the honours to signify the end of the festival and to personally thank people. Amanda performed her role with some sadness, remembering that Patricia Hughes should have been in her place.

In the bar, waiters were ready with trays of champagne glasses. Each guest was given a programme sheet, which contained information about the characters in the mystery drama shortly to be performed and some advice about paying attention for clues. An element of realism was attained through some of the actors mingling with the guests. There were also some mystery characters not listed on the cast sheet, so who knew who was an actor and who was 'real'? It all made for an interesting evening.

Oldroyd and Deborah arrived in good time. Deborah was excited at the prospect of the murder mystery dinner, and thought it would be great fun. Oldroyd was less enthusiastic about what he considered a 'busman's holiday' type of evening, but he was quite happy to accompany his new companion. He also knew the food at The White Swan was good and he was looking forward to his dinner.

'Good evening, Chief Inspector,' said Amanda. The strain on her face was still clearly visible.

Oldroyd introduced Deborah, and they went through to the bar, Deborah clutching her programme notes. They got their champagne and, as they were early, managed to find some chairs.

'Ooh, let's have a look at this!' exclaimed Deborah, sipping her champagne and smoothing out the sheet of paper. 'You'll have to give me a chance to work it out. You've got an unfair advantage with your professional skills,' she laughed.

'Of course,' said Oldroyd, relaxing into his easy chair. 'I'm quite happy to take a back seat. I'm sure these things are not remotely realistic anyway, just a bit of fun. It probably comes down to guesswork in the end.'

'Maybe, but I like a nice puzzle.'

Oldroyd smiled at her. He liked puzzles too, but solving them wasn't quite so entertaining when people's lives were at stake. He didn't say anything, not wanting to spoil the evening.

Without realising it, they had sat in a position that allowed them to see the guests as they arrived. It wasn't long before familiar people started to enter the bar holding their champagne glasses. Carol Ashworth, looking flushed and excited, came in with a man. She saw Oldroyd almost immediately and came over.

'Oh, Chief Inspector, I didn't expect to see you here! This is my husband, Dennis.'

Oldroyd shook hands with Dennis, a bald-headed, glum-looking man, who looked as if he'd been dragged along to the event. After this, Oldroyd introduced Deborah to the pair.

'We come to this every year, don't we, Dennis?' Carol said, and then continued, not waiting for a reply. 'It's a bit expensive, but I always look forward to it. Last year's was so good. The actors were so convincing and you'd have been proud of me. I worked out who the murderer was, didn't I, Dennis? Anyway, with you here, Chief Inspector, it's going to be difficult for the rest of us. We're going to be up against a professional.'

'I'm sure you'll do fine,' said Oldroyd, smiling and hoping that the couple would quickly move on.

'Well, we won't hog you, Chief Inspector. I'm sure other people will want to talk to you, but no giving out advice – that would be cheating.' She wagged her finger at him and laughed. 'Come on, Dennis, we've got to read through the notes. Oh, I'm so looking forward to it all!' They went off to the far end of the bar, where there were still seats available.

'I think we should move,' said Oldroyd, 'or I'm going to get collared by everyone who comes through the door. How about over there?' He indicated two seats in a corner with a little table, which were not visible from the bar entrance.

'OK,' replied Deborah. 'As long as you point out anyone interesting. This is so odd. Here you are taking time out from working on a real case and some of the actual suspects are also here watching a piece of crime drama. And some of them are crime writers themselves! Fact and fiction overlapping. I'm sure some Cultural Studies student could write a thesis on the ramifications!'

'I'm sure they could, but that little encounter has made me all the more determined to keep a low profile. She works at the Baths, by the way. She was there when the body was discovered.' Oldroyd was beginning to have the same weird, confusing feeling he'd had during his appearance at the festival, and he was beginning to be weary of it. How disturbingly odd it was to have all these people who were suspects in the real murder case around a festival about crime fiction; it was even worse tonight as a fictional murder was to be acted out. He shook his head to dispel the disorientating complexities and sipped his champagne.

When they were ensconced in their new seats, Deborah began to consult the programme notes. There were short descriptions of the characters, with a photograph alongside.

'So the drama's called *Who Killed Lord Willoughby?*'

'It's always the butler, isn't it?' quipped Oldroyd.

'Shut up! How many times have you arrested a butler?'

Oldroyd laughed and had to admit that he'd never even met a butler, never mind arrested one.

'Apparently he'd had affairs with his solicitor's wife and the woman who ran the estate riding stables, and his wife knew about it. Now there's Lady Willoughby – she returned the favour by having an affair with her brother-in-law. Kathryn Willoughby, the daughter, has a boyfriend her father doesn't like and he's threatened to disinherit her if she doesn't dump him. Then—'

'Wait there a moment,' interrupted Oldroyd. 'This big bloke is Charles Derryvale, one of Penrose's enemies. By the way, you're sworn to secrecy about anything I tell you about these people or the case, OK?'

'Yes, Chief Inspector. I don't want you to arrest me,' said Deborah with mock seriousness.

Derryvale lumbered into the bar, flamboyantly dressed in a top hat, with a black cape over his dinner jacket and carrying a black cane. The cape was wet and glistening. Luckily he saw someone at the bar and went straight over, twirling his champagne glass. He didn't notice Oldroyd, who watched him arrive at the bar and heard him say, 'Filthy night, Roger; I'm ready for a drink. Fancy something a bit stronger than this champers?' He looked deprecatingly at the champagne glass and downed the contents in one gulp. 'Never been a fan myself.' He remained at the bar, his loud voice and laughter audible throughout the room.

'He looks like something from a stagey 1930s thriller,' said Deborah. 'Are you sure he's not one of the actors?'

'I think he's one of those people who are acting all the time. Hello! Here comes another. This woman's conducted a long campaign against Penrose's alleged plagiarism of other writers' ideas. She goes on about it all the time; she can scarcely talk about anything else.'

Esther Stevenson entered, embellishments galore on her art deco dress. She was accompanied by a tall, bespectacled and immaculately dressed man, who was presumably her partner, Leo, the solicitor. What a strange couple they made, thought Oldroyd. He looked extremely conventional compared to her general air of artiness.

'Excellent charity shop buy there,' whispered Deborah, winking at Oldroyd. 'They look odd together,' she said, echoing Oldroyd's thought. 'There's no accounting for who gets off with whom, is there? Sometimes it's the most unexpected; the old attraction of opposites.'

'Like us, you mean?' teased Oldroyd.

'Oh no, we've a lot in common: after all, you're concerned with the criminal mind, and I work with people who are troubled. Not a million miles apart, I'd say.'

'Ah, here's another!' Oldroyd had noticed John Sinclair entering the bar alone. His rather glum expression suggested a lack of enthusiasm, so why was he here? 'You'll like this one. He was the first murder victim's lover years ago, when they were both young in London. Then they fell out over money.'

'Ooh, a juicy bit of scandal. I bet it was him. It usually comes back to sex and money in the end, doesn't it?'

'In fiction as well as in fact, judging from what you've read out about this evening so far. If only it was so simple, and anyway, in this case, who would we go for, Sinclair or Penrose's two ex-wives?'

'Well, Penrose sounds a colourful character. He seems to have got around a bit and played both ways. Is there a lot of that stuff in his books?'

'A fair amount, though I've not read many; not my style. They're all about the machinations in the rich set: millionaires, yachts, affairs, jewellery, sex, money. Very popular books, though; I think they feed into people's fantasies of the high life.'

'Seems like it. He was obviously into those fantasies himself, by the sounds of it.'

'He certainly rubbed a lot of people up the wrong way and seemed to enjoy doing it. Anyway, carry on.'

'Right, so Elizabeth Merryfield runs the estate riding stables, but it's not doing well and Lord Willoughby had been threatening to close it down, even though she had a brief affair with him. What a bastard! He deserves to end up murdered, never mind who did it. By the way, wasn't there a famous female murderer called Merryfield?'

'There was: Mrs Louisa Merryfield, the Blackpool Poisoner. Killed an old woman she was housekeeper for with phosphorous from rat poison. She and her husband had got the old lady to change her will and leave them the house. She was hanged by Albert Pierrepoint in Strangeways Prison, Manchester, in 1953.'

'God, you know some gruesome stuff! Do you have to memorise it all as part of your police training?'

'If only it was all as interesting as that, and not tedious and mundane stuff about procedures.'

Deborah continued. 'So we've also got Henry Cavendish – that's the daughter's boyfriend. No job, bit of a waster – fond of Kathryn but also of her money. Sounds like a bit of a fortune hunter. Kathryn has told him that her father has threatened to change his will. Pretty strong motive there, then. Now, Angela

Willoughby is Lord Willoughby's sister. She borrowed money from him to start a business as a fashion designer, but is not doing too well. Unfortunately, her brother has insisted that she pay the loan back, as the estate has hit a few cash problems too. Finally, we've got Simon Henderson, the solicitor, and his wife, Margaret. She also had an affair with Lord Willoughby, remember, and was devastated when he ended it. She was dazzled by his money and title, and had fantasies about being the "lady of the manor". Poor deluded woman! Her husband knew about the affair: that's motive one. Also, Lord Willoughby had found out that he had been involved in some fraudulent property deals and was blackmailing him by making him do the family's legal work for nothing: motive number two. So there we are. What are your first thoughts?'

'I still think it was the butler,' said Oldroyd.

Deborah kicked him under the table and finished her champagne. 'Fancy another drink?' she asked.

'Not for me. And I'd go easy if I were you. There'll be plenty of alcohol with the meal and there's a bar in the ballroom. You need to keep your mind clear if you want to solve this mystery.'

Deborah frowned at him. 'You don't think I'm going to solve it, do you? Well, I'm going to prove you wrong, even if I do drink. I'm off for a glass of white wine.'

The bar was getting full and Deborah had just got back with her wine when Oldroyd again noticed someone he knew arriving. 'Ah, here she comes. I knew she'd make a late entry to create an impression.'

Susan Lawrence made a grand entrance, literally glittering as the light from the chandeliers hit the sequins on her body-skimming silver evening dress. She swept into the bar and caught the attention of numerous people. However, when some of them saw who it was, they immediately turned away. Undaunted, she marched over with her glass of champagne and engaged Esther Stevenson and her husband in conversation.

Minutes later, Barry Evans and Amanda Rigby entered the bar, a sign that it was time for the evening's events to begin.

Barry began to speak, and the room went quiet. 'Good evening, ladies and gentleman, and welcome to The White Swan. Once again we are here to mark the end of another successful Crime Writing Festival here in Harrogate, and I would like you to join me in thanking everyone involved this year, whether as an organiser, participant or sponsor.'

There was a round of applause.

'Of course, this year's festival has taken place against the background of some tragic events, which I will not dwell on tonight. We decided that it would be best if the festival continued despite what has happened and I want to pay a special tribute to Amanda Rigby here.' He turned to smile at Amanda. 'Amanda took over the running of the festival at very short notice and in difficult circumstances. I think she deserves our special thanks.'

Another round of applause and calls of 'Hear, hear!'

'So now I think it's time to—'

There was a sudden disturbance at the bar and a woman screamed. Everyone turned to look. A man had fallen off a bar stool and was lying on the floor. A waiter was crouching over him. Then he stood up and announced, 'He's dead.'

Barry Evans smiled. 'Well, ladies and gentlemen, I think we'll find that that poor individual is Lord Willoughby.' There was some laughter, and people looking relieved. 'It is now going to be your task to discover who murdered him. So please, will you all come through to the dining room, where the story will continue.'

'I wondered what was going on then,' said Deborah to Oldroyd, who was chuckling as they made their way through to the dining room.

'I thought they might start with some kind of stunt like that,' he replied. 'It creates a bit of excitement, doesn't it? That little bit of confusion about what's real and what isn't.'

There was a lot of chatter as people took their seats at a series of large round tables, each place being marked with a card. Oldroyd was relieved to discover that no one involved with the real case was on the same table as him and Deborah. There were eight people on each table, and all over the room people were introducing themselves. Oldroyd picked up the menu; the meal was going to be the best part of the evening for him. Duck liver pâté with toasted seeded bread, chicken chasseur with potatoes dauphinoise and green beans; a nice bottle of a smooth Italian red. Deborah chose French onion soup and a goat's cheese parcel with red pepper salad and fries: all too lightweight for his liking.

As soon as orders had been taken, an actor dressed in a smart suit and trilby took the empty area in the centre of the room.

'Ladies and gentlemen. Allow me to introduce myself. I am Inspector Drake and I have been called here this evening because a murder has taken place. Lord Willoughby collapsed in the bar and was pronounced dead. We now know that he was poisoned.'

Here there were some cries of 'Ooh!' as people began to enter into the spirit of the evening.

'In order to solve this murder,' continued the detective, 'I am calling on you all to assist me in the investigation. After all, however many brains we have here tonight, they're better than one!'

Here a ripple of laughter went round the room.

'I think you all have a copy of this briefing.' He held up the programme notes. 'Which tells you a little about the suspects. And now I'm going to introduce them to you and ask each a few questions. Think carefully about what they say and what you've been told about each one.'

'I could pull rank on him and take charge of the investigation,' Oldroyd whispered to Deborah. 'But that would be greedy, as I've already got one to be getting on with.'

'Shut up and listen,' she whispered back.

The inspector proceeded to call out the characters in turn. They had all been sitting at different tables with the unsuspecting guests, which caused another frisson of excitement. The inspector confirmed the identity of each and interrogated them about their relationships in the family and about their motives.

After this, the starters were brought out and the actors toured the tables, answering any questions from the guests. Oldroyd ignored all this and started on his pâté. Deborah had written down a list of questions on the back of the notes, and neglected her soup while she listened carefully to everything that was said.

'You're wasting your time,' said Oldroyd between mouthfuls, affecting a superior disdain. 'There won't be enough information to clearly incriminate any particular suspect. You'll have to go on your gut instinct in the end and make an informed guess.'

'Is that how you work, then, spoilsport? I thought it was all about the patient gathering of evidence.'

'Oh, it is, but sometimes you have to use your instincts when deciding which line of enquiry to pursue.'

Deborah shook her head, put down her notes and made a more determined attempt to eat her soup. She looked at Oldroyd's plate and decided to get her own back by reigniting their discussion about meat eating. 'You shouldn't be eating that; producing pâté is cruel.'

'I thought that was only foie gras, where they force-feed the birds.'

'That's the worst, but imagine all the poor ducks slaughtered for their livers.'

'Well, the rest of the bird is eaten too, isn't it?'

'Does that make it any better?'

Oldroyd smiled at her. 'Nice try, but you're not going to make me feel guilty tonight. I'm enjoying myself,' he said, and popped a piece of toast smothered with pâté into his mouth.

Deborah stuck out her tongue at him.

The rest of the meal was eaten amidst a hubbub of whispered conversations as couples who were engaged in solving the mystery tried to discuss their ideas without giving anything away to the others on their table. Oldroyd was glad that Deborah was keen to do this without his specialised help, as it gave him the chance to relax his mind and savour the meal and the wine. It wasn't possible to forget the case completely, as he kept catching the eye of the suspects. Directly across from Oldroyd's table, Charles Derryvale smiled and waved a languid hand at him.

Sinclair, on the next table, greeted Oldroyd cursorily and then turned away, seemingly embarrassed. Susan Lawrence, on a table in the corner, gave him nothing but a frown. Only Esther Stevenson came over briefly to introduce her partner and say that she was pleased to see Oldroyd here.

'Well, what do you think of this, then?' asked Deborah. Having finished her goat's cheese parcel, she was writing notes. 'My chief suspect so far is the sister, Angela. I thought she was very shifty when the inspector asked her questions. I don't think she was close to her brother, and her business would have been at stake if he'd called in her debt. I think we're being pushed towards suspecting the solicitor, who came over as a nasty piece of work, and he had a double motive, but I think that's too obvious. What do you think?'

'Do you really want to know?'

'Yes, but don't you dare say the butler again.'

'Well, I'm not telling you yet. I often play this game with my detective sergeants. It makes them think for themselves instead of relying on me.'

'Don't give me that. I don't think you've been listening to what's been said at all. Too busy eating and drinking.'

Oldroyd twirled his wine glass cheekily. 'Don't worry, I'll tell you what I think towards the end.'

Desserts were brought in, and Oldroyd treated himself to a lemon-and-sultana cheesecake. Deborah declared herself too full for anything else but was persuaded to have a raspberry sorbet.

'Do you always eat like this?' asked Deborah.

'Well, not really, but I enjoy treating myself on special occasions.'

'No wonder you're a bit on the chubby side.'

'I beg your pardon?' said Oldroyd good-humouredly.

'It's time you started working out a bit. I'll bet you don't go to the gym or anything.'

'I do plenty of walking.'

'Yes, at a leisurely pace around the Stray, I'll bet, and then you go into the pub to recover.'

'Are you going to take me in hand, then?'

'I might do. We could go running together.'

Oldroyd grimaced. 'I'm not sure about that,' he said as he finished his cheesecake, and Deborah laughed.

'You're afraid I'll beat you.'

'I know you will. I'm not fit enough for that.'

'Not yet. We'll see.'

When the tables had finally been cleared and coffee served, the inspector reappeared. 'Ladies and gentlemen, I hope you have enjoyed your meal. We are now ready to progress and I need your assistance. Each of the suspects will appear in turn and you can ask them any questions you want. It is your chance to pursue your ideas and find out a bit more about which of these characters you think is a murderer. You will be helping me to bring them to justice.'

The inspector placed a chair in the centre of the room and, as promised, each character in turn sat in the chair and was questioned by the guests. Oldroyd listened but didn't ask anything. He noticed that none of the real suspects did either, apart from Carol Ashworth, who took part enthusiastically. Was it because some of them were writers and found all this a little crude? Or did they find it all rather weird, as he did himself, to be observing this piece of fiction when they were involved in a real case? Instead of listening to the actors, he looked around at the expressions on various familiar faces. Were any looking uncomfortable because of a guilty conscience? Maybe the real murderer would have found it impossible to attend something like this. But then again, ruthless killers were often very good at dissembling.

At the conclusion of the questioning, the inspector announced that it was now time to progress to the ballroom, where there was a jazz band ready to begin playing. Just as people were getting up, there was the sound of shouting. An argument had started and it soon became clear that it was between the actors playing Henry Cavendish and Kathryn Willoughby.

'How could you, Henry? I can't believe it!' Kathryn shouted.

'Darling, you don't understand. Let me explain.' Henry tried to grab her arm but she pulled it away.

'Don't touch me!' she cried and, bursting into tears, hurried from the room pursued by her maybe now former boyfriend.

This caused a great commotion, with some guests claiming to have expected something like this and others expressing their surprise.

'Well, you can't be off your guard for a minute,' said one man, laughing as he passed Oldroyd. 'There's certainly plenty of action. What did you make of that?' he said to his wife as they headed off to the ballroom.

Oldroyd looked at Deborah and clapped slowly and ironically. 'Very good show,' he said.

Deborah frowned. 'Well, I'm enjoying it, fatty,' she said, and headed off rapidly out of the room.

'What!' cried Oldroyd with mock outrage, and pursued her at a more sedate pace.

It was now dark outside, and in the ballroom subdued lighting came from beautiful glass chandeliers, which reflected on the polished parquet floor. Tables were arranged around the edge. A jazz band on the stage, consisting of piano, drums, trumpet, saxophone, clarinet and double bass, was lit by spotlights. The bar was small, so waiters were moving between the tables, taking orders for drinks.

Oldroyd was feeling pretty stuffed and a little lethargic after all he'd eaten and drunk, and he wasn't a keen dancer at the best of times. However, he was prepared to make the effort for Deborah and wanted to avoid further comments from her about his figure and fitness. They sat at one of the tables and listened to the music. The band was playing some slightly improvised version of a slow Glenn Miller tune. Oldroyd had learned a bit of traditional ballroom dancing when he was young, but he was very rusty.

'Shall we dance?' he asked Deborah as other couples were taking to the floor.

'Yes, but I'm not very good.'

'Me neither. We'll just shuffle round to the music. It's the taking part that counts.'

They took their place on the parquet floor and moved around slowly.

'This seems very old-fashioned, doesn't it?' said Oldroyd. 'My parents went dancing every week in the early fifties. Everybody learned the waltz and foxtrot.'

'Mine too, but this is becoming popular again, isn't it, with *Strictly Come Dancing* on the telly?'

'Yes. I wonder how many viewers go to classes and learn it, though?'

'There's certainly a lot more skill to it than jerking about in a club to rock music. I went for a few lessons once for a laugh, and it's damned hard to do it properly, I can tell you.'

After a while the music changed to something much faster. They both decided this was a bit too much for them and retreated to their table.

'I'm enjoying listening to this,' said Oldroyd. 'I like a bit of traditional jazz.'

'Me too, actually,' replied Deborah as a waitress came to see if any drinks were required on their table. Oldroyd consulted the drinks list.

'Fancy a cocktail?'

'Why not?'

'How about a mojito?'

'Ooh, yes, two of those. I love rum-based ones.'

Oldroyd ordered and sat back in his chair. It was turning out to be an extremely pleasant evening.

After several dances, the band stopped and the inspector took to the dance floor. Deborah and Oldroyd sipped their cocktails. Deborah turned to her notes.

'Ladies and gentlemen, I assume you are comfortably settled here in the ballroom and are ready for the next stage of our murder enquiry. We will now—'

He stopped as his attention was drawn to a slight disturbance at one of the tables at the other end of the room from Oldroyd and Deborah.

'What's going on now?' said Deborah. 'It's so exciting; you don't know what's going to happen next.'

Oldroyd didn't reply. He'd seen the puzzled expression on the face of the actor playing the inspector. He stood up and looked over at the table, concerned, just as a woman screamed. Something was wrong and Oldroyd hurried over. There was a hubbub of noise in the room and other people were starting to stand up and look across. At the table, a man had his arm round the woman who'd screamed and now looked hysterical.

'It's all right, darling, she's just acting; it's part of the show. There's been another murder, do you see?' he said, trying to make light of it, but sounding uneasy.

'But she's not one of the characters. She's just slumped there; I don't like it!'

All around, people were looking uncertain. Oldroyd reached the table, where a woman was indeed slumped face down. She'd knocked over her wine glass. He put his hand on her shoulder.

'Are you OK?' There was no response; there was now a crowd round the table. Oldroyd gently raised her head. He was looking into the dead, staring eyes of Susan Lawrence.

The woman screamed again. 'She's dead! I know she is! What's going on, Ivan?'

'Move back, please,' said Oldroyd firmly. 'I'm a police officer, a real one.' He saw that the fictional inspector was by the table, looking horror-struck. 'I know this woman, and I know this is not part of the act. Go quickly and find Mr Evans. Tell him to call the ambulance and police HQ. It's too late for her, I think, but I need some help.'

The actor ran off. People were shrinking away from the table and its corpse; nevertheless, Oldroyd had to take precautions.

'Do not touch anything. There's evidence here.' He looked at the glass and some of the contents, which had spilled on to the table. He leaned down and sniffed at it. The faint smell of bitter almonds was enough to tell him that the drink had been poisoned. With cyanide. Deborah came up behind him.

'What's happened?' she whispered in a shaky voice.

Oldroyd looked at her grimly. 'I'm pretty sure she's been poisoned. She was one of the suspects in the case – the real one,' he added sardonically. 'That woman who made a big entrance when we were in the bar, remember?'

'Yes.' Deborah put her hand on Oldroyd's shoulder. 'That's horrible.'

'It is. I'm sorry the evening's spoiled,' he said quietly. 'I should have warned you. This is the kind of thing that happens to me. Maybe you shouldn't be seeing a detective.'

'Rubbish. It's not your fault. The murderer wouldn't have killed her just because you're here. In fact, that would have made it more risky for them.'

'True, I suppose. It's just that—' He was interrupted by the arrival of Barry Evans, speaking into his phone as he ran to join Oldroyd.

When Evans saw the body, his face turned white. 'As quick as you can,' he said into the phone and then put it into his pocket. 'Good God! Is she really dead?'

'I'm afraid so. I'm sorry to say you'll have to bring the evening's entertainment to an end, but everyone will have to stay until we've questioned them. I suggest you provide some calming refreshment. Tea might be a good idea. I need to stay right here until my colleagues arrive.'

'Yes, yes, of course. I'll . . . I'll say a few words.'

He walked up on to the stage, where the jazz players were solemnly looking towards Oldroyd and the body, which was still in exactly the same position.

'Ladies and . . . er, gentlemen.' Poor Evans was struggling. 'There has been an unfortunate, er, incident, and the police and an ambulance have been called. Chief Inspector Oldroyd here' – he indicated Oldroyd – 'is of the view that, er, foul play may have occurred.' There were gasps from the guests, who were variously standing around or cringing at the tables.

'Is this all part of the game?' shouted a man, slurring the words and obviously very drunk.

'Patrick, shut up!' shouted a woman, who could have been his partner.

'No, sir, it emphatically is not. I only wish it was. The chief inspector has asked me to tell you that it will be necessary for you all to remain here until more police arrive to take statements.' There were some shouted objections to this. 'Those are the police instructions. Now, please remain calm. My staff will serve tea. I suggest you simply return to sit at your tables and keep away from . . . from that one,' he said, pointing to where the crime had taken place.

There was a buzz of conversation as he left the stage to rejoin Oldroyd, but everyone seemed to be obeying his instruction, even if reluctantly.

'Well done,' said Oldroyd. 'We just need to keep everything as calm as possible until they arrive.' He turned to Deborah. 'You don't need to stay, as you were with me and we can take a statement from you later.'

'Jim, I'm not leaving you by yourself to deal with all this, even if you are a professional. I'll stay out of the way, but I'm not going home until you do.'

'That might be very late.'

'I don't care.' She squeezed his arm and went back to their table, where she talked reassuringly to the other shocked-looking people who were sitting there.

To Oldroyd's relief, it wasn't long before officers from Harrogate HQ arrived, closely followed by Tim Groves, who shook his head at Oldroyd and smiled sardonically. 'Well, Jim, I'm truly sorry for you. Death often seems to follow you around, doesn't it? Even when you're out for the evening enjoying yourself. Why can't these murderers have a little more consideration?'

'Please put a word in for me if you have any influence, Tim. Anyway, I think you'll find she's been poisoned by cyanide. I've smelled the faint whiff of bitter almonds.'

'Keep away, then. The gas is worse than the liquid.' His tall figure stooped over the body and he examined her skin and mouth. Then he picked up the glass and smelled it. He turned to Oldroyd. 'You're probably right, Jim. She's a bit pink and I can smell the almonds too. This drink, whatever it was, was probably poisoned, and by a pretty hefty dose, I would think. They weren't taking any chances, though when it's ingested in liquid form it takes about twenty minutes to take full effect. And right under the chief inspector's nose.' Groves could never resist teasing Oldroyd.

'It's not the first time, Tim, and probably not the last. Maybe it's the thrill of the extra challenge.'

Groves smiled. 'OK. Well, we'll get her back and do the full post-mortem. I'll report to you as soon as I can.'

'Cheers, Tim.' Oldroyd left the removal of the body to the forensics team. Some officers were slowly working their way through the guests, taking names and brief statements. Oldroyd turned his attention to the other guests on Susan Lawrence's table. They were sitting some distance back from the table, as if fearing contamination.

'So tell me what happened.' He tried to be as gentle and encouraging as possible. One or two looked too stunned to say anything, but a confident-looking middle-aged man replied.

'She was OK when we first got here from the dining room: chatting away to everyone and quite full of herself; said she was pretty sure who'd committed the murder – that is, the one in the mystery.'

'Yes, I know what you mean.' It certainly sounded like Susan Lawrence, and he was sure it would now transpire that she knew who had committed the real murders too, which was why, like Patricia Hughes, she'd been disposed of.

'Then she went quiet and was clutching her stomach. I was sitting next to her and I could see she was struggling. I asked her what was wrong. She said she felt sick and a bit dizzy – said she'd drunk too much. Sylvia – that's my partner – and I went to dance. We weren't away for long; when we got back, she was really in trouble. She seemed to be gasping for breath, and then she tried to stand up and just fell forward on to the table.'

'I thought it was all part of the act,' said the tall man who'd tried to calm his screaming partner. She was sitting on his knee with her face buried in his shoulder.

'That thought crossed my mind too,' said the first man. 'But I was closer to her and I knew she was either a damned good actor or it was serious.'

'Where did she get this drink from?' Oldroyd indicated the glass, which would shortly be removed as evidence.

'One of the waitresses who was serving our table. She took orders and brought the drinks over.'

'Any idea what the victim ordered?'

'It was a cocktail; a whisky sour, I think.'

How convenient, thought Oldroyd. The strong and bitter taste would have masked any unusual flavours.

'Can you describe this waitress?'

'She was quite small – dark hair; wearing the same uniform as the others, and glasses with quite thick, dark frames,' said a woman.

'Her accent was a bit Geordie, wasn't it? Oh, and she had a birthmark on the side of her neck.' She pointed to the spot and looked for confirmation from others round the table; people nodded.

'And it was definitely her who brought the drinks back?'

'Yes,' replied the first man. 'She brought me a beer, and you had a glass of white wine, didn't you?' He spoke to another woman in the group.

'Yes,' she confirmed in a weak voice. She looked very pale. 'Oh my God! We could all have been killed!'

'I don't think so,' said Oldroyd reassuringly. 'Unless you'd swapped drinks with her, of course. She was targeted. There's no random maniac poisoner on the loose, so don't worry. Can you all confirm that the victim didn't leave the table after the drink was brought?'

'No, she didn't.'

'And she definitely drank it?'

'Yes. There wasn't much left when she knocked the glass over. No one else drank any. Thank goodness.'

'OK. Thank you for your help. A police officer will take a statement from you all shortly.'

Oldroyd joined Deborah at their table and sat down, looking grim. He'd been outwitted again but at least the reference to the size of the mysterious waitress gave further confirmation to an idea he'd been considering for some time. He'd been thinking that the murderer was a small female. He wouldn't have been at all surprised to learn that she'd been wearing very high heels to conceal her true height. But who was this person?

He turned to Deborah. 'I just need to get Andy Carter over here and then talk to the manager and the staff who were on duty. After that we can probably head off. I can leave the rest to the others once Andy arrives to take charge. There's nothing more I can do tonight.'

'Fine,' said Deborah, and gave him a comforting smile.

Oldroyd got out his phone and rang Andy's number.

'Sir?' answered a sleepy-sounding voice.

'I'm sorry to wake you and everything when you're off duty, but you're going to have to come over. I'm at The White Swan and there's been another murder. It's definitely part of the series. Susan Lawrence. I knew she was keeping something from us. It's cost her her life. She obviously didn't listen to my warnings.'

'Bloody hell!'

'Yes, and I want you to take charge, clear up. Something crucial might turn up.'

'Right, sir. I'll be over as soon as possible.'

Oldroyd put his phone away and went to find Barry Evans, who was standing in the corridor outside the ballroom, looking agitated. 'Chief Inspector!'

'Mr Evans. You and your staff are doing fine. Don't worry. But I have to ask you about the waitresses who were serving in the ballroom tonight.'

'Yes. What about them?'

'I need a list of all their names, please, and I want you to get all the waiters and waitresses together and the bar staff. I need to speak to them.'

Evans looked surprised. 'Why?'

'I'm afraid it's fairly clear that the victim was poisoned by a drink that was brought to her table by a waitress.'

'Good God! But couldn't the poison have been put in later when the drink was on the table?'

'Well, that can't be ruled out but it's very unlikely if you think about it. It would be very difficult to lace someone's drink right in front of them. The other people sitting with her confirmed that she never left the table after the drink was brought to her, and I've no reason to suspect any of them at the moment. It's possible the drink could have been poisoned by the person who prepared it, but again unlikely. How could you make sure that it got to the right person?'

Barry Evans got out a handkerchief and wiped his brow with a shaky hand. 'Right, Chief Inspector. The problem is that on a big occasion like this, we obviously need to employ extra waiting staff and we get them from agencies. It's the job of Neil Andrews, one of my deputies, to organise that and he's not here tonight. It means that we don't necessarily know all the people if they're here on a casual basis.'

'Yes, I understand. The list will do tomorrow, but I need to see the staff now.'

'Very well.'

He went away to gather them together, and Oldroyd followed them into a smaller room nearby. They looked very subdued and sombre.

Oldroyd introduced himself and then said, 'OK, just to confirm what's happened. A person has been murdered here tonight – not a fictional murder, a real one. We are fairly certain she was poisoned by a drink, a whisky sour cocktail, which was taken to her table by a waitress.'

There were gasps and cries of 'What?' Many eyes turned to look at one of the bar staff, who'd turned white.

'I take it you're the cocktail maker,' said Oldroyd.

'Yes,' stuttered the young barman, who looked absolutely terrified.

'Don't worry. I have no reason to suspect you. We are working on the assumption that the drink was poisoned after it was collected from you. Do you remember preparing a whisky sour? Were there a lot of them during the evening?'

The barman's eyes looked startled as he frantically searched his memory. 'No . . . there weren't many whisky sours . . . Just two, I think.'

'Can you remember which waitress collected them?'

'I took one of them,' said a tall waitress, also looking terrified. 'But it was for a bloke, and not on that table where the woman collapsed.'

'Yes, I remember that,' said the barman. 'And I know Jackie.' He indicated the tall waitress.

'What about the other one? Think hard; it could be very important. Who took it from you?' Oldroyd tried to be insistent without being too alarming.

'It wasn't anyone I knew, I don't think. It's hard; it's very busy behind the bar. I think she was not very tall – dark hair.'

'Did she wear glasses?'

'Yes, quite heavy frames, and she had a birthmark on her neck.'

'That's the suspect.' Oldroyd turned to the group. 'Do any of you know a person like that? Mr Evans has told me that extra staff are employed for big occasions like this, and they come from agencies, so you might not know them, but do you at least remember her?'

'Yes, I do,' replied another waitress. 'I was serving the tables next to hers. I'd never seen her before tonight. I remember she was quick to volunteer to serve those particular tables when we spread out into the room. She didn't say much apart from that; sounded a bit north-east. She's definitely not here now.'

'No, she targeted the table she wanted and would have made a quick escape after delivering the poisoned drink. Did anyone else speak to her?' The staff looked around at each other, but nobody answered. 'No, I expect she just quietly appeared and blended in with the rest of you and everyone thought she was an agency worker.' Oldroyd sighed. He was dealing with a very clever and deadly assassin. 'OK, thank you. One of my colleagues will take statements from you all.'

He returned to the ballroom and remembered that this had been the venue for Penrose's last appearance. Was this just a ghoulish coincidence? Many of the original suspects were here. He looked round and located them all. Derryvale was sitting back in his chair, a glass of whisky on the table. His large body was flaccid, and his expression uncharacteristically solemn. Esther Stevenson was talking to her partner. She looked up, saw Oldroyd and glanced away. John Sinclair was sitting with his arms folded, looking completely miserable, as if he wished he'd never come to the event. Carol Ashworth was close by. She looked as if she'd been crying, and was being comforted by her husband. The exciting evening to which she'd looked forward for so long had been ruined.

Oldroyd considered them all. Was it possible that one of them was behind the latest murder? Had they arranged for an accomplice to deliver the poisoned drink? He was increasingly questioning many aspects of the case. The people who had seemed the most obvious suspects to begin with now seemed less likely to be guilty. Nevertheless, he needed to speak to Esther Stevenson about something.

'What on earth's going on, Chief Inspector?' Oldroyd turned to see Ben Poole, who was formally dressed like everyone else.

'Where've you sprung from?' Oldroyd asked.

'I've been here all evening.'

'Have you? It's the first time I've noticed you.'

'I've seen you a number of times. I was on a table behind you in the dining room and in that far corner in here.'

'No wife?'

'No. Geraldine doesn't like events like this. She finds crowds difficult.'

Oldroyd nodded. 'The answer to your question is that we definitely have another murder on our hands.'

'Related to the other ones?'

'I would think so. The victim was Susan Lawrence, Damian Penrose's first wife.'

'Do you think she knew something?'

'In all probability. By the way, I'm telling you all this because you're a local journalist and not a nasty so-and-so from one of the tabloids, but you can't print anything yet, not until the formal announcements have been made. At least you'll have a head start on the others.'

Ben smiled. 'Thank you, Chief Inspector.'

Oldroyd went over to Esther Stevenson and took her aside. She looked as shocked as everyone else. 'I was about to call round to interview you again,' began Oldroyd. 'In the light of what's happened, it's become more urgent. We're pretty sure that the murderer this evening was a small woman disguised as a waitress and she had a birthmark on her neck. Now, we have Damian Penrose's diaries in our possession, and he refers to a "little bitch" at one point and "not giving in to her", whatever that means. He never uses her name but this is all in the context of a row about stealing ideas, so I need to ask you: does that description fit anyone in your group of women who were Penrose's victims?'

Esther listened to him very intently. She thought for a moment. 'No, Chief Inspector, I can't honestly say that it does. No one in the group could be described as small.'

'You're sure? It's very important.'

'Yes, I understand, but the answer is no, apart from the fact that I'm sure none of us would resort to violence. We did our best to harass him and make him realise we were monitoring him, but that's all.'

'OK, but I warn you, be careful. This person is highly dangerous and if they think anyone knows anything about them, that person is in peril. If you remember anything else, let me know immediately.'

'Yes, Chief Inspector, I understand.' Oldroyd turned away but Esther continued. 'Chief Inspector, there is something you ought to know. Charles told me you'd mentioned that Penrose's murder had some similarities with something in one of his novels. I wrote a crime novel called *The Mystery of Murder* and in that story one of the female characters is killed at a Murder Mystery Evening in a hotel like this, though I had her shot, not poisoned.'

'I see,' replied Oldroyd, and he told her what Carol Ashworth had said about Liz Simpson's book and Patricia Hughes's murder. Esther put her hand to her mouth.

'Oh my God, I never thought of that. What's going on, Chief Inspector?'

'You're the second person to ask me that. I'm not sure. At first I thought if there was a connection, someone was trying to implicate all you writers who were Penrose's enemies. Now I'm not sure. It seems as if someone is just enjoying the ghoulishness of it all. I need to speak to more people, if you'll excuse me.'

Oldroyd called Derryvale and Sinclair over to speak to him and asked them about Penrose and a small person. 'No, Chief Inspector,' replied Derryvale in a flat voice. 'I never saw Penrose with anyone like that.' The genial wit and humour seemed to have left him.

Sinclair shook his head. 'Me neither,' he said tersely. 'I wish I'd never come. I hate these evenings but I always get invited as a publisher and I don't like to be absent from a local literary event.'

Both men were either superb actors or genuinely shocked at this third murder, reflected Oldroyd.

Oldroyd returned to Deborah and talked to her for a while, and it wasn't long before Andy arrived.

'Well done,' said Oldroyd. 'I hope you managed to get away without waking Steph.'

Andy looked at his boss rather ruefully. 'Actually, sir, I was sleeping in the spare room. Steph banned me from our bed because I was making such a stink. It's your fault for getting me to drink that foul water.'

Oldroyd laughed, and made an exaggerated move away from Andy. He was grateful for a moment of comic relief. 'Oh dear, I'm sorry but those mineral waters do often have that effect; too much sulphur. Never mind, hopefully it'll have passed through you by tomorrow.' He explained to Andy what had happened. 'So I want you to supervise the statement taking and check out the backgrounds of the waitresses and the barman who mixed the cocktails. I don't think you'll find anything but we have to make sure. Ask the guests if they saw this mystery waitress or saw anything else suspicious. Then you can let them all go home.'

'Right, sir,' said Andy, yawning and not relishing getting to work at this time of night. 'Are you getting off, then, sir?'

'Yes. I can't do anything else, and to be honest I've had enough for one evening. I also need to take my, er, my companion home.'

Andy grinned. 'Right, sir, well, that's fine.' He was amused to see his boss a little self-conscious.

'Yes, I'll, er, see you tomorrow,' said Oldroyd, and got out his phone to ring for a taxi.

Deborah was still waiting and talking to the now exhausted-looking people at their table.

'Thanks for staying,' said Oldroyd as they walked to the hotel entrance and waited for the taxi. 'I really appreciate it. Are you feeling OK?'

'I'm fine, and you're welcome. Anyway, I'm a nosy old so-and-so; I was interested in seeing what happened.'

'Nothing else exciting is going to happen now, just the slog of getting statements and checking on what people saw. It's nice to be in the senior position and be able to leave all that graft to the lower ranks, but I've done plenty of it in my time.'

'I see. You're the brain worker now, is that it?'

He laughed, loving the way she made fun of him and punctured any tendency to self-importance.

'Not only brain work, as you've seen. I have to take practical charge sometimes when things get dramatic.'

'I was very impressed. I suppose you get used to seeing dead bodies.'

'Well, it helps when you've got someone like Tim Groves around. He's always good for a black-comedy moment.'

'I suppose that's how he survives in his job.'

'Yes, I certainly wouldn't like to have to cut them up and take their insides out, like he has to do.'

'No.'

The taxi arrived.

'You take the taxi. I'm going to walk back over the Stray. I need some fresh air.'

'Are you sure?'

'It's fine and, well, what can I say? Sorry the evening turned out like that.'

'Not to worry. It was even more exciting.' She put her hand to her mouth. 'Oh dear, I shouldn't joke about it; someone's died!'

'Don't worry; as you've just said, humour is sometimes how we deal with these things.'

'The only disappointment is,' she said as she got into the taxi, 'I'm never going to find out who did it. In the murder mystery, I mean. Fiction turned into reality and took over, didn't it?'

'Oh God, no more of that, my head's spinning! Never mind, just think about me: I've got to solve the real murder mystery.' He leaned into the taxi and kissed her. 'See you soon.'

'Yes,' she replied, and smiled. 'Though we'll have to stop seeing each other nearly every day. I bore easily, you know.'

Oldroyd laughed and shook his head as the taxi drove off. It had finally stopped raining as he walked over the wet grass of the Stray towards his flat, musing on how in this case everything seemed to always return to this strange confusion of fiction and fact. They still seemed some way from solving the case, but nevertheless, he had a spring in his step and a lightness of heart. The relationship had already surpassed all his expectations and he was looking forward to seeing her again. As he walked along, he started to sing patter songs from Gilbert and Sullivan, and a late-night dog walker gave him a wide berth and a funny look.

On the following Monday morning, another drama played itself out at Harrogate Police HQ.

Derek Fenton was in his office, feeling self-satisfied. His arrangement with Jack Sandford was proving to be very lucrative. As for Steph Johnson, it was only a matter of time before she cracked. She wouldn't want the possibly career-damaging humiliation of having those photographs made public. He smiled to himself and licked his lips lasciviously at the prospect.

There was a knock on the door. For his further entertainment, young Sharon Warner came in. 'Well, it's my lucky day! What can I do for you, love?'

She smiled demurely. 'I can't get the photocopier to work. There's no one else around. Could you give me a hand?' Was there a suggestion of flirtatiousness in her manner?

'Of course. There are times when you just need a hunky man, aren't there?' He grinned at her and then followed her down the stairs to the printing area. This was a series of small connecting rooms that housed various machines. Sharon stood by the photo-copier, which was against the wall at one end of the room.

'You see, it's saying there's a paper jam, but I can't get the top off to see inside. I can't reach.' She leaned over the machine, and Fenton, standing behind, found it irresistible. His hand stretched towards her bottom.

'Thanks. That will do fine.'

Fenton turned to see Steph, who'd taken a short but damning video with her phone. She must have been hidden outside, and quietly followed them in.

'What the . . . !' exclaimed Fenton. A door to one of the other rooms opened and Nicola Jackson and Cynthia Carey came in.

'We saw what happened,' said Nicola. 'We were watching through a crack in the door.'

'You ought to be ashamed of yourself, you dirty old so-and-so,' said Cynthia.

Fenton looked rapidly from one to the other. His eyes bulged like those of a trapped animal.

'Who the hell do you think you're talking to?' he shouted, but his tone was desperate.

Steph had shut the door, and they all stood round him, block-ing his way out. 'We know exactly who we're talking to,' she said menacingly. 'A serial abuser of women, who's made life here difficult for a lot of people. But now it's all over.'

Fenton laughed. 'This is bloody well right out of order. So you think you can set up some kind of trap for me, your superior officer? It's downright insubordination. I'll have you all disciplined.'

'Before you do,' continued Steph, 'just consider a few things. We've now got evidence of how you behave. But that's not all.' She looked round the group of women, who were all staring defiantly at Fenton. 'You've harassed everyone here, and we're prepared to go together to the authorities and call you out about it. They won't be able to ignore four of us, whether they like it or not.'

Fenton looked down and seemed to be struggling with himself. 'OK,' he said finally in a sullen, angry voice. 'What do you want?'

'I want those photographs back,' said Steph, 'and you'd better destroy any copies you've made.'

'And?'

'We'll be watching your behaviour, and if you try it on with anyone ever again, we'll shop you. We'll be warning the other women here at HQ about you, so if anything's going on, we'll find out. We're together now, so you can't pick us off individually.' She held her phone in the air. 'And I'll be holding on to this video.'

Fenton glared at her with contempt. 'I knew it would be you behind something like this, you . . .'

'Careful, don't make things worse or we might change our minds.'

'If you did anything, those photographs would be straight out.'

'I'm sure they would,' continued Steph calmly. 'But it might be worth it to see you brought down and humiliated. I think it would be worse for you. Anyway, it's up to you. Are you going to accept our arrangement or not?'

Fenton's face looked tortured, as if he was desperately trying to think of a way out. But he couldn't. 'OK,' he said quietly after a long pause. 'Now move out of the way.' The women moved back and Fenton stormed out of the room. Cynthia sighed with relief.

'It worked, thank goodness. Sharon, well done; you were brilliant!' The others congratulated her too and she beamed.

'Well, it worked up to a point,' said Nicola, striking a more downbeat note. 'The bastard's still got away with it, though, hasn't he? I know we had to protect you,' she said, turning to Steph, 'and well done for planning this, but it still sticks in the gullet to see him escape without any consequences.'

'He won't do anything again, though, will he?' said Cynthia.

'No,' replied Steph, 'and other things are going on that will have a big impact on him.'

'What?' said Nicola.

'I can't say, but trust me and watch this space. I think you'll soon see it all come to a satisfying conclusion.'

'That's terrible, Jim. This is happening to you far too often. It's one thing to have to investigate these terrible crimes but quite another to actually witness them when you were at the Murder Mystery Evening.'

'Yes,' said Oldroyd.

'Well, it's really grotesque.' Oldroyd's sister, Alison, shook her head, and drank some of her coffee. They were sitting in the large, rather faded kitchen in what Oldroyd called the 'Jane Austen Vicarage' at Kirkby Underside, the village in the countryside between Leeds and Harrogate where Alison was the vicar. Badly in need of a break after the traumas of Saturday evening, Oldroyd had driven out seeking some relief and sustenance from his sister.

'It certainly was, but Deborah was wonderful. She refused to leave, and just sat there patiently waiting for me until backup came and I could leave them to get on with clearing things up.'

'That's great. I can't tell you how pleased I am, Jim, that at last you've found someone.'

'Well, it's early days. I've known her for hardly a week. You're like Louise. She was rushing things along too.'

'She's also pleased for you and she's sharp; she can probably tell, like I can, that you sense something good is happening.'

Oldroyd was grinning. 'Yes, I can't deny it. We enjoy each other's company and share the same sense of humour. I'm not seeing her for a few days and I'm missing her already.'

'Good Lord, the man's in love!' laughed Alison.

'That might be stretching it a bit after a week. It sounds very teenage.'

'Why should it? Why should romance be confined to the young? I married a couple in their eighties the other week and it was a very joyous occasion.'

'Good for them. I'm not sure marriage would be for me second time around.'

'No point in even thinking about that yet. Now who's jumping the gun? Anyway, I'm fascinated by this case. All about writers, isn't it?'

'Yes. And rejected wives. There are plenty of people with motives. Two people have been killed, almost certainly because they knew too much. We still can't make much sense of the first murder scene either, though I've got a few ideas.'

'I see. Sounds about normal for you, then. You don't make it easy for yourself, do you?'

'I never have,' laughed Oldroyd, reaching out for another of Alison's homemade chocolate brownies and then pulling back as he remembered Deborah's remarks about his figure. 'Incidentally, Deborah agrees with you that plagiarism could definitely have been the motive, but I have to set that against some other deep personal grudges that people had against Penrose. We've also got an idea of the kind of person we're looking for in terms of who carried out at least one of the murders – a small woman – but I can't see how it all fits together. There's definitely more than one person involved.'

'Well, you're as good as anyone in putting the pieces of these puzzles together and—' Alison's phone rang and she looked at the screen. 'Oh, I'll have to take this, Jim. Just excuse me for a minute.' She went into the sitting room.

Oldroyd sat in the quiet. He always found it soothing to come to this oasis of rural peace when he was feeling frazzled. Of course, he knew from experience that rural places were not always peaceful, and so it proved today when Alison returned.

'Jim, I'm really sorry but I'm going to have to go out. That was a young woman in the parish. She lost a baby a couple of years ago – miscarriage. She's pregnant again but having some problems. She's feeling very bad today. I said I would go round.'

'What's the problem?'

'Oh, I think it's one of those cases when the umbilical cord is wrapped round the baby's neck. That's not usually a problem these days: they'll be able to put it right but obviously she's over-anxious after what happened before. I'll have to go right away; she was in tears. Stay and finish your coffee; just put the latch down on the door when you leave. Bye for now.' She gave him a quick hug and kiss and she was off. Moments later he heard the car scrunching down the long drive.

Oldroyd sat there very thoughtful and guiltily excited. Alison often provided him with important clues, even when she didn't intend to. Yes, that was how someone could have stayed in that place for long enough. That was a crucial piece of the jigsaw! He was nearly there. He needed to get back as soon as he could.

Eight

Theakston's Brewery in Masham, North Yorkshire, dates from 1827. It produces a strong beer called Old Peculier, a reference to the time when the parish of Masham was a 'peculier', with its own ecclesiastical courts. Theakston's sponsors a Crime Writing Festival that takes place each summer in Harrogate.

Andy Carter was at HQ waiting eagerly for his boss to appear when Oldroyd suddenly burst into the office in a state of excitement.

'Andy, I think I know how they did it! We need to go to the Royal Baths, now.'

'Right, sir, but before we do, I've got some interesting news too. The techies have finally tracked where that call was received from Patricia Hughes on the night she was murdered and I've followed it up. This is who lives there.' He showed Oldroyd a sheet of paper.

The chief inspector raised his eyebrows. 'Good, well done. That fits in with what I've suspected all along. Come on, let's go. It's finally all falling into place. We just need to be very careful, and this is what we're going to do.'

~

At the Royal Baths, Carol Ashworth was surprised to see the police back.

'Oh! Chief Inspector, it's you again,' she said, turning a little pale. 'I'm afraid I haven't got over that awful business at The White Swan the other night. You've just reminded me all about it, but it's a good job you were there. That poor woman! It absolutely ruined the evening for everyone. I hope your nice lady friend wasn't too upset. Oh, and did you know the murder was like one in a book by—'

Oldroyd didn't have time for this. 'Yes, we've made that connection, thank you, and my friend is fine. We need to go down to the scene of the murder again. Is there anyone down there?'

Carol's face fell. 'Oh dear, we won't have to close down again, will we? We've only just got on our feet again after that terrible day.'

'No, that won't be necessary.'

'Oh, good. Well, it's been fairly quiet this morning, but there are a couple of people in.'

'Right, well, if you could go down and just make sure there's no one in the pool and that everyone's decent. Just tell them that the police need to look at something. We won't be long and there's nothing to be alarmed about.'

'I see. Well, I'll tell them to wait in the changing rooms. Is that OK?'

'Yes, that will be fine.'

'I'd ask Steve to do it, but he's not here at the moment.'

The detectives followed Carol down the marble steps and waited while she alerted the customers.

'You can go in now,' she said, and went back up the stairs.

'We won't be long but don't let anyone else come down while we're here.'

'I won't, Chief Inspector.'

'This is all very mysterious, sir,' said Andy as he followed Oldroyd to the swimming pool, but his boss didn't reply. The door to the boiler room opened and Sid Newman came out. When he saw the detectives, he took a step back with alarm.

'Oh, it's you again,' he said. 'I'm just doin' a bit of maintenance work. I—'

'That's quite all right, Mr Newman, we won't be here for long. You just carry on,' said Oldroyd, who was looking intently at the pool and seemingly examining every part of it. Newman went back into the boiler room, looking relieved. Andy was puzzled.

'Sir, you surely don't think the murderer was hiding in there underwater? We were down here for a long time. They would never have been able to hold their breath, and I did look in there in case anything had been thrown in. I certainly didn't see anything or anybody.'

'That was the whole idea, Andy. You weren't able to see them but what I can't—' Suddenly he clapped his hand to his forehead. 'Oh, but of course. It was staring me in the face. That's how it was done.' He knelt by the steps that led down into the pool and seemed to be looking for something. 'Yes! Excellent.' He laughed. 'It's ingenious and daring and it was hiding in plain sight, as they say. Deborah used that phrase at the Murder Mystery Evening, and it made me think then.'

'About what, sir?'

Oldroyd stood up and turned to Andy, looking very self-satisfied. 'I once heard a tale about the Vietnam War, Andy. I don't know whether it's true or not, but according to the story the Americans were trying to disguise an air base from the Viet Cong, so they removed any sign of their presence and covered things with camouflage and so on. Then a few days later, despite all their efforts, the base was attacked. They couldn't understand it but then someone realised that they'd left a big McDonald's sign up, which completely gave the game away. It was so big and everyone was so used to it that no one in a sense noticed it. So with this. The murderer was hiding quite close to you and the method is obvious now I know, but we completely overlooked it, even though we were standing by it and touching it.'

Andy grinned. 'You've lost me, sir. What happened?'

Oldroyd pointed to the changing rooms. 'The murderer was already down here that morning when Penrose arrived; they'd probably been here all night and they'd made all their preparations. Penrose was caught completely off guard because he wasn't expecting anyone to be here. The killer would have come up behind him and strangled him with some kind of strong cord, which they took away with them.'

'Then what happened? How did they disappear?'

'They didn't; they were hiding.' He pointed to the pool.

'But how, sir? Did they have gills or something?'

'No. Remember I spoke about camouflage? I started to think about it when I saw a chameleon on my screen saver at home and thought about how it changes its colours to blend in with its environment. Now, let's look at this pool.'

They stood on the edge by the steps and looked into the water. 'First of all, the bottom and the sides are covered in blue tiles, so if you were wearing a completely blue, close-fitting diving suit with a blue cap and something blue on your feet, you would be camouflaged. Also, notice the edge of the pool; it's an old-fashioned design and the rounded edge sticks out quite a way over the water, which means you can't actually climb out. You have to go up the steps.'

'So if you lay right up against the wall of the pool down there at the bottom in your camouflage, you would be difficult to spot.'

'Yes, Andy. Now you're getting it. You actually have to lean over to see where the tiled wall joins the tiled floor of the pool at the bottom. You wouldn't do that if you were just having a quick glance.

Now also notice that the water pump is conveniently pushing water out of a grille into the pool just below our feet next to these steps, so the water is moving and you don't have a clear view. So even if you did peer over the edge, all you would see is a swirl of blue at the bottom, which is exactly what you'd expect. You wouldn't be able to distinguish a camouflaged human form. Also, remember that the killer had turned up the steam and opened the steam room door so that everything down here was misty and indistinct.'

'OK, but you still haven't explained how the person would breathe.'

'I couldn't work it out myself for a long time. When I was walking with my sister in Wharfedale, I saw a memorial to a diver and I thought: you could stay underwater with an oxygen tank. But that would be so cumbersome; how would you disguise it? And how would you get rid of it afterwards? We didn't find one. So I was back to square one with that problem. Then this morning I was at my sister's, and she told me about a case of a baby with the umbilical cord round its neck. And the mention of that cord, which is the tube that connects the baby and its mother, gave me the answer. It could be done with some kind of blue plastic tube, a breathing tube.'

'But how did it work?'

'This is another really clever bit.' He knelt down by the steps. 'These curved rail supports you get hold of when you're going up and down the steps are tubes of metal; they're hollow. Now look at the back here. Someone's drilled a hole where it's connected to the floor and where you wouldn't notice it. You can bet there's another one where the support is connected to the wall at the bottom of the steps in the water.'

'So a breathing tube was fed through and they could stay underwater?'

'Yes. It worked like an extended snorkel. They would have had a mouthpiece on the end and maybe a face mask, again all blue.'

'Bloody hell! The clever sods. So the murderer was lying at the bottom of the pool underneath my feet the whole time?'

'I'm afraid so. The small holes would have been drilled out well in advance, but no one noticed the one at the top because it's hidden at the back of the support. The one at the bottom is in the water and effectively invisible. Part of the preparation during the night before the murder would have been to secure the tube at the top with some kind of waterproof glue so that it wouldn't fall back down the metal tube. You can see bits of the glue around the hole. After the murder, the killer got into the water, put the pipe in their mouth, blew out any water and then sank to the bottom, waiting and breathing through the pipe. They would have lain face down to conceal the mask, and they would have kept very still. Partly to remain unseen, and also to conserve energy because a pipe that length would not have been very efficient. It would have been tricky, but with practice it's possible.'

'How did they know when to come out? We could have still been here.'

'The murderer and the accomplice probably both had a kind of diver's watch where you can send a signal: a buzzing noise or vibration from one to the other. That signal would mean the coast was clear.'

'And the accomplice was Steve Monroe?'

'Yes. Of course, the person who discovers the body in those kinds of circumstances always comes under suspicion, but at first sight, his story seemed genuine. No one had come up those stairs since Penrose went down and there was no other way in or out. There wasn't time for him to have killed Penrose himself, and we couldn't find anyone concealed. Another advantage for the murderer is that they didn't need to stay under the water for as long. They didn't need to hide in the pool until you arrived. Monroe told everyone here he'd searched the place but I imagine the murderer was hiding in the changing rooms at that point. Monroe may have used the diver's watch to send a message that the police had arrived.'

'And the murderer is a woman?'

'Yes, a small but powerful and ruthless woman. The same woman who posed as a waitress and poisoned Susan Lawrence and who probably killed Pat Hughes too.'

Andy was shaking his head. 'So, sir, that's all fine up to a point but then how did she get out of the building? She still had to get up those stairs without being seen.'

'I'm afraid she was carried out.'

'What? Not in that basket under our very noses. No way.'

But Oldroyd was nodding ruefully. 'Yes.'

'But I checked it twice. It's impossible.'

'But think back to what actually happened, and how the rooms are configured. Before I arrived, you quite rightly checked the basket, got all the dirty towels out, and found nothing. Then you went back up to call me. You might have left a constable down here but that was in the hot room where Penrose's body was. You can't see the swimming pool from there. That was their opportunity. Monroe gave the signal from wherever he was; she quickly got out of the water and into the changing rooms, taking the breathing pipe with her, or she may have stuffed the whole length of it into the metal tube and Monroe removed it later. She didn't need to pass the hot room, where the body was. She dried herself with one of the old towels from the basket and then got into the same basket with the pipe, the mask and any other bits and pieces, curling up and flattening herself as much as she could at the bottom. This is where her small size is crucial because they then placed some kind of false bottom over her, which they'd custom made. That false bottom would have already been in the basket lying over the real base. Then Monroe filled the basket with the towels again.

'Enter us, the gormless coppers. Monroe comes down to remove the basket. While we're preoccupied with other things, he probably wiped over where her footprints were with his squeegee. If we'd asked him, he could have said it was water streaming down the walls because of the steam. I see the basket, and you say you've checked it. I say check it again, so you have another cursory look, pull some towels out and feel about a bit. But there's nothing there. Monroe carries the basket up the stairs and into that laundry room near the entrance. He locks the door. She gets out and hides in there and changes into her clothes. Shirley Adams, the cleaner, told us there was a door out of there into a side street, and you can be sure that Steve had acquired a key. She slips out and that's it. There's no CCTV at the side of the building.'

'Oh my God – and we let him carry her out!'

'Yes. It was skilfully done and we were concentrating on other things. That's the great thing with tricks and illusions like this, as I've said to you before: misdirection; get people to look at the wrong thing and perform your trick while they're not looking at what you're doing. We were searching for ways out of the building and paying a lot of attention to the body. It was all over in a twinkling before we realised. They must have practised it many times.'

'What put you on to it, then?'

'Nothing at the time, obviously, but when I was in the café at Riverstone's, I looked out of the window and I saw men loading up a van with containers; they were struggling because they were heavy. It stirred something in me, a kind of idea that I'd seen something that was not quite right but I hadn't processed it, and then I remembered that Monroe had seemed to struggle with the basket going up the stairs to the entrance. Why would he struggle, a strong young chap like him, with a basket of towels? That basket would have been light if it hadn't also had a person in it; admittedly a small, light person, but still a significant extra weight compared to just towels.'

Andy was shaking his head and his hands were over his face. 'I'll never live this down with people back at HQ, sir. "Here's Andy, Sergeant Stupid, who let a murderer be carried away in front of him." Bloody hell!'

'Well, tell them Chief Inspector Oldroyd watched the same basket go past, and if they want to laugh at me, send them up to do it.' He slapped Andy on the back and laughed. 'Cheer up, we're nearly there now. We've just got to bring them in.'

He looked away and his smile died. Doing that could be the most dangerous bit of all; he and Andy had already survived one murder attempt.

Meanwhile, the net was also closing in on Derek Fenton for the second time, although he knew nothing about it. Ben Poole sat at home at his computer and smiled with satisfaction. His shots of Fenton and Sandford meeting had come out well. This, together with Steph's evidence about Fenton curtailing the investigation for no good reason and the information from his council contact, should be enough to at least trigger an investigation. Fenton should not have been meeting in secret with a man he was supposed to have investigated. When bank accounts were examined and Fenton's conduct of that investigation was scrutinised, Ben was confident that everything would start to look very dodgy.

'What are you doing, Ben? I've brought you some coffee.'

Geraldine was calmer after Ben had given her reassurances following Clare Bayliss's visit. He wasn't going to explain to her what was going on, but exposing this would be a big feather in his cap, as far as the world of journalistic investigation was concerned. There was a good chance that he would get opportunities with one of the national papers. Also, Amanda Rigby had called to say that they were in fact going to continue to employ him next year at the Crime Writing Festival, so it was good news all round.

He got up. 'It's just the story I'm working on. Trust me, everything will be OK. I'd never do anything that would cause you stress or risk our happiness.'

She looked at him and smiled. She did trust him. He took her in his arms and kissed her.

At Harrogate HQ, DC Robinson was interviewing Steve Monroe in Oldroyd's office. Robinson sat behind the desk.

'OK, sir, we've just called you in to ask you something. Did you know anyone who regularly used the Baths who wore a diving suit?'

'You mean, like for diving underwater?'

'Yes. People sometimes practise going underwater in swimming pools, don't they? Anyway, Chief Inspector Oldroyd is interested in someone who might have possessed a blue diving suit. Maybe they just wore it to swim in.' A bead of sweat appeared on Steve Monroe's brow.

'No, I don't. Why do you ask?'

'Just because you know the people who use the Baths better than anyone else.'

'I see, but no, I didn't. It's an odd thing to ask, isn't it?'

Robinson smiled. 'Yes, I admit it's unusual, but "Ours is not to reason why", as they say; I'm just doing my job and—' Robinson's phone rang. 'Oh, that's the chief inspector now. I'll just take this in the next room, if you'll excuse me.'

Robinson went out. Steve watched him go.

'Yes, Chief Inspector . . . I'm just talking to him . . . No, I don't think so . . . Oh, right. What takes you up to Harlow Carr, sir? . . . I see. Oh yes, that case . . . You're going to walk back through the Pinewoods? . . . Good idea, sir; get some exercise . . . You'll be back at four . . . Yes, I'll see to it, sir. Bye.'

Robinson returned to the office and had the distinct impression that Steve had just sat down. 'That's all for now, then, but it would be very useful if you could ask around the regulars at the Baths about this blue diving suit business. The chief inspector seems to think it's important.'

'I will,' said Steve, and left the room and the building very quickly.

Later that afternoon, Oldroyd was walking through the Pinewoods between the Valley Gardens and Harlow Carr. He had just reached the densest part of the woods and there seemed to be no one around. Birds were singing and squirrels were scampering up the trees. Suddenly a small figure wearing a balaclava appeared from behind a large beech tree, scuttled quickly and silently towards Oldroyd, and then jumped up and stabbed him in the back with a knife.

Oldroyd wheeled round and threw off the assailant, who leaped up and lunged at him again, but more hesitantly, perhaps wondering why the first attack hadn't had more effect on the target. Oldroyd moved quickly to one side and then produced a hand gun. 'Don't move,' he said in his sharpest, most commanding voice. 'And drop the knife. Now!' She did.

Meanwhile, Andy had managed to locate another person hiding in the undergrowth nearby. He signalled to DC Robinson to join him and they carefully crept up to the person and pounced.

There was a struggle, but they quickly subdued their target and got the handcuffs on.

'Andy, over here!' shouted Oldroyd. Andy and DC Robinson appeared, pulling along a handcuffed Steve Monroe. 'Get the cuffs on her as well and let's have a look at her face.' He lowered the gun. Robinson picked up the knife.

'OK, sir.' Andy removed the balaclava to reveal a ferociously scowling female face. He vaguely recognised her as someone he had seen around the festival. He tried to apply the handcuffs but she lunged forward and tried to bite and scratch him. He had to use all his strength to control her. She was like a wild cat.

Oldroyd raised the gun again. 'That's enough of that!' he shouted. She spat in his direction.

Andy finally got the cuffs on with her hands behind her back. He took a firm hold of her wrists and they walked through the woods back to a road that bisected the green area and where two police cars were waiting. Oldroyd took off the old coat he was wearing to reveal the protective clothing underneath.

'That was a strong thrust for such a small person. I'm going to have a bruise there.'

He looked at the handcuffed figure in the back of the car. She was bent forward, concealing her face. There was no sign of a birthmark, as witnessed in the bar at The White Swan. It had clearly been a fake applied to confuse them. Steve Monroe was in the other car. Neither of them had said anything.

'She's a fierce little thing, sir. I've no problem believing she could have committed those murders, now that I've seen her.'

'No. Let's get them back to HQ. They're silent now, but let's see what a bit of cross-examination will do. They know the game's up.'

At Harrogate HQ, Steve Monroe and his girlfriend, Jade Darton, had been charged with the murders of Damian Penrose, Patricia Hughes and Susan Lawrence. They were in the cells, ready to be questioned. Oldroyd, Andy and DC Robinson were in Oldroyd's office.

'Well done, Constable,' said Oldroyd, relaxing in his chair. 'It worked like a dream.'

'Thanks, sir. I like a bit of play-acting, you know.'

'Well, it's been a feature of this case. So he fell for it quite easily?'

'Yes. He came in after we phoned him and I asked him about the blue diving suit. I could see it was a shock, but he tried hard to conceal it. I played it as though we didn't suspect him at all and were just asking for his help. In the middle of this, I got one of the lads in the office to call me. I told Monroe it was you and went to take it in the next room, leaving the door open and talking fairly loudly.'

'They were desperate to find out what I was doing and where I was, having failed to get rid of me before. Once you mentioned the blue diving suit, he knew I was on to how the first murder was done. From that the whole thing would start to unravel. They knew they had to try to dispose of me quickly. It was their only hope.'

'So I improvised a conversation with you, sir,' continued Robinson, 'in the course of which I mentioned you were up at Harlow Carr and you were going to walk back through the Pinewoods. And I asked you what time you'd be back here and repeated that time. I finished by requesting that he try and find out a bit more about the diving suit.'

Oldroyd chuckled. 'Brilliant. I'm sure he never suspected you knew the truth, but by that time he was probably panicking so much that he was caught off guard. He never paused to think whether or not it could be a trap. I'll bet he nearly ran out of the building to alert his partner.'

'He did.'

'And what a partner she is, sir,' said Andy. 'She's bloody dangerous, like a little wild animal. She'd be capable of anything.'

Oldroyd shook his head. 'Indeed, and I'm sure she was the force behind the scheme.'

'You took a risk out there, sir,' said Andy, who knew that Oldroyd was occasionally willing to break the rules and that DCS Walker was prepared to turn a blind eye. 'That gun wasn't even real.'

'I know,' replied Oldroyd ruefully. 'But I wanted to catch them before they could do any more damage or before they got wind that we were after them and disappeared. I've no doubt she had some great hiding places lined up. They would have been difficult to track down. I was the best bait and they took it. Thankfully, we don't go around with firearms all the time in the British police force. This replica' – he took it out of his pocket – 'has served me well over the years. Criminals never think a police officer will draw a fake gun.' He clapped his hands together. 'Anyway, come on, it's time we found out what it was all about, though I have a pretty good idea.'

Jade Darton faced Andy and Oldroyd, with a solicitor present. She sat impassively, staring ahead with her hands on the table. She had very short hair and fierce blue eyes. Oldroyd could see that her small frame, only five feet or five feet one inch tall, was powerfully built. She blew out air, as if she was bored, and tapped on the table.

'Right, I'm not going to pussyfoot around with you,' began Oldroyd. 'I don't think you'll blame me, as you've tried to kill me twice.'

'Give me another chance. Third time lucky,' she said abruptly, giving Oldroyd a twisted smile and laughing in a sinister way, which made the blood run cold in everyone who was present.

'I can see that Damian Penrose had no chance against you,' Oldroyd said. 'We know how it was all done. You must have been planning it for years.' She shrugged. 'What I want to know is the motive. Did he steal your stories too?'

Oldroyd was surprised to see her smile at him again. It was like the smile on a crocodile's face.

'Oh, Chief Inspector, you're so keen to tie up all the loose ends, aren't you? Well, since I can't kill you and escape, I'll tell you everything – let's say as a mark of respect. We have a lot in common, don't we? We both have minds that can create and solve puzzles, and we love illusions. By the way, I knew it was probably a trap today, but we were in a corner, and poor Steve was in a panic. He's found it all difficult. If it hadn't been for that wretched Pat Hughes ringing me at Steve's house, you would never have tracked me. I knew then it was only a matter of time before you'd find out where I was. So we had to try to finish you off at Brimham Rocks.' She shrugged again. 'Luck didn't go our way, and you always need luck.'

Oldroyd sat stunned. The violent, spitting and struggling little creature had been transformed into an articulate and thoughtful presence, but one that was nevertheless deeply criminal. Before he could say anything, she resumed.

'Anyway, to begin at the beginning, as the narrator says in *Under Milk Wood*. Do you like that play, Chief Inspector? I know you studied English at Oxford.'

She was taking delight in surprising Oldroyd, and it was unnerving. This all seemed to be well prepared. Was she expecting to be caught? Even pleased about it in some strange way?

'That bastard, Penrose. Yes, he betrayed me in many ways. You see, I was his mistress for a time. I'd been interested in writing crime stories since childhood; I've always had a penchant for the criminal.' She smiled sardonically. 'I first met Damian up here at the Crime Writing Festival several years ago and I followed him back to London. You probably think I was in awe of him, but I wasn't. I had sex with him so that I could get him to use his influence and get my novels published.'

'I take it this was during the time he was married to Susan Lawrence.'

She grinned and shook her head. 'Yes, poor Susan. All bark and no bite, as they say, Chief Inspector. She couldn't survive for five minutes without someone to support her with plenty of money. But we'll be coming back to her, won't we?'

'We will,' replied Oldroyd, who was feeling somewhat overwhelmed.

'After a while, of course, Damian moved on to other women. He deceived me but, even worse, he stole my stories.' For a moment her eyes blazed and Oldroyd thought she was going to be angry again but she kept her control. 'I had written some excellent crime stories with ingenious plots, and I gave copies to Damian. He said they were OK, but needed quite a bit more work. He promised to help me but he kept stalling and I sensed something was wrong. When his next novel came out, I knew what it was: he'd stolen the main idea from me.

'When I confronted him, he laughed and denied it. When I showed him the similarities between his book and my manuscript, he said that the idea needed to be developed by a talent such as his. The ideas were nothing without the writing ability. It's a wonder I didn't finish him off there and then. I thought about it. We were in his kitchen, and there was a lovely row of sharp kitchen knives within easy reach. But no, I would never have got away with it.'

'You tried to take legal action against him, didn't you?'

'Yes. Complete waste of time; don't know why I bothered. No solicitor would touch it; said there was no real evidence. I couldn't even prove I'd written mine first. I wrote letters threatening him with exposure, said I'd go to the press. He never even replied. He knew that no newspaper would take me on either without evidence.'

Oldroyd glanced at Andy. This confirmed that she was the 'little bitch' referred to in Penrose's diary. 'I presume you knew that you were not the only woman from whom Penrose plagiarised. Esther Stevenson has a group of his victims who campaigned against him.'

She frowned. 'Oh yes, Chief Inspector, but I didn't want anything to do with them. Their protests were mild compared with what I planned to do. I kept a low profile. The only people who knew about me and Damian were Susan, whom I'd met in the early days in their apartment in London, and Pat Hughes, whom I'd known in Harrogate when I was a volunteer years ago at the festival. She knew that I'd met Damian and that he'd eventually cast me off. She must have put two and two together, the same as Susan, who knew how Damian treated all his young female writers. She must have seen it happen many times. Eventually, of course, he ditched her as well for that Clare Bayliss, and then he got rid of her too. I could have formed an alliance with those two but they wouldn't have been as reliable or as useful as my devoted Steve. He'll do anything for me. And I'll do anything for him, if you see what I mean.' She flicked her tongue wickedly around her lips.

'So you developed a plan together?'

'I wouldn't say that, Chief Inspector. Steve wouldn't be capable of such ingenuity, but his help was invaluable.' She sat back in her chair. She's enjoying herself, thought Oldroyd. 'You see, the thing about Damian is that he thought he knew me, but he had no idea who I really was. His understanding, like his writing, was very superficial. He might have thought twice about treating me the way he did if he'd known how' – she searched for the right word – 'implacable I can be.'

'So it took a while to plan your revenge?'

'Yes, I can be very patient until the moment comes and then I can be – fatal.' She suddenly jerked forward. Like a praying mantis, thought Oldroyd. 'Damian had used his influence in the publishing world against me; my career as a crime writer was effectively ended. So I thought: if I can't be a success in fiction, I'll triumph at the real thing. This plot was my masterpiece and it takes a lot more guts, imagination and attention to detail to enact a mysterious murder than to merely write about one. Just think of it, Chief Inspector: I was acting out my own narrative! How much more intense and real than being the author of some book that people take off the shelves or download on to their Kindle! The postmodern critics will be in ecstasy over it: "Jade Darton: The Crime Author for Whom Writing Was Not Enough".'

'So this was your bid for fame?'

'Yes, and it's worked. I'm almost glad you solved the mystery, because now the full story can be told again and again in all the newspapers and true crime magazines. My place in crime history will be unique.'

'Carry on,' said Oldroyd, aghast at this twisted desire for infamy.

'I came quietly back to Harrogate and laid low. I met Steve at the Baths and I knew I'd found my faithful accomplice. I told him how Damian had treated me and how upset I was. I played it up, of course, and he was outraged. The poor man dotes on me. I knew Pat Hughes was potentially a problem, as she was the only person around the Crime Writing Festival who might have remembered my relationship with Damian, so I monitored her by turning up to offer my PR services.' She giggled. 'That's a good one, isn't it, Chief Inspector? Me offering advice about public relations.'

'I imagine you'd be very good. PR is all on the surface, isn't it?'

'Well, thank you, Chief Inspector, and you're right. But you've seen how good I am at acting parts. Pat and Amanda were hugely grateful to me for my help. It's a pity about Pat. I liked her; right up to the moment I smashed her over the head.'

Oldroyd took a moment for that comment to sink in before continuing. 'I take it you have some experience of diving?'

'A little. I've done a lot of sports in my time. My gymnastics was useful when I had to squash into that basket. It makes you very supple. I've always kept strong and fit.'

'So you were ready in time for this year's festival. How did Steve take to the idea of murder?'

She smiled at Oldroyd. 'He didn't like it to begin with, but Steve is round this, you see, Chief Inspector.' She held up her little finger. 'It didn't take long for me to persuade him that Damian deserved to die. Steve wanted to prove himself to me. He said he'd always lacked determination to get what he wanted, so I goaded him. I said if he really wanted a future with me, he would have to show he was made of strong stuff. Poor fool. He did it by helping me with the murders.

'Steve had access to everything at the Baths, so I developed this plan. Brilliant, wasn't it? You'll have to admit. Steve drilled the holes for the breathing tube and smuggled me in. You know what happened next. It was extremely satisfying to be carried out of there right in front of you. I don't know how I stopped myself from laughing.'

'It started to go wrong when Pat Hughes rang you, didn't it?'

Her demeanour changed and, for a moment, she looked like a cross, sulky child. 'Poor Pat. Why didn't she keep her mouth shut? Actually, it was my fault. There's never a perfect crime, is there, Chief Inspector? Always something the killer forgets. I was beginning to think she'd forgotten about Damian and me. It was a while ago and she never knew much about it, only that Damian had shown an interest in me. She never said anything to me when I was playing my PR role, so I thought we were in the clear. Unluckily for her, something must have jogged her memory. We had to get rid of her as soon as possible after she called me in case she went to you. I took her phone but I knew you'd trace the call to Steve's flat eventually, even without it. So we had to turn our attention to you.'

'I see.'

'I know all about you, Chief Inspector, and what a fine mind you have. I thought if we eliminated you, then we'd have a better chance of toughing it out. No one else would be able to work out how the first murder was done, and Steve could explain the call somehow. I had a hunch that you were the kind of person not to share your theories until you were sure about them. We're proud of our ideas, aren't we? We like to keep them secret and ours.' She leaned forward to Oldroyd with a chilling air of intimacy. Oldroyd drew back. 'Then the police would fall back on the mugging theory. They're mostly mugs themselves, aren't they?' She giggled at this witticism. Oldroyd thought how accurate her hunch about him was. Andy bridled at the insult to the police.

'I was surprised how easily we were able to lure you to Brimham Rocks.'

'I was off my guard that day. I'm not perfect either.'

'No. I had Steve to help me push the rock over. I was looking forward to seeing you crushed underneath but your dashing sergeant sprang to defend you.' She blew Andy a kiss. He had no idea how to respond.

'And then Susan Lawrence appeared.' Oldroyd prompted her to continue.

Jade sighed again. 'She did. I never expected her to come up from London. She hated Harrogate and she wasn't shedding any tears at Damian's demise, but, of course, as he was dead, he would no longer be paying her allowance. She called and threatened me with blackmail. She was a scheming bitch too. It takes one to know one. She had no real evidence but she must have sensed that I was involved and she, like Pat, had only to mention me to you people and that would have been the end. It was too much of a risk to take, so I poisoned her.'

'That was a very effective disguise,' admitted Oldroyd, although he was privately shocked at the matter-of-fact way she described the murder.

'It was. She made the mistake of telling me she was going to the Murder Mystery Evening. I love a bit of dressing up and impersonation too. I thought the birthmark was a nice touch: just a bit of make-up. A real murder at a Murder Mystery Evening – irresistible! Incidentally, if I'd known you were going to be there, I would have tried to deal with you too.' She smiled sweetly at Oldroyd, who shivered at the prospect. 'But I missed that chance: one missed chance and two failed attempts. You've got a charmed life, Chief Inspector; not many people escape from me when I've decided on their fate.'

'How did you get hold of the cyanide?'

She looked at Oldroyd, as if pitying him for his naiveté. 'You can get anything you like on the Dark Web or if you know the right people. No problem.'

'At this point it sounds like you were running to stay still, as it were. You were having to deal with more and more problems, and you knew I was on your trail.'

'We were, and I suppose the stress put us off guard. Earlier this afternoon, Steve came running very agitated to the flat, where I'd been staying ever since I strangled Damian, saying you were on to the blue diving suit and that must mean you were starting to get to the answer. He said you were going to be walking through the Pinewoods and it was our chance to finish you off. I should have stopped and thought about it, but we were desperate by this point.

You don't think clearly when you're in that frame of mind. So here we are. It's been exciting and great fun. I'm delighted you've been involved, Chief Inspector; it's been wonderful to pit myself against such a person as you. I've always fancied myself as an Irene Adler to a Sherlock Holmes. By the way, I hope you noticed another layer of irony and ingenuity I worked into things.'

'I suppose you mean the copying of the murders from stories written by enemies of Penrose.'

'Yes.' She smiled. 'I knew you'd appreciate it, Chief Inspector. It took some working out, especially as we ended up doing more murders than we originally intended. I bet the first got you think-ing about those writers and whether someone was trying to frame them. And they were! I had to research the second two a little but fate was kind to me and I found the incidents in the books by Stevenson and Simpson. By then you were probably confused and thinking what sort of a mind thinks of things like that. Well, now you know!' She was beaming with pride. 'The only murders that didn't come out of books were the attempts on you at Brimham Rocks and the Pinewoods. Of course, I didn't expect that I would have to deal with you, so I had nothing planned and had to move quickly. I didn't have time to research anything from fiction. How strange that they were the ones that failed! But at least I was pleased with how I managed to lure you to Brimham, Chief Inspector.'

The last sentence was spoken in the Scottish accent of the fictional Fiona MacPherson. Oldroyd squirmed in his seat. She seemed to have reached the end of her narrative, and sighed.

'Hey ho! There we are. It's a shame about Steve, but at least he had the honour of assisting a master.'

Oldroyd had had enough for the time being and brought the interview to an end. She was escorted out of the interview room by two female officers. Andy and Oldroyd went back to the office. Andy collapsed in a chair and blew out air.

'Well, what did you make of her, sir? Do you think a lot of it was bravado?'

Oldroyd shook his head and looked grim. 'No, I don't. She's one of the most dangerous psychopaths I've ever dealt with. She enjoyed the whole thing. There was a staggering lack of empathy and a truly shocking casualness about her accounts of killing people and manipulating Steve Monroe. I'm starting to feel almost sorry for him. I seem to have been constantly reminded throughout this case that she was small, first in Penrose's diary and then that line I heard from *A Midsummer Night's Dream*: "Though she be but little she is fierce." But the character of Hermia in that play is not in the same league for fierceness as this woman. I knew from when I realised the murderer had been carried out in the basket that they must be small. I didn't think it would be someone who packed such a punch.'

'She seemed to be doing it all because she couldn't be a successful writer, but wanted to be famous. It was bloody weird, wasn't it?' said Andy. 'She was creepy as hell.'

'Yes. The worst psychopaths are the clever and imaginative ones, the ones that can act parts and adopt an imitation of care, tenderness, trustworthiness, if necessary. Beneath it, they're utterly ruthless and self-motivated. Penrose, Monroe, Pat Hughes, Susan Lawrence, even you and I, were all characters in her complex drama, some of it planned and some of it thrillingly improvised. So even though she's been caught, she regards it as a success: she's got her revenge on Penrose and the drama will ensure her infamy.'

'I'll tell you what else was weird, sir. Do you remember at that second press conference, there was a reporter from some tabloid who suggested the whole thing could be the work of a deranged lunatic acting out a crime story? Turned out he was right.'

'Hell, yes, I remember! No doubt they'll have a field day with that but we'll just have to live with it. I'd love to know more about this woman's background. I'll bet this is not the first time she's been involved in criminal activity. Psychopaths are very good at covering their tracks. Anyway, we'd better talk to Monroe.'

∼

Steve Monroe, sitting in the same interview room with a different solicitor, presented a contrasting figure from that of his partner. He looked exhausted and bewildered, like a man waking up from a nightmare. Unfortunately for him, thought Oldroyd, the nightmare was real and there was no waking up.

'Ms Darton has confessed to everything and given us a detailed account, including your part, so I think it's pointless to deny it.'

'How do I know that's true?'

'I could go through it, if you like.' Oldroyd began repeating what Jade Darton had told them. He saw that Steve was shocked and desperate in the realisation that it was all over. 'Is this what she said she would do, Steve?' asked Oldroyd. 'Did she say she was going to tell us everything?'

Steve looked around frantically, like a trapped animal. 'No, but I bet you put her under a lot of pressure, didn't you?'

Oldroyd smiled at the prospect of trying to put that woman under pressure. 'No, we didn't. She enjoyed telling us. She doesn't mind being caught. It's all part of her drama. She told us how brilliant she was and how she'd got you to help her. She never once expressed any regret about what's going to happen to you now.'

Steve was wild with denial. 'What are you talking about?' he shouted. 'Jade and I love each other. That Penrose got what was coming to him.'

'And the others? They were a bit different, weren't they, especially poor Pat Hughes?'

Steve looked sheepish but tried to stay defiant. 'They were . . . They were in the way. We were going away together after this to start a new life. We couldn't let anything spoil it. We were going to have our own business: massage, alternative therapies. It would have been wonderful.' He looked down.

Oldroyd thought about the bizarre idea of going to Jade Darton for therapy. Then he looked at Steve closely. His voice was soft and kind. 'Steve, she's fooled you. She's a psychopath. It was all clever manipulation, making you believe she was in love with you. She needed an accomplice. She told us that she could twist you round her little finger. She called you the poor man who dotes on her; she said it was a shame.'

Steve erupted in anger. 'No, she didn't, she wouldn't. She loves me and . . .' He couldn't continue. He tried to get up and his arms flailed around pathetically. Then he collapsed in tears, leaning over the table, with his hands covering his face. Despite what the young man had done, Oldroyd found it difficult not to feel sorry for him. Steve began to shake and was unable to speak.

The solicitor intervened. 'I don't think my client can continue at this point.'

Oldroyd nodded. 'Very well. Interview suspended.'

When Oldroyd and Andy arrived back at the office, DC Robinson was waiting with a folder of papers.

'Sir, you need to look at this. It's what we uncovered in our search about Jade Darton. I think it will explain a lot.'

'Thank you,' said Oldroyd, sitting down heavily in his chair and feeling exhausted. None of them had expected this twist at the end of the case: the revelation of the true nature of the perpetrators and their relationship.

He skimmed through the main parts of the report and raised his eyebrows. Andy sat opposite him, feeling similarly drained.

'Good God!' said Oldroyd at last. 'You're right, Robinson.' He pushed the file over to Andy. 'She's got enough form to fill an old filing cabinet. She came from Harrogate originally. Her birth name was Diana Pearce. Her mother was a drug addict and couldn't cope, so she was brought up in care. She got expelled from school for attacking someone with a razor blade. At sixteen she was out of control and running some kind of drugs racket in Leeds. Then she stabbed someone and served a sentence in a juvenile detention centre. This is where she must have got her education, and she seemed to reform for a while. When she was released, she went to college to do a mature access to higher education course and then to university in Manchester to do English and Creative Writing. She must have decided she wanted to be a writer. She was disciplined for plagiarism at one point. That's ironic, isn't it? She'd also changed her name to Jade Darton and was supplementing whatever grant she got with a number of illegal activities. Manchester police arrested her for soliciting and she was suspected of dealing in drugs again.

'She drifted back to this area after university and presumably was looking for ways to get established as a writer. She thought Penrose was her way in. She searched him out rather than the other way round.' Oldroyd laughed and shook his head. 'Bloody hell. He had no idea what he was getting himself into. He thought she was just another naïve, young, aspiring female writer that he could exploit and string along. Little did he know he'd met his match big time, and he ended up being part of her drama.'

Andy was scanning through the report as Oldroyd was talking. He put the folder on to the table. 'God, that's dark, sir. I can't even begin to get into the head of someone like that. It's just too strange. I can cope with ordinary motives. Money, jealousy, you know . . . but this is beyond me.'

'People like that don't think and react in the same way as the rest of us.'

Andy looked up at his boss. 'What makes somebody like that?'

Oldroyd thought for a moment. 'Good question. All badly damaged people have been through traumatic experiences as a child, and I'm sure she was no exception. Whether that's enough to explain it, I don't know. And I don't think anybody really knows; that's the uncomfortable truth.'

'What about Monroe? He looked completely wrecked. I'm not excusing what he's done but what you said to him was right. He was completely manipulated by her. I was almost sorry for him.' Andy looked guilty.

'Don't worry, me too. He was a good subject for her: physically strong but emotionally weak, nowhere near as clever as her and easy to control.'

'He must have known that what they were doing was wrong, though.'

'With part of himself maybe, but he was obviously infatuated with her and did what she told him. People like her can be oddly magnetic, even though it's all an act. It's strange how sometimes people, like Steve Monroe, can't see the truth, usually because they don't want to. He believed in the dream of their future life together.'

'Well, his infatuation has ruined his life. He's going to go down for a long time.'

'Yes. Maybe if she admits actually carrying out all the murders and he cooperates with us, a clever barrister might be able to argue that she was exerting psychological control, especially with the evidence of her background. The problem is that when they see how small she is beside this tall, strapping chap, it's not going to be easy to make that case; the instinct of judge and jury will be to think the opposite.' Oldroyd shrugged. 'We'll have to see.'

Derek Fenton was called in to Chief Superintendent Walker's office early the next day. He was puzzled to see the presence of another DI sitting at the side of Walker's desk.

Walker was reading papers in a folder, but he stopped when Fenton came in, and took off his reading glasses. He looked at Fenton with a grim expression and the latter began to feel alarmed.

'Right, Derek, sit down.' He took up the folder. 'I'll come straight to the point. There are some serious allegations against you concerning your relationship with a councillor, Jack Sandford.'

Fenton's stomach lurched. 'What allegations, sir?'

'That you have taken bribes and not investigated allegations against him properly. You were assigned to that case in which Sandford was accused of favouring his wife with a contract for some designs for the Royal Baths.'

Fenton was stunned and speechless.

Walker continued. 'I've seen your report on that case and another on the evidence you had and how you conducted the investigation. I've also seen photographic evidence that you have had recent meetings with the man you so recently investigated. That in itself is highly suspicious, is it not? There's also some suggestion that this may have been going on for some time.'

Fenton was sweating. This had all come out of the blue; he'd had no time to prepare a story. Then he suddenly realised who must be behind this.

'If Detective Sergeant Johnson has been giving you information, sir, I wouldn't trust it.'

'Why not?' asked Walker sharply.

'She . . . She's young and inexperienced and she jumps to conclusions about things. She and I have never . . . got on together.'

'What on earth are you implying? That she has some grudge against you and is trying to get you into trouble? I've always found her a very reliable officer.'

'But I—'

'I'm sorry, Derek. I'm not making any judgements now but I have decided this is a matter of sufficient seriousness that I'm going to report it to the PCC. There will need to be an investigation by members of another force. In the meantime I have to suspend you from all duties pending the said investigation. You will need to organise representation.'

It was all very formal. Fenton decided to say nothing more. He was stunned.

'Ian here is going to escort you off the premises. I have to say that I'm very sad that this has happened, but I can't say any more at the moment.'

Without a word, Fenton got up and left the room, followed by the DI. As he collected his jacket and was accompanied out of the office, he was watched by Steph, hiding behind a storeroom door. When he'd gone, she looked up to see Nicola, Cynthia and Sharon peering round another door. She gave them the thumbs-up sign.

As Fenton was leaving the building, Hancock and Turnbull, together as ever, were just coming in. Their mouths dropped open as they saw their boss being frogmarched off the premises.

'What the hell are you staring at!' growled Fenton as he strode past them.

Esther Stevenson and Charles Derryvale met for coffee for the last time before Derryvale headed off back to York. They had somewhat recovered from the traumas of the Murder Mystery Evening.

'Well, what a festival it's been this year!' remarked Derryvale, munching on a croissant. 'I don't think I'll ever be able to see this town in the same way again but I'm quite sad that it's all over. It's been so exciting.'

'Honestly, Charles, it's been terrible!' replied Esther. 'I'm glad it's all over. I think I'll find it better in future years. I can see now that Penrose was becoming a bit of an obsession with me, so much so that I couldn't really enjoy the festival. I was concentrating on how we could disrupt and annoy him with our protests.'

'I suppose that's the end of all that, is it?'

'Not entirely. We're going to pursue things with his publishers. It's a question of justice. The women he stole those ideas from need recognition. It might be easier now that he's no longer here.' She sipped her coffee, looking as focused and determined as ever, in spite of what she'd said about her obsession.

'I'll tell you what, though,' continued Derryvale, wiping crumbs from around his mouth. 'We'd better book in early for next year. After the exposure in the press the festival has had this year, people are going to be flocking here.'

'Maybe.'

Derryvale's eyes glinted mischievously. 'I'm sure the police have finally found the real culprits, but did you ever consider that the whole thing could have been masterminded by someone on the festival committee? What an amazing publicity stunt! "The Crime Writing Festival Where Real Crimes Happened". It's guaranteed to get the punters in.'

Esther pursed her lips. 'Charles, that's positively bad taste again and it's not funny. Three people have been killed, including poor Pat Hughes.'

'Bah! Yes, I suppose you're right.' Derryvale finished his coffee and looked at the cup with dissatisfaction, as if he'd have preferred it to have been filled with something stronger. 'But what an amazing crime fiction story it would make, don't you think?'

Stevenson shook her head. 'You're incorrigible, Charles, and no, I don't think it would make a good crime novel. If you wrote a plot based on what we've seen here, in the last two weeks, no one would accept it as being remotely credible.'

John Sinclair heard on the radio that arrests had been made in the Penrose case. Good news at last, especially after that ghastly Murder Mystery Evening at The White Swan. It was a relief to him that no one he knew had been involved, and the effect on him was cathartic. A line had finally been drawn under his long relationship with Damian. While the killer had been on the prowl, he somehow felt that the malign spirit of his former lover was still brooding over the town.

Amy brought in the post, and there he read further good news: one of his authors had been nominated for an award, which was marvellous publicity for John's business. This made him realise that he had been wrong in the first place to ask for Damian's help. Making a success of this business by himself was important for his sense of self-worth. He needed to free himself from his reliance on his charismatic but unreliable friend. Damian's influence on him had been too strong, too long and, as the years passed, increasingly a burden. He rang Ed to tell him the news.

'Yes, great, isn't it? It's all been cleared up. He was killed by one of his victims; those women that he seduced and stole ideas from . . . I feel fine about it; in fact, I feel that a burden has been lifted. I'm going to make this business succeed . . . I know I can do it. Look, let's go out and celebrate this weekend . . . Yes, book a table at that Italian place you like for Friday night . . . Yes, that one . . . Why not? Things are looking up, Ed. We've got some happy times ahead.'

'You stupid fool! How could you do such a thing? Do you think you're some kind of Mafia boss who can control the police? When you said you were going to deal with that detective, I didn't know you meant like that. I didn't know you already had an agreement with him when he came to interview me. He was very unpleasant.'

Clare Bayliss was in an incandescent rage and the barn conversion on the edge of Nidderdale shook with her shouts and screams. Jack Sandford sat looking sheepish on the sofa. His shoulders were drooped and he looked away from Clare, who stood above him with her hands on her hips.

'What else could I have done?' he said. 'He was on to me; he uncovered evidence a while ago that I'd accepted bribes. Your contract just added to the suspicion, although that was a genuine mistake.'

'A mistake that also made the police suspicious of me; they thought I'd got the contract for the Baths so that I could somehow plan Damian's murder.'

'I know; I'm sorry, but my agreement with Fenton worked well until now. He had to act up being tough when he interviewed us because he had that sergeant with him.'

'And what was the plan in the long term? You had a bent copper on your hands, who could have blackmailed you any time he liked.'

'He couldn't have said anything because I know things about him too. He's taken bribes from me to stop any investigations.'

'And who do you think would have been the most likely to be believed? A detective with years of experience, who would know how to present things to his own advantage, or Mr Big, the failed businessman-turned-councillor, who's left a trail of evidence about his corrupt dealings. Mr Bean, more like.'

'Hey, that's not fair. My business hasn't failed.'

'Huh! Don't think I don't know why you don't go into the office much. It's nothing to do with your council work.'

'What do you mean?'

'I've been doing a bit of investigation myself. You don't have a bloody office anymore!'

Jack shifted uncomfortably on the sofa. 'The rent was too much. I decided to run the business from home. I didn't tell you because I didn't want you to worry.'

'You didn't tell me because you were embarrassed. And what happened to your dynamic workforce?' Clare asked sarcastically. 'You let them all go, I presume; doesn't sound like a flourishing concern to me.'

'Well, things have been . . . difficult.' All his confidence and charisma had drained away. He was almost whispering. She looked at him with contempt.

'You're a huge disappointment to me.'

'Clare!'

'Yes. After Damian, I thought I'd found someone who would be straight with me, someone I could trust. You've been plotting behind my back and keeping me in the dark about your business and your shenanigans on the council, and you've made me a suspect in these murders. Now you've lost everything.'

Sandford squirmed but he knew it was true. He and Fenton hadn't covered themselves well enough and someone, probably Ben Poole, had turned evidence in to the police. Once the investigation into Fenton uncovered everything, he would have to resign from the council and would probably face prosecution. He made a weak attempt to go on the offensive.

'Anyway, you said you could put a stop to people prying. What happened to that?'

'What? So it's my fault, is it? I tried to warn off Ben Poole by putting the frighteners on poor Geraldine. I wish I hadn't now. You make it so easy for people like him, there's no point. I think you deserved to be caught.'

'Clare!' he repeated but it sounded weak.

She gave him a steely glare.

'So let's be clear. You're going to have to rely on me from now on and I'm going to be calling the shots. I'm sick of men messing up my life and I'm going to be in control. Understand?'

Sandford looked into her implacable face and saw no mercy. He felt the bitter taste of defeat.

'Bloody hell!' said Andy, shaking his head. 'I can't believe it.' He and Steph were in the sitting room of their flat in Leeds, over-looking the River Aire. They were sharing a bottle of red wine as Steph told Andy all that had happened with Fenton, including her alliances with Ben Poole and with the women in the office. She'd decided it was time to share things with him.

'Well, it all happened, I can assure you, but you don't say a word to anyone, not even the boss.'

'That bastard, Fenton!' said Andy as a spasm of rage went through him. 'You should have told me he was harassing you and I would have—'

'Exactly, which is why I didn't tell you. You would have prob-ably got yourself into huge trouble assaulting a senior officer or something.'

'He would have bloody well deserved it.'

'Maybe, but it was better this way. We didn't want to go to the men to sort it out for us, as if we're helpless. That just confirms us as weak, needing protection, subordinate. You know what I mean. There comes a time when you need to deal with it yourself.'

Andy's anger subsided, and he smiled at her with admiration as he drank his wine. 'I'd like to have seen Fenton's face when you all sprang out of your hiding places and snapped the photograph.'

Steph laughed. 'He wasn't pleased, I can tell you. If looks could kill. He knew I was behind it. I don't know whether he suspects I was involved in uncovering the corruption business, but as I was on that enquiry with him and objected when he closed it down, he must wonder.'

'He won't be coming back, that's for sure. Good job too. It would have been really difficult for you to work there if he'd still been around, wouldn't it?'

'Yes, so it's worked out well that we've got him over the other business too.'

'God, that was risky, though. Following him around and investigating without permission like some kind of private investigator in a thriller! You could have got into serious trouble.'

'Which is why you have to keep all this to yourself.'

'So that journalist, Ben Poole, sent in a dossier of stuff about Fenton and Sandford?'

'He did, and it ended up with DCS Walker. None of it was conclusive, but when they start to explore and find that Fenton shut down the investigation without reason, and when they look at phone calls, payments and council records, they're going to discover exactly what was going on. They'd had a cosy arrangement for some time, I think. Fenton was just acting tough with Sandford and his wife when we interviewed them.'

Andy looked at her again. 'Tell me one thing, though. How do you feel about Fenton getting away with all that sexual harassment and blackmailing you? Wouldn't you rather have called him out and let the authorities deal with it?'

Steph thought for a while. 'Good question. Yes, ideally, but we were worried that, as women are in the minority at work, Fenton would have been investigated by men and maybe let off with a slap on the wrist. They would have had to do something but it still might have been fudged.'

'Surely they would have taken it seriously these days?'

'You might think so, but you're a man. It looks different from our perspective. There's still a lot of chumminess between men and thinking that all this stuff with women is just a bit of fun, which the women can't take because they have no sense of humour.'

'Right. Well, what can I say? Good on you. I'm proud of you.'

'Steady on, nothing patronising!' replied Steph, but she was smiling.

'You're joking – I wouldn't dare! Anyway, here's to you.' He raised his glass and drained it. Steph did the same.

'Yes, it's been one of the strangest cases I've ever been involved in,' observed Oldroyd as he sat in an armchair in his flat. Outside, the evening light was slanting over the smooth acres of grass, as it had at Ripley Castle only a few days before. The pace had been hectic since then, and it was a relief to be able to relax. Deborah and Alison were sitting together on the sofa, and all three were sipping coffee after a meal prepared by Oldroyd. 'Prepared' was a little overstated. Like many men of his generation, Oldroyd's cooking repertoire was very limited, but he rejoiced in the good selection of food now available in the better supermarkets. Tomato and red pepper soup from a carton, linguine with seafood and a sticky toffee pudding, all from the top range of prepared foods, had made an excellent meal. He sat with a satisfied smile on his face but this was more to do with the fact that, as expected, his sister and Deborah had seemed to get on really well from the moment they were introduced.

'The seemingly impossible murder of a crime writer at a Crime Writing Festival,' he continued, 'and at the end we discover the whole thing was a kind of weird play devised by the psychopathic killer with herself in the starring role. It's all enough to "do your head in", as I think they say nowadays.'

'You say the killer was hiding in the swimming pool?'

'Yes, it was ingenious, but you gave me a hint, Deborah, at The White Swan, when you said the murderer could be hiding in plain sight. It reminded me about camouflage and how the person could be somewhere obvious but we couldn't see them. I'd seen a picture of a chameleon that set me thinking, but you sort of confirmed that train of thought in my mind: that they were there but at the same time invisible. Also, she managed to stay underwater because she was breathing through a tube that ran through the tubular metal supports at the side of the steps into the pool. There was the answer straight in front of where we were standing, but we didn't see it.'

'Well, I'm glad to have been of assistance.'

'Oh, that's always happening, Deborah,' said Alison. 'He's always picking up clues from things you say or things he sees when he's with you.'

'That's right,' said Oldroyd. 'I got the idea of the breathing tube when you were talking about the umbilical cord when you went off to see a parishioner.'

'Oh my goodness!' laughed Alison.

'And all this in Harrogate, of all places!' said Deborah.

'Yes, I've long since learned that the more genteel and ordered a place seems, the more darkness is being concealed beneath,' observed Alison. 'But Jim, didn't you say she had some real motives? It wasn't just to do with her dark imagination, was it? Hadn't that writer seduced her, stolen her stories and then left her?'

'Yes, he'd pinched her ideas, but I'm not sure you could say he seduced her. She was always well in control and was using him to try and get into the publishing world, and she bitterly resented his theft of her ideas, like they all did. The problem was that she reminded me of Iago in *Othello*. The motives given don't seem to properly explain the actions: the twisted and almost exuberant way in which she enjoyed orchestrating the whole thing; just to gain fame? I've always thought that Iago is Shakespeare's depiction of a psychopath, and it was the same with her: manipulative, remorseless, with an ultimately inexplicable darkness at the centre. She's a highly intelligent and well-read woman, but her education is only a kind of civilised veneer over her ruthless and violent nature.

'I've been meaning to ask you, Deborah, for your professional view about psychopaths. My detective sergeant asked me what causes them to behave like that and I couldn't answer him.'

Deborah put down her cup. 'Wow, that's a big one, Jim! The honest answer is, we don't know. There are theories about deficiencies in the brain, but as a therapist I believe that our identities result from our experiences. I would say that people who exhibit those behaviours have failed to form attachments and learn what love is. They're unable to empathise, and therefore live a completely self-centred life. It's tragic for them as well as for the victims if they turn out violent.'

'I agree,' said Alison. 'There are explanations for many of the bad things in the world, but sometimes we just have to accept that evil can be a mystery, a darkness we can't always explain.'

'That's why Iago is the most terrifying character in Shakespeare,' continued Oldroyd, 'because in the end there's no satisfactory explanation for what he does. He gives us plenty of motives himself but ultimately we're not convinced. He thwarts our need for behaviour to be explicable, and that's alien.'

The three of them went quiet as they contemplated one of the insoluble mysteries of life.

'Well, on that rather sombre note, I'm going to get off,' announced Alison, laughing. 'You'll have to watch him.' She pointed to Oldroyd. 'He has a tendency to melancholic reflection on life's problems and he's also a bit of a workaholic.'

'Well, thanks, Sis. I love you too!'

'Don't worry, I think I've got the measure of him,' replied Deborah with a smile. 'It's all been very interesting and exciting so far, though I don't know how many real murders I can witness before I've had enough. The fictional kind are good enough for me.'

'Don't worry, he has plenty of good points too.' Alison chuckled as she got ready to leave. 'Deborah, it's been a pleasure to meet you.' The two women hugged each other. 'And I hope it's not too long before we see each other again. You must come out to the rectory and see how the clergy *used* to live.'

'I'd love to,' replied Deborah.

Oldroyd gave his sister a kiss and they accompanied her out to her car. She waved to them as she drove off back to Kirkby Underside.

'Fancy another drink?' asked Oldroyd as he and Deborah settled back down inside.

'Why not?'

Oldroyd poured out two small brandies and they talked for a while about what had happened since they met.

'There is some truth in what Alison said,' observed Oldroyd. 'It can be difficult being around me. I don't follow a regular work pattern and I tend to become very deeply involved in serious cases until they're solved.'

She looked at him with her head on one side. 'Being a bit self-deprecating, are we? Let's just say I like what I've seen so far. It's the liveliest time I've had for years. And now,' she said, finishing her drink and standing up, 'you need to stop talking and come with me.'

Oldroyd downed his brandy and got up. They held hands as they walked out of the sitting room and towards the bedroom.

Acknowledgments

I would like to thank my family and friends for all their support and encouragement over the years.

The Otley Courthouse Writers' Group has been a wonderful source of help and inspiration.

The lovely Harrogate Turkish Baths were the model for the Baths in the story. In the novel they are extended and include a swimming pool. The Turkish Baths were originally part of a much bigger complex, which included rooms for the various spa treatments. I have used the original name: The Royal Baths.

The Royal Pump Room Museum in Harrogate is a fascinating place to visit but, due to Health and Safety regulations, it is no longer possible to sample the waters as Andy did! When I was a small boy, there was an old-fashioned pump on the wall outside the building and I used to enjoy cranking the handle and pumping up the smelly water. The pump is now electric and you push a button. The water still appears but it is nothing like as much fun!

Theakston Old Peculier Crime Writing Festival takes place each year at The Old Swan Hotel in Harrogate. It has become one of the most important crime writing festivals in the country. The Old Swan Hotel, with its link to Agatha Christie, was clearly the model for The White Swan Hotel in the story. I would like to thank the hotel and Theakston's Brewery for presenting such a good festival every year.

Brimham Rocks has been a fascinating place to me since childhood, when I enjoyed climbing over the giant rocks and exploring the tunnels. I would like to thank the National Trust for its care in maintaining this unusual landscape.

The West Riding Police is a fictional force based on the old riding boundary. Harrogate was part of the old West Riding, although it is in today's North Yorkshire.

About the Author

John R. Ellis has lived in Yorkshire for most of his life and has spent many years exploring Yorkshire's diverse landscapes, history, language and communities. He recently retired after a career in teaching, mostly in further education in the Leeds area. In addition to the Yorkshire Murder Mystery series, he writes poetry, ghost stories and biography. He has completed a screenplay about the last years of the poet Edward Thomas and a work of faction about the extraordinary life of his Irish mother-in-law. He is currently working on his memoirs of growing up in a working-class area of Huddersfield in the 1950s and 1960s.

Printed in Great Britain
by Amazon